Meanwhile in
Dopamine
City

DBC Pierre

faber

For Katz of Friday Night City:
it's always five o'clock somewhere.

First published in 2020
by Faber & Faber Limited
Bloomsbury House
74–77 Great Russell Street
London WC1B 3DA

This paperback edition first published in 2021

Typeset by Faber & Faber Limited
Printed and bound by CPI Group (UK) Ltd, Croydon, CRO 4YY

A CIP record for this book
is available from the British Library

ISBN 978-0-571-22895-9

MIX
Paper from
responsible sources
FSC® C020471

10 9 8 7 6 5 4 3 2 1

We cannot wait for favours from nature;
our mission is to take them from her.
Ivan Michurin

SEPTEMBER

I

East Palisades

She looked like a sawn-off tramp. The day was going from bad to ratshit but this was one thing he would fix. A tramp and he couldn't lie, there was a whiff of pride in his disgust that made it worse. Lon stood his gunk-spangled bags by the fence as she padded up the road on half tiptoes. She was barefoot.

She didn't see him, then she saw him.

'What can I smell,' he said. It wasn't a question; there was a scent, just not olfactory. A sight-smack of lip gloss, legs and lies.

'Don't be bizarre.' Now she dawdled. Her eyes were cuts in the beery light, the swimmy twilight. Sphinx moths were out.

'Smells troubley.' He blocked the gate.

'Why would it?'

'Trouble in the air.'

'What is your problem? Why're you home?'

'Tell me who it is because I saw. He bully you into this?'

'Into what?' She checked her nails. 'It's not like anyone's teabagging.'

'*Excuse me?* Where did you get that?'

'School.'

'Who at school?'

'Kim Stern.'

'*Ms* Stern? The teacher?'

'Sex ed. What is wrong with you?'

'They teach *teabagging*?'

'You're freaking me out now.'

'They teach you *teabagging* at *school*?'

'Seriously freaking me out.'

'You know I'm going to check up.'

'Why are you here?' she said as if to a vision.

'I live here.'

'So early, duh.'

'Let's talk about you, out on the road dressed like I don't know what.'

'I'm trying to go inside. I supposedly live here now too, y'know.'

He went to the road from the rough-shorn grass and planted work boots apart like a bull rider. He lived on the edge of a suburb, was employed in sewerage till earlier that day, his knowledge of bulls was zero; he just was one of those men who had stridden from the womb in the shape of a husky cowpoke. Even his brow was built for hatshade, down-raked like his eyes and with a national-anthem lofty pitch that could slip from aloof to dismayed; but his lips belonged to a baby boy, and these slightly parted could mesmerise his prey. 'Tell me who it was.' He scanned the stubble plain they called the flat, which buffered his town from the world. 'If it's someone from Number Fourteen you have to say – we don't even know who they are.'

'Tch. Is this going to be one of those awkward deals where you just assert your authority or whatever because in all honesty, Lonnie, I have limited interest right now, it's getting fresh out here.'

'Try *Dad*.'

'Whatever.'

Technically, Shelby was dressed. White T-shirt big enough to be her brother's. Three cardinal-red patches of bikini underneath, cherries through fog, and they were wet or something was wet because she was wet. He took a tail of her hair. She was blonde but it shone mauve and wrapped cold around his finger like a swirler in a drain. 'Is Ember inside? She see you come out like this?'

The girl crossed her arms and huffed like a freckled boy's stepmother. 'What matters here is that I'm trying to do what I'm supposed to be doing according to all the rules including yours, and now it's you holding me back from doing it.'

'Nanny Mona wouldn't let you run around like this. If she knew, I'd be right back in court. That what you want? Back to Nanny Mona? Leave Egan and me again?'

'Let me go-*ho-ho*.'

Her bones caught his eye in the syrupy light. She didn't use to have bones but now she had them, under her back, her face, her shoulders. Bone and tender muscle. Character. *Structure.* Her structure loomed out with her bones as the mosque wailed up from Molan, the suburb to the west, and the day didn't feel like his life any more.

She stabbed a toe at the road. 'So random and bizarre.'

'Tell me about it. Beachwear this far from the beach.'

'Swimming! Remember – Wednesdays? That you pay for?'

'With lipstick? And today's Thursday.'

The street lamp pinged on beside them. Another four lamps lit up along the road but theirs for some reason flickered. Shelby's edges shimmered and buzzed.

She made a break for the gate. He tangled in his bags.

The washing machine thruffled inside. TV laughter clanged over it. Ember already on the red, lips as purple as an eel's.

'*Wha*—' She flinched off the sofa.

'See this?' He pointed at Shelby.

'*What?* Why are you home?'

'He's being bizarre.' Shelby went to the stairs.

'Too much to ask for these kids to be watched? Where's Egan? EGAN!'

'Somewhere.' Ember looked around.

Lon snapped a finger from Shelby to his boots. 'Come here.'

'Stop it.'

'HERE.'

'What is *wrong* with you?'

'NOW.'

Ember scraped over instead. Regarding her: it wasn't romantic; she minded the heretics for cash. Lon raised the palm of his hand to enact an authoritative fatherly force field; but that force only flows when you're winning a case, and this one wasn't won by a mile. The force withered back to a grumpy thirty-six-year-old's, a newly laid-off man who felt that a girl's choice of clothes should allow for bumping into a nun.

'WHAT IS YOUR PROBLEM!' Shelby bent double on the bottom stair. 'I SAID I WENT SWIMMING!'

'Lonnie, *what is it*?'

'Swimming's Wednesdays. TEN SECONDS OR GROUND-ED.'

'SO UNFAIR! Ember, tell him.'

'The Hub does girls Wednesdays *or* Thursdays.'

'Seven – six – five – four . . .'

'STOP IT!'

'Three – two – one . . .'

'GET AWAY!'

He hammered up three flights behind her. She flew into her room. *Bang!*

Ember followed like a sigh, with the same fallenness as her mood, carefully riding the swing of her behind to keep from spilling her wine.

A hand-drawn sign on Shelby's door said *STAY OUT*.

Lon opened the door. *Click*.

She was in there breathing hard. 'Go away! This is all over NOTHING!'

'Which way do you come from swimming? You come east, which is not the way I saw you come, and there was someone else down there.'

'Who cares which WAY I COME? YOU'RE IN MY SPACE!'

'Lon.' Ember tapped his arm.

'You're not her mother.'

'Oh. Thanks.'

'It's *ridiculous*!' Shelby thrashed the bed. 'If you're so obsessed with where I am all the time you'd get me a PHONE LIKE A NORMAL PERSON!'

'Don't count on it now.'

'*Yuh*, so Egan gets one.'

'Egan wears clothes in public.'

'You need a frickin girlfriend. Take your mind off non-issues.'

'Don't you swear at me. Tell the truth.'

'Which one if you don't like the swimming one!'

'The only one.'

'I TOLD YOU!'

'WHERE WERE YOU?'

'STOP IT!'

'Lon, what the hell?' Ember lowered her wine.

'Stay out of it.'

'This isn't the way.'

'Oh, this is the way. Surely, surely the way. Keep this family straight till I can bail us out of this hole. Bail out and never look back.'

'If you were really that serious you'd take market price for the house.'

'Yeah, the bank'll just forget the rest.' He loomed over Shelby: 'TELL ME!'

'I TOLD YOU!'

'NOW!'

'GET AWAY! Loser.'

'*Excuse me?*'

'LOSER!'

Crack! He slapped her. For her own good and with a sudden hatred he would later suppose was love. The noise of it shocked her quiet. Him too. A heartfuck.

You'd think Ember's skin was being sucked off her face: 'WHAT IS WRONG WITH YOU TODAY!' She yanked Shelby out of the room and slammed the door behind them.

Ribs clenched. Skull rang. The less Lon could afford to lose battles, the more he lost them. He even lost some respect for himself, doubly so because it wasn't just respect he was losing, it was power. Nothing makes you lose respect more than losing power.

In a corner of that cotton holocaust he spied a My Little Burro toy. Formerly adored like the Godhead. Mint in its box. My Little Burro. Until recently wrangled by a girl with loud breath and loose socks in a pact with a universe that wanted things shiny in the original box. That wanted things awesome.

Her skin had been firm when he smacked her. A future adult lurked under her skin. Future old woman with her memories. He as good as slapped an old woman. She might remember that day as she died. Down to the front step he tramped, beaten. Creatures barked over the wasteland flat as the light bruised to ash under clouds.

Oh, Shelby Shall-be Shel. Shelby-Ann. Could be the name was a problem as well. Racy name. She was provisionally called Annie until three weeks to the day after her mother Diane left Alma Hospital in an unmarked white hearse like a butcher's van. Vents on the roof spun fast in gusty sunshine. Lon followed sweating in traffic before losing her behind a bus at the corner of King and Wisteria, up past the fire station. News of her death was in his thinking mind, the information was there all right, but it may as well have been in a bank vault because his gut knew he physically lost her behind that bus. That's when he really lost her. Lost sight and power and care of her. For ever. Some vulture, a stranger driving a butcher's van, hauled her away in a bag and tried to lose him and succeeded. Her last ride in town.

The funeral home was a sandy brick bungalow wedged between Amos Disposals and Dan's Outdoorland on the westbound exit where the speed camera sits. By the time Lon found it she was yellow. He had carried a bag to hospital that morning with aloe vera gel, mini pretzels, more books, fresh underwear – including the pair that said *IT WON'T SPANK ITSELF*, a therapy meant to run on wrongness – and a hastily framed picture of little Egan and baby Annie like hampers in the crooks of his thick arms. The bag was still on the front seat. She was in a coffin. He never lost the pressure to deliver that bag.

A hovering black suit processed their credit card within sight of her straw-coloured hair. It was swept up in a way she hated. She really hated that. The suit offered a 'viewing' with gauze over her face because 'some people prefer the distance', he said. It was wedding veil material – what kind of zombies were they? Lon ripped it off. He wanted to roll her on her side the way she always slept. He wanted to stroke her belly. He wanted to climb in beside her and have the suit nail the box shut. People always come back from these places saying *She looked so peaceful*, and it's bullshit: she was a mess. If you saw her like that on any other day you wouldn't say *peaceful*, you'd fucking call someone. Her head was small and loose on her neck; it wanted to roll when he stroked it. He settled it back as the terminal beeped and declined his five-grand payment. He'd thought it would. He lied about it. Better to vaguely pretend to have the money, although what were they going to do – stand her outside till he paid? Organs played over his lying and at one point were in concert with air brakes on the road. He looked out and it was another fucking bus. How could he let one between them? How, after hustling and chasing and hitching her up, could everything slip this way?

This is what he lived with.

The bag stayed on his front seat because she might still need it. He was ready to deliver it day and night. It sat with its handles neatly crossed until he got body odour and a big enough collection of empties at the gate to freak her mother out when she brought the little ones back. That's when Shelby got her name. Named after superstar Shelby Mykura because the world's fastest female would not have let a bus between soulmates.

*

A breeze fiddled up. To his left along Palisade Row sat the abandoned Moyle estate, trees bristling out like rearing dogs. That was the way she'd come, from the edge of the flat and not from Molan. He totted up the facts: she claimed she had swimming but that was Wednesdays at Molan Hub. The Hub was reached the opposite way, and nine times out of ten one of the other girls dropped her back. She wasn't carrying her bag. She was still wet. She wasn't wearing the one-piece they used for club swimming. Against that, there was just no water around the palisade. Aside from a reservoir breach years ago that had swept through downtown, over the palisade and into these properties' chimneys, there probably hadn't been water down here since whatever upheaval had caused the cliff in the first place. Probably also wiped out the dinosaurs. As for the jungle of ash and yew at Moyle's, it might look like Shenanigan City but it wasn't a place any stranger would come from further afield in town. Apart from it looking spooky, you just wouldn't come out of your territory to creep past Lon's place, or risk your neck on the so-called Palisade Stairs. One thing about company towns: territories as snug as condoms. Comes from a lack of workmates you want to bump into off the job.

Whoever he'd seen with her must be local. Extremely local. Apparently not Egan, as he would've appeared and anyway was allegedly inside. The only other household nearby was Number Fourteen. An unknown quantity.

She'd been cagey about it.

Palisade Row was an unusual road, serving only two homes along a lane that led to Moyle's abandoned mansion. The houses sat at a distance under the long sandstone cliff, like cigar butts clenched in a sneer. Though mostly forgotten by the city upstairs, an outbreak of planning in the twentieth century had led it to suddenly number the properties; not One and Two, but Thirty-Seven and Fourteen, reflecting a hope of one day filling the arc between them. Lon Cush was in Thirty-Seven, the nearest to Moyle's estate. Who knew who was in Fourteen these days, at the main-road end of the palisade, but he was about to pay them a visit. New people had moved in nearly a year before – he'd waved at one on his way from work once, hadn't seen exactly who. Foreign. In his mind the wave passed for a knock at their door with a card and some cake and a welcome to the Row, as Diane would have done on day one. He felt bad about the neighbourly thing for a month or so. His Monday-to-Saturday excuse was late shifts, Sundays he blamed fatigue. But look at it: he wanted Shel to grow up like Diane and take cake round on day one. While he found it easier to feel bad for a month than buy cake. This was what he was up against. Then look at flying time: he was finally going round with no cake but with a threat to ram a boy's head up his ring if he touched her. Which also came at Shelby from the other side, showed her he had the perimeter. She was his Little Burro, safe and pink in her room; the kid was a stalker from a cheaper house, thirty to forty grand cheaper and still no lawn after almost a year. Which kind of thinking was indigenous to a breed of older parent who saw life in black and white, he was well aware. But this was the time for it.

Back inside to drop his overalls. No sign of the girls. Canned laughter still played – how bitter. You had to wonder if human sanity hadn't ended the day the species started living with disembodied laughter everywhere. He was about to change out of his work boots but ended up thinking better of it: ballast if things got pushy. As he hung his workwear behind the door, a shadow slid over the landing upstairs. Egan, apple of his other eye. Lon nailed him before he crawled into his hole: 'Eagle. You just come in?'

'Down to turn off the TV.'

'And failed?'

'Changed my mind. Didn't know you were there.'

'What are you up to really?'

'Just reading.'

'Reading what?'

'Mm – *The Dog That Said Ely.*'

'What?'

'You know. The dog. Ely.'

'A book from the lie shelf.'

'It's not.'

'You're gambling I won't come up.'

'I'm not.'

'What other books are there? Shoot me some titles.'

'*Truant Under Spline, Mesmer the Snail, Hello There Pointless, Is It Safe Yet?*'

'There's no book called *Is It Safe Yet?* I'm coming up.'

'There is. A safety book.'

'Uh-huh.'

'Mm – *Where Donald Found Larvae, Return of Mrs Gremet, The Gremets: A Life in Disgrace, Rowdy Stays at Your Place, The Diabolical Nuns, Bonjour Heini, Eight Steps to Who Cares, Zambar the Avigator, Spell It or Die . . .*'

Lon paused to scratch his jaw. It was pedigreed bullshit, that's what got him. Good enough to cancel out the need to read. As if the talent spent in avoiding the thing was as much as he'd gain if he did it. That's what got him. And the kid wasn't twelve till June.

God only knew what Shelby'd be like by that age.

2

Kinbassa Lounge

Little Burro Avenger sounded extravagant but it had rhythm. It bound to the tavern region of the brain and kept Lon focused under his breath. He wasn't out to stop the heretics making friends, he just wanted them inside with games and juice and some 'Hello, Mr Cush – thank you, Mr Cush', not hustling around at dusk.

His seatbelt stayed off for the two-hundred-yard drive to Fourteen, another tall house against the rock face, simpler and somehow duller than his. No foliage to speak of, the plot was still a beach of the cereal-coloured sand that flew off the face like wheatgerm before rolling to a tidemark with the flat's motley grit. You wouldn't see it in the shadows. Just then an eggy light spilled out of windows at the side of the house.

Lon supposed he should've walked, but a car is a territory and an embassy. The old car was a gunboat from Number Thirty-Seven, Little Burro Nation. He coasted along until the exhaust started farting at idle and it hit him how lame it might seem to drive two hundred yards to deliver a warning, then drive two hundred yards back. What if it turned sour? Get in, slam the door, get out ten seconds later and slam it again at home? Do a burnout and try to brake before overshooting his own front gate?

He put on the belt and cruised past without looking. A better idea was to sound the issue out, workshop it over a beverage. Then later when he knocked at Fourteen he'd at least be on his way back from somewhere with the car pointed east towards home. The Environmental Services pipeline crew, day rats and some flexitimers, plagued the Kinbassa Lounge on Thursdays to stab sacred cows and each other. Boges and Feral and other sideburned types who were born to wield heavy-duty root cutters. Lon must have been one too; he looked like one, although his dream had been to wield a guitar.

Diane had encouraged the dream, heartened him along by letting his plucking prolong her feel-good years in sarongs and windstrung hair. She might have been influenced by a song he wrote about her, but anyway.

Lon made a pass by the bank to get cash, keep a rein on his unemployed spending; but he entered Sebastian Road and saw that his bank and even the teller machine were gone. Menus were scribbled on chalkboards instead under a sign that said *Nom Nom*. Raffish bobs and beards gobbled noodles off trestles behind the window. He pulled alongside a beard puffing vapour outside. 'Know where the bank went?'

The man looked around. 'The Capital? It was clicks-and-mortar for a while there, but I think it went full clicks. Isn't it called Josh now?'

'Josh?'

'Yeah, didn't they have the public vote for the trustworthiest name or whatever, where the winner ended up being Satan Rocks? And they fired the agency?'

'Wasn't that a radio station?'

'You mean BUTI-FM – they got Satan's Bitch or something. Satan's Yo Mama. Anyway, I think Capital's Josh now, or Jared or something. Pretty sure it's Josh.'

'Josh Bank?'

'I spose, or just Josh.'

'Hm.'

'And you know what's really weird?' The man grinned.

'What's that?'

'My brother-in-law's called Josh.'

Lon waited for him to say 'And my sister's called Satan', but he just kept grinning and puffing. 'Okay,' said Lon. 'Well, thanks.'

He decided not to look any further. He drove back down City Hill to Leonard Road with the price of one beer in loose change.

The Kinbassa was a timber box on a weed-and-gravel car park cowering between industrial units, two streets north of the palisade edge. The faded tiki-sports-bar theme was still not unfashionable in Palisades. Nothing was really unfashionable except for the fashionable. Lon went in past the smokers at the door, past the artsy-farts in wingbacks by the window. Past the girls and orbiting apprentices on the long and sticky mission into their pants. You could hear Lon's crew in the gloom beyond the pool table, the meanings in their voices twining together as they do whenever a brain slides into a crowd. That eve his brain was sliding into the Wide World of Man:

'Want to see my penis?'

'Fuck off.'

'Anyone want to see my penis?'

'The fuck's wrong with you?'

'It's a joke, for fuck's sake – just say no!'

'Who the fuck says *penis*? What are you, my mother?'

If you didn't go to the Kinbassa for voices there was no point in going. Not drink but reckless voices was why you went to a hole like that. Like a crow to caw the week's trigger words, or else to hear others caw them. Doesn't work on a screen; the descent to your crew through a tavern is a plunge through layers of personal space like levels of chill in the sea, ending here with the blind who lurk by feel where nothing grows because light doesn't reach it. Types you talk down to your wife but secretly hope for. Types you talk down to yourself but secretly hope for. Fellow defectives.

It was early enough that only Dennis 'Feral' Farrell, Janos 'Boges' Bogdanovic and Jorge 'Hordy' Almibar were there; Feral a scrawny polecat on the permanent verge of offence, Boges off a communist labour mural and Hordy a Latin pretty boy with pyramid schemes in his eyes. Boges was the first to stop pretending not to see Lon.

'Behold,' he grunted. 'A personage of leisure.'

'You next.'

'Fuck off, I'm on the safeguards team. They'd need a better than average reason and I'm not of a mind to give them one.'

'Robots need no reason.'

'Buy me a beer. Make you feel better.'

'Not getting into rounds, I'm on a mission. Caught Shel up the Row in a swimsuit with someone just now. Shotgun time.'

'Still got the over-and-under?'

'Uh-huh. Time to oil her up.'

'Gonna happen sooner or later,' Boges rasped into his bottle. 'I'm riding Joelly like a fascist – already owns more make-up than her mother.'

'And isn't Swim Club in a one-piece? Shel's out in the little red thing she got in Calabrava that time we went.'

'So it's either a calendar shoot – or someone from Caveney's.'

'Is what I'm thinking.' Lon waved for a beer.

Fourteen Palisade Row had been Ernest Caveney's house when the men were boys, back before it needed a number, before the Company came to town. Ernest ran Caveney's shoe factory. He used to host an Easter fair with rides out on the flat to thank the community for its support. The boys sometimes went, although they never wore his shoes. The factory died with Ernest but his Caveney Thor-Gard work boots are considered fetish objects today.

Hordy – English for Jorge, which is foreign for George – listened through the back of his shiny ears. 'Caveney's.' He turned to Lon. 'Isn't refugees in there now? From the war zone? Wasn't that batch of reffos from Al Qemen housed down here?'

'Makes sense,' nodded Boges. 'Supposed to be temporary but it's already a fucking year. If they're in limbo it's less reason to keep their noses clean.'

'What's that?' Feral turned.

'Reffos. Baiting Lon's kid.'

'Didn't think they were refugees,' said Lon. 'House doesn't look that crowded. Not that it matters. Foreign is all I can tell.'

'Silver four-door?' Hordy lifted a brow. 'Lives at the mosque.'

Feral lowered his beer to stare at Lon. 'What do you mean, not that it fuckin matters? Who else d'you think it's gonna be? Reffos are like fuckin seagulls: if it's not locked up or nailed to the ground you can kiss it fuckin goodbye!'

Tyson blew in with more crew. Squalls of cologne came before him, a feature of drain rats who couldn't leave work without showering. After the usual exchange about brothels he said, 'What's the current?' and Feral piped up:

'Reffos at Caveney's seagulled his kid.'

'*No way*. We'll all fit in the van – let's go.'

'I'm on it, I'm on it,' said Lon.

'Alone?'

'It's a residential address, not the fucking war zone.'

Feral stabbed the air. 'But there goes the street. Isn't your place on the market? There goes the street. May as well be the fuckin war zone now, boy.'

'We'll all go down there,' said Boges.

'No, we won't,' said Lon.

'Every which way, these fuckers.' Feral trained a finger on the door. 'In public, in daylight, tail, tail, tail. It's all over the news.'

'Don't include my family in *tail*. I can see their house from my gate – you think they'd hit the road they live on when there's only one other address? Anyway, have some fucking heart, not their fault we bombed their places.'

'Forced marriage is a growth industry there.'

'Fucking *what*?'

'And they kill the used ones. Why do you think they pick em young?'

'Don't just kill em,' said Tyson. 'Stone em. Look on the grid.'

'Jesus, you mongrels.'

'Not all bad news,' said Feral. 'She could end up with a goat butcher.' He crouched as if they were all hunchbacked. 'Another happy man'll be Bogesy – Boges, like goats as much as sheep? Fuck a nice goat on the cliff edge? *Baa* – get out the Velcro gloves!'

Backwash emptied to froth on Lon's tongue. Backwash was how you skipped dim-witted moments, it was an edit-replace. He swallowed too soon, just as Tyson took the floor with his cultural insights: 'Some reffo tried it on with me once in a fucking taxi. I said Arcadia, he said ten, I said fine and he went no, it's ten right now. And I said get away and he said no that's the rules and I said no way and he said yeah because we have to get paid first. So I go to get out of the car, I just open the door and start getting out, and he goes okay listen I can see you're a good guy, and he pulls right back, just like that. Fucking no sense of reason at all.'

'The fuck you doing in Arcadia?'

'Connie's olds.'

'They that loaded?'

'Pre-Company, been there since Moses. Loaded if they ever sell.'

Conversation stalled as a bell chimed a tip at the bar. Music plinked and went *branggg*. Quiet swelled and the crew swigged together like herding beasts. Perhaps Lon shouldn't go to Fourteen. Perhaps he should watch and wait. Perhaps he should enter a pact with Ember to harvest more details from Shelby. He gazed into the middle distance, where a pencil-necked apprentice was trying to charm a gothy girl by looking indifferent. She with spackled face and cobalt streaks was winning because she genuinely didn't give a shit. Human relationships were bent. Didn't conform to advertised standards. No one ever shut up about them but it was all largely bullshit because they never threw light on the bent. Lon didn't want his rug rats settling for bent. They were too little to enter that fray. He stared at the apprentice. The boy's head was bobbing from too much beer, the wrong starting point for indifferent. The kid saw Lon gazing and took a chance to boost his cred: 'Goats, hey, Boges?' he quacked like a pal.

A tenth of a ton of Boges rotated and slowly refocused.

'Velcro gloves! *Ha!* I just mean from like the goat thing.' The lad's head buoyed around like a cork. He could sense it was all or nothing, but his only real hope was if Boges knew his folks and had swung him by the ankles as a child.

Now the girl looked interested.

'I *beg* your pardon?' said Boges.

'Like from just now, you know.'

'The *fuck* is your problem?'

Train wreck. The girl curled her fingers into a little clutching wave, not at the boy but at the crew. She shuffled away to the future. The only tool left to the apprentice was to pretend to be drunker than he was, as if he'd lost his mind, as if the rub and grind of his feverish life had left him incoherent. Lon waited but he was even too green for that.

'Just saying yo,' he mumbled.

'Say yo somewhere else, dickhead. And the name's Bogdanovic.'

The boy spindled off like a broken spider. Part of Lon wanted to buy him a beer, the stupid part, because then he's all over you like a pox until you're manoeuvred into being seen with him by his rivals. When the brutal truth was that they and not he would end up on your crew. There was justice in it and injustice in it.

Relationships. Just too bent.

Out of control.

Lon had to go to Fourteen.

'Hey.' Boges waved a hand across his face. 'A job's a job – a beer is life.'

'Pessimists,' said Feral. 'It's re-*training*. Sacked is sacked, retraining is retraining. Not that *I'd* need it, I could always go private, give classes or something . . .'

'In fucking what? Sewerage?'

'I have a trade, thank you. I'm saying for Cushy, he doesn't have a trade. Don't knock retraining, you never fuckin know. Could even be a ticket up the hill.'

'*Over* the hill,' grunted Hordy.

'Farrell,' said Boges, 'how many boys you know on retraining?'

'I'm not saying anything's guaranteed.'

'Because I know the same ones and so far the training is Shut Up and Wait.' He play-punched Lon. 'Sorry, Cushy. Replaced by a flying pig – who could've guessed.'

By *pig* he meant the giant bullet they shot down pipelines to treat or clean or inspect them. Early models had been made of straw wrapped in barbed wire or leather, making them squeal as they went along. Lon had boasted that little fact to his kids after a week on the job, as if the pigs had come out of a fairy tale. He hadn't boasted that the boys were known as rats, or that they called the pigs Zacs in honour of a particular apprentice and the noise he'd made when he saw his first corpse in the sewers. It hadn't sunk in to Lon how much he'd miss his pipes and drains. You were a free agent in pipes and drains. Paid to emulate nature, because after a while pigging mains and walking sewers you came to see how everything under the sun was plumbed to bring good stuff in and take bad shit out. You couldn't help but absorb the model into your thinking; you looked around and every system was the same, cells, creatures, crab boats and countries. Good stuff in, bad shit out. Don't block it and don't let it mingle.

The rot had set in for pipeline crews when smartpigs arrived that made the workforce look pointless on paper. It meant the boys worked more gutters and bullied more rodents as they whiled away the wait for a retraining notice, as good as a straight termination. What Boges was talking about wasn't even a pig at all but a sewer drone that synchronised with robot dredgers known as gators. The rats had been doubtful when the system arrived, expected it to be like the auto-checkouts at Supa-Lo that needed as much staff as before, or auto-immigration at the airport which was slower than a person in uniform. At first it looked the same with flying pigs, and the crew won weekly bets with the control room until Brayan Basauri got gnashed by a dredger. Instead of boosting the case for a human workforce, department brass made it a case for pulling crews out altogether before anyone else got gnashed. New drones were launched to watch the drones, gators to watch the gators, until fuck only knew what was in the drains any more. New ecosystem that didn't play well with others.

Lon had a week to report to Human Resources at the Octagon to exercise his option to retrain. It still could take them weeks or months to suggest anything to retrain in. The Octagon was Company headquarters: an ecologically sustainable architectural marvel and equal opportunities 'achievement space' committed to the global community. To the rats it was a wealthy day care with optimistic drainage, full of trendy gamers who looked like they didn't do much not doing much and spending the rest of their time designing spaces where doing anything looked wrong. There was sushi. There was a slide and an indoor beach bar. Real work was underway overseas without a slide and a beach bar. Slaves overseas built the slide and the beach bar.

Lon drained his beer and turned to leave.

'Wait for us,' said Tyson.

'It's my neighbours, for fuck's sake. I'll deal with it.'

Feral huddled up with his phone. 'I'll get a last selfie.'

'How about some bowling on Sunday?' asked Hordy. 'Now that you have leisure.'

'I'll think about it.' Lon nodded around the clump of his crew, saluted the bar and thudded away in his work boots. Voices swirled behind like filthy cinders in his wake:

'Call if it gets too heavy down there in Palistan!'

'If any are wearing backpacks get the fuck out!'

'They're not gonna wear backpacks in their own home, you fucking idiot.'

'Why not? *Be Ever Ready* and all that.'

'*Be Ever Ready* is fucking Pup Pioneers.'

'Ha! Reffo Pup Pioneers.'

'Got my suicide badge, my asylum badge, my tail badge.'

'My forced marriage badge.'

'My stoning badge.'

'My goat badge.'

'You're not gonna earn many badges after your suicide badge, you dipshit.'

'Why not? My martyr badge, my headlines badge, my virgins badge . . .'

'Payout to my next-of-kin badge who thought I was a cunt anyway badge.'

'Feral, it's your buy.'

'How's it always me?'

'It's not always you; it's you now.'

'What about Tyse? Bit of fuckin democracy?'

'Okay, democracy: hands up who tells Feral it's his fucking buy.'

The air outside had purchase. Weeds were crispy, gravel crunched bright after beer.

So went the Little Burro Avenger.

Giddy-up.

3
Apple Meadow Flashback

'I said get your kid away from my daughter's swimwear.'

'You send your daughter out in swimwear?'

'I said get your kid away from my daughter's swimwear.'

'At least till he can afford the full service.'

'I said get your kid away from my daughter's swimwear.'

'That explains those sores, Laila.'

All this plus beards and wailing and the thud of a mortar on dust run amok in your mind on a Thursday like that. Already whipped by lunchtime but the lash of ratshit chance kept hissing down. There was Lon coasting down City Hill Road to his false riviera, past sheds that could be freight cars under a rusty glow of sodium lamps in West Palisades and Molan. Behind them huddled alleys built for homecoming soldiers more than a century before, minus the old mattress place, the chicken place, the laundromat, the foreign food place and the goat butcher, as Farrell would have it, or anyway a butcher with trays of heads and tongues and ruffled guts they didn't do at the Supa-Lo. All this rattled past on his right but he was lost in the rear-view mirror, where the dark above town was aglow like a hotplate on full.

He had to move there.

Crawl north in life. Climb upstairs.

The physical cliff they called the palisade was why the town hadn't spread at this end. Renewal ran upstairs with all the money – Arcadia, Reynes, Stresnan Heights. Up with the high-end sports utilities, Harville and around there. The further south you got the less successful you were until you hit the edge he was driving past now. Once you were there you were fucked. 'Definition of confusion? Father's Day in Palisades', et cetera, a culture in a laboratory dish, a state of permanent waiting for the stinking truck with flashing lights to haul away your semen in tissues or socks before any more freaks grew out of it. The secret life of the southernmost suburb, and who could blame anyone; nothing says forget it like a seventy-foot rock face: you're either above or below it.

In or out of town.

In or out of sight.

In or out of luck.

The car whined down to the T-junction, another falsehood because it was really a bend to the right into West Palisades with a small feeder left on to the single dead-end lane of Palisade Row, which was unsignposted. The main flow was west and this was a filter valve where Lon departed town. Good stuff in, bad shit out, don't let it mingle. To the west, barely over City Hill Road, the palisade narrowed and fell to the ground, making all persons equal, if still somewhat scummy. Take the left turn and it flew into a cliff that also curved inwards so that nobody in the world who wasn't on the Row could see you. People in town lived a lifetime without turning left there. It just looked like you shouldn't. If anyone wanted to play on the flat they did it to the west, where there was parking and a kiosk with drinks and calcified snacks in a warming cabinet. Some kids had tried to launch skateboard-kiting but it had only lasted as long as the kite shop lasted, which was until the first lease ran out. Place wasn't windy enough.

Lon's headlights swung over the flat like a puke of bleach. Lights were still on at Fourteen. Grey sedan in the carport. He pulled on to the sandy shoulder across the road and cased the place for mayhem. There was none, so he crossed the road, went in the gate and up to the door, *rap*, *bap*, *bap*.

He checked his fly. Thumbed a nostril. The boys had primed him for explosions and screaming and he was ready to go in like a soldier; but holding his violence was like holding his breath and it was fast running out. He glanced back at the car. It wasn't that clean but it glared like something molten. Their street lamp worked just fine.

A shadow spread over the door glass. A rounded figure approached that wasn't as tall as Lon. The door opened, warmth fell out, and there, thought Lon, stood a lightly olive-skinned man, although olives are purple or green. In truth it was a peanut-butter-skinned man, and he came with a you-take-care-now brow and an upturned mouth on the way to a smile. Soft and shiny as a wholemeal bun. Early forties.

'Can I help you?' Not a refugee.

Yes, I said get your kid away from my daughter's swimwear, Lon didn't seem to say. 'Lon Cush, from Thirty-Seven.' He pointed up the road to his flickering lamp.

'What a nice surprise!' An accent but confident. There would be no explosions or screaming here. 'Al Medina,' said the man, interrupted by a voice from behind. It was followed by an even smaller person than he.

'Who is it, Albert?'

'Our neighbour.'

'No!' A woman emerged. 'Please come in, come in! I'm Marta.'

Your son is the Little Burro Stalker, Lon didn't seem to say. Who knew how this position had come to the party after he'd laid a table in his mind for the other position. His mind made up the difference by assuring him he could pounce from where he stood – 'Delicious cake, Marta, *I said get your kid away from my daughter's swimwear*' – but he could no sooner pounce than piss his name. The mind has a region that does this for a living, makes new positions look better than old ones when they're not necessarily.

Marta pulled him into her slipstream. 'What was the name, excuse me?'

'Lon – short for Lonregan.' His face already said yes to cat-sitting, mower-lending and selfies from the beach. Rapport: the silent killer.

If Lon was five-nine, Al Medina must have been five-five. Marta five-two. Folksy scarf and rustic bangles meant she gave a shit about libraries. A nicer type of person, vibrating and beaming and full of warm plans. Her power probably came from picturing friends with apples in a meadow, whereas Lon's only thought as he entered the house was what a monumental dimwit Feral became after a drink.

'Oh, Thirty-Seven.' She led the way through her cosy home. 'We admired that house so much, didn't we, Albert? With the lovely plants. I can't get ours to grow at all.'

'Not all species can deal with the sandy soil,' said Lon. 'When did you move in? Probably only missed my place on the market by a whisker.'

'When, Albert – a year ago?'

'Not even, we arrived for the fair.'

'That's right – oh, our first week we didn't have a fridge or a stove or anything; we spent the whole week eating fairground food. Can't look at pizza since!' Marta bounced with the humour of it. They both had the zest-for-life thing going on – plain good people, as you say before you have to face them in court. Now came a kitchen-diner with a breakfast bar in wood-effect Formica. A matching hexagonal table suitable for cards. Decor that lulled the mind into waiting for gravy.

'Carnival food.' Lon nodded. 'My kids account for half their business.'

'Oh! *Ha ha*.' Al pulled out three chairs and shuddered at such a great joke. 'Ours was the opposite: she went on a diet. I saw her buy a burger, take off the onions, soak the grease out in a napkin and throw away the burger! She called it onion salad!'

'Ha!' Lon's head tossed more than it would for a gag at the Kinbassa. Strange how infectious behaviour is. 'Kids will be kids,' he added like a failing talk show host. He was already wondering where the boy was, or if there was a boy.

'Well, but Galatea's nearly twenty-six, not a kid any more. It's crazy but she feels all this pressure, sees her life flashing before her eyes.'

'Alberto, we all feel it at that age. My God, back when you had a moustache you'd spend hours with it in the bathroom. I was like a widow to it.'

'Not hours, come on. Although hair is a big responsibility.'

'Don't want to sound cheesy,' said Lon, 'but you don't look old enough to have a twenty-five-year-old. Is that cheesy? How many kids do you have?'

Marta folded her hands on the table. Her head dipped, her smile drained, her eyebrows floated up. Enter the human moment where the shell cracks open and you're sitting facing someone like yourself, mealy breath, wayward flesh, secret lover of bad music. Susceptible as a naked prawn. Happened here as surely as when love sucks your brains out. Lon clasped his hands and waited. Albert looked down and waited.

'Gala's not our biological child.' Marta lowered her voice as if she'd built the girl from a popular but unfashionable kit. 'She's my sister's girl. Some difficulties with rebellion, and my sis had health issues, so she came to us. Win–win because we wanted a child and she's family, and anyway we couldn't have supported more than one.'

Lon nodded towards a statuette of an ugly cross-legged warrior with a bowl in his lap where a pear rested, bruising from inside. A calendar on the wall said *Don't Look Back You're Not Going That Way*. A fridge magnet holding a photocopied schedule said *OOPS*. Their dishcloths were seagrass and aqua and blue, faintly nautical like everyone's knick-knacks who fell for the flat, which after dark was an unshining sea. Everything in the place was just over the line from blue-collar into white. They would have classical music somewhere, and something instrumental with a flute. Lon was the closer to explosions and screaming.

'So let me get it straight.' Marta sat back. 'Did you also move into Thirty-Seven quite recently? Or is it you who was selling it?'

'I'm selling. Trying to move upstairs.'

'Do you mind if we ask how much it was listed for?'

'It still is, for two-fifty.'

'Oh!' Her face fell. 'We could never have afforded that.'

'No?'

'We paid a hundred and sixty for this.'

'Even that was a stretch,' nodded Al.

'A hundred and sixty? *One-six-oh?*'

'Even that was a stretch.'

'But the place is fine.' Marta blinked up at the light. 'Could've been more accessible, but it's a nice open space, kind of feels like the edge of the world.'

'With the protection of the cliff.' Al pointed. 'Those flowers and ferns growing out of the face? They line up with our back windows like a rock garden.'

'Alberto, go and call Gala. It's so nice to finally meet our neighbour. We weren't sure if to come and introduce ourselves – you know, because of privacy?'

'No, yeah, we were the same.' Lon cleared his throat.

'How many of you? We've seen a pretty girl on the road.'

'Shelby. There's her and my son, Egan. Sometimes Ember, who looks after them when I work. Not romantic or anything.' The truth bit him back as soon as he said it, namely that he and Ember had once done the dirty deed after weed and discount wine. Fast and sloppy like tossing a hot dog up City Hill Road. Regret, regret, regret; he was suddenly a traitor to the memory of his wife, and he felt just as bad for Ember. He'd been so damn lonely, she must've been too, and that night was so pouting and warm. The force of it had locked them into a twilight ever since, where they alternated hoping for more or for less, never together, one-up-one-down like a silent piston engine; and the twilight only stayed by never talking, so they didn't. Who knew why people did that. *Relationships*. Just too bent. Lon moved over it by mumbling, 'Their mother died when they were babies.' What a thing to say but it was context.

'*No!*' Marta flinched as if it were happening on the table. 'Oh *no*! I'm *sorry*. They're welcome here any time, *any time*. Albert carves puppets on weekends and there's always food on the table – well, you can see!' She patted her belly. 'And maybe the girl . . . ?'

'Shelby. Shelby-Ann.'

'Maybe Shelby would look up to Galatea – she's great with kids.'

Al went to the stairs: '*Gala!* And put on some clothes! Not that she walks around naked but she might not expect a guest.'

'Tea, coffee . . . ?' Marta stood and smiled. 'Are you hungry? Well, you don't have to be hungry; let me get you something to taste, a treat from our part of the world.'

'Which part? Please don't go to any trouble.'

'San Uribe. No trouble, I insist. *Insisto*, as we say.'

'San Uribe, San Uribe.' Al sat with a sigh.

'Blessed in its people and its nature.' An oven pinged in the kitchen. 'Just the crime can be a problem. Life's too short to tolerate violence.'

'The whole world's going that way,' said Albert. 'What's the saying – where the jungle meets the city only the colours change?' A plate of folded bakes arrived, *timpas*, Albert called them. 'You're with the Company too?'

'Environmental Services.'

'Publications Studio,' said Albert. 'Instruction manuals. Strange first year. I've said goodbye to more colleagues than are left on my floor.'

'In the Octagon?' Lon didn't want to be seen at Human Resources.

'Second floor,' said Albert. 'You?'

'We have our own bunker behind Knox Park.'

'Lucky. Cost-cutters might forget you're there.'

'Doesn't seem right – Company value grew by a third last year.'

'Efficiency increased as much, that's the problem. New technologies. Although I met someone from Legal who said their team is set to triple.'

'Huh. So they're just killing manual jobs.'

Talk was interrupted by a flash of cornflower blue. A smile like a searchlight led a young woman into the room, barefoot under a short fitted dress thrown on moments before, still finding its fit from the shoulders down. Slim bendy girl with big eyes, glowing skin and the short frisky hair of a boy on a raisin box label. Something about her was hungry for life; her gaze delved around with fingers.

Lon's clothes creased loudly as he stood.

'And this is Galatea.'

'Lon.' Hot silky hand.

Al reached for a *timpa*. He waited till his mouth was full then covered it to say: 'She wants to be a welder. With a degree in media. Work that one out.'

'Yeah?' Lon worked it out.

'Why not?' She grinned. 'Heat and sparks, it's honest.'

'I do some welding here and there.'

'There you go,' said Marta. 'Lon might have some realistic advice.'

'I'm realistic, I just need a start.'

'A start can take many forms.'

Some forms came to mind as Galatea settled her dress around her body using her hips like a tongue in a cheek. A tattoo on her shoulder gave Lon a licence to stare.

'Nice ink there. Leopard?'

'Ocelot.'

'*Nice?*' Marta recoiled. 'Why anyone would damage such beautiful skin is beyond me to understand. I won't make a big deal, what's done is done, but – seriously?'

'Giving up the big deal after only six years?' said Gala. 'Such a quitter.'

'Shh. The problem is, Lon, a boy talked her into it and she's only lucky it isn't his name printed there. Imagine if she ended up with *Humberto* written all over her, because anyway by three days later she never saw him again.'

'No one talked me into it.'

'Nooo, weren't you his little *tigre*, his little *gatita*, his little *poosy* . . . ?'

'*Marta!*' hissed Albert.

'Ush – too much info, sorry. But we're all adults, I'm just trying to tell Lon that kids don't understand permanence at all, they don't get that it's for ever. I hope you've been lucky so far with Shelby and your boy.'

'Mm? Oh – they're obviously too young, a parlour wouldn't do it without a parent's consent. I'm safe for a while, anyway.'

'It goes fast.'

'It does go fast. You're right there.'

All of them studied their hands until Gala broke in: 'And I guess your wife . . . ?'

'Shh!' hissed Marta. 'She passed away! I'm sorry, Lon.'

'Ow.' Gala frowned. 'So sorry.'

Marta rapped the table. 'Get your little ones over here. Gala just loves kids, but Gala – don't encourage them with tattoos! Tell them only about the pain!'

'There was no pain. I love my *ocelote*.'

'No pain for you, perhaps. Try feeling *our* pain. Honestly, Lon, and if you saw the boy you'd seriously scratch your head.'

'Thanks for not making a big deal!'

'I'm not making a big deal. What's done is done.'

'Still you feel obliged to discuss my love life!'

'Ush.' Marta shifted in her chair. 'First of all, you can't call a few days *love*. Think about it. Anyway, let's not make a big deal.'

'And why can't it be a few days? Lon, you're a neutral party: is it better in life to find a small amount of love, even a promise of love – or no love at all?'

'Don't go there, Lon!' Al flapped a hand. 'A little too much college – don't get her started. A little too much and not quite enough.'

Gala cocked her head and waited. A lock of hair fell over one eye.

'Some must be better than none,' mused Lon. 'No?'

'Thank you,' she said. 'So the only question is: can it exist in a few days?'

'Mm – why not?'

'Ouch.' Marta buried her face. 'Another one from the "Why not?" school.'

'Oh no,' said Al.

Gala's tongue peeped through her grin. She bit the tip at Lon.

'That's it, Lon' – Marta shook her head – 'bad move. Next thing you know she'll be packing her bags and moving to your place.'

'*And we'll help her pack!*' Al thumped the table.

Like the tremulous birth of an undersea bubble they all surged up together, heads tossed back to where necks at the Kinbassa would snap. Marta struggled for breath, Gala glistened in her mouth, Al blasted the tabletop with thundering dark hoots, *ho ho HO*, finally drawing himself up, wiping an eye and whimpering, 'Great – we know the neighbour twenty minutes and we're *quarrelling about love*!'

As they sniffled and whined back into their skins, a shout clanged in from outside.

'*Cushy!*' It was Dennis Farrell.

The table dabbed its eyes.

'*Don't fucking scream, you moron.*' Boges.

'*Should I knock or what?*' Tyson.

'*Don't! They might take it for gunfire.*'

'Strange.' Al froze. 'Don't think we've ever had a caller here.'

The voices rippled round on a breeze. 'Must be for me,' murmured Lon. Mirth turned cold in his eyes.

The women scurried up to the front curtains. Al beat Lon into the hall, approached the door as a knight approaches a castle. He opened it slowly. Lon quickly followed. A posse arrayed on the road, its shadows an open-jawed trap between picket gate and street lamp. Boges's old van puffed smoke behind Lon's car. In a flash the scene appeared to Lon through Al and Marta's eyes: non-Palisades eyes, clear eyes. A sinker fell inside him. He knew the view. Diane's old view, where boys like these were just a pack of chewed crayons, where thugs were thugs and dirt was dirt and there were plenty of nicer people in the world who would still take your bullet.

'We're having a chat,' Lon called down from the step.

'Fine,' said Boges. 'We got your back.'

'You *know* them?' hissed Al.

A filmy membrane stretched between this apple-meadow household and the rats at the gate. The membrane was Lon. He needed to stay on the meadow side. The Diane side. Why don't the sides of a membrane mix? Why can't they mingle? He didn't know. He only knew he had to stay in the meadow.

'D'you nail the little seagull?' Feral leered over the gate. He'd enjoyed more drinks, and still had a bottle in hand. 'You look like they've got a gun to your head.'

'Get out of here, Farrell.'

Al caught Lon's gaze. 'Is this *okay?*'

'They're just passing.'

'Passing to where?' He looked up the dead-end lane.

'Probably saw my car.' Lon said it loud enough for at least Boges to catch the drift.

'What – *what?*' Feral gaped around. 'Not how things go in the desert? Pals don't come over for beer?'

'False alarm.' Lon's fingers twitched for a stone to throw.

'False *alarm?*' queried Al.

'Lucky man tonight.' Feral jerked himself upright. 'Need more than a fuckin backpack to mess with us.'

'Shut it, Farrell. Boges – for Christ's sake.'

'Come on, dipshit.' Boges lumbered up to the gate.

Broad ancestral lines pressed up through Al's skin. A different time and place pressed up that knew the scent of ignorance. 'Why do I feel I'll be calling the police?'

'They're okay,' mumbled Lon. 'Few drinks.'

'Oh, the *police?*' Feral sneered.

'Yes! When I have drunks outside making threats.'

'Boges – before I kill him.'

'Can't drink yourself so you fuck everyone else up, that how it goes in Al Qemen?'

'They're from San Uribe *will you piss off!*'

'Tell me to piss off, it's between me and the camel-jockey.'

'Did he just say *camel-jockey?*' The shine fled Al's skin.

'C'mon.' Boges jimmied Feral off the gate. 'You don't need cops.'

'You're welcome, Cushy, cunt.' Feral teetered into his shadow. 'Next time find a posse up your fuckin asterisk.'

'I didn't come for a posse.'

'Nooo, we all had the same dream that your neighbour was a stalker.'

'I will break your legs.'

'Fuck's sake.' Boges shoved Feral to the van. 'We got the drift.'

Al's lips pulled taut as catapult rubbers. 'I don't know what just happened here but it leaves a bad taste. Some agenda, I don't even want to think what. Thanks for dropping by.' He made himself large in the doorway. 'If in two minutes I see anyone still out here I am calling the police! Now go home!'

'*Go home yourself!*' Feral rallied. 'Come to our fuckin place and tell us what to do!'

'Huge misunderstanding, Al.' Lon blinked at the sky.

The door double-locked behind him.

He scraped down the path and out through the gate, looking back.

Gala's face was there between curtains.

Then it was gone.

The night was chill.

One final thought quivered down like a spore:

Dennis Farrell was a welder.

4
Owl Light

Gazing out across the Palisades flatland at dusk, the stranger stood and marvelled at how the smoky band on the far horizon did not conceal a sea, no crashing tide on its way to his feet. Around him instead swished the grasses and trees of the abandoned Moyle estate, its chimneys rising up in silhouette. It was an otherworldly view in bands of ochre and twilight blue, as clear as backlit satin. The mansion was the last place he'd looked at that week, an eleventh-hour wild card, but no doubt about it: it was the one. A renovation to sink his teeth into, a sideline to the high-pressure Octagon project he'd come to oversee. Bastian Matanick scanned the scene with open mouth, as if deciding where to bite first. A videocall underway in his hand had almost been forgotten.

'Wait, wait till you see,' he finally hissed at the phone. 'Before the light goes.'

'What time is it there?' asked his aide, Anouk. 'Aren't you back at the hotel?'

'No, no, wait.'

The shiny young man with straked golden hair like the undercoat of a hedgehog wove between ash trees as clean as pool cues to stand on the shore of the flat. The plain was neither sand nor dust, solid enough to drive over yet soft enough to tread barefoot, if you watched out for fuzzy plants like nestling crabs here and there. The palisade's face of foxgloves and ferns rose behind him to curtain the scene, a shine above the cliff the only hint of any settlement beyond. Ash and yew reverently tapered towards it, leaving grasses and shrubs to storm a snaggled side gate in trousers of runaway ivy. An old iron arch framed Palisade Row as it curled like a brook past a tall, narrow house not far along the road, and one solitary other like a miniature in perspective, whose windows beamed dairy rays through the owl light outside.

He took off a backpack and produced a tiny drone, tapping its gut to his phone. The view from those two houses must be of a dry riviera, he thought; an anchorage you could stroll on. The device set off like a firefly towards the Row.

'Bastian?' said Anouk. 'Still there?'

'Wait, check this out. You inside or on the street?'

'At home.'

'Throw it to a big screen – watch.'

The aerial view flashed up.

'WOW.'

'See what I mean? It's like *Oh my God.*'

'*Wow!*'

'Can you believe it?'

'A dreamscape. What's that other building?'

'The nearest house to the estate. There's that and one other, further away again, and that's the whole road, just these three old places along the curve of the cliff.'

As if on cue, low sun broke through a slash in the sky at the end of the Row, making the tableland creep like quicksand, vaporising chimneys for an instant over City Hill Road. Its beam came to light a moving figure before shattering among ash leaves, the figure of a man on his way to a car at the nearest house.

Bastian Matanick saw so much in the place, so much that wasn't there – exotic flags and horns, land brigantines and schooners, a city of coloured tents, herds of impala, pram-wheeled gondolas punted by liveried gondoliers; to him the place was a drug and a canvas in waiting. Miniature flowers shimmered up from the grasses like fishlings, leaves rushed around as if sucked in the wakes of small birds. He guided the drone with the screen of his phone, looping high over the flat for an inbound approach to the Moyle estate behind him. 'Check this out.' The drone spun head-on. 'Hardcore, isn't it?'

'I'm just waiting for the orchestral score.'

'You're right, it's totally cinematic. It needs a banquet under flaming braziers, a bicycle polo team out on the flat, a child with a lute, a hot-air balloon, a touring carriage, uniformed bloodhounds, tapirs in armour. It needs an eco-estate like a desert market powered by solar sails. It needs me, in fact, Anouk. Hah! The hell. Doesn't it? In fact?'

'Where on earth are you?' Anouk's dusky face bobbed over the screen as Matanick caught the drone mid-air. 'Is the hotel around there?'

'Well, the story so far, I've spent since Tuesday with the liaison guy checking properties selected by the Company. But no luck till now.'

'Or no *Bastian* luck? Tapirs might be difficult for them – it's not that big a town.'

'Every place was like a nineties cartoon of a nerd pad, just skateparks and hot tubs and bowling alleys, you know? Ay-ay-ay. And this one place had a pool with a boat in it that was a waterbed. Just really small ideas, buzzwords on the walls and shit like that. So after watching me laugh for a few days I guess the guy took it as a challenge and finally showed me this place.'

'The big place? Can you stay there? Looks abandoned; it's spewing ivy.'

'I could fix it up. Make it a workspace *and* a home. It's perfect, and far enough away from the crunchers at the Octagon.'

'They own it? They can just sell it to you?'

'The City apparently owns it after a fight between the heirs and the Tax department. And the Company owns the City, more or less.'

'Would it fit your budget?'

'I'll make it fit with spare. The place with the skatepark was five mils; the dude told me this must be two as it is. Use the rest to fix it up.'

'Mm.' Anouk blinked around. 'Big job.'

'Sure, but if you think about it this is probably our last somatic project – of its kind, anyway. Need to dig in, make a base, think ahead to phase three.'

'And those two houses along the lane, do they come with it?'

'No, they're private homes – but I'm already thinking of one for Professor Roos. Perfect office with apartment upstairs, and not too big, the way Toby says she likes it. Maybe the nearest one, what do you think? According to the liaison dude there's only like a sanitation worker or someone living there.'

'Shouldn't you ask Roos herself? She might be around a while.'

'I hear she's really difficult. Also super-old. I don't think she'll want what we want. Sounds kind of beige. I just don't want her on-site where she can be a pain.' Matanick wedged his screen in the crook of a tree to capture himself in the scene. 'I also just think she'd prefer an independent space like that. I think the key is to have it all done before she lands and present it as a fait accompli.'

'Ten days? Good luck with that.'

'Wasn't born hyper for nothing.'

'And when she sees you kept the mansion and she got the gate-house?'

'It's not a gatehouse, and anyway the view must be even better. I'm being thoughtful and taking on the ruin as a construction site – she's getting the charming quiet home, all ready to move in and put her feet up.'

'Hasn't she written papers on people like you?'

'Come on! I swear I feel like walking over to that house right now and throwing the sanitation guy an offer. It could be painted and furnished the way Roos likes by the end of next week. Fix her up first and leave my mess for later.'

'Maybe easier to find tapirs than that much beige.'

'Looking at the general area I don't think it'd be expensive. Half a mil or less. My instinct's just so strong on this place – I mean, look at it. It's peaceful, it's dramatic, it's self-contained. It's surreal. And we could run secure feeds between here and that house, duplicate some systems, make her feel part of a team.'

'She's not part of a team?'

'Not tech, anyway. First time we've had like a research scientist.'

'And she's going – *why*, exactly?'

'Window dressing. The board wants her in to keep the regulators sweet. Likely Institute Prize winner, obvious prestige. Maybe she'll do some media if things get weird. Beyond that, I guess she'll continue her research, or who knows. All I know is I'm going to buy her that house and play jazz as she opens the door.'

'Now it's a visit from your grandmother.'

'Another tip of Toby's. He also said to leave her some booze in the fridge.'

'So we're off to Planet Bastian. At least talk to an agent!'

'Tie the deal up for weeks and end up paying *more*?'

'You can't go playing developer – the project's going to start. They showed you the place with the skatepark so you can chill and prepare for the job, not run around rebuilding the town. If you don't want to skate, paint it blue and put water in it!'

'And start wearing deck shoes.'

'Why do you have to deal with her, anyway?'

'Part of the dressing. She's advisory committee and we sponsor a member each. I'm technically her host. Hope it doesn't end up being ironic.'

'It's already ironic. Have you even read her work?'

'You know, Anouk: you never lost the ability to help me channel decisions. I bought a nice wine on the way over just now, and I suddenly see it's for the table in that nearest house with a straight offer of three hundred grand, negotiable to four for immediate possession. Has to belong to the guy we saw leaving – it was the only car on the street.'

'And he drove the car away. Drink the wine and think about it. Anyway, it's getting dark already. Do some research and look again tomorrow.'

'I swear, if he's back before I go to the hotel I'm taking this bottle and sealing a deal. Come on, it's just too perfect. You have to admit. Otherwise even the furthest house would do, closer to the main road. Maybe even better.'

'You haven't even signed for the ruin!'

'It's not a ruin! Anyway, a project like this, they can't say no.'

Bastian ended the call walking back to the Moyle house. He climbed the stairs by screenlight, lingering on the threshold of an overgrown chamber like a primeval dinosaur's garden, less of a room shanghaied by parkland than a coincidence of palisade landscape resembling a boudoir. Not only had nature reclaimed the space but long slow nature had settled there, not homeless detritus like mulch or mould but nature as it came to an empty planet, laughing at time, digesting its grime till the site was a virginal glade. Stalks of *Fallopia* hovered like kelp over a froth of rude life on the floor, a shaggy burlesque that must bask now and then in a sunbeam through a tall window. Abreast of the windows were petrified drapes as gnarled as the yew outside, and where moss tumbled under a derelict chair, itself grown over with algae, flowers no bigger than pinheads strove up the legs like hairy socks. A bed also stood under a linen of moss as clean as the quilt once laid there, while shorelines of plaster and green brick shallows etched worlds in the wall behind.

Bastian looked around. 'Screen could go here. Knock through here. Screen here.' He muttered and paced through the yawning space, losing himself till seven o'clock when the cold chased him back down the stairs. The door stood open across a grand hall; a breeze rustled treetops outside. He could see a white car under a lamp on Palisade Row, and as he reached for his phone to call his driver to collect him, another car approached from further along. It was the car he'd seen earlier, at the nearest house. The sanitation worker's car, it could only be.

Bastian grabbed his bottle of wine and swung it under his arm like a crop.

5
Society

Lon crawled home in first gear. He squinted around for hints on the flat as to how the fuck he'd wound up here. Seven o'clock and beaten in life. As if the wasteland itself were pulling him down, ant-ridden Palisades tableland where birds were nervous and bunnies were grim, where a barrow could languish for a hundred years, where even if there were homes they would be bare, even if there were owners they wouldn't be there.

Explosions and screaming would've made an easier night.

And Galatea: an impossible prospect, he didn't kid himself. But the spark alone was unsettling. Nine years he'd kept a T-shirt in a freezer bag that he swore still smelled of Diane and now this other flicker played into the years like a disembodied cigarette. A signal from outside a trap he didn't know he was in, a flare on a horizon that showed there was an outside at all. Now he felt a chill. It was a pipeline of years he'd been hiding in, a tunnel of time, and it wasn't that he hid there in pensive times, it wasn't a grieving that he went to like a shrine, but rather his life was lived there entirely, years of history strewed behind him, the people he'd looked at and the people he hadn't, the ones he'd liked and the ones he hadn't all lined this channel in a sideshow row where they froze as they were when he knew them.

His mind managed turmoil by simplifying time. Time came from behind and went forward in sections that were sealed after an upset or a change. He could have no perception of parallel scenes lapping alongside or outside or overhead, other potentials or viewpoints. His model of time was this fore-and-aft line that could only track along and never sideways. In the smell of old upholstery and the dimness of the night he saw a storm drain in his mind that he'd been wading through. Trawling for love in her bathwater suds as they cooled running down to the sea.

Perhaps here was finally the sea. The spout of the drain where the first winter rain would unleash the deluge that drowned him.

This was the headfuck concerning Diane.

She was dead and he was still inside her.

Lon turned his mind to his collateral headfuck, Diane junior. She even looked like Diane in that satirical way genetics so loves, his satirical lovechild with her Little Burro Stalker. Obviously hadn't been Gala baiting her out in a swimsuit – she was too tall and clearly a woman. Had to be someone else. That he didn't dwell on it more at that moment owed to a white late-model sedan in front of his gate. Of such self-consciously standard equipment that it reeked of volume leasing, which reeked of the Company or the City. He didn't know the car. At best it was someone for Ember.

Frogs fell quiet under the catmint and sea holly as he pulled the gate shut behind him, lifting it on its hinges to dampen the squeak. He went up three steps and billowed into his house like a sailor in a black-and-white bar scene. A woman sat inside amid his decor. Not Ember but a stranger with lank molasses hair. She rose from the table, ending a soft exchange with Shelby. He caught the rising sigh that meant they'd run out of things to say. Egan was on the floor by the window, pretending to be alone with his phone. Shelby had a sudden bow in her hair like a child, although she was a child, and a Sunday-school dress although she'd never heard of Sunday school. Both suggesting his memory of them after news of their deaths in a bus crash.

Shelby watched him close the door. 'He's been drinking,' she sighed.

Lon weighed the scene from the hall. The L-shaped haven had a blue-and-grey living room flowing to a maize-and-apple dining space where the kitchen ran through saloon doors streaked over with a spider's remains. Something was now amiss in it. The woman regarded him strangely, gazing for a moment like a long-lost cousin, faltering at first as if torn between opposites to say.

'Mr . . . uh?' She raised a lanyard ID from between her small breasts. 'My name is Julia Sturdevant.' She was casually dressed, with a camera clipped to her lapel. A little red light blinked as if she might explode.

'Can I do for you.' Lon craned around for Ember.

'I'm afraid I'm responding to a report of assault.'

Lon's mouth fell open at Shelby. She huddled over the table, scratching a secret word with a finger. 'And where's Ember?' he demanded.

'Gone.' She didn't look up. 'What do you expect?'

'*Excuse me?*'

'What do you expect?'

Julia Sturdevant was about to speak when Egan sprang up off the floor. He sidled over to Lon and hissed, 'Some guy's coming in the gate.'

Lon heard the squeak but didn't turn. 'Skinny or big?'

'Skinny. Carrying a bottle.'

Lon slumped to the height of his son's small ear: 'Tell him your dad still has his boots on to break his legs if he sees him round here.'

'Serious?'

'Tell him, I just told him myself. Then lock the door. Shout if he doesn't leave.'

Egan padded off in his socks.

Lon's gaze hadn't left Julia Sturdevant. She shifted uncomfortably, a game show hostess in a remedial class where the table stood in for a prize. She wasn't that old, thirty or so, but the kind of not-old that did young by the book, whose friend who had danced on a table one time was as wild as life needed to get. Mindful, fretful, outspoken young. 'First and foremost I'm here to help.' She didn't sound convinced and she blinked a lot, flickered like a silent film. 'Not all disturbances are police matters; I'm responding in advance to assess the situation.'

Lon's mouth hung waiting at Shelby. Egan locked the door and came to watch.

'Don't look at me.' Shelby shrugged. 'Ember called them.'

So the twilight had ended. Lon grabbed his phone and jabbed Ember's number.

'You have Ember Mullock to thank that police didn't attend directly.' Julia nodded that good news as if hearing it for the first time herself. 'I'm satisfied this isn't a routine situation. Shelby, why don't you leave us now, honey? Can you run up to your room?'

Shelby stretched and yawned. 'Yes, why don't I put Burro to bed.' She swished off her chair and took a kitchen route to the stairs, avoiding her father.

'And work on your acting.' He shot her a look. 'You too, Eagle, show's over.' Ember's call went to voicemail in his hand. He pocketed the phone.

Julia waited for the heretics' footfall to die overhead before speaking. 'I shouldn't have to tell you how seriously we take assault on a minor,' she said.

'*Assault?*' Lon slumped a notch more. 'When I was a kid it was called boundaries.'

'Are we even old enough to have known the day when violence passed for parenting? And she's not just a child, she's a *girl*. Apart from anything, isn't it about time females could start associating males with something other than just *violence*?'

Watercolours, he thankfully didn't say. 'Hey, I'm not celebrating.' He propped his weight against a chair. 'Believe me. But she lied and swore and was rude. She was unsafe, out of control. This is Palisades, in case you hadn't noticed.'

'Would've thought the west was the problem area; you seem to have a nice spacious backwater here.' She looked around as if the house was the backwater.

'Listen, I don't wake up wanting to discipline anyone. But this is a wider battle and I tell you that little bundle of beans knows how to play.'

Julia bookmarked the moment on camera. Checked her watch. 'You have admitted to me that you struck Shelby-Ann Cush, your daughter, at the address of the report, for reasons, according to you, of setting boundaries.' She seemed to blurt it. She didn't blink for a moment, held her breath – then: 'Mind if we sit down?' She exhaled, blinked again and even smiled. 'I can run through some options and give an indication, according to my assessment, of the appropriate way forward from here. Outcomes following early intervention after an assault are shown to be four times stronger than going it alone. Clears the air before any more pressures build up.' She nodded as you nod to a baby. 'I also note that you lost custody of Shelby once before, to her grandmother? But you managed to keep your son? Which can be worse than losing both, in a way, splitting two siblings like that. I'm just trying to say that I get what's at stake here, and hope you do too. There's everything to play for, and we can help – but you have to work with us.'

Lon tousled his head as if badly awoken. 'It's just not assault.'

'Did you touch her?'

'It's just not accurate under the circumstances, I'm sorry.'

'Did you make physical contact at all?'

Lon spread his hands.

'It's assault.' Julia's mouth clamped shut. 'Part of the process we now have to go through is you coming to terms with the fact that you assaulted a minor. You may never have wanted to do it, may never have dreamed of doing it, may never think of doing it again. But as we stand here today you are the assailant of a minor, none other than your own daughter. Start getting used to it because we will not make any progress until that fact is agreed. It's not even a case of the child calling in a malicious report – an adult witness, outside the family, not resident at the address, saw fit to call us.'

'It's not accurate, not under the circumstances. Did you see a bruise?'

'The bruise in her little mind could take years to heal, possibly a lifetime. That's what we're talking about here, that's where our attention needs to go.'

'I'm her dad! How am I going to teach her right from wrong!'

The volume pushed Julia back a step. She sighed and softened her tone. 'Look: we're having this discussion at a time and in a place where you can't hit a puppy. You know? If you can't hit a puppy you can't hit a person, especially not a little one who relies on you. It's really that simple. I mean, honestly. Would you hit a puppy?'

'Damn right, because it wants to know who's boss! Until it's smart enough to handle itself! But it's not *hit* – it's *tap*, it's *reinforce*.

The sound is what does it. Nobody gets beaten up. Or how do they learn if they can't reason? It's a duty of care!'

'Have to be one hell of a smack to be loud enough to frighten it.'

'Oh, for crying out loud.'

'Look: Shelby has rights. Isn't that what we spent however many millennia trying to achieve? She has a right to not be assaulted. By anyone.'

'Assault is just not an accurate word.'

'Can we sit down?' she asked again.

Lon tapped the chair she had earlier vacated and straddled his own like a cowboy. There was much to say, but nothing to be said. His whole recent life had been that way.

'It's important that you grasp our position.' Julia hauled her bag on to her lap like a fender. 'Especially on the back of a confession. A while ago we wouldn't have even explained, we'd have removed the child to safety and passed the assailant on to police. But the area's been better studied: we're now seeing stronger outcomes doing everything we can to keep a family together, even in the presence of some tension. We have new instruments, like the ESA – Enforced Surveillance Agreement – or VSMA, Voluntary Short-term Monitoring Agreement. The operative word in both, of course, is *agreement*.'

Lon shook his head at the ceiling.

'Hear me out, news gets better: I'm satisfied enough to say I won't be seeking removal. Nor am I inclined to go the enforcement route, subject to your cooperation going forward. What I need to establish is a lifeline for Shelby. She needs to know we're a community team, that we're in it together, that you're not battling alone. It's a safety net and a witness, for all of you.'

'AKA parole. I cannot believe this.'

'Keep an open mind – it's minimally intrusive. In the old days you would've been opening your door to all kinds of random visitations. You know? But now: I gather from Shelby that she doesn't have a phone. A couple of ways around that: a TCP – Temporary Contact Point – which is in effect a monitored camera somewhere you can easily reach it, such as a family area.' She peered around some cornices, the door frame, the cabinet by the kitchen. 'Or' – she blinked – 'in the case of a Voluntary Monitoring Agreement, there's a two-way device that Shelby can carry to contact us. As might be used in a care home – not particularly fun but suited to purpose.'

'You're worried about us having fun?'

'Work with me here. If she had a phone you could install our app, which has games to play and a tracking function for you to keep tabs remotely. But it's not our brief to intrude any more than we have to for the child's safety, so whether or not she's ready for a phone is up to you. Between us, knowing many single parents as I do, I think you'd find it a blessing. And if you're thinking it's a can of worms, well – she's going to get one sooner or later. Peer pressure being what it is, I'm surprised you held out this long. So. The app is friendlier than anything else we can do, but it's up to you. I guess you'll also be aware of the staff discount on phones through the Company?'

'I'm laid off. Not sure it applies any more.'

'Sorry to hear. Busy few weeks coming too: the Monitoring Agreement involves intensive anger management, group and solo therapy, and a reorientation club for the whole family, although that can be a lot of fun.'

Lon dragged his face into a silent scream.

'In a team-bonding kind of way. Outdoor activities for parents and kids, and it's open to non-offenders. As for anger management, it's tailored to issues like yours; you'll partner with others who crossed the same line. Our experience shows outcomes up to seventy per cent stronger following the course.'

He had to wonder if this meant seventy per cent were cured of their violence, or everyone's violence reduced to thirty per cent. She didn't look like he should ask. 'And if I don't want to go? If I want to argue my case?'

'If you breach the agreement or decline to enter, we go back to doing things the old way. Protection warrants may be enforced, although let me explain: your agreement tonight doesn't waive any charges arising from this; enforcement is simply suspended pending the outcome of our agreement. Think of it as an opportunity. I'll say again: not long ago you could've been arrested and carted off to jail. Any arguments would've been made before a judge. But thanks to the twenty-first century, social sciences and the law are coming together in a whole new way.'

As rope comes together in a noose, he didn't grunt. He swayed under a weight of bleak ideas until his mind, in the end more compelled by immediate discomforts than by any kind of long-term threat, took control and refocused his will. What he most wanted now was Julia Sturdevant out of his house.

She leaned over as if she'd heard. 'Look, we do this all the time. It's six weeks that can change your life, not only in this way but in lots of ways. I strongly urge you to sign with us and get the show on the road. Then I'll be out of here and you can get back to your life. Shall we enter into an agreement?'

He nodded at the tablet and stylus she pulled from her bag, shifting side-on to avoid what he thought was a glimmer of triumph.

'Excellent.' She blinked with new confidence. 'Moving forward.

While we fill in the details I'll let you in on a little reorientation exercise that can put some power in your hands straight away. Based on the finding that power and control are the drivers of life, and when they're lacking in one area they can pressure others, including relationships and the home. But now this can be fun, and it really works – I do it myself religiously. I want you to think of three small things that irritate or defeat you, three things over which you could exercise some power. And I want you to write them down. They can be anything at all – bad patch of lawn, faulty appliance, creaking gate – and between now and your first session I want you to take control and fix them.'

'Long list. And if I'm technically unemployed, I mean . . .'

'*Small* things. This isn't about solving the world's problems, it's about the brain acknowledging that you have taken power back into your hands. For instance, not to be rude but I did notice your gate squeaks. Should it go on the list?'

'That's how we know anyone's out there.'

'Work with me here.' She readied the screen. 'They'll be entered into our system, and we will follow up. But seriously: it's worth it. It's a question of training ourselves to win again. Winners don't resort to violence. You know?'

'Anybody'd think I stabbed her.'

'Work with me.' She held the stylus poised.

'Okay, okay. Mm. One thing: the system on my laptop seems to have changed all by itself. Now I can't find my old—'

'If you mean the auto-upgrade, forget it. Act of God. Don't nominate anything that can defeat you: this is about *winning*. How about for now just pick one or two doable things. The list can expand over time.'

'Mm, okay. I opted in to a package with my network, and . . .'

'Act of God. Pick something you can plausibly control.'

'Well. Mm. Shelby came home with some very adult ideas that she said came from school. Made a note to chase it up and see what's going on.'

'Okay. Does it have anything to do with today's issues?'

'Not at all – separate issue.' As Lon gazed along the table in thought, the front curtains blurred into heaving live organs to the timbre of the street lamp beyond. 'And that lamp needs attention, outside,' he added.

'Perfect.' She tapped the screen. 'Here, item one: what can we say? Meeting with the school. And item two: attend to faulty street lamp. See how easy?'

'Okay. Pretty much what I did before starting work shifts.'

'Excellent, then you have a head start.'

His compliance was like an ignition to Julia; the outcome seemed better than not being an assailant at all. He watched his stats fly off her stylus in the form of words and ticks and taps: height, weight, race, hair, eyes, education, income, convictions, alcohol, smoking, religion and sex, for the last two of which she ticked *Other*, explaining that it saved some court time if clients then changed them as they couldn't later cite discrimination.

Her mouth now seemed lighter, lips smaller, better formed. Lon even came to feel her distantly familiar. Diane had also been 'together' like this.

By eight thirty she was done. She glanced at the ceiling in reference to the two little lives up there, his foul and ruthless heretics. 'Do you eat together?' she asked. 'One of the first things they'll say on the course is to share at least one meal a day and treat it as a religious vow, no excuses. Share a conversation point too, watch a show together or play a game. We recommend the news because at least it's real events, which can also give civic and global awareness. It's even a point of power for you, filling in the stories, explaining the right and wrong.' She ambled with her bag. Lon overtook her to open the door. 'Finally, it might take some bonding to get over the day's bad feelings.' She turned in the doorway. 'Send out for food, watch a movie, play games till late. A visit from us is even grounds to take tomorrow off – go to the zoo. Only one hard rule: steer clear of any topics that were issues today. Does that all make sense?'

Lon followed as far as the step. As he came into the night, flashing lights jabbed the air up the Row. Police lights. Julia looked across. A patrol car stood flashing in front of Fourteen, three figures milling around it.

'See what you mean,' she muttered.

'Telling you. Palisades.' He hitched the moral ride, although police were never seen here, and Feral was a Molan Gardens problem.

'Well,' Julia sighed. 'We have it on camera. And believe me, we don't argue bad circumstances. As rich as this town is, it's getting poorer round the edges by the week. Anyway. We're done. Thanks for your cooperation.'

She widened her eyes before he could turn, as if to retain his attention.

An intrigue.

He paused on the step.

'*Wait*,' she mouthed. A finger rose up out of camera range. 'Have a peaceful night and let's look forward to a healthy outcome.' She stepped on to the path, checked her watch – 'Interview terminated at twenty thirty-five' – and switched off the camera.

Her arms fell limp at her sides. Shoulders melted down.

She looked up like a child left behind at a bus stop and said: 'Lon? I am so, *so sorry.*' She freed her hair with her fingers, shook her head. 'You don't remember me: Diane used to hang with my sister when you two were first going out. I didn't know if to say anything, but then I was like . . .'

'As in – Tania Holie?' Lon's brow collapsed to his nose.

'Yeah. I was the annoying teen.'

'Julie? *Little Julie Holie?*'

Her frame seemed to crumble under her clothes. Her knees knocked, her arms swung, her head flew back like a frisking foal's. 'I was such a little— oh my God. And look, really, I'm so sorry about tonight. You know? I mean for you, and everything, and, well, for me.' She made googly eyes. 'Like I really needed to lay shit on my teen crush! But Lon, hey, most of this is bullshit – obviously we have to go through the motions, but all you really need to do is show up at these things, tick the boxes, you know? We're a public–private contract, part of Gideon Hovis's care mill, hence the crappy little care home buzzers. And who knows how long he'll last, he's getting outed every week over something – racism or whatever. So I mean just roll with it: you don't fit the profile that rings any bells upstairs. For a fact, half our last intake of anger clients end up at Ali's Bierhaus every week – you know? Nobody'll see the video unless it comes to court.'

'Hard time you gave me to end up saying that.' He stepped on to the path.

'I know, I'm sorry. The camera has to be running from the moment we leave the car. They're all over us since the Baby Perry thing.'

'Hope I'm not in a folder with Baby Perry.'

'Of course not. But you know how it is – one slips through the net and the only way the media shuts up is if we treat every call as infanticide.'

Lon shook his head and smiled. See how things clustered on rat-shit days like this, and how many connections swirled around. All these connections around the mouth of his drain. Old and new. All this life milling around outside. He took a moment to remember Julie Holie when she was gangly and listless and her ass peeped from seedy pyjamas. When she'd ambush him with buckets of crap propped over her sister's door. Whole little montage on the step there. And an irony: probably the only person she would ever have seen dancing on a table was Diane.

'You haven't changed.' She stood staring.

'Jesus, you have.'

She buckled and swayed and they laughed as she opened the gate, looking back. 'I'm still sorry, Lon. You know. Always the good ones.'

'Thanks. I hope Tania's fine? Tell her I still have the tin. And the scar.'

'I'll get out of here before you hate me. But you owe me a long chat, and I'll fill you in on everything from our side. Are you on Rike?'

'The social thing? No.'

'Okay – well, you owe me.'

'After today?'

'Never said I grew out of annoying.' She latched the gate behind her. 'And can I ask a big favour? You might get a call with a survey about my attendance. I need all the likes I can get right now – my super's being a five-star bitch.'

6

Heretics

'Things are going to have to change around here, Lonnie.' Shelby stomped around in front of the screen. 'BIG time.' She spat it like a pebble.

'It's *Dad* and those are my words, young lady, not yours.' Lon was croaky. 'I'm going to leave the unanswered questions for now, but I want you to grasp what happened today. I'm here to bring you up, not be your best friend.'

'Duh *yuh*' – she rolled her eyes – 'as if I didn't work that out when you *assaulted* me.'

'No one assaulted you, Shelby.' His head slumped on to the backrest.

'No *yuh*, except according to the law. Except for that little fact, you could go around killing everyone you want. Well, I am here to tell you *it-has-got-to-stop*.' She flicked her head from side to side and flounced her hair off her shoulders.

'Sit.' Lon patted the couch, where he was sitting with Egan. 'We're going to watch the news and hang out. Make a fresh start. Make some deals.'

She came and perched as if on a nail. 'If you mean deals like cash or a phone, then phone wins. Also, after all this trouble, I just think a phone would look better for you, you know? Like you were at least a little bit sorry.'

'I *am* sorry. Doesn't mean you're getting a phone.'

'Okay, but then cash would need to be like . . .'

'You're not getting anything. Not until I see some responsibility.

What makes you think today was a win for you?'

'Because I mean, what, you're just going to let me go around with like an old person's buzzer or whatever, like a panic button? Oh yuh, *really*.'

'Who says you have to go around with anything?'

She flew off the sofa and stamped on the spot, jaw hung as slack as an imbecile's. 'And, duh, *what do you think I just spent all night talking to the lady about*? Jesus, Lon, see, this is what's bizarre, this is what gets me – major assault, carnage in the crib, and now you're just like la-de-da, like la-la-land Lonnie.'

Lon was still. His tongue glided gently over the inside of a cheek. He levelled his brow. 'Come here,' he softly said, pointing to a patch of rug.

She approached but not too close, and not to the patch he was pointing at. She stared, hunting signs of weakness. There were none.

Lon's head wavered slightly, swayed by extreme restraint. 'Shelby,' he finally said. 'First of all, we can get our points across without swearing.'

'Yuh, what did I even say? If you mean *Jesus*, that's not even swearing – he's like A-list. He *wants* you to say his name. *Wants* you to say it.'

'Not in that way.'

'Is that all you have to tell me? After everything?'

'No.' Lon slouched in his seat till their faces were level. 'Underneath all the laws in the world, Shelby, there is a natural law. I see it at work in the pipes every day. Things come in, things go out. You can put all the laws in the world against them, but if they're natural they come in and go out how they want. And people are natural too. Underneath all our laws is a natural law; you can push and shove against it or be quiet as a mouse, but things will still go where they're trying to go.'

'Serious bus trip to the point here.'

'This is the point: if someone takes away all you have to lose, then they have a problem; because you have nothing left and you don't care any more, which means you'll do anything. After today, you grasshoppers are all I have to lose. And imagine my surprise, Shelby, when I see that the only one who can take you away from me is you. Imagine that. And you seem to want to do it. Because your little attitude and your behaviour will be my fault and the court will send you back to Nanny Mona.'

Shelby bent to adjust her socks. She overbalanced, flailed, propped a hand on his knee. But didn't interrupt, which was a win.

'How families work,' he went on, 'is that I will protect everything you have to lose. With my life. *Everything*. Little Burro, your freedom, your space, your dignity. And your respect. That's the deal. And how it works is that you protect what I have to lose in return – in this case *you*. But as I see that you're not motivated to do this, as I see that it's all a big game to you, because you're so grown-up and so above it – then natural law requires me to tell you that being grown-up means only one thing: making decisions. Life-changing decisions. And as you're so grown-up I need you to make a decision right now. One of the biggest you can make: I need you to decide if you even want your dad in your life any more. Because the courts won't let you play ping-pong with this, back and forth to Nanny Mona. If you go back you're going back till you're an adult and we're strangers. So – Miss *Yuh Whatever*. Your father who loves you in ways you don't get, who has a sacred duty to your mother, who loved you very much, to bring you up the way she would've wanted;

your father who paid too much for a house just so you could have your own room, your father who feeds and clothes you – not *Lonnie*, your *father* – asks you to make that decision right now. Because you are risking everything I have and I will not sit by and watch you play with it.'

Shelby's gaze roamed the ceiling till a chuckle hissed up her throat. '*Kh kh kh*, protect Burro with your life, oh my God. Priorities.'

Lon didn't blink. He reclined with his chin on his chest. 'I am now going to make a call. Either to tell Nanny Mona we'll be over in the morning with your bags. Or to Hog's to get a pizza for a picnic on the floor and do some deals and get over ourselves like people who love each other. Your decision. Make it.'

She was quiet. A glow rose off Lon. Not a bad little speech. He turned it in his mind, picturing the pair of them as accomplished adults with heretics of their own. Then a flash of Shelby in an alley, caked in vomit, jerked him back.

Maybe the image flashed to her, natural law being what it is. She stood tracing flowers on the rug with a toe. Slowly. Downcast. And by the time she looked up, her composure was gone. Her lip started twitching like a worm on a hook and she was back at the slap with its whiff of dry fright as if the evening between had never been.

Lon reached out in the nick of time. She fell like a bundle of saplings, spattering his arms with tear-chips. 'You don't even look sorry.'

'I *am* sorry. I never want to hurt you. Sometimes you make it hard to protect you – it can be grubby out there, you don't even know.'

She shuddered and sniffed at his sturdy neck, lips squashed aside, guyed by cords of spit. After a minute she burrowed a hand down his back and rubbed as if to comfort him. He closed his eyes as his brain sucked the drugs that resolve busted souls and forge wisdoms, that bring on a binge after bloodshed.

'Your mother would be so proud. Strong, pretty girl, smart girl. She'd want you to grow up generous and true, kind but able to stand your ground. Able to follow through, go the distance, build your dreams step by step.'

'If I brought you a beer could I have a phone?'

'No.'

Egan the Invisible stirred from his screen. 'The grid-ready models still have issues. Better either find the last version or try the new Sagui.'

'Beer and nuts?'

'Forget it.'

'Can I just get the case and practise?'

Lon slid his mouth to her ear. 'One day I'll get you the awesom-est phone you ever saw. Just be a *good girl*. Make a deal that we stick together, support each other, play on the same team. And one day I promise I'll surprise you.'

'Huh,' she grunted. 'Unlike today. Ew, it's gross down here.' She slap-wiped some spit over his shirt. 'And can we workshop this *Dad* thing? Just seems a bit bizarre in this day and age. Like *The Gravy Years*, or whatever I caught you watching that time.'

'I can watch *The Gravy Years*. And since when is it bizarre to call your dad *Dad*?'

'Show's like a selfie of you. *The Lonnie Selfie Years*.'

'Or *Daddy*, like millions of other kids?'

'Oh *yuh*, then I'd need like some bling and one of those dancing poles.'

With this gentle exchange the oil-blue leatherette sofa on the trendy-ten-years-ago rug was restored to a human nest, awaiting the cream of the day's violence on the living room screen. And although in their minds they gave less of a shit, the heretics – one much like Lon only sandier, one like Diane only finer-boned – imprinted vague warmth from his breath and his sweat and were soothed by his chemistry unbeknownst to them. He was made masculine, a strutting cock in a small way, also feminine, a clucking hen in a way, while the rest of him stayed Lon and thought ahead to the future, going to the school for some answers, raising the City Lighting crew, and tightening a grip on his floundering life.

The news came on as he rallied this way. He elbowed Egan off the remote as a bombing flashed up over fanfares and drums in the faraway Al Qemen war zone. 'If you want to feel lucky' – he pointed – 'just imagine being a kid over there.'

Shelby stood. 'I'll bring you the beer and nuts anyway.'

'I think Ember ate the nuts.' Egan's legs swung on to the sofa.

'Pretzels, there might be?' said Lon. 'Or leave it, we'll order pizza.' He turned to Egan as Shelby scampered off. 'What are you playing?'

'*Donkey Kull.*'

'Thanks for muting it.'

'No worries.'

'So what's your take on the war?'

'How do you mean?' Egan didn't look up.

'Know what's going down?'

'Heh – bombs.'

'Okay, yes.'

Egan counted on his free fingers: 'We're bombing them, about

65

four other places are bombing them, and they're bombing themselves. And when the bombing gets slow they blow themselves up individually.'

Lon's brow had been set for formal argument. It could only retract. 'Fair enough. And do you know how it all started?'

'We said to them stop bombing your own people and they said they're all terrorists and we said no they're your people so we bombed them but then the people ended up being terrorists so we bomb them too.'

'Mm. Fair enough.'

'Signal must be terrible there.' Shelby returned, smiling and frowning like a corporate hostess. 'No wonder they're all running away.' She was gripping a beer with both hands. She thrust it at Lon. 'Here you go – *Dad*.'

'Why, thank you, Shelbubby.' He wiped the mouth on his wrist. 'But connectivity must be the least of their worries, don't you think?'

'That and skincare – looks seriously dry.' She perched on Egan's legs.

Bombing gave way to the unfolding national hunt for Keeley Teague, a twelve-year-old runaway thought to have eloped with a fifteen-year-old boy from her school. The nation was engaged in the most extensive trawl through CCTV in the history of camera security. 'Like a fairy tale,' sighed Shelby, coiling her hair.

Lon waited for the frantic parents to appear. 'Might sound fun from where we sit. But they could be in danger – they haven't been seen for days.'

'But they're in *love*.'

'Well, Shel – that's arguable. Twelve's a weird time.'

'How can you say that? If they feel love then it's love.'

66

'Not necessarily. Anyway, you can be in love without starting a manhunt.'

'But isn't it better to have love and a manhunt than no love? I mean – Egan?'

'I spose.' Egan shrugged his lips. 'Why not?'

The news went on to say that babies today could look forward to hundred-and-twenty-year lifespans. Shelby yawned as if hers was spent. She wiped a spit mote off the couch, probably imaginary as she didn't focus there but turned to Egan with the air of a date sidelined at his card game. 'Hm, so – shall we go up? Let Dad rest?'

'I'm okay,' grunted Egan.

'What?' Lon sat up. 'Don't run away, we can watch something else – here.' He flicked through the guide. '*Filter Cops*, *Bubu Don't Cry*, *Little Pam Big Jeff* – how about that? *Little Pam*? . . . *Undercover Shrink*, *Closet Billionaire* . . .'

'Oh *yuh*, "I need the four jobs to take my dying kids to the beach."'

'Ouch, Shel!'

'I mean – *really*? And love the way you skipped *Youngest Moms*.'

'*Wowlie the Pope*, look. Shall we watch? With pizza?'

'Nah.' Shelby crinkled her nose.

'But it's hilarious. I mean—'

'It's not, it only has like three stars.' She bounced on Egan's legs. 'E-gun! Been a long day for me too. *Really* long.' When he still hadn't moved after a moment, she latched a finger and thumb to his waist fat and twisted him on to his feet.

'Okay, but guys – weren't we going to hang out?'

'School night – we usually go up. You're usually not around.'

'No, but today I am. And hey – we'll take tomorrow off, how

about that? Executive decision. Drive up to Reynes Gorge? Have a picnic?'

'We can workshop it.' Shelby bundled Egan to the stairs.

'But what about pizza – guys?'

'Can you leave us some? Or no – message Egan, we'll pick up.' They took three plodding steps out of view and hammered up to Egan's room. The ceiling throbbed as they bounced overhead. Something was afoot with the heretics.

Lon tuned his ear and sat like a stone but there was only one thing to do: risk the landing's creaks and pings to go snooping. Privacy was privacy but security called for intelligence. He slipped off his shoes and went to the stairs. You could hear Shelby's hiss from halfway up; she was louder trying to whisper than if she yelled.

'Fuck, Egan, we could've done this hours ago!'

'Chill for a while, he's suspicious,' drawled Egan.

'Well, he wasn't even supposed to be around! And you can just tell he's going to make a whole ratfuck out of getting me a phone.'

7
School

How much more pressing it is to recall a stranger's face when you're on your way to talk teabagging. A whole ratfuck, as Shelby would say. Lon mouthed the word over his steering wheel. Absolutely fucking insane that his kids should be au fait with stuff that he was going to find awkward saying to another adult, not counting the crew at Kinbassa. Or work. Or scratch that: awkward saying to a teacher. They shouldn't be au fait, was the point. Or what could be next? Not a lot, after the old teabags.

Lon spent the rest of the drive to the school trying to recall if he had even met the teacher, Kimberly Stern. He hadn't been near the place apart from a parent–teacher evening on the heels of Shel's return, almost straight off the plane from their week in Calabrava, where they'd gone to break the ice for their new lives together. Shel had been away for almost half of her life after Diane's mother convinced a judge that Lon couldn't care for both rug rats. Truth is she needed Shelby to fill the hole left by Diane, which must've been why she only applied to keep one heretic. Lon kept Egan by the skin of his teeth, as courts don't like splitting siblings. By the time he persuaded the court that Shelby should come home, school was the last thing on his mind. His thoughts flew back to that time. Seismic shift all round, the Eagle adjusting to his sister again, Shel adjusting to less info about Pap smears, and Lon working nights to pay the bills. All this with Mona still ready to pounce.

He felt a vague dread as he approached Palisade View. As if he might arrive to find a parallel universe inhabited by his kids where things were out of hand. Where he was the only parent who'd missed the clues. La-de-da Lonnie.

His foreboding came from the heart: Diane had grown up in a leafy suburb where kids were busy with tennis. She'd warily gone along with his Palisades world, but hadn't lived to see her kids at school there. That little debate hung pending. Lon in a way was still braced for it. And now that unspent bracing led him to see the school through her eyes, with its raucous cliques and parenty shit from the blue-collar end of a company town where flick knives passed for tennis. A habitat like a millpond where all of nature's slimy panache would carouse, given any excuse; because the southern suburbs culture that lived, worked and played together got pretty good at ignoring hook-ups at barbecues, bake sales and open days. Palisaders had all spotted someone in a Knox Park bush, a bouncing car down the back of the Hub car park, a store room floor with empty jeans strewn warm and still in shape; 'ah', 'shh', 'there'.

Diane had wanted better for her babies than that.

That was the point here.

Neither of her babes could serve a tennis ball.

Both could tell you about teabagging.

That was the fucking point.

Lon followed a fringe of shuddering poplars along the fence beside the school. The breeze upstairs was firm with a sunny chill. A vertical banner saying *Neighbour Day* was crackling beside the entrance. The Medinas came to mind. He would have to apologise there, which also brought Ember to mind. Whole flock of duties, but meanwhile his duties were greater: no less than saving young souls.

Palisade View School had no view of the palisade and never had; it was a low-rise brick bunker upstairs in the suburb proper, all barren airport floors and doors wide enough to push beds through. A clock stirred the air in reception. A prison buzzer sounded when the hands hit twelve, and a froth of jostling midgets filled the hall. Lon stayed near the entrance as the gush kept flowing through, though it quickly ebbed away through other doors. The scene brought a pang for his kids, who on the evidence presented would be among the least well dressed in the place. He chewed his lip until a teacher emerged down the hall. Ms Stern; a brow-flash confirmed that she knew who he was. A boy appeared caught in her wake until he spun like a top through a door, a random little demo for the width of them.

Ms Stern was someone Lon remembered meeting, but there was no comfort in it as she was also petite and pretty and clearly smarter than him, her presence more open for business. He would have to suffer the shame of saying the word, or tiptoeing around it till she guessed. She approached in short, fast steps, head listing aside in that way of parrots and certain teachers. Jeans, sweatshirt and trainers on her, hair in a tail like the flow of a hearty spigot.

'Can I call you Lon?' Her hand unlatched from a stack of folders. 'Perfect timing: my classes are out on a tour of biophysics labs.' She smiled and sagged with relief. 'Let's find us an empty space. Coffee? Tea?'

'Coffee's good. Thanks.'

'I use the term loosely.'

'It's fine, I'm immune.'

She led the way down the hall. 'Missed my Cush fix this morning. Shelby often helps with my bags from the car park. Hope everything's fine?'

'Little bonding day at home. I'm supposedly out arranging a picnic, thought it a good time to swing by, while they're not here. Hope it's okay?'

'You're fine for a one-off – their records are good. Just be aware they'd need a note to miss Monday as well – new absence penalty scheme.' She heaved open a door with her shoulder and showed him to a long white table while she went to fetch coffee. Screens stood idling on a bench along one wall. The place stank of school, a mixture of plasticine, toes and fear. A chart on the wall was titled *The Eight Stages of Genocide*. Lon read as far as stage three and realised his culture hovered there permanently against its enemies. Stage four, if you listened to Feral. Something about the place was a slap in the face; there was a blunt edge to the light, a whiff of time running out, of doors slamming. It was in the smell and in a chill that swept the hall and blew under the doors, a prodding like the edge of a cyclone. Lon lately knew the taste, not from cyclones but from life in general whenever he lost step with routine. That's why he had a routine: it was a blind against that chill in particular.

Sobering place – he couldn't put his finger on it. Alien sense to it. His school project at that age had been the life cycle of a silkworm; now it was eight steps to genocide, which didn't even fit in a shoebox. The kids went up a notch in his estimation.

'Ignore the staffroom humour.' Ms Stern came in with a mug that said *GOSH BEING A PRINCESS IS EXHAUSTING*. She kept a hand over whatever hers said. Lon half expected *IT WON'T TEABAG ITSELF*, but then felt bad for thinking it. 'We could've gone to the office for the full hospitality treatment' – she sat on a folded leg – 'but I'm thinking you're here with a specific issue? Can probably even guess it.'

'Don't let me stop you.' Lon settled in.

'Okay, first up – Egan, I'm presuming?'

'Actually not. Unless, if his work's . . . ?'

'No, no, work's solid, no issues there. Hm, so. Top-ten reasons for a chat lately . . . How about our change to flexitime – right track?'

'No, but please carry on. I hadn't heard.'

'Okay, well, after weighing the results of national trials, the board has decided to roll it out here. Takes effect in January, so no panic yet. As we said in the circular, outcomes were so overwhelmingly positive that it suddenly seemed cruel not to switch. Kids have later sleep cycles, so there are real benefits to starting the day at eleven, in improved mood, attention, general health. Turns out the rest of us grew up sleep-deprived.'

'Explains my report cards.' Lon trod water with lukewarm asides like this, a sure sign of floundering. Ms Stern's reciprocal nose-crinkles for a second made him feel like one rabbit meeting another in a clearing. It made him think of her as Kim and not Ms Stern. Then he was in a bunny suit, then she was in one. Who knew why brains did this. He dropped his gaze and shut up.

'Yours and everyone's,' she continued unawares. 'And to the next question, yes, in future when a format is agreed we hope to go full flexi, where attendance is more ad hoc. And yes, it means more computer; yes, we'll tailor programmes; and no, the City won't sub-sidise working families, but savings should add up long-term.'

'Must've missed that circular.' Lon blew wisps of steam over the glint of his coffee. He almost excused himself by saying he worked nights, but that wouldn't explain why any circular in the last four months was still in a pile on the sideboard, older than the spider smeared across the kitchen door. Neither would it explain his having missed any email, but he hadn't opened his laptop since it auto-updated to a format beyond his abilities. In the end he scratched the whole thread because he didn't work at all any more. This all broke pretty fast in his mind, little pang-cascade down a drain.

'Hm, so let me see.' Kim sipped and frowned. He was wasting her time and she was letting him waste it. He didn't interrupt. 'Code?' she said.

'Code?'

'Shelby will soon be writing code. She'll want a device.'

'Don't say that – she's hardly off my back over a phone.'

'Ha.' Kim tossed her nose. 'You're looking at a veteran: mine went from doll's house to smartphone in three days flat. Then auctioned the doll's house on the smartphone. I can point you to some security software, if that's what's holding you back? Heaven knows she's going to get one sooner or later.'

'So everyone keeps telling me.'

'Anyhoo, before I spoil your picnic – what was it today?'

'All right, so. Mm – Shelby's coming home with some ideas that she says she picks up in sex ed. Describing, uh – sexual practices.'

'O-*kay*.' Cautious grin poised for shock or mirth. 'As in?'

'Teabagging.'

'*Ah*.' A dawning. 'O-*kay*. Couple of things probably going on there. I mean, obviously we don't get up in front of a class to teach that vocabulary specifically, but it will be in the air. Let me answer your case in particular: first up, Shelby doesn't take full sex ed, not until next year. So anything beyond the birds and bees must have come from somebody else, perhaps an older friend – maybe Egan? – or it could just be around the halls, but let me explain: from Shelby's class upwards the entire student body spends its days surfing the grid. If we don't answer questions, they answer them the easy way and it's out of our hands. We can't even specify filtering on a child's device, so it only takes one with good access to let all the toothpaste out of the tube.'

Lon caught himself slouching like the night before, chin on chest, legs outstretched and crossed at the feet. He shuffled back up in his seat.

'And there's another issue we're dealing with.' Kim stooped as if to a confessional grille. 'Might go a way towards explaining. I'll cut straight to it: a competitive new culture has taken hold among boys where they want their sexual conquests categorical – as in "no means yes, yes means anal" or worse, excuse the lingo. Blame what you like, blame music full of big shaking booties, media full of big shaking booties, content full of booty booty booty. Fact is booty came to town and boys are going there, and going without passing go. This all exploded in the last twelve months, followed by some nasty incidents with schoolkids, a few of ours included. Meanwhile a national study reported an equal new culture among girls – but in their case a culture of fear. Of stress, of pressure, of pain – even suicide in a couple of cases.' She swallowed a lump. 'Girls with all the right petals unfolding, good families, good habits, good minds . . .' She paused to fan her eyes. 'Sorry. Then boys can spread the diseases, share the pics, some even weaponise them, post them online – and pop goes your weasel.'

Lon was still. 'Booty. You mean . . . ?'

'All kids. But getting back to your question, how these ideas came around: the upshot is that sex ed policy had to change across the district this year to target the problem aggressively. I wish I could tell you it hadn't but we can't put our heads in the sand. Psychological risks, hygiene risks, health risks are just too steep. It's a battlefront and the best we can do is explain and empower before kids find things out the hard way.'

'So – you're basically teaching it.'

'Trying to head them off at the pass, shall we say. It's curriculum now, so out of our hands. I mean, I really hear what you're saying; put yourself in my shoes at nine in the morning in front of a classful of cannibals when the new booklet turns out to have line drawings. Hell, and I was fourteen before I knew oral didn't mean food! Thing is, take my word for it, the curriculum isn't calling the shots in this case. It's just trying to sweep up the mess. Or put another way: this ball's already in play, we're simply trying to kick it in a more hopeful direction.'

'Need to find a convent school. Divinity school or something.'

'Price of freedom.' Kim shrugged. 'Supposedly.'

'Drag me into it kicking. Can I opt my pair out?'

'You might opt out of the classes, but not the halls. Get me? Some of our minorities are out, but it's not that simple. Egan's already in the thick of it – I bet you haven't heard a wrong word from him? He won't be one of our problems. We may just have to face it: it's probably too late, in our part of the world anyway. It's wildfire.'

'Pox, more like it. It's just too young. I'd want them at least sixteen before thinking about any of this. You know? Or eighteen. Or twenty-eight.'

Kim huddled in a shrug with her mug to her lip like a shield. 'Hate to be the bearer of bad news' – she bit the lip – 'but things ain't what they used to be. Remember the junior boys' choir? Scrapped for the first time this year after too many voices broke. There's just no stopping it, kids are blossoming younger than ever. Studies have shown it's a bodyweight switch – they hit a certain weight and bang, away we go. Blame fast food. Though honestly, if it's any consolation, you're really only here because Shelby's smarter than the average fox. I think as long as she knows these aren't topics for public use, she'll be bored within a month. My Mallory just started the year ahead of her and already finds sex ed a drag. Those girls are pretty cool for their age. We should give them some credit – they're smart enough to take this on board.'

Lon stared at the wall. So much to say; nothing to be said.

Kim unfolded her leg and lowered it to the floor like an undercarriage. The flight was preparing to land. 'And you have such good leverage with Shelby. I'm sure you can spin her a healthy perspective. She's so your biggest fan.'

'Oh yuh.'

'I'm serious! Oh my God, you should hear her! Everything you say, all your songs, your tours – little bombshell's the last girl in class without a phone, but I've seen her put everyone to bed on the subject of you.'

He lost Kim's gaze for a moment. When he caught it again she was mentioning his site, how it linked to their Rike page, how they loved his pictures, his tours, blah, blah. Fucked if he should tell her that he knew of no site, no pictures, no tours.

'The others are green over it, and it's just so ace that she gets to call you Lonnie, like an old buddy. Everyone else comes from boring nine-to-five, then here's this golden siren with a super-cool dad. So don't ever tell me she's less than diehard.' Kim reached behind them to rattle a mouse. 'You must have seen this?' She clicked to a class page. 'Ha – and speak of the devil.' The first image up was a video of Shelby in her T-shirt and swimwear the day before, out on the flat where Lon found her.

'The ice bucket challenge,' Kim chuckled. 'We do something every year in aid of the children's ward at Alma. Or at least we propose something every year – the ice bucket always wins with that age group. I'm so glad she got to do it; we always ask for parental supervision, but then we didn't hear back after the circular we sent you.'

The video was one of a series of kids pouring buckets of water over their heads. Most in swimsuits. Shelby among the modest ones who also wore a shirt.

Kim scrolled to another link and hit it with a flourish: 'And looky here.'

Lonnie Lonregan appeared in rustic billboard lettering. Filling most of the screen underneath was an old shot of him on a stool in a hat with his guitar on one knee and little Shelby on the other, beaming like a night light through a muss of tawny hair. The flash caught half of Egan behind them, a spectre with one red eye. And Lon did have some crooner in him, smouldering out from the picture, lips all poised and proud. He struggled to find words, could only mumble and lean to squint as Kim scrolled down the page. He was finally saved by a commotion outside in the hall. Kim sprang to her feet and opened the door.

'You're early. Do you know where to go? Quietly!' she barked.

Lon's gaze echoed back from the screen.

Shelby must have been four. Egan seven. Both happy.

A pain dawned in him. Dear God, what had he done.

Kim turned without closing the door. 'Hope I didn't blow any surprises with their little grid project. I just think they did really well.'

'Hm? No, no. Thanks for your time today, seriously.'

'You're very welcome.' Scrunch of the nose. 'So, Lon, unless I'm mistaken you're listed in our system as Mr Mom for the time being? I just want to say if things ever get too girly with Shelby you can always phone or ping me.'

'That's good of you, thanks. Thanks a lot.' A pile of papers behind the screen was weighted down by a bright-orange book: *Is It Safe Yet?*

Light gushed streamers through the entrance up the hall, as through an ice-hatch seen from the deep. Lon surged for it before his lungs burst.

'Oh, and Lon?' Kim caught him up. 'Do you mind if I put you down for a little survey about today? Not a problem if not, you can just say no . . .'

*

Swarms of dapples like hatching spiders fell on the car from the trees. They flickered in time with hard feelings, in and out of sync with speeding clouds, or speeding time, or speeding shame, or who cared, Lon couldn't dick around the truth any more when the one idea he had to climb to, away up the list of explanations for the last twenty-four hours, sat flashing like a newborn's bruise. He went and it stung and retold the truth this way: yesterday he surprised his child doing a good deed for the children's ward of the hospital where her mother had died, a fun civic duty in good faith, and his response, when she had been too wary of him to tell the truth, had been to browbeat and corner her and smack her. In the only safe space she had in the world. Sweet Lord, what the fuck.

The other figure was probably Egan, skulking in via the kitchen, saying he'd come from up the stairs; they would have uploaded the video in his room after abandoning Lon on the sofa. Both kids too leery of their father to confess the simple truth. Because earlier simple truths they confessed must have proved a bad idea. Now the ice bucket fucking challenge, and that little girl still had the spark in her to stand up to him and launch a case for reason and freedom and peace.

Birds eddied around as if the wind were his fault as well, as if each little bird were a jettisoned hope of motherless children simply look-ing for an ally, for a hero, for the man with the guitar in the picture they posted, the man who made them beam and glow, the laid-back man with time in his life for music, for life, *for them*; not a pipeline pigger, not a sewer rat, not someone plodding against their will to make a buck, but someone being who they wanted to be, who they had to be, who they *could* be in life. The sorcery this implied was that *they knew who that was*, and that maybe it was the same person Diane had thought it was, which also implied it was someone other than who he was being, and it might take some effort to become. *Lonnie Lonregan*. The name had started out as a heretic gag: he'd used it to sing funny songs about them, to wrinkle his brow, deepen his voice and croon them into hysteria. As for tours – sure, he'd done some gigs, played some taverns back in the day, had even stayed over in Eastwood; but the tours the kids meant on the page they'd built were the tours they'd taken together, lined up on stools like passen-gers as he sang them around the world and into bed.

It was as if the heretics were throwing Diane's voice. From the grave or genetics or instinct or magic, they were nursing that better world, of music and gags and laughter, where things felt rosy ahead; reserving his seat in that universe till he came to his senses, went back there himself. So disheartened in the meantime by who he was being that they had to make it up at school.

Lon gazed around through the windscreen. An old man was rippling against the wind beyond the poplars by the playing field. Yellow leaves a-frenzied around his legs while he flapped greyly in his coat that probably rattled and cracked if you were close enough to hear it. He rattled and cracked through scraps of amber scenery that detached and flew as calcium might scud through his blood one day and kill him. Lon's eyes filled quick as a snakebite. Because although the wind whipped many things to their deaths, over the nearby cliff his babies were alive and young and well and wondering and waiting.

A scent of rain took the air. Dapples washed to shade. One of those jiffies that lifts the skirts of time to show its sausagey flesh, all mottled and real, too real, and gristled and fatty and indifferent. Lon's chest began to chug all by itself; he couldn't stop it jerking and heaving and fusing his brain to his skull. Upholstery smell melded with showers and truths, that his children would one day be old and then dead, and he would be all out of power. He juddered and snorted and hissed at it.

The ironic fact was that he'd chased idle dreams for too long post-Diane. He'd been harmed at that time chasing dreams. The few jobs on his worksheet when she was around just hadn't grown big enough wings. He'd had to stop and get real and pay bills, and he hadn't stopped soon enough. Those bills and a lack of accessories for the heretics were all Diane's mother had needed to snatch Shelby-bean away. Took him four more years to build strong enough figures on paper to pull her back. And it now turned out she'd come banging a drum for the old days.

Maybe it wasn't too late. Shelby was alive over the palisade with her brother.

The car boomed to life. Tyres sizzled over the wet, the indicator tick-tocked loudly and he made for the nearest Foneflash outlet, up by the Company Octagon. Where the successful went. Where people on quinoa went, cool-talking people whose kids were proud of them being who they were meant to be. All the fun shopping was up by the Octagon; it was a wellspring that radiated out. A battered heart and the smears of old tears gave him bravery and abandon, lent an unthinking certainty to his quest. He had the promised picnic to arrange, although the day had since turned showery; responsibility pressed because the kids were home alone. But more important now were their unsuspecting souls to make good to.

They would gambol and squeal today.

A high-end phone cost over a week's gross wages even after the employee discount. He didn't buy one. He saw the new Sagui and got that instead for half the price, as recommended by Egan, no small endorsement. It was silky and powerful, came in a silky box, and the box came in a bag that was powerful too. The flutter rose in him that causes tears in the tender or weak. It was pride and it was excitement. It was trepidation, because the tool in the box was nothing less than a key. The moment would be her communion, her marriage to the wave of human freedom – and, as importantly, to him and their family team. The moment was big. Shel would accept the terms and conditions, click the buttons and say *I do*. And her life would start anew.

For another hundred bills he got Egan a *Donkey Kull* gift card, a big deal this side of Christmas. Then he slid home with the silken phone in the silken box in the silken bag, silken, silken, silken, and the sun broke through as it does at such times, kept beaming as he edged around two furniture vans in front of the Medinas' – strange as the place had seemed furnished, but he was too absorbed to wonder about it.

Shelby spotted the bag before he was even in the door, flew at him and latched like a bat. 'Oh my *God*!' she shrieked. '*Oh God, Daddy, I love you!*'

She ran off with the bag. Egan shuffled away with his voucher. And the house fell strangely still. Lon stood and stretched for a moment. Took a step towards the stairs. Listened. Took a step back. The fridge started to hum in the kitchen. A bird peeped in passing. Sunbeams rolled cubes over the floor, sharpened hues on the wall, captured dust motes inside, thunderbugs out.

Nothing else.

Number Thirty-Seven fell still and silent.

A still,

silken

silence.

8

Sunday

'I am going out this motherfrickin window!'

'Shel, open up! We're a team, remember!'

'I am not leaving this godfrickin room EVERFRICKIN-AGAIN!' Every grinding note evoked a thread of blood. 'Except out THISFRICKINWINDOW! Bah-ha-*haaaa*.'

'Shel, we can work through any issues, okay? Any problem will wait while we take a deep breath. Okay? You don't have to shout.'

Egan and Lon stooped around like oncologists, observing the landing floor. To the wailing, the clattering birds and muted daylight add old carpet and battered skirting, the scene of a private asylum, a place where light was usually dusted through with stewing veggie smells and swishing trousers.

The phone rang at the bottom of the stairs. As loud and unwelcome as a weapon. Ember had cranked the volume up from the purr Lon preferred to this car-yard uproar, to hear it over comedy laughter. The hysterical jangle spiked Shelby's bawl to even eerier heights, with whines and gasps of tragedy. The boys watched the stairs in case the thing crawled physically up, but after three more rings it went to voicemail. 'Pick up, Lon, I know you're there.' Mona Winbourn's staring voice. 'Shelby? If you can hear this, pick up, darling, Nanny's here.' Then a pause. Lon tried to unremember her cushionlike face. 'If I can't reach you I'll have to drive *da-hown*.' She delivered the threat as a lullaby.

The boys exchanged glances. Egan ran for the phone without a word, brought it swinging to Lon like a censer puffing her breath this way and that.

'Bad timing, Ramona.' Lon turned from the door.

'What are you doing to my granddaughter?'

'Nothing, she's fine. Says hi.'

'She's not fine, she's in meltdown – it's all over her Rike page.'

'She's too young for Rike.'

'As if that ever stopped anyone, and thank God if it's the only way to get any damned news about your flesh and blood. Total utter meltdown, I mean—'

'Growing issues. We've all been there.'

'It is not ISSUES' – Shelby bashed the door – 'it's frickin CEL-LULITE!'

'For crying out loud' – Lon covered the mouthpiece – 'you are *nine years old*! You *cannot get cellulite*! And see if we can tone the language down.'

'Don't you think we'd better do something? Lon? Poor little pumpkin. Are you calling someone or will I? I have Dr Kirchner's private number.'

'Don't panic, I'm on it. Bit of drama is all.'

'Don't *panic*? But I can hear her in the background, I can actually *hear* her, Lon. Are you just going to stand by? I mean, is this, are you . . . ?'

'I'm dealing with it!'

'She was never like this over here. Say what you like about me – and I know you will, and do – I never had her like this. Not once. I mean—'

'Mona, this whole scene probably isn't an hour old. She'll be fine.'

'Have you seen her Rike?'

'I don't need to see her Rike, I'm standing right here.'

'Strange that everyone else should know what's going on. Is it just me or is that slightly strange, in this day and age?'

'I'm right here – she's three feet away!'

'Then put her on, if she's three feet away, as you say.' Mona did a great line in 'as you say' traps; she could volley words back like live grenades from any angle or distance, followed by her trademark little grunt of satisfaction.

'She's obviously not in the mood or she'd answer you herself.'

'But if, as you say—'

'Ramona, she's fine and healthy, grew an inch since May. Her school-work's going well, she's enjoying her swimming. She's going through a crap afternoon is all. I'll get her to call when she's feeling better.'

'Why are you lashing out like that? Lon? I'm just concerned, and you seem to want to throw it in my face? I never asked about her school or her swimming. I mean – why are you avoiding the elephant in the room? When she's crying out like this?'

'The elephant's supposedly cellulite. That's the elephant.'

'I have creams – I mean, she needs a woman's – Lon? Are you, I mean, that's what you don't seem to get, she's a *girl*! My God, what'll happen when she gets her moons? What then? Is this like, I mean, are you . . . ?'

'She has all the support she needs – we still live in town, you know. Things may have changed since you grew up. There's support around every corner.'

'Now you're calling me old.'

'I'm not calling you old.'

'Well, if I'm *sooo* decrepit, as you say, how is it I can see her up-dates and you don't even have an account? When it only takes a minute? I mean . . .'

'Listen, thanks for your concern. I'd just better get back to the situation.'

'Speaking of updates, I see the Holie girl found you looking well.' She served that up like a rat on a platter. 'Oh, wait – Shelby messaged me! And there's a picture! Oh, poor little pumpkin. Okay, well, I'll deal with her direct, Lon, and if there's anything to worry about I can message the pics to Dr Kirchner.'

She left Julie Holie in the air like poison gas and went off to influence his child in her bedroom on the other side of the door from where he stood. Masterpiece of timing as well. This was how she rolled, Ramona: scary starey type, some kind of vampire on a squirmbinge. Stereotypes sucked, Lon didn't hunt them, but they did exist and here was this mother who genuinely felt he was not good enough for her daughter, even dead, and in fact felt that her death was down to him too, for having put her through the risk of another pregnancy. As if the decision had been his alone. It rankled hard because he remembered the night that Shelby had likely been conceived – he'd swear he felt her little soul erupt – and now Mona with all her crap made him feel as though she'd been at that bedside watching. It was that, more than any blame, that got to him. That and you'd think he'd given Diane the lupus in the first place. So, due to this bright animus, a thing of nature, a nesting crow even Mona would struggle to shift, Lon had resolved not to match her spite but just plot a straight course and push through – tally ho.

New implications were clear: he would have to assume she knew he was retraining, or on childcare parole, or both. One would be enough to make him sweat in court, if not lose him a child again. Both would just lose him a child again. When all he wanted was to bring them up smart, make them ready, make them capable, patient and prone to living well, disposed to fine if not flashy luggage.

Meanwhile one of them was grunting and wrestling a latch for the purpose of throwing herself out of a window. Lon pressed his head to the door, crunched stubble along it. 'Honestly, Shel: cellulite is not a possibility.'

'*Yuh*, that's why there's a zillion results for *CHILDRENAND-CELLULITE*.'

The home phone rang in his hand. Aneurysm. He answered by slamming it on the point of his knee, half willing the handset to crack, but instead his own phone started ringing in his pocket. Another day was going from woebegone to what-the-fuck. He passed the landline to Egan – 'Answer that, will you?' – and dragged his screen from his jeans.

It was Boges. 'Any survivors?'

'Wouldn't have picked you for a grid stalker.'

'Joelly saw it. They link through the swimming club.'

'And you give a shit?'

'Very well – ach, I'm so transparent. You still bowling today?'

'Never said I was bowling. Anyway, I'm dealing with this.'

'Well. Hope it's really serious.'

'Thank you.'

Egan meanwhile had the invalid face beloved of boys protecting their apathy, the one meant to kill any hope that they might lend a hand. Lon presumed Mona was on the home phone again, to rub it in, or to put him in debt to her lovechild Kirchner in Harville; but Egan was being especially useless, stunned as a landed fish. Lon finished with Boges and snatched the receiver back, one ear on Shelby's fumbling.

'Is that Lon?' – it was Marta Medina. 'Don't want to intrude but we were looking you up and saw Shelby's Rike and, well, it's not why we wanted to call, but . . . ?'

'Thanks, Marta, we're fine. Bit of drama.'

'IT IS NOT DRAMA!' Shelby bashed the latch and hurt her hand. There was a pause followed by her low rising howl with tears.

'Ush, well, I'm glad for that. I just wanted to say I hope there's no hard feelings from the other night? Albert felt bad and we just—'

'No worries, Marta. I wanted to apologise myself. I'm afraid those boys got the wrong end of the stick with some drinks on board.'

'Ended up being such a lucky night for us anyway – crazy, really. We're back living out of a suitcase at the Cornado while we hunt for a new place around Arcadia or Reynes. Thing is, we didn't want to leave a bad taste; it was nice to meet you. Will you come to our housewarming when we settle?'

'Arcadia, eh? Must've scared you away!'

'Just the strangest thing, proverbial offer we couldn't refuse – and we almost had the man arrested! Oh my God, anyway, we'll save the story until we see you. It can only be good news for your property too. We're still trying to digest it ourselves! I can see you have your hands full, so let us know if there's anything we can help with. And please thank Shelby for passing on the number – although you should tell her to be a bit careful about sharing her details on the grid!'

'Thanks, Marta. I'll let her know.'

Something smacked the latch. Shelby grunted and hammered and bashed till whatever it was cracked into pieces.

The window scraped open. Lon tested the door with his shoulder. It used a knob lock, easy enough to work around but not immediate;

probably best to bust in and surprise her. He didn't know how far she might go, he just couldn't say, and she knew he couldn't say, which was how the drama thing worked: she only had to go far enough that he just couldn't say any more, then spin him on her finger like a ball. Lon tallied the cost of a knob and new fittings from Providers, probably twenty or so, plus wood filler and paint to finish the job. 'Shel!' He gave her one last try. 'Listen,' he said, 'I will take everything you have to say on board. I'm not making light of this – you're upset and we will do something about it. Might not be cellulite but the quicker we get started finding out, the quicker we can fix you back up!'

The gambit caused rattling and bitching. A whine, a sniffle, a shivering sigh. Then the door burst open. Shelby huddled there like a slave-driven laundress, tragic and swampy in shorts. She squatted to her haunches till a smooth half-inch redundance rolled out of her thigh-tops. 'DUH, DUH, DUH!' She jabbed.

'What! You're totally trim and normal!'

But she'd reached that stage of despair where facts not only confirmed her worst fears but proved how alone she was. She sobbed herself into a ball. A halo settled on her from her bedside lamp. By the window beyond lay her makeshift hammer: My Little Burro, all busted to hell.

Lon cradled her up and nodded Egan aside. Her phone was still gripped in her hand. She'd barely left the room since she got it; he'd placed a sun in her hand, and what could compete with a sun? Whatever it was – hobby, puppy, pal – he needed it fast.

The landline rang again. Now it was the teacher, Kim Stern:

'Wild guess,' she simply said – 'the cellulite troll?'

*

They landed like chic paramedics, Kim and Mallory Stern, a jangle of car keys and shower scents and duty. 'We need a vacuum cleaner, some baking paper and a towel' – Kim didn't wait on the doorstep. 'And kitchen roll.'

Lon watched the lean, somehow lonely pair bustle inside with painted-on leggings and untainted trainers, mincing high like royal ponies, straight-backed, slim-necked, long tails of hair wiping taut, tan shoulders. Partnerless souls in a way, confident but self-conscious, tidier than need be, although that alone didn't say partnerless, and it was there that Lon's theories fell down. Truth is he didn't know if Kim was single but figured the shrink-wrapped buttocks at least were for flouncing through a singleton's door on a Sunday. You'd be able to read braille on them.

Nice of Ms Stern to arrive. Caped crusader with sidekick. It wasn't all about booty, though what creature doesn't revel when new vistas come around – something else was also triggered, a sense of a jigsaw feeling around for a missing piece, a picture trying to complete itself of a family on a runaway locomotive.

Even Mallory twinkled with purpose. A miniature of her mother down to the wingtips at the corners of her mouth that flickered, trying to dampen her smile. She was full of the authority of double-figure age and carried a tapestry-covered case like a hatbox as big as a toolbox. Perhaps the cellulite defibrillator.

'What do you mean by *troll*, exactly?' Lon dragged the canister vacuum from under the stairs. 'I'm guessing not a fairy-tale ogre?'

'Oh my God. Innocence.'

'Try keeping up with email down a tunnel.'

'*Email?* Oh my God. It means a few of our ice bucket challengers got nasty comments on the site. Probably an inside job, a classmate.

Already wonder if I don't know who. Bit of detective work for the morning.'

'Ksenya Ululay,' said Mallory.

'Shh,' said Kim.

'Anyway, good of you to come and clean.'

'In your dreams. This is a life hack.'

'Vanilla Lipo,' said Mallory. 'Really works.'

'*Shhh*,' said Kim. 'Secret.'

'Just tell her it's a troll. No? Problem solved.'

'So, so innocent. Don't you know information is useless now? The mind needs action, it needs a hack, a narrative, something to vlog.'

The nozzle banged up the stairs behind her behind. She looked back to see if he was watching and he turned as if he wasn't, but they both surely knew they were bended to mandrill law. Uncanny how you can know. Though maybe less uncanny when you've groomed your rear to be looked at and people look at it, or you're hardwired to look at the ass of the species and a good one comes along and you look at it. But what differed here from the high-octane days before kids and Diane was that Lon's mind didn't skip from her leggings to her lathered and moaning form. Instead he flipped forward to twanging the elastic on greying old familiars on the sofa on a Sunday, a haze of sleep and toast and a junk sale to get up for. He might not have known it but he was skipping ahead two years past saliva, past the panicky abyss to the accomplice, the line of coke to the muffin where he'd left off with Diane. Muffin of muff'n'love.

He went to the sofa, switched on the screen and listened to the hubbub upstairs. Some chattering, squeaking, the vacuum in bursts, even the chorus of a song. They were singing up there in Drama-land, a land where information was useless. Apparently wasn't useless as a cause but just as a remedy, so they were singing. Singing and vacuuming cellulite. Lonnie floundered and lolled and idly watched the screen, where a report tried to explain scientific breakthroughs in the field of ageing. Turned out science had discovered that people age – first breakthrough – and that some people age faster – second. 'Look around a school reunion,' the presenter implored through her nose. 'You might wonder why some of your classmates look so old. Do *you* look as old? *Not necessarily.*' She turned away as if deciding whether you were still young enough to hook up. 'We now know that some age clocks run faster than others. John is thirty-eight and still looks young.' She walked around a frozen image of John, someone you'd have a beer with. 'How's it going, John?' Lon mumbled the dialogue. 'Beer?' 'We now know it's because his true genetic age is twenty-seven. His cells decay that much more slowly than Leon's, who at thirty-eight looks over *fifty*.' No hooking up for Leon. He didn't look happy about it. 'Now scientists have isolated markers in cells that can indicate a body's true age, a kind of genetic speed gauge. We mightn't yet have the tools to adjust it, but the implications are already far-reaching: imagine if an inexpensive gene test led to health coverage being based on true age and true risk. Today's system of averages, simply counting the years since your birth, would seem as absurd as expecting everyone with legs to run a marathon. Imagine if jobs were targeted at your true developmental strengths, imagine workloads and lifestyles individually tailored to the year and even the month of your true age.' John's life ran behind this in a montage. It involved him scrunching his chin to put on a tie, and kicking a ball in a tracksuit. Easily pleased, young John, mused Lon. Unambitious – probably what made him such a prospect for a drink. Last thing you wanted was someone itching for achievement over beer. Achievement is the bitch of beer. But then Lon was a beer drinker and he worked in sewers, while John swanned around in a tie. Bit of blue and white striping there, collar-wise. Truth be told, John probably drank cider, or worse – low-alcohol beer. Lon killed his little dialogue when it hit him that John could as easily turn him down for this beer. Strong-nosed, sideburned, sewer-working type, out of nowhere, his kids either sullen or rude. A beer was really going to happen between that and a stranger in a tie from the type of watering hole John frequented. Lon didn't think himself scum, it wasn't that. He was raised by good people, could've probably done tertiary, technical school at least if he'd had a mind to. He wasn't your local badly inked fatberg with the tadpole-headed dog. Still, here was the thing: he wanted to be welcome at John's watering hole. Wanted to be candid and jocular in razor-pressed shirts and waxy skin. Backslapping instead of play-punching. Upstairs in life, with upstairs kids. He was ready. Upstairs was smiley because intelligent people had the guts to pursue smiling fortune, to enjoy the fruits of their labours and set a high bar to keep aiming for. A bar of standards. *Standards*, for fuck's sake. Lon scowled at the presenter, who had the relentless edge only three hundred grand a year can bestow. 'While detractors warn that such a system would create an underclass of the faster-ageing,' she urged, 'with all the stigmas known to the elderly, scientists say we can't unlearn new truth – that life-speed plotting can boost . . .'

Lon went for a beer. Blame John. Beer and admit he was floundering as a father and drowning as a worker and a lover, though in the latter you can only drown when you're in the water and he hadn't even made it to the beach. The long-shot up in Shelby's room had accused him of innocence already, not a premium quality in Palisades, plus she had tertiary education, knew life hacks, probably lived at Stresnan Heights and drove a sexy hatchback, making him stoop to the curtain and look. But it was a dusty gunmetal people carrier and now he felt as bad as if he'd rifled through her bag. What had he really become? Snooping around a crisis, trying to get off with his children's teacher? He retracted to the sofa. That's what was happening: a little subplot was growing under the drama. He'd become nothing less than your typical Palisades predator.

Perhaps he was coming round. Coming good. He settled back to consider this, recalling that his life in the tunnels had only started post-Diane. It had even been due to her, in a way. Her funeral had no sooner been paid than he'd descended underground to wrangle bulks and tangles, even occasional cadavers in the foamy hurrying waters beneath the town. Now fortune seemed to have sprung him and sent along Hackgirl.

Plus another window had opened with unemployment, a brief one at least – hopefully it was brief – to weave himself into the heretics' lives. Fill Egan's days, fill Shelby's days, fishing and riding and building and playing and dragging them like zombies over the lawn, suffusing and infusing and evoking and invoking and pumping them full of good values. Values, for fuck's sake. Without which vices get passed as virtues.

The report on screen was about time in general. Wouldn't usually have kept Lon's attention – wasn't keeping it much, come to that – but time *was* feeling strange lately. He could remember ten years ago as clear as today but the month before last was prehistory. Now cameras were entering a physics lab where a man like a castaway in sandals said everything happened in parallel realities, and time didn't exist at all.

Fuck that. Lon was all for the future but he wanted a part of it that geeks didn't own, a part they couldn't dose out like pay-per-view sex. Anyway, how did Professor Sunstruck meet anyone for lunch if there was no time? Fuck that.

Lon was busy deciding between the news and a movie when the girls chattered out of Shel's room. He went for the news, listening out for nouns or verbs on the stairs: 'So, but, like', 'He was like but then I'm just like', 'No like but so but like . . .'

Shelby arrived wearing cat ears. She bounced off the stairs as runaway Keeley Teague came on the news, a timely foil for leggings around the sofa. Turned out the runaways had been found but the girl was pregnant. They'd run away *because* she was pregnant, because no one would understand. Now she reunited with her family while the boy was helping police decide if they could charge him over it.

That was barely the story's fuse. Most of the report was taken up with the *response*, not the story, the *response* to the story, the social media tizz from Chinicalpa to Chaolin as the left, the right, the middle, the top, the bottom, the possessed, the dispossessed and the broken weighed into the chinfest: feuding rappers, movie legends and influence peddlers swarmed behind the homeless man who had found the pair entwined beside a shopping-centre grate. The Supa-Lo whose vent it was had quickly sent a hamper in a giant bassinet, which had then gone viral by itself as a healing sofa for all ages that increased one's sense of closeness to the womb. The homeless man would be partying with cyberstars that night. Millions were offering Josh as their baby-name suggestion upon hearing that the foetus tended male. Accounts proposing Satan were being suspended on the spot despite complaints from kids called Satin who had issues with autocorrect. Human love hearts were forming on playgrounds and fields, brands of perfume were pitching fat licensing deals, and one more fraud had been detected among the apparently genuine crowdfunders trying to float the young lovers for ever. OUTRAGE! was otherwise the gist of it. OUTRAGE for the pristine young rebels who had done what was right for their love and their child and were heroes oppressed by an old guard obsessed with this rigid anachronistic bullshit, was the gist of it. A dewy little family shattered by lumbering old white people, a velvety coupling as luscious as peach skin, squirming like sperm with young love – with LOVE with LOVE, for Christ's sake, with LOVE, which we always said was the only thing to live for, TRUE LOVE, which every fucking song was about yet whenever they actually saw it the generation that taught us indifference set about crushing it as soon as possible, and that's just what happened HERE – now trapped in a knot of impenetrable codes run by silver-haired golfers whose sex lives were lies or illegal or paid for. A pure nascent life in turmoil before its first breath, an outrage, an OUTRAGE!

Was the gist of it.

Kim added her outrage in six seconds flat. She hit send and turned to Lon, raising the baking-paper roll like a standard. 'Kitchen?'

'I'll take it. You'll never come out alive.'

'Maid's day off?'

'Again.'

'Like mine.' She slapped the roll on to his palm. 'Can't count the days he's *on*, let alone off' – and that was unnecessary to add, strictly speaking, for maximum cool, which meant the pair were flirting like mandrills all right, running scripts through their mouths while their glands tested senses, weighed auras, assayed particles, or simply confirmed them after mingling at school.

'Coffee?' Lon mouthed over the girls' longer outrage.

'Don't let me intrude on your family time.'

'No intrusion – hey, you saved the day.'

'Hack Force. Waiting to take your call.'

'Milk, or . . . ?' Lon tossed the roll into the air and dropped it, grunting as he bent to pick it up. Unnecessary move altogether.

'Please. And grab your devices, I'll hook you up to the future. Speaking of which, Shelby – you never showed me your new phone!'

Oh my God oh my God oh my God, and the girls clamoured round, the carpet hissed beneath, the screen implored behind and the afternoon mutated in the time the coffee took, as if time itself renewed for Lon's return. Sunday light hurried in through the window, softening from white through gold to mauve, to eventually cooling and deepening the room into a pond where faces were bobbing like fruits.

The girls flew up the stairs to stream some clips on Mallory's phone, a hack around the fact that Lonnie's screen wasn't smart – 'Smartscreen,' said Kim as they banged overhead, 'if you want the activity out of their rooms and back on the couch where you can see it . . .' Which sounded like a plan to Lon; he swigged some beer and pondered this as Kim installed apps on his phone. She went on to configure his laptop and revive his old desktop, her lips pursed and pert as a pianist's. Lon was close enough to hear her hair on her shoulder. He listened to her hair and joined Rike as the news announced that forty-six per cent of young *Donkey Kull* gamers found physical contact distasteful and even repulsive. More just found it blah. The room drowned in shadow as this plagued the Kullsphere, but Lon didn't switch on the light. He didn't have to: five glowing screens – the television, his laptop, three phones including Shelby's, kept back on a pretext of loading school apps – placed their skin in a late-night sports bar. To news that fertility in affluent males had halved in forty years, the two leaned in to configure parental controls, their voices warm and pebbly. Antivirus loaded to news of a breakthrough in animal-to-human tissue grafting, a boon for the future of life-saving surgeries; messaging to the case of a woman falling pregnant from a tissue found discarded in the waste bin of an upscale hotel; and Kim's breathing rose and fell, rose and fell, rose and fell so softly through it all, so softly.

'You can thank me later for this one.' She cocked an ear to the ceiling and tapped her phone. Mallory appeared in a clip. 'Live from upstairs.'

'That's what they're watching?'

'Uh-huh.' Kim trawled remotely through Mallory's phone, through images, contacts, calls and chats. 'Snooperware. This is the bomb.'

'Does she *know*?'

'Oh, please. Do I look like someone who'd spoil her fun?'

'Evil.'

'Isn't it? I'll set you up for Shelby. You'll have to load Egan's yourself.'

'Invisible Boy? I don't think he has any activity, apart from slaying donkeys.'

'Oh, he's a kulla? Too addictive – I had to stop at level two. Is he into *Donkey Kare*, the sequel? It's only been out ten days and already something like a sixth of the world's population is massing against the kullas. He a karer or a kulla?'

'Who knows.'

'Donkeys either sigh or die screaming.'

'Kulla, then.'

The girls thumped on to the stairs, and Shelby yelled down: '*Lonnie!* Get the guitar out and play something! We can shoot a video!'

Kim smiled. Lon paused. Campfire moment. He hadn't played the guitar in a year or more, but the idea did cater to the moment. 'Mm – it's behind my door. *Carefully!*'

'Yay, sing "The Badass" – wait'll you hear "The Badass"!'

'"The *Badgers*"!' he corrected, but not too loud; he was touched and surprised she could remember a song at all. When the heretics were little he would sing them 'The Badgers' at bedtime, racing through the bunny verse to chase them into bed.

'Cool,' said Kim. 'Should we rally Egan, make it look like a crowd?'

'I don't think he'll rally. He'll say he's in the middle of a book, *The Gremets* or who knows what – he'll make something up on the spot.'

'Gremets are awesome, though. No harm there.'

Lon looked at her. She shrugged and stowed her screens as a newsflash announced that a van had mown pedestrians down in the third attack that week.

Headlights passed by the curtains.

Then dimmed.

Lon hauled himself up and went to the door, glad of a pause to call songs to mind.

Then not as glad.

He opened the door.

Thunderbugs caught in his scalp.

Moths grazed the light.

Julie Holie was at the gate with a vacuum cleaner.

He propped a smile on his face as one props a length of fence against a wall to smash it to fuck with an axe. He propped it and glanced up the Row to see Fourteen lit up like a building site, on a Sunday no less, like a movie set where a fleet of vans and a swarm of men were taking things in, many more than when the Medinas had come out. A renewal was underway, some kind of rebirth at Number Fourteen, of bad shit out, good stuff in, or old shit out, new shit in, or who could even venture a guess any more, who could even say what shit it really was; the only certain thing was that it wasn't mingling and it wasn't blocked. Shelby fluttered to the door, assessed the scene with a frown, said '*Awkward*' like a robot and bolted back upstairs.

Lon sucked a blast of crisp air through his nose, rinsed it around as if to renew his brain as the world renewed around him. He didn't know if it was bad shit out and good stuff in – nobody knew if it was bad shit out and good stuff in any more. For Lon's money the Medinas hadn't been bad shit, Capital hadn't been a bad bank, waiting for the hair to arrive on your parts hadn't been a bad time to start talking teabagging, but now it was shit out, shit in, and nobody knew which was which any more, nobody seemed to care – it didn't matter if it was bad shit, there was no bad any more, there was no good, no scientific basis for either, it was all shit out, shit in, except for one forgotten pocket under the cliff, one little festering backwater in the form of so-called Lonnie Lonregan and his pat little Palisades life, his pat trope life of the blue-collar-round-town, your sturdy chum from the Row with his rhythmic days and rhythmic ideas and pat little answers, his pat little dialogue and fear of the untimely, his leeriness of all that didn't rhyme; Lonregan Kennedy Cush, who chided his kids for being unrhythmic, now stood with a lie of a smile on his face as his wife's childhood friend's little sister came hauling a vacuum up out of the cold to a place where his lay in a cosy repose with a tidier person than she, a prompter hero with a rounder behind; he snorted the air like a dungareed farmer expanding his chest with the dawn, filling himself as the Row changed its shit, the world changed its shit and her vacuum came calling his vacuum in the midst of its post-coital smoke. This was all happening when the landline rang, and Ramona left a voicemail saying that Shelby had a date with Dr Kirchner tomorrow at ten – 'Promise me, Lon, don't fight me on health' – and as he weighed this new maths of ravening shit, he reached into his pocket for the first time in his life to fondle his phone like a genital, grip it and whip it to view like his fellows, as if it were a ray gun, as if it were a prayer, as if it would save him; but as it all sank in, he thought only one thing, felt only one certainty under a fading stripe of sky, the faintest beige skidmark over a black tumbling world – he snorted it up, gazed out, smiled falsely, and knew:

He didn't stand a fucking chance.

9

A Fibonacci Bacchanal

'Professor Roos?'

'Yes.'

'It's Bastian Matanick – from the project?'

'What is the accommodation? My partner isn't very well.'

'Sorry to hear that. I think you'll like it, I—'

'How do you know what I'll like? Some cancerous suburb, I already sense. I'm smoking in it – I don't care. And playing music.'

'You can smoke, of course. And duplex apartment upstairs.'

'I need at least two hundred interior metres. I'm pacing a lot.'

'It overlooks a huge open flatland, just a surreal, beautiful space. I'm already thinking of a drone festival here. I could time it for our first big announcement, as a background to the news. A literal buzz in the air!'

'I can't be sharing an office, it just doesn't work.'

'Stand-alone building, just for you.'

'Nowhere near the complex?'

'Miles away and out of sight.'

'Who is this calling?'

'Bastian Matanick?'

'I'm asking you.'

'Bastian Matanick.'

'Ah, the wunderkind.' She made it sound like an intimate rash.

'I wouldn't go so far. I'm twenty-seven.'

'I'm seventy-two.'

'Ha, the wunderkind. Ay-ay-ay.'

'Do you have news on?' asked Roos. 'There's an echo.'

'In the background. I can turn it off.'

'The runaways story. I'm tracking it. Lovely Fibonacci spirals – see these graphs?' She swung her phone to a pair of screens, where sophisticated geometries spun in 3D. 'Building in real time.'

'Graphs of the story?' Matanick peered back. 'Tracking news or what?'

'Social media.'

'Oh-*ho*. Interesting. Cool graphs. Could also be hurricanes from the air, same graceful spin. What are those coloured lines peeling off?'

The professor stood for a moment scratching her raw-boned pelvis through a grey business shirt. Cornelia Roos looked like a tall, angular boy, and handsome with it, her back only now growing round at the shoulder. Large curious eyes on the verge of surprise spilled through undersized tortoiseshell glasses. 'Top to bottom' – she eventually pointed – 'the alleged homeless man has been recognised on the grid as a tollbooth repairman who was cruising for sex the night he found the runaways. The orange tags on this arm – see here? – are threats of harm, the red of death. This branch is a feed from the prostitute he was with, says she saw the children first, and that he tried to talk her into an enema.'

'Ay-ay-ay. Ha!'

'Not *ha*, Mr Mantik.'

'Ma-*ta*-nick, Professor. Bastian Ma-*ta*-nick. People always—'

'Not *ha*, Mr Matanick. It's good that you call this evening: I want to show you what's developing on these screens and then I'm going to ask you to stop what you're doing on this project until I get there.'

'*What?* But no can do, I mean—'

'Can do. Do not launch another algorithm.' Cornelia sat to light a panatella, waving it outspokenly as if to serve it like a tennis ball. 'Watch and understand.' She lodged the cigar between her teeth and pointed to a line curling out of the charts. Tags flickered along it like aircraft on radar. 'This arm here, anterior' – she traced it with a finger – 'is news that one of the crowdfunders is related to the runaway boy. This tip growing out is police getting involved and accounts being frozen. The veins under here are reactions to security video of the boy getting drunk two days ago. This one – curling now, but I predict it will straighten and fall – is old posts coming to light of the girl saying she was abused by her father. This grey one sinking is the mother moving out to her sister's place as a result of that. Then da-de-da, here, da-de-da, threats on the father, da, here, to the bad marriage, trouble at work, de-da de-da . . .'

'What's that one climbing? Wow, look.'

Cornelia peered over her glasses. 'Ah – now the boy is dyslexic. Daaa, look at it go! It's breaking off this vein about his lack of response. But now – plink, plink, plonk, look – his picture with another girl, his picture with another girl, da-de-da, and bop! – his line joins the abusive father's. And wait for it – plop! – all-men-are-abusers, de-da de-da, women-are-whores, de-da, and here we go – *Satan* – and boom, the runaways exit here and the arms attack themselves, de-da de-da . . .'

'Ay-ay. Like a flower in time-lapse.'

'Yes, a *Galactites tomentosa*. This one is going for fifty-five petals, I'd say.' Roos swung in her chair. 'Except it's killing itself. Do you see?'

'What's *that* one about?' Matanick pointed.

The professor turned as sections of the graph began to flash. 'Ah – a parallel study. The system looks for arguments also used in gaming.'

'So . . . is that geometry *natural?*'

'The mathematics of it forms a flower – work it out for yourself. If you want to see gardens in bloom I'll show you the war zone feeds. Can you see where this is going?'

'Unaccountable dynamics like that? Can I just say we're not responsible for the platforms? I mean, is that where you're . . . ?'

'You're not responsible for anything.' Roos flicked ash at a waste bin and missed. 'That's the problem we face. And nothing's unaccountable – what do you think I'm doing with this data? It's not for my entertainment.'

'Ay, okay. But look, Professor – this was a courtesy call, a welcome aboard, and I'm sure we'll sit down with the finer points when—'

'There are none. This is wholly an outrage.' Cornelia Roos sucked her cigar as if its smoke were the oxygen of reason. She knew that her eminence was more attractive for the project than her mindset. She knew that extremely good pay was meant to soften the slap of her true job description: to make intelligent noises without interfering. It wasn't uncommon among older academics, who wanted their last earning years to be as bountiful as possible, to lend the glow of their eminence without their hands-on support. But this project had misjudged Professor Roos. It had selected her for her achievements and not her convictions. When her convictions were stronger by far. And she knew that it fell to Bastian Matanick, under the guise of simplifying life for consumers, to connect and centralise grid applications that harvested personal data – and from there to control the public. But that wouldn't be happening on her watch.

She had seen too much in life.

Roos believed in freedom. Genuine freedom.

And that conviction overrode all other needs.

'An outrage,' she echoed, exhaling.

'But – seriously?' Bastian stifled a sigh. 'That's your position? I know it's trendy to dump on the platforms, but so many global users—?'

'Do not cite users to support this fiasco. They're innocent.'

'But I mean – *fiasco*? Are you referring to . . . ?'

'I'm referring to the mind. To the matrix and rhythm of life. Do you have a closet? Or are all your clothes across the floor. Do you have cupboards and drawers in your kitchen? Or is it all across the floor. Do you have a door to your house, a window? Well, the psyche and the brain are the same. If a stranger broke into your mind to use your resources without your control, you would quickly end up their slave.'

'Okay, but – it's relevant to this because . . . ?'

'By six o'clock my local time a hundred million people had focused their wills on a pair of runaway children in preference to matters in their own lives. As a proxy for those matters, breeding value in their brains without the risks of real life. And those children are unknown to them. They would stay unknown if they lived for a thousand years. The chemistry being deployed is there to encourage us to wave at the postman, meet a stranger's eyes – this is how it's relevant. Whereas their angst-by-proxy via advertising platforms designed to exploit vulnerabilities in the brain is making users happy to intrude until they crush to dust the status quo of anyone involved in the story.'

Bastian paused. 'Like I say, Professor, the platforms aren't our remit. And I think it's proven that humans are comfortable multitasking. I don't see how, uh . . . I mean, you're really launching into the heart of free—'

'Do not use the words *free speech*! Free speech I practise with you directly to promote a meeting of minds. This is not free. Every second an arm like a blade combs the surface of the earth for dopamine, yours and mine, our whims and arguments, our relationships with others, our attempts at love, our anger, our caring, to embezzle it as revenue for a dozen male college dropouts.'

'Oh wow. So females would be better? I mean, we're talking about the most basic rights of expression, not only that but—'

'We're talking about masturbation sold as purposeful life. Pay attention, I tell you now: the model that made you boys rich, of selling the market unfinished ideas built to decoy routines in the brain, is not honest or agile enough for what we have to do. Life is real now, not beta. No longer progress, not the future, not version 2.0 or 3.0 or 5.0 – it's a *culmination*. Do you hear? A *culmination*. Do not enter this project thinking kitten emojis will fix anything, some drones and PR will make a difference. Wake *up*! It can be real and it can be elegant! Nature can be elegant, maths can be elegant, humans can be elegant. We have a choice. Let us be elegant. Now is the time. Look up from your screen, don't sit in the north playing games! Somewhere a mother curls around a sick child, a woman hides shoes in a stranger's coffin to deliver to a lover buried barefoot, scientists launch rockets with peanuts in their pockets for luck! Look at us! We're a susceptible biomass! This is who we work for now!'

'Wow. I'd vote for you if I wasn't so offended.'

'You should be offended – things are starting badly. As the local man said, "I know where you want to go but I wouldn't start from here."'

'But why give out to me? I didn't build any of this. Never mind freedom of expression, never mind the voice this finally gives to—'

'You are working on integration. Is that not phase one? Integration? Into a *synchronous human lifestyle*, as the document says?'

'Ay, worried face here. I am just really concerned that we're coming from such opposite positions. I may have to speak to the committee; I can't see this working at all.'

'Follow me.' Cornelia turned to the graphs. 'You're someone who works with algorithms – look carefully. What would a student ask?'

'I don't know, I mean . . . if the axes forming those shapes are coming from complex opinions and not simple trigger words – why so many?'

'You see?' She pulled on the cigar till it glowed like a jet. 'And I'll tell you: *people are receiving different data. They* are being *targeted individually.* They have clicked and liked and favourited themselves into their own hermetic worlds, where they receive what an algorithm gives them. They are forming ever-smaller *tribes.* Haters with hate, lovers with love, the obese with diets and food.'

'But what makes them loop? There must be another axis?'

'Mass human nature makes them loop. Whoever got a rush from making heroes of the runaways can only match it now by cutting them down again.'

Matanick was silent.

'You see the future before your eyes. Flowering, look at it. The big issue. And it's not technology, oh no no. This is neuropsychology en masse, the madness of crowds, a century of it to come. So I ask you now: what other pubertal gamer-boy shit were you thinking to launch in my absence?'

Slightly Frowning Face

Fifty-nine messages from the school chat group stole into Lon's life as he slept. Every messenger a stranger to him. They massed on the bedside a foot from his head thanks to Kim hooking him up to 'the future'. Only a weekend had passed since he lost his job and blew his cool with Shelby; things were moving fast. Time was sliding like quicksilver.

And now here was the future.

As lean early birdsong punctured the grey, activity on the school account stepped up. A central argument ran between emojis: that the heretics' school nativity play should be switched to *The Ninja Monologues* to honour non-Christian values. The louder voices were soon agreed, while the weaker – life's followers and the less interested, a constant majority – fell in with a show of thumbs-up. But as Lon rolled around in the shallows of sleep, the exchange refocused its will: not only did *The Ninja Monologues* make light of capital punishment, it was a cultural appropriation from overseas. Moreover it was written for performance by children dressed as foreigners. To a newbie these might seem subordinate points to the need of some people to be right. But newbies hadn't learned the inviolable rule: never acknowledge the need. So the debate slid along for sixteen more comments till someone suggested *Trout to the West*, then twenty-one more before *The Kittens of War* sparked an unbridled shitstorm to hell.

Light relief was collecting elsewhere. Lon's phone had notified friends of his arrival in the future. His old crewmate Hordy was first to respond, sending five dirty jokes, a picture of a bear being shot out of a tree, and another of an ass spread wide with a map painted on in which the anus was the suburb where they lived. Ads sprouted between it all, for anger management, family therapy, legal advice and Coypu beer, while alerts to a targeted newsfeed warned that a storm was on its way.

Lon opened one eye. Saw the notifications.

And faced a new dilemma.

His brain had learned over millions of years to sift data for meaningful patterns; but the maths had changed overnight. The number of events in the stream of his mind was now multiplied by the number of his contacts and feeds, till he was suddenly connected to a greater sum than there were atoms across the universe. They wouldn't all trigger at once, but they didn't have to: under his sheet-creased skin he was vaguely aware of the low-level buzz of potentials. The effect may have been subtle, but like a submarine's hum it was enough to lure whales up a beach. And it would soon partner up with a weakness of his, that his real-life duties were enough of a drag to make beaching a welcome escape.

He opened both eyes.

Looked at the bedroom window.

Then at the screen.

One was real life.

The other was the future.

Or something.

One was here and now.

The other was – something else.

Information.

A binary life had started.

A binary, ternary, sky's-the-limit life.
A golden age, some were saying.

FACE WITHOUT MOUTH

Lon Cush, 37 Palisade Row, East Palisades. When your life reloads in the morning and all you can say is what the fuck. Have to learn how to ride this thing; notifications gang up like one of those maths questions – 'If twenty pilots make twelve mistakes in forty minutes, what is the distance to the sun?' – and when I was so nicely surrounded in a dream by willowy independent straw-haired women. Woke up when it dawned they were clones of my wife.

It was the dream's burning quest to find out why, what meaning there could be in so many of them. They seemed to be saving me.

From something.

I didn't find out.

Morning gushed in.

My legs are still in bed but the phone's in my hand. Silken ruthless screen to help escape the realisations. Kirchner today, for one thing. With a sawn-off straw-haired girl. Normal Healthy Shelby off to Keen and Kindly Kirchner. With Gentle

GRID STREAM

0: Campaigners for twelve-year-old runaway Keeley Teague will lobby lawmakers today seeking a review of laws governing age-related consent. A spokesperson for up to five thousand Early Choice activists said of the action: 'For having fallen in love, for having made tough decisions, for having simply sought the adventure of family life – a universal birthright – a young woman in her physical prime has been hunted down and captured like a dog. It's time we admitted that life waits for no one, and the young know it too. It's time to take the blinkers off and get behind Early Choice.'

Caring Lon. No More Tears Lon. Win him over. Make him an ally. Comrade Kirchner.

The newsfeed says a storm's on the way. Storm *Ashley*, apparently. Rash of red exclamations around it but the only thing that comes to mind is if it hits my bank the headline could say *Ashley Batters Josh*. Scrolling further down I see they're calling it *Ashleygeddon*. Must be a monster storm. Better be a monster storm, we got this far in history without the weather needing a personal name. We don't get hurricanes over here so maybe we compensate by making ordinary storms dramatic. A toddler-sandbox storm – you'd think Shelby ran the show.

Drama plus smileys equals Shelby.

And as if everything has to be sexy all of a sudden, risky and sexy, even the weather has a porn-star name. *Ashley Storm*. Here she comes, a dirty haze out over the flat. *Dirty Ashley*. Punish me Ash I've been a bad boy *ah, there, ah*.

Looking out I also see two City crew in a cherry picker up at our street lamp. It's Gunny and Keller.

1: The storm warning in effect for the metropolitan area and northern districts has now been extended to Belvoir as Storm Ashley gathers strength in the south-west. Currently a depressive idiomobile air-mass event, Ashley is expected to bring strengthening winds, high precipitation and possible electrical events. Danger to life from flying and falling objects cannot be ruled out, nor risks from slippery road and pavement conditions with transient micro-flooding, especially in exposed and low-lying areas. Residents are advised to avoid all but the most necessary journeys and to take adequate shelter until at least two o'clock today.

Gunny I know from occasional bowling. Middling bowler. There for the beer and admits as much, which makes him an okay type. They're obviously aware of Ashleygeddon – they're hurrying as if they are. Don't want to get fried up there.

I step into shoes without lacing them up, and head down the stairs and outside. The breeze is fresh. Earthy scent. *Earthy Ashley*, bend me over, *ah*. The boys finish work on the lamp and pose like wealthy cruise ship passengers as the picker whirrs down to the fence. What took you so long, I say. Gunny adjusts his tool belt. Wouldn't have come at all except it got listed as an urgent job, he says. Company job, we have to do the Row.

We look down the lane to the Moyle property. Construction hoardings are going up. Scaffold going up at the house. New shit in. Big swinging dick in there now, nods Keller. Company nerd, he says. At Fourteen too, I think. He points up the road with his nose. They grin at the ground and laugh: You're the only iffy cunt left on the Row! I guess I am, I say,

1: The case of a person falling pregnant after contact with a tissue from a hotel wastebasket has sparked a string of similar incidents around the world, leading to tightened security and increased guest profiling at many hotels and guesthouses. The viral Serviette Roulette craze, popular with teens and young adults, has so far not resulted in any more confirmed conceptions. Health authorities have warned of the extreme hygiene risks associated with the practice, and the Police Association has advised that in many countries, personal waste at the time of disposal becomes the property of the establishment owning the receptacle in which it is discarded.

and we laugh under the unlit street lamp. I additionally laugh at the house price going ker-*ching*. Sudden whiff of chickpea and rose petal salad, of bags being packed for the Club de Pesca Calabrava.

We stand looking up the pole. The pole itself is the same but the lamp's long and thin, more tubular. It's going to look green, says Gunny. Green like a lit aquarium, he says, and soft, might shimmer sometimes too – there's a life cycle to these things. I spose when the young are born it might light up strong, and even sparkle sometimes, he says. It does sparkle, says Keller, but I think it's when some of them die. They must burn out like little suns, the ones that don't make it, he says. They go too hard at life, I guess, some of them. He nods to himself. Well, says Gunny, we all know how that is. We chuckle watching the cherry picker fold itself away, reattaching to the van like a robot. Shiny new kit, with the latest City slogan on it: *Forward!*

We turn to the lamp as if it might do something. Nothing to see yet in daylight. So what exactly lights

2: A twenty-five-year-old in Iltania has become the first person to receive a live animal-to-human transplant for cosmetic purposes. Benjamin Ehrlich of La Reata had a pair of markhor goat horns grafted to his skull in a procedure that doctors say will pave the way for many more interspecies transplants. Those involved in the groundbreaking three-hour operation were quick to play down the risks, pointing out that the nature of animal horn and the graft site on the skull made the procedure more akin to a hair transplant than actual surgery, as the body wasn't invaded. Both patient and goat are reported to be recovering well.

it up? I ask, and Gunny just says: *Bacteria*. He rests his hands on his tool belt, looks up as if to count them. Bacteria is all we know, he says, or something like bacteria. Billions of little scummies. They react to a gas and light up – *bioluminescence*, see? We get the units pre-loaded, we don't grow the beasties, although I think they're designed at the Octagon.

So, I muse – you replaced the shimmering lamp with one that shimmers by default? Not definitely, says Keller, adjusting his crotch through his green City overalls. They might do, he says, that's all. Not many went up yet, the plan was to wait until the sodiums burned out, but then today, urgent ticket, Company order, Palisade Row, blah blah blah.

I squint up at the lamp. So how do they know it's night? Or are they on all the time? No, no – Gunny shifts his weight – a contact goes live, same as before, just takes a shitload less current to activate. Real environmental. Doesn't light anything, just stimulates the population of whatever they are, puts a charge up their bangholes, and they start to glow.

3: A judge is considering referring to a higher court the case brought by star DJ Wim Behre, which seeks to challenge the authority of hotels and other civil establishments to claim legal ownership of human DNA-bearing material disposed of on their property. The law currently states that any waste becomes the property of the venue owning the receptacle in which it is discarded. The case is being closely watched as a test for wider physical dominion law reforms, in line with shifting culture. Appearing outside court after the first day's proceedings, Mr Behre told reporters: 'A bar may own a jukebox but it cannot own the tears I leave behind.'

Greenish, looks great around trees, he says. Keller nods at this. Kickass, he says, like in a park or something, shines like underwater, there's one at the Octagon Zen garden. We all look around for a full-sized tree but the nearest are all at Moyle's. Hoardings cover all but the tops of them. It won't be as light as before, says Gunny, but still enough to see by. Not enough for a selfie, says Keller. Yeah it is, says Gunny, my phone'd do it. Maybe not your piece of crap, but who wants a selfie of you?

They grunt and jab and I gaze down the road as two figures pass Number Fourteen. They're pointing around and taking an interest in things. It's busy on the Row this morning. The pair look like religious canvassers, neat and preppy, lanyard IDs on them, shades although it's overcast. Not hostile – you can tell just by looking. Body language.

Gunny and Keller take the cue to clink away, jiving as they go, *You'd fuckin light up too if I put a charge up your banghole*, which still counts as work time to them, not that I can talk.

5: A third crowdfunding page has been launched by supporters of runaway Keeley Teague, despite two earlier accounts being frozen while authorities investigate a number of claims of impropriety. Half a million in cleared funds is thought to be tied up in the two previous accounts, which came under scrutiny after allegations were made of phantom beneficiaries and theft by the minor's guardians. It follows the closure of four unrelated accounts that were later traced to a number of beneficiaries who had legally changed their names to Keeley Teague in the story's wake. Ms Teague herself has not been available for comment.

The strangers pass them by and veer up to my fence: Hello, hello, cheery types. They tell me access to Palisade Row will be restricted for up to a week during the next few months due to Company events on the flat. They ask if I plan to be in continuous residence. Instead of in Cala as usual. And actually Shelby's birthday will fall in that time; she's getting a bike. Shame if she couldn't ride it on the day. I ask what events they're talking about, remembering the rattly old rides at Caveney's Easter fair. But I can tell before they open their mouths that their events don't rattle. The first, they say, will be Dronestock, which is a mammoth drone festival. Day two is Holoforest, a hologram robotics event for Company guests. They point up at my top windows – You'll have the best seats in the house! – but stop short of specifying actual dates or inviting us to any shows.

The pair move off towards Moyle's, pointing around like surveyors, and I look across to Fourteen, the Medinas' old place. Wistfully, I don't know why.

8: Casualty departments across the country have reported a surge in paediatric cases following the recent viral phenomenon Vanilla Lipo, also known as Kitty-Tongue Lipo or Cookie-Dough Lipo, depending on the method used. Health authorities report that more than a dozen children have so far been hospitalised, and dozens more checked, after using vacuum cleaners to try to shift subcutaneous fat. Medics have warned that even under new limits governing suction strength in vacuum cleaners, the devices pose a serious risk when used on the body. The craze follows a recent focus on the plight of infantile cellulite and stretch-mark sufferers.

Now a lawn's being laid in strips, as clean as a golf course. Small palms going up as well.

This is Monday on the Row. Ashleygeddon in the air, spank me, *ah*. Kirchner to see. And as I hang at the fence scrolling crap on my screen, trying to avoid waking up altogether, Shelby comes howling downstairs. She flies past the door and into the kitchen, where the howls bang off the benchtops. I run inside and find her with a box in her hand and her top lip swollen to twice its size. Looks like someone punched her. *What happened?* I grab her and kneel. Her eyes shine red at the ceiling. They got away, she cries, the *bees*! I pull her close. Her lip's inflating like a life raft. Did a bee sting you? I shake her: *Where did you find bees? What's going on?* Duh, she blubbers, *I bought them!* My head starts to spin with the mystery of this, till she drops the box, wipes her nose, rubs her eyes and ogles me. Jesus, Lonnie – Honeybeetox! Or don't you even want me to look pretty for the doctor?

13: Health authorities have issued a warning highlighting the dangers of bee venom following a surge in emergency-room visits on the heels of viral cosmetic craze Honeybeetox, in which live honeybees are used to sting the lips and cause swelling. Doctors report seeing patients as young as four years old, some suffering critical allergic reactions, and have warned that any allergy to the potentially lethal venom can't be ruled out until a child's first bee sting, making the practice especially dangerous for minors. Medics went on to add that skin on the lips is amongst the most sensitive on the body, making it especially vulnerable to toxins.

Ramona Winbourn, 64 Sun Village, 144 Kaylor Road, Harville Downs.

I hate to do it but I mean, what else – what other choice is there? It's always just the, well – why should I always be the one to sit by? And watch her slide downhill? Could I ever forgive myself? Later, I mean, and then, it's just . . . you know? I want her to see Darryl, he can tell me what the hell's been going on. Like blood from a stone getting anything out of Lon, and I mean. Is that such a . . . ? And Julie Holie so coy about him on Rike and I just, well, is he, I mean . . . What else can I do? Is it too much to ask for my surviving flesh and blood to be properly cared for . . . ?

Darryl promised to call when he's seen her, and if they miss the appointment he'll give me a letter and I can apply to have her back. I mean, or am I, why should I . . . ? And if he sees her and finds something dubious he'll still give me a letter, and I can . . . Or what's the alternative, just watch her go downhill? Is it always just me who has to . . . ?

She's not cut out for a rough-neck lifestyle. Diane

21: Scientists in New Peyrouse reveal they may have discovered a natural remedy for symptoms of the menopause, and the unlikely source is none other than *beer*. The unusual discovery was made following claims by female consumers of a microbrewery pilsner that their symptoms had lessened or vanished, prompting a series of studies showing that symptoms were reduced in over two thirds of cases, while a third saw no appreciable change. The ingredient responsible for the effects is still unknown to researchers, and further chemical studies are now underway. The microbrewery in question cannot be named here for legal reasons.

wasn't and she isn't, and no one can challenge me on that. My own daughter? And granddaughter? Egan possibly yes, he's a boy, but not Shelby-Ann. I just don't, I mean – why should I be the one to fret my life away? Concerned all the time? *When I've lost one to him already!* And he just *brushes me off*!

Darryl will see her at ten, and I'll. It's the least I can do! When she's alone like this, without the influence of a, I just . . . It's almost nine now. I hope he keeps that appointment. I hope for all our sakes. And *his* sake. You know? Don't mess with her health, Lon. Don't jeopardise that. Lost one to him already, and *that* was down to healthcare. God only knows what he put her through to cause a flare-up like that. He should've known another pregnancy, so soon after the, you know? Not again, Lon, not this one too, oh no. Enough is enough. He dialled me twice just now but I'm not picking up, uh-uh, no excuses, not today. Is that such a . . . ? For your own flesh and blood? I mean.

34: A number of andrologists and urologists have cast doubt on claims by a woman that her pregnancy came about through contact with a tissue from a hotel wastebasket. Specialists said in a broadcast earlier today that the lifespan of human sperm outside the body is limited to a few minutes at most. To conceive via sperm found outside the body would require almost immediate application to the reproductive system, they asserted, casting further doubt by adding that acids and other chemicals found in sanitary tissues would speed the sperm's death even further. The woman at the centre of the wastebasket scandal has yet to comment on the claims.

Lon Cush, 37 Palisade Row, East Palisades. Shelby pouts at herself in the mirror – trout face, kiss, tongue, smile – while I try and raise Ramona. Changed my mind twice: called first to put the appointment off, then to get Kirchner's address. She won't pick up. For example's sake I eventually go to the trouble of finding our last paper phone directory to look up the address the old way. Nuts idea, must be centuries old. Hoping he hasn't moved. But Shel needs to see that not everything's faster on the phone, and see, here's his address, Harville. At least the phone book, which someone went to the trouble of checking and printing on paper, won't tell you to sting yourself with bees. Otherwise they wouldn't be able to print it. As I scribble the address on paper as well, my phone pings a concert with Shelby's. Fucking casino parlour here. I decide to leave her phone at home. We're pushing shit uphill as it is with Kirchner; he'll be looking around for our pit bull. We're going to treat the mission as a human experience, go with heads up and eyes forward.

55: Responding to claims by experts that conceptions from sperm found outside the body have a minimal chance of success, a health advocacy group has countered with a warning that up to sixty per cent of current medical knowledge may be wrong. The group cites a study of ten thousand doctors, which found that almost a third held wrong assumptions about biochemistry, physiology and pathology, a finding it says adds to the sixty per cent of current 'facts' likely to be proven wrong by future advances in science. The group advises patients to be prepared for an accuracy rate as low as thirty per cent for any current medical opinion.

We march in silence to the grubby outdoors, frowning around for threats. Ashleygeddon is a gust and a rumble so far, barely a spit in the face. Monageddon's the one we're on edge for. There's nothing in the feeds about her. It's a problem with the news that most of the threats don't ever apply. We must prefer the threats of others, except for Ashleygeddon. Ashley G, the poor man's whipping. Our own little threat to nurture and love, to dress in grown-ups' clothes. Thing is, Egan's at school, can't be that big a storm if the school's still open. And Shel's obviously absent for Kirchner. Can't be that big a storm if Kirchner's still open.

This morning's mission is to stop him spreading panic to Mona. Have him spread joy to Mona. Have him spread Mona! Easier when Shel doesn't look like a duck, but fuck it, kids will be kids, and to be positive about it, her lip might distract him from bigger things. Doctors always want to find something, private doctors especially. Their job is to find shit wrong and they're pretty good at it. Years

89: A landmark precedent has been set by a judge ruling on the case of a nine-year-old whose phone was confiscated by his parents as a form of punishment. Ordering the device to be returned by the couple on grounds that the child's human rights had been violated, the judge stated in summing up: 'A child's forced isolation from his peers, from his sole source of information and possibly his greatest if not only form of distraction, can be said to constitute as stark and cruel a punishment as any meted out in the isolation cells of prisoner-of-war camps, where such practices would surely have done violence to the letter and spirit of many human rights conventions.'

of study. Want you to get your money's worth; the more you pay, the worse they come up with. So today we're being as normal as possible under the circumstance of looking like a balloon sculpture. We're out to win him over and avoid the subject of Mona, another straw-haired girl, come to think of it, flaxen like a crop in the wind, although she must dye it by now. But good old Kirchner, let's be positive. Shel's already whiney about leaving her phone, already sniffling over previous howling, which was added to last night's whining about wanting to leave swimming for gymnastics. Your pool membership's paid until March, I reminded her, and anyway you like your swimming. But no, she doesn't like her swimming. It's boring and shows *no potential for growth*. It's not a *scalable platform* and is *bizarre*.

This is our whiney safari this morning. Fucked up and phoneless under a shadow of Mona, trying to beat Ashley to Kirchner's. The paper with Kirchner's address sits where my phone would sit in the dashboard console. We check it periodically as if it'll

144: The woman at the centre of the wastebasket baby scandal has been granted permission to sue the unborn baby's alleged father for paternity. The man in question, who can't be named for legal reasons, had occupied the hotel room where a used tissue was stolen to which the woman attributes her pregnancy. Lawyers for the plaintiff argued that even given her agency in applying the stolen article to herself in such a way that conception ensued, the man's actions had effectively turned the tissue into a live weapon, his abandonment of which caused at least as great a contribution to her condition as the tissue's application to her body.

ping. Shel with her hair in a shining golden sheet, a mini sphinx with a fat lip and a handbag.

She moderates her sniffling on City Hill Road and starts to look at me sideways, weighing some risk or other. Then out of the blue she says: For a fact you can rent at least one tiger in town. Carly saw a white one, and if there's a white one there must be other like normal orange ones. Pause for a rumble of thunder. Cubs are obviously preferable. She catches my gaze in the mirror. Her face shows real concern. I can only gently nod. She fumbles in her bag for a sparkly notepad and opens it as if by accident. *TIGER* is written in capitals amongst a mess of other writing. An *s* has been added later in a different ink. Now it says *TIGERs*. I scan the page in sidelong glances till the lights at the top of City Hill. She frowns when I get to *PEACOCKs* and *SWANs*. Their *s*'s have been tacked on too.

Daddy – she pulls out all the stops – it's not just any birthday, it's my *Perfect Ten*! Nine can be *bleh*, eleven can be *meh* – but my *Perfect Ten*! Really the

233: The most comprehensive survey to date of animal numbers in the wild confirms that the majority of the world's tigers now live in captivity. Private pets form the largest part of their number, followed by zoo, park and party-hire animals. Pets alone outnumber wild tigers by a factor of three, and for the rare white tiger the figure is ninefold. Although proponents of captive breeding claim the pet market is a crucial hedge against dwindling numbers in the wild, wildlife activists were quick to point out that in under a single century humans have mostly eliminated the world's large wild species, and from there can only turn on themselves.

only next stop is my Sweet Sixteen, in terms of like milestones. She sighs at the blur of it all.

I look at her. One thing I learn is that it's harder to pull off matter-of-fact when your lip's blown up like a life ring. She more or less pulls it off, though, little tangle of nerves and will. I resist the urge to sigh or tell her the tigers sound illegal, but I still pick a crap reply. Okay, but Shel – I also commit the sin of smiling – won't the tigers eat the peacocks and swans? Just to be practical for a moment, tiger insurance might not cover us for peacocks and swans. Don't you think? I shift the smile to apologetic. It seems a valid argument to me but she quickly goes to the truth of it. *You're not even taking it seriously!* Her voice begins to break. It can take a few volleys to break her voice but here it is broken in one. She's heavily invested in the tigers.

And frickin *duh*, Lonnie – she slaps the notebook down – they don't just run around loose, I mean, *he-llooo*! They don't just leave them loose on the flat to frickin run away, like *duh, really*! Okay, okay, I say.

377: The bill for toy-testing celebrity vlogger Minus Wardy's seventh birthday party came in at over sixteen million bills, it was revealed today, and involved construction of a living fantasy forest complete with unicorns and tiger cubs. The party was attended by a number of royal baes including Princess Leela, previously linked to Wardy as BFF and possible crush, arriving in a Kiz Kitty helicopter and matching onesie. Wardy's vlog went ahead as usual this week, probing the ins and outs of the latest *Donkey Kull* release, *Bray or Slay*. A number of special birthday episodes are expected in the next week for premium subscribers to the channels.

I harvest another clue from this: that she wants the party on the flat. The light turns green, we pull off towards North Road, and I ask her straight out – Is this party on the flat? – but I make the next mistake of calling it *this party*, which Mona would do to wash her hands of it: *this party of yours*, she'd say. Shelby fields it mid-air, has an ear like a bat for backhanded comments, tuned by Mona herself. *Just frickin forget it!* she squeaks.

All this time she's stroking her notebook with her thumbs as if it'll do something. Scrolling: the new worry beads. You can sense the rupturing pressure inside the pipeline of her body, hissing with powers trying to find a way out. Her breath and pulse bang away like a bird's, you can feel it from here. Can't bring myself to tell her the flat might be closed on the day of her birthday. Better to wait till I have a Plan B. We head up North Road in such supercharged air that a sigh would crack and die in a shower of sparks. I get to thinking if Diane were here she'd laugh us out of the car – *Tigers in your*

610: A panel of leading technology experts said today that recorded personal history has begun to disappear as digital file types change. Once marked as a concern for the distant future, experts now report that many among the first generation to convert records such as photographs into files have begun to see those files become corrupted or obsolete. Anyone who destroyed or lost their original records stands to lose their entire history. Even more concerning, they say, is the vast first-generation legal and civil archives cache, about which one expert said: 'It's unfortunately not that unrealistic to imagine us literally losing our past.'

dreams! she'd say. But times have really changed. Ten years coming up and times are a different country now. Different fucking planet. Would've been outrageous to think about tigers back then, whereas now it's perfectly rageous. I steam in my shell as well, boiling in the knowledge that Diane was both a person and a time. Not only is she gone but her time and everything around her is gone, the life, the vibe, evaporated. Throughout history we must've been able to walk in someone's footsteps and still tread the world they knew. But no more.

Shel once asked if I'd kept Diane's Rike alive so she could see what her mother was like. I told her none of that really caught on till the year or so after she'd gone, that we'd only heard of chat groups up to then. She was quiet for a moment when I told her. Her lashes flickered and she filed her mother away like a black-and-white TV cowboy's wife. And who can really blame her – for all intents and heretic purposes there are only three stages in history: dinosaurs, black and white, and now. Anything that

987: A whistleblowing site has published the name of the man thought to be the father of the Wastebasket Baby, conceived after a woman stole a napkin from the wastebasket of an upscale hotel. The man is said to be forty-two-year-old Qumau real estate developer Edmund Wei, who was named in hotel receipts published by the site that appear to show his reservation on the day and in the hotel room in question. Mr Wei's office refused all calls and closed early today, adding to the growing mystery surrounding his whereabouts. It is not yet known if paternity court papers have been issued or served on him over the affair.

isn't a dinosaur is black and white like some old movie. To Shelby her mother is just a black-and-white name in history. *Diane*. Even sounds olden to me now. *Diane Marie Winbourn*.

My throat grows a lump and I reach for Shel's hand – Listen, I say, do they hire them out for parties, with a handler, is that it? Be a little bit patient with me; when I was a kid the only tiger was at the zoo, called Teddy, with one eye. So let's just see about it, we can see, let's just see – okay? Well, she says, unsure if to go on sulking or get back in the game – Ksenya Ululay had one. Burp of thunder. Not a white one, she says, just a normal one. Aha: the motive. She leafs through her notebook to a folded colour printout of Ksenya's party pictures. She's done some groundwork.

I take it in like a tax bill. So – I reach over and touch a picture – is this the kind of thing you were thinking of? She cranes over my hand as if to confirm what I'm touching, as if I'm proposing it myself. Y-*es*. She hesitates. But in the act of seeing

1597: A study has found that being a child today is equal to life in a prisoner-of-war camp, in terms of hardship and stress. Responses by over two thousand children to thirty specially designed questions were matched with records from survivors of some of last century's most crushing wartime plights. The surprising results reveal that childhood is perceived as comparable to the battle of Al-Hakoum, the Din Internment Camps and even the notorious spider pits of Ho Mui. The report follows recent assertions that many common practices in households and schools today would be universally forbidden in war.

my rough-veined hand over her wildest dreams, the blue-collar hand of reality, tigerless hand of a burger-bar birthday with paper hats at best – the scene suddenly hits her through my eyes. *Bang*. Her lip falls and she stares at me, face all doughy and wide. Shel, I softly say, what you're showing me is like a celebrity wedding; there's concert lighting and flamethrowers, there's palm trees and waiters. I mean – it must be thirty grand's worth. I reach for her hand. She retracts it under her legs. Listen, I say, we'll make a big effort, something really cool, we'll . . . But she explodes into the back seat, gasping, *I'm just so sick and tired of being poor!* My whole life's flying past so *fucking poor*! Hey, hey, I say, but she throws herself flat on the plastic and screams, Even your own *wife couldn't take it*! You even made your *wife so fucking poor* that she *died of it* and now LOOK AT US! TEN YEARS LATER AND WE'RE STILL JUST AS POOR AND YOU DON'T EVEN SEEM TO CARE! WHO YOU *KILL*!

2584: An Eastwood man has been allowed to bring a test case against an air passenger whose sneeze he captured in a sick bag. The man fell ill following the flight and sent the bag for testing to a laboratory, which was able to identify pathogens from the sneezing passenger's fluids. Commentators say a ruling in the plaintiff's favour would have far-reaching implications, as the law's newest branch of interest, bioliability, remain largely untested. Lawyers will argue that the sneeze, delivered by a person with full knowledge of his illness, and aware that he would sneeze in proximity to others, fills all the judicial requirements of assault causing bodily harm.

**Jorge 'Hordy' Almibar, Environ-
mental Services Liquid Waste
Management Patrol, Knox Park East.**
Feral goes Heh he. Heh he. Heh he,
and it makes a flock of echoes. Drives
me up the wall. He just received his
retraining letter, halle-fucking-lujah, so
this is the last fucking day of him.

He always did stop in the cathedral
here, humongous brick junction in
the town's old sewers, place with a
signal you don't have to climb for. So
bing bing bing bing, heh heh heh heh,
and finally he shows me his screen.
I take off a glove to receive it but he
only wants to point it at me, like I'd
steal it or something. He's worse than
a fucking toddler. Then I expect to
see porn but it's a vid going viral of
two girls in a checkout line at a Supa-
Lo. Huh. Go figure, Feral. He skips
to the beginning and I see they're
baiting some other girl over the way
she talks. Doesn't look like she even
knows them. They're trying to make
her say the word *butter*, steering the
conversation to trap her into it. Then
she finally says it and it comes out as
munner. Huh. Nasally girl.

And now the cashier supervisor twigs. When they get the girl to say *later* it comes out as *laner* and he almost cracks up. Then they try *latte, battery, better, hotter, fitter, tutti-frutti, tittle-tattle,* and are about to fucking lose it when the girl up and says, *Everymony says munner nase menner mun I han nase the nifference.* They go off like fucking fart bombs. Haha! Okay. Pretty funny. And the girl's like *What the . . . ?* Hottie babe too, in a twisted kind of way.

Then, uh-oh, under the vid you can see the backlash growing. It's in the news already. And oops – she's multi-disabled. Cashier guy got sacked eight minutes ago. Baiters are in hiding as of forty minutes ago. One released a statement that she suffers from depression. Now Butter Girl's going on BUTI-FM to talk about *haners* and *mullying.* Huh. Doesn't look disabled. Looks pretty hot, if you ask me. But multi-disabled, they're saying. Her name's Melinda Meims, goes by Mindi or Minda. I elbow Feral to send it to Lon but he says, I don't have his number and I don't fuckin want it, after the other fuckin

6765: Two social media servers crashed today after responses to a viral video broke service request limits. Octagon spokesperson Will Sullivan blamed the spike on an event-cascade in advance of the surge in demand. The video in question shows eighteen-year-old cupcake vlogger Mindi Meims being bullied in a supermarket checkout queue. During the angry response phase a monitoring service in Doriton recorded a topical surge in excess of the global levels demanded by porn and religion combined, making Ms Meims the single most sought-after person on Earth for just under eighteen seconds.

night, fuck him. So we study the screen for disabilities. Maybe just her speech? I suggest, but Feral says, Nah, that's just vlogger voice – they drop their *T*'s and *D*'s or it makes the mike pop and slows them down. We search Minda Meims and there's a fan page already. Redirects from *Butter Girl* and *Munner Ngirl*. The disabilities are listed as RDFD, ASTTS and SRDT. Huh. We look up SRDT but the first thing we see is *Steered Rotationally Directed Transmission*. So fuck knows. Nothing you can see by looking at her. Or else her transmission's fucked, ha. We set off down the main again and after a while Feral just says, I'd give her a fuckin disability – she wouldn't be able to sit down for a fuckin week, heh.

Lon Cush, In Transit, North Road, Harville Downs. Ten minutes to Kirchner and she looks like a victim of napalm. Boiling in our shells, the fucking both of us. Glad it's a slow drive to Harville. Already ten o'clock. Everyone forgets how to drive when it rains and it's not even raining yet. Just the panic

10946: The man at the centre of the Wastebaby scandal, real estate developer Edmund Wei, is being sued for divorce by his wife, according to documents filed with the courts today. The woman, who can't be named for legal reasons, has reportedly been estranged from Wei since his removal to a safe location following news of a paternity suit, and is said to have been removed herself after groups of NO WEI! supporters were seen gathering near her home. Crowdfunding receipts for the birth have meanwhile inched closer to a million bills, threatening to eclipse the six-figure sum raised for runaway Keeley Teague's unborn child.

makes them forget. Lash me, Ashley, *ah*.

In the end we get to Kirchner's fifteen minutes late; shady uphill street, new cars, no people outside. Bamboo and contract mowing. The place looks more like a house than an office, no sign at all on the door. I check the piece of paper and this is the address all right. Takes five more minutes to rally Shel and make her look human again. She won't say a word and it suits me fine – if I get around her triggers she'll only go bang. Between Mona, Kirchner and Child Protection Services, she has an armoury of weapons all loaded for bear. I'm the fucking bear.

My power defaulted to her and she knows it as brutally and simply as bacteria knows how to spread. Sawn-off heretic despot. I wipe her down with the cuff of my shirt and drag her up the path. Carved wooden doors ahead. There's a buzzer but I don't need the buzz; I knock on the wood instead. Shel is still and quiet, head down on her chest. I really need Kirchner to see through this shit. Need him to know what kids are

17711: The wife of the man at the centre of the Wastebaby scandal, Edmund Wei, has been named by a whistleblowing site as Margaret Wei, née Zhang, a thirty-nine-year-old marketing graduate thought to be a partner in the company that last year was forced to withdraw a campaign for Chikkistix snacks after its branding, featuring a long-eared zebra resembling a donkey, was found to belong to a San Uribean zoo. Ms Wei was removed to a safe location after crowds were seen gathering near her home. Supporters and activists are also reported to be gathering near the court where Edmund Wei is expected to answer paternity papers.

like, especially divas like this one. You'd think she was attached to the mains for the amount of water she can put out in a day. But Keen and Kindly Kirchner will see through the swelling and tears. Years of study, after all.

A rattle comes to the door and I pump Shel's hand to raise her head as a bare-chested man with a tan opens up, a forty-something man with a gym membership that he only uses for biceps. I break out a smile but he lunges through the doorway with his knee out like a fencer. *What do you think you're doing!* We scatter on to the lawn like pigeons. Get off the PROPERTY! This is a PRIVATE RESIDENCE! – what the fuck. Anger issues. Probably see him at anger management, in which case I can knock his head off. Feel much better – boy, this management really works. It takes me some seconds to muster my wits – Uh, we're here to see Dr Kirchner? – and he goes, Yes, I've been waiting an hour to have screen time with Shelby! Screen time! Screen time! SCREEN TIME!

28657: Experts at this year's quantum expo have predicted that QT – Quantum Time, also known as Curlytime – could be rolled out in a Lifestyle Option format as early as the end of next year. Curlytime is possible, they say, because time doesn't exist as a linear reality under many interpretations of quantum mechanics, making it more informally divisible to fit real-time needs. Under Curly, work can condense into microbursts a few seconds long, and household bills can be paid irregularly. Digital financial transactions already use a new version of time, and experts say a wider move to Curly will free us from a raft of inflexible old norms.

I glimpse a dusky young woman in the dark of the doorway behind him. He was probably making love to this woman. At ten in the morning. Between tennis and golf. And now it's Kirchnergeddon. I should probably punch him but instead I turn to Shel and ask if she knew it was a video date. She barely gets to the rolling eyes and *duh* face before his knee charges out and he runs us off the lawn in little bursts like a bull. I WAITED AN HOUR! he snaps, which is an incorrect statement anyway. I suppose morning sex can be disorienting. Probably only lasted three minutes, shot his load when he saw his own tan. Videocall within the hour! he barks. I'll make an exception for Mrs Winbourn, but THIS IS CLEARLY A PRIVATE RESIDENCE!

Gideon & Arielle Hovis, 41 Reynes Parade, Reynes Park. Nice tan on them, mm? For this time of year. Let's just say. Arielle. Mm? No reply as usual. Say what you like around teenagers, they're lost in their own little worlds. The only thing that

46368: Three more private doctors have denied leaking video transcripts of patient examinations on to the worldwide grid, after at least sixty clips in which patients were clearly identifiable were spotted on a foreign porn site. All three doctors use the same videoconferencing software to attend to patients remotely, prompting some developers to speak of a security breach. The software in question has been praised up to now for allowing doctors to increase consultation numbers and retain detailed evidence of examinations. Some practices are switching back to written notes until security risks with the software are made clear.

gets their attention is silence. The stress of silence. Takes about a minute with Arielle before she looks up from her phone – *What?* – and then she makes it sound as if I've woken her.

I point down to the street, where two women and a man, of ethnic provenance, are apparently bringing luggage into a neighbour's old place, which is up for sale three doors down. Foreigners or something, I tell her – they seem to be going into the Wards'. She twists upside down on the sofa and stretches to the edge for a look. Teenagers: shape-shifters like snakes. Would've taken fewer muscles to stand.

She mumbles, Maybe they're staff?, but I soon disabuse her of this. Reynes Parade might rank among the sixteen most desirable streets in the city but the Wards' is a compact three-bedroom property, where would they fit any staff? The younger female – I point – looks too old to be a daughter of the other two, mm? Arielle hits the roof at this, just like her mother: Do you always have to call us *females*? Makes us sound like hamsters or something!

75025: A new study has found a marked polarisation effect in the IQs of economic migrants and refugees, as measured by a new generation of intelligence tests. Research on local populations revealed that nearly half of those studied had lower-than-average IQs, with many falling into the subnormal range, while middle ranges accounted for less than twenty per cent of the total number studied. Instead a spike was seen in upper-range intelligence among men who had a criminal record of three or more offences since arrival, with a significant rise where the offences had been ideologically motivated or had involved more than three victims.

You're not hamsters, obviously, Arielle, I say. Although I think: Teenagers – hamsters. If you could take your eyes off your phone for one minute you would see the implications for yourself. But who even cares? she retorts, and I push right back at her, *You* should care, young lady! For one thing this place will form the bulk of your inheritance when I'm not around any more; you'll want it to hold its value. You'll only blame me if it doesn't. All well and good to be touchy-feely but life is not a game, Arielle – generations of hard, honest work grew these assets, protected them and nourished them like forests, I say. But she's back on her screen. She just doesn't get it, doesn't care.

Can you stop saying *When I'm not around* all the time, it only gets my hopes up – she mutters the last words but I hear them. The prickle of guilt she gets off that little outburst, so high up the bitchometer – needle flying *off* the bitchometer, in fact, and which I don't dignify with a comment, leaving her to fester in its juices instead – has the effect of stirring her up

121393: Two Molan men have been arrested and charged with attempted murder after the car they were travelling in was seen mounting a kerb and narrowly missing a pedestrian near Molan Hub yesterday. Abu Hanifa Taban, twenty-three, and Asim Fadlalla, nineteen, were traced through the vehicle's owner, another Molan resident, and held under anti-terror laws while investigations were underway. Police later reported that the thirty-year-old victim, Mustafa Saleh, had left the scene unharmed. They added that a security cordon will remain in place until investigations are completed. The offenders will appear in court later today.

off the sofa. So I'm victorious in the transaction and we stand together watching Reynes Parade as those people go into the place three doors down.

She lets me take her arm like a ventriloquist's dummy and point it at the *For Sale* sign. You see, Ellie, I explain: the place went on the market back in April, but flabby conditions over the summer made the Wards drop the price last week. They did this to observe an equation between the difference in the amount they originally wanted and the discounted price of today, versus the cost in overheads and lost liquidity of the time it might take them to achieve the original price. Arielle pulls her arm away but I carry on because it's about damn well time she woke up and smelled the coffee.

When a price drops like that, I go on, it can open the property up to a different class of person, a class not usually able to live on a street like this. I pause for this coffee to hit her. She stands so limp I feel like massaging her joints. *So what?* is all she says, and I tell her in no uncertain terms why so what:

196418: A linguistics think tank in partnership with the Octagon has reported that communication by the young via emojis may be making them more intelligent. The head of the groundbreaking project, which studied the effects of emoji communication on the developing brain, has likened early results to what is known of hiero-glyphic readers, who have been shown to develop stronger intelligence through hieroglyphic study. The specific effect is thought to stem from the nature of pictographic languages, where characters expand and exercise both sides of the brain at once, compared to languages formed of an alphabet, which use only one.

Because otherwise we may as well pack up and move to Molan is why so what, Arielle, to a damn property and an environment built on less hard work than ours, and in fact mostly funded by taxpayers, which also means me. Is why so what, young lady.

Her face gets so ugly when she's like this. The ex-wife floods into her like a nightmare. She's like an ex-wife flashback system, that and a disposable-income drain. A drain and a spy. And now she sneers, Well, what do you expect *me* to do about it?, and I take her shoulder to spell it out: It just might be more appropriate for you to go and say hello, mm? Than me. Seem more casual. Say hello, see what they're thinking, if they plan to buy. Mm? Not right now, but if you see them around. More likely you will than I will – it's a hostage situation at the office. I soften my features, make an olive branch out of my face, but she stares like a zombie into her screen, says *Whatever* and drifts away. Mm? Teenager. If you find a better case for abortion, buy it.

317811: The latest demographic survey has revealed that less than two per cent of migrants who arrived under economic migrant guidelines, or as refugees, live outside the southern suburbs, with a vast majority never leaving Palisades and Molan. Commenting on the survey, government spokesperson Ron Kidd said figures reflected an organically healthy population, where people of all kinds were free to cluster around the neighbours and amenities most in line with their comfort zones. He dismissed opponents' claims that figures revealed a failure in integration, telling us: 'There's nothing stopping anyone from moving wherever they want.'

143

Lon Cush, In Transit, North Road, Harville Downs. Whatever. Fuck him. Running us off the lawn must be his way of saying he does his appointments by video. Don't even want to guess how he palpates anything. How he checks down your throat. Harville doctor, set things up to fuck around instead. Palpate girls instead. Check down their throats. With small instruments. *Modern world, modern world*, I sigh, and Shelby's will to live goes out the window. She huffs: Is there any heat around here or am I stuck with your sexist temperature? I reach down and flick the heat on. We cruise past Shaky's along North Road, where I could honestly spend the rest of the day in front of a charitable, glistening beer. Then Leonard Road, where I could happily drown the rest of the year at Kinbassa. Modern day, modern *day*, I sigh.

Ashleygeddon's a washout too, six fat raindrops like birdshit. She spent her charms elsewhere. Sun already lurks on the horizon. Can't even get laid by the weather.

514229: Cyberstar megababe Mindi Meims, the most sought-after person in history after a bullying video went viral, has revealed on her site that her favourite animal in the whole wide world is the tender fennec fox. Sources around the country have reported a surge in fennec pet enquiries, with one grid trader reportedly landing a six-figure deal for an unborn litter of cookies'n'cream fennecs. Fennec foxes weigh little more than a kilo and are known for their large alien ears, soft fluffy fur and bushy black-tipped tail. They are the world's smallest species of canid, or dog, and make active, intelligent pets, according to fans.

We eventually get home and Shelby sprints to her phone, in a box under the stairs where she hid it. She goes to call Kirchner from Egan's room, jabbing her screen to try and staunch the social bleeding.

Wait for me! I call after her.

It's *private*! she snaps, and I shout up the stairs – *We're a team, remember!* – in case she has a mind to get dramatic. Which she almost certainly fucking has. I distract myself with my own little workload of pings from Boges and Hordy, including a parrot that dances to bagpipes. I read nine messages, answer three, delete four in case I drop dead and detectives look into my character, five more come in, I answer one and delete two, by which time Shelby's back to send me up to Kirchner. *Darrylzilla*. The *Kirch*.

But this brainwave: before heading up I can score some points by sharing the bagpipe parrot video with Shel. Make Kirchner wait for the duration while I bury the hatchet with her. And I actually do it, fuck him, but she hears the first note and sighs, *Old*. Do we have any cinnamon? she

832040: Legislation being proposed today aims to make parents criminally responsible for any harm suffered by children falling from ladders, chairs, stairs, trees or any platform higher than a yard off the ground. Set to apply to children under twelve, the law seeks to combat thousands of injuries sustained every year through unnecessary falls, a toll the government has warned is unacceptably high. Children's advocacy groups have welcomed the proposal, while the leader of a senior citizens' lobby has commented: 'Childhood is for running, climbing and jumping, for going crazy – it's when we grow our damn wings in life!'

asks on her way to the kitchen. Don't know, I reply, what for?, and she says, Forget it if it's another interrogation. I give up hatchet-burying and take a beer up to Egan's sock-brothel.

Kirchner's head and shoulders are on the screen. He's put a shirt on. A little logo's on it – maybe he's even sponsored. He speaks without acknowledging me: There's redness and swelling on her face and thighs – *rubor et tumor*, he casually adds in case I only speak Latin. She's a child, I reply, their limbs are in constant use. Perhaps she climbed a tree. He drops his voice and looks up: You and I both know she didn't climb a tree. Well – I pick at the beer label under the table – perhaps it's not redness, perhaps it's the video? He doesn't respond, doesn't like my tone. He has a habit of pushing his lips into a pout as if something's trying to be born through his mouth. I wait for an egg or a dove. He does it now, and says: I've seen tough love before, Mr Cush, and I note from the system that your address is on a social services watch list. I can't say anything back to this.

1346269: The race is on between funders for Keeley Teague's unborn child and the Wastebasket Baby, with pledges on both sides exceeding a million by this morning. DAB Betting has reported a torrent of wagers on the outcome of the births, with odds shortening past four-to-one for the so-called Wastebaby, which doctors predict will be delivered last. Industry sources report that much of the activity originates in the Far East, where the size of the wagers is said to be prompting fears of criminal involvement. Tote cryptomarket futures also spiked dramatically as markets opened, giving an early boost across the board in alternative trading.

He doesn't like me, told me to fuck off once today already. Now he's looked me up on the system and his feelings have been confirmed.

My intestines shift. Don't let her get dramatic, I say – she can get dramatic. What concerns me, he goes on, is that everything described adds up to a pattern. Drama, anxiety, depressive dysphoria. Altered affect. The *DSM* would say *Predispositional Defence Disorder*. Lips push out. I think the lips are meant to suggest a space where things can sink in at my end. Wasted on me because all that sinks in is *So much to say, nothing to be said*. She's fine and healthy, I protest as if I'm selling her. Grew an inch since May. I mean, who knows what they get up to, don't let her get dramatic.

He's going hard at this due to looking like a prick in front of that girl this morning. This is the true operation here. Busy fucking then I came along. By now I'm zoning out, scrolling my phone for self-esteem. He toys with his fitness watch – I'll have a swab kit delivered for a DNA work-up – then he

2178309: The company behind *Donkey Kull* has responded angrily to suggestions that the viral game may have influenced a recent spate of attacks on donkeys in farms and sanctuaries around the world. Calling the claims part of a troll campaign, the company went on to warn through a legal spokesperson that any suggestion in public that the game in any way promoted violence towards animals could be met with litigation. Celebrity kulla Minda Meims was quick to back the company, saying: 'If it were that simple that we just went out and did whatever we saw on screen, there would be mass attacks on people every week, never mind on donkeys.'

tinkers away at his keyboard and mutters, Very smart girl, sharp as a tack. Don't underestimate her needs at this age. I'll follow up for PDDD when her DNA comes back, but Mr Cush – his lips fall heavily pregnant – you'll know I'm obliged to report any apparent contusions. Do we understand each other? His mouth goes into labour and he vanishes with a *bloop. Donkey Kull* desktop returns. Donkeys flinching through a gunsight. I swig some beer in sympathy, toast down to the foam on the donkeys' account, in a spirit of charitable sacrifice.

With the beer gone I get up and move out to find Sharp-as-a-Tack herself behind the door. As if it's her natural habitat. She doesn't look up. Her screen shows a panel of vital statistics: pulse, temperature, breathing. Must be a Kirchner app. I wait till she twists an eye at me, and go: Okay, Smarty, four times three minus two equals what? A clusterfuffle, she says. She wipes her nose along her arm and scrolls down her contacts to Mona.

3524578: A study released today reveals that declinism – the belief that things are getting worse instead of better – is on the rise in the over-thirties. Declinism takes hold when 'cognitive bias' tricks the brain into thinking that things are much worse than when a person was young, and is especially active in older people. But researchers now say that those endless summers were just normal summers forming a larger percentage of a young person's lifespan, while the truth according to indicators is that things are measurably better than ever before, with more people enjoying a voice, and global poverty on the decline.

Bastian Matanick, Thomas Carman Suite, Cornado Hotel, 212 Sienna Boulevard, Reynes. When I tell you his idea of a perfect Sunday is a Scotch-and-steak dinner at a hotel, you'll get the type. My dad is one of those guys who wears a tie for no good reason, who's capable of wearing knitted ties, who gets friendly on three brandy-sodas and spreads his legs, talks more than he should, about stuff he shouldn't. A lover of fishing who has a cap that says *Fish!* And I remember this day at our house, special guests around the table, connected to his work but not high up, lower than him, or they wouldn't have been there – he has the keenest sense of higher and lower, probably having worked his way up, and would rather hang out with lower so he can play the seer with his pithy pronouncements – maybe they came from another plant, I don't think they worked in his office. Anyway, among those guests was a man with timid features and bloodless lips, a quiet man with straight, lifeless, neatly parted hair, who just observed and said very little. I

5702887: A research group has found that on average only one in five senior members of a sitting government is a declinist, while four in five members of an opposition party are. The finding follows earlier research showing that virtually none of the country's wealthiest people were declinists, regardless of age, while most of the poorest were. Analysing the data, experts have pointed to intelligence quotients and upbringing as possible factors, explaining that high achievers by definition will have used intelligence and a positive mindset to achieve their goals, qualities also likely to have been fostered from an early age by high-functioning parents.

watched him and he didn't smile when talk got loose, when jokes got spicy. I don't recall exactly what Dad was saying, but he was boasting about liberties he took at work, vehicles out of hours, data off the record type of thing, to make himself out a maverick, a cut above it all. And as I recall it, later that week he was in big trouble at work over those same liberties. Not just one but a bunch of them. I gathered it from all the hissing in the kitchen. He came home astonished, couldn't believe it – but I knew there and then that it was Timid Features who'd shopped him. This must've been fifteen years ago and to this day he hasn't worked out who fingered him. Hasn't worked it out because none of those guests were in positions of power, none had an interest in his job. Meaning they would've practically had to file a complaint off the street, go to the effort of writing or calling for the principle of the thing. But I knew then that Timid Features would do it. I was only a kid but I knew he'd do that. And did it.

My dad never worked it out but I did, and I

9227465: An estimated hundred thousand copies of the banned *Terrorist Fennecs* wall calendar may be in circulation despite numerous grid outlets having been shut down. The satirical calendar, featuring 'the twelve cutest fennecs' posing in improvised combat gear, first appeared a week ago and was promptly banned under anti-terror laws. In spite of this, early sales now make it a candidate for the most popular year-end gift calendar, set to beat even *Booty Call* and *Fennec Friends*. A security spokesperson warns the calendar may be a fundraising tool for terror, while proponents argue that it dilutes the imagery used by terrorists to cause fear.

remember it now because I get the same feeling off Roos. Same sense that even though her theories are arguable she won't be putting any of her differences aside for the sake of team spirit. She's out to sink us with her data and any other data we give her to sink us with. She may have some points, from a certain oblique angle, reflecting humans in a process of accelerated change, which is never going to be easy as I see it. But to her it's not a process, it's a black-and-white fait accompli, and she is out to fight it like a mongoose. It's her perfect storm, age versus youth, tradition versus change, college versus capital. Could even be her last project – who knows how long she expects to live but she could be set to rattle the cage, go out in a blaze of glory.

Ay, Roos. Declinist technophobe battleaxe. Full of human truths but there's one she doesn't get: lucky people don't do what they must, they do what they can. And we are lucky. We are riding a wave. We are doing what we *can*. I am doing what I *can*. Which is to say going over the committee's head and

14930352: There's a buzz around town and it comes from the word *singularity*. Sources close to the Octagon reveal the recent influx of scientists and techies is here gearing up for what one source calls singularity beta, an immersive social test phase ahead of superintelligence trials. For the uninitiated, the 'technological singularity' will be the moment when machine intelligence surpasses human intelligence, the point in history when the affairs of humankind as we know them can go no further on their own. Sources have said that it probably won't come down to a single moment but a runaway phase that could soon be underway around town.

speaking to the executive about her, to Evan Specovius himself, up in cloud heaven where the capital lives, the project lives, where they eat their sushi alive. Let them attach her to the robotics group, the environment team, the quantum applications think tank. Let her research her own buttocks, just get her out of my way. I'm stroking my lobes, poking for earwax, kneading an arm of my glasses, fast and in rotation, as the screen on the bed hooks me up to the honcho Specovius. He'll spit his nigiri across the room when he hears what she had to say. Evan Specovius and I haven't spoken that much but he's cool, accessible, has a mentor vibe going with me, though he's only a decade older; not a million miles from my dad, the vibe, come to think of it, with his pithy little pronouncements.

In the distance through the window I see the southern edge of town, where the palisade drops to the flat. Looks like the edge of the world from here. I scan along to the Moyle estate, which now has a crane in place. The race is on to get the western side clean before Holoforest and Drone-stock. As I wonder if the buzz of massed drones will be able to reach this far up in town, Evan Specovius appears on the screen, heat flaring off his bald head. He tokes on a joint, blowing smoke at the ceiling and watching it. Seems he's on a yacht, all the furniture's built in. I grab a bottle of Lahiti water – an IOU for a yacht, in a way – to mess with more than to drink, as he chimes, Baz! What can I do you for?, and I get down to the nub: So I spoke to Cornelia Roos, I say; and it seems she wants to kill our model, starting with platforms integration.

I wait for this to bite. Uh-huh. He gazes away. So I'm wondering your position, I add. On the model. Being killed. This late in the day. Uh-huh. He frowns to the side and pounces off-screen – thud, *bang*, a leg flies up, a deck shoe – then settles himself back with a gecko in his hand: Dino rampage! What should I call him? I suggest it has to be Gary, but he sucks his teeth: Too obvious. How about, I don't know, Jared or Justin or – *Josh*? Josh is good, I nod, and sniff my

39088169: A technology watchdog has invited three more tech industry leaders to answer questions about the so-called Hada Wormhole, an operating-system backdoor that was found to have been gathering user data from personal computers for the last eight years, and possibly even longer. Industry notables were quick to distance themselves from the breach, saying it was common programming practice to leave a hatch during product development, but that these became redundant in versions reaching the market. The watchdog has labelled Hada 'potentially the most extensive data heist the century will see'.

skin, fondle my jaw, graze my crotch very lightly. Can't help but detect an absence of nigiri being spat here. And I can't put the case any stronger – *kill the model* – what does he want. But now he gets up to go aft, or fore, with the gecko – boat's too big to see which way it's pointed – says *Sorry* when he returns, nods *Uh-huh* as I repeat myself, then gazes up with twinkly eyes as if to break into song:

So I hope you treated her nicely, he says – it does come out in a sing-song – I hope you found some common ground, because the aggregate reach of phase one is a flat-out backstage pass for regulators to clip our wings or cut our balls off. The advisory committee's our firewall, Baz, the professor's part of our firewall, we have to be smart how we handle her, and it. He relights the joint and sits back: If we were flipping burgers for a living we'd still have to dabble in politics. Price we pay for ambition, necessary evil, it's not all burritos and beer, he says.

He inflates his neck with smoke and croaks from the back of his throat: Also bear in mind, Baz, that

63245986: In findings released today, the rich were shown to be as much as fifty per cent more intelligent than their poorer wage-earning counterparts, and in the case of the ultra-rich the figure rose to a startling sixty-one per cent. The ultra-rich were also found to be twice as likely as average wage earners to discern opportunities for gain, although one leading expert pointed to flaws in the experiment, saying the rich have been shown to consume different foods, a fact which in itself could account for some of the results. He went on to add that the group's lower rate of declinism would influence the figures even more significantly.

the overall footprint is bigger than you'll see from the lifestyle products at your end. Cough, snort, exhale. If you look from where I sit you can see the integration ploughing a bow wave like a tsunami. We need to look worthy of ploughing it. Skateboards out of shot, know what I mean? He waits for me to nod. Tsunami of social change, Baz, and our one sticky issue is this reek of direct democracy coming off it, a cookie-dough ozone that people can fucking smell, a scent of collective power. They're already bypassing courts, governments – look at it, he says.

I frown at my nails: Not often you hear democracy tagged as a by-product. Anyone ever think of making it a product? I grin but he misses the joke: Yah, right, not this form of it, he says; we'd depose and elect governments every second of the day, execute and pardon them in a heartbeat.

I can't help but hear shades of the professor in this, and I tell him so. He simply replies: It's the accepted position – we knew it in the sixteenth century and governments know it today. That's why

102334155: Physicists at the Octagon's quantum mechanics lab have broken the record for the most subatomic particles entangled in a single cluster, beating the previous record by thirty million. It came as part of a series of experiments to prove the Diffusion Interpretation of quantum mechanics, with which physicist and mathematician Mangeta Flause proposed that we inhabit a multiverse where every action that can be taken is taken, splitting into a world of its own and rendering us immortal, as at least one of the actions would lead to our survival. DI has since become a mainstream theory, and Octagon teams are on the trail of more proof.

they're shitting kittens. The smoke and mirrors that get them elected are a bust against our models. Look at the last six months, regulator snouts to the ground. They caught the scent. Cookie-dough ozone. He whirls a finger to illustrate either diffusing ozone or a cookie. As I watch I'm reminded that visionary and paranoid are the alternating current of people who earn yachts from a garage in their underwear. And once they get the yacht they like you to play, so I wade in: If the amount of memory a grand can buy is the only flying curve on a graph of the last seventy years – what government can now be surprised?

Specovius lets his head roll: They thought it meant jetpacks and mono-rails. Now the old guard whimpers in bed at night, it can see the game's moved beyond tech, the brain's re-wiring, the battle's gone to nature, to neurochemistry, *influence*. Name any human battleground, all are now battles for territories in the brain, and the armoury's the screen in your hand. Think of this: if you subtracted the empty space between atoms in all our brains, the

165580141: She's our awesome princess bae and this is her tender fennec fox! Carlos the tiny fluffball with his succulent wet eyes and heart-melting love begs Princess Mindi for a mouth-watering snack. He's a rascal lol! BFF Melinda Meims is known to her vast number of soulfans as Mindi or Minda and you can see with your own eyes that it's true love at first sight with the tender helpless fennec, omg it's like stab me! Can they ever bear to be parted again without breaking their less-than-threes – like, *wut*, people, hellooo, nuh-*uh*, heh heh, idts! Check out Mindi's crib and go premium for streaming sacred updates yay! Oh Minda it's L-O-V-E. Sigh. *Melt*.

mass of global intelligence would barely fill a shot glass. He serves his eyes like canapés – *We hold that shot glass*. That's what gives them the jitters. We own a shot glass containing the species, Baz. Hence the advisory committee, we hope the powers come to see it as their embassy, somewhere they can whine and we can defuse before things get out of hand. Hence therefore also Roos. She doesn't have to agree with anything – in fact, it looks better for us if she doesn't. We have to look like a global congress, a philanthropic mission, a hack from God. He tongues his joint to keep an even burn. Anyway, all I think you're saying is that she's older. And you're probably sensing an irony – please don't repeat this – but an older person, maybe nearing the end of her life, on a project which won't turn us all into bots as your whiners love to predict, but will probably force us instead to face the deepest truths of nature, including the ultimate truth, one she'll know too well, from her own field of study. That all human life – *every little pizza crumb* – is only coded for youth.

267914296: A panel of leading dentists has voiced concern over the increasing number of patients who believe that gum disease can whiten teeth. The trend follows assertions by more than one celebrity blogger that gum redness associated with swelling and irritation makes teeth appear whiter by contrast. The blogs in question have since disappeared, but dentists say the myth has grown among members of the public, as evidenced by an increasing number of patients ignoring, and in some cases promoting, gum disease. A leading dentist warned of major health risks if left untreated, adding that *disease* was in the name for a reason.

That no contingency or capacity beyond our early thriving is designed into any person anywhere. DNA is a code to be *young*. Designing golf courses, cruising the islands, shopping for sensible shoes are all subordinate expressions of a program optimised for one sacred thing alone: to make the young ride the pony. To make our hanky-panky so contagious and enslaving that we'll hurry to do it again, that we'll get butterflies over it, kill rivals for it, sing songs about it, build palaces to it, so intrinsic that a coin in a slot will set it off, so impatient it'll blow in our PJs whether we like it or not. *Boom.* Life is the trivia between booty calls, and here's the crux – please don't repeat this – *as servants of the future we now serve that code alone.* We are working for the *genome*, Baz – he throws himself back as if falling through air – because it's how things *are*. It's what there *is*. We didn't invent it, nobody invented it, it's what there *is*, it's truth, it's honest, *we're* honest. He takes a toke, examines the roach and looms to the screen like an inmate: Just try and work around her,

433494437: It's finally official: we share ninety-six per cent of our genes with chimps, and a whopping ninety-eight per cent with pigs. While it's been thought for centuries that we were essentially 'high-end ape-pigs' – our long arms, tailless backs and lack of fur are a clue – the true extent of our likeness is only now being uncovered by new technologies, prompting one researcher to admit that science has barely pulled the curtain on our true links to the ape. What's more, as if we couldn't have guessed it watching celebrity derrières on our screens, new evolutionary research confirms that one of the least-changed features between us is the brain.

can you? She'll be slower than you boys anyway. She hasn't even clocked in yet – last thing we heard was that her partner was having treatment in Vierne, which we're sorry to hear, it's a tough, tough break. But it can't be helped. Life intervenes. Meanwhile our markets await, and if you're in the mood for an early launch – what's coming up on the list? The trust-scoring matrix? UFS? And you got to town ahead of schedule, a damned fine idea – then, well . . . Know what I mean? Make hay while the sun shines, Baz. Sun's shining. Go make some kickass hay. Specovius stares for ten seconds straight, flaps his hands like a child and logs off.

I sit for a minute very still. May appear to nod but it's the velocity effect of the ground falling away from my feet. I wet my lips with my tongue. Stroke the Lahiti bottle. Wonder how early I can launch. And in the distance through the window follow the arc of Palisade Row from the crane at Moyle's to Number Fourteen, where Roos will soon be staying.

701408733: Three men have been arrested on suspicion of stealing the medical records of Wastebaby father Edmund Wei, who faces another day of arguments in the case arising from a wastepaper theft which left a woman pregnant. It's thought the heist of medical files may have been ordered by any one of a number of gang leaders behind growing gaming interest in the birth of the child, as the records could help predict the baby's gender as well as hint at any issues leading to early or late delivery. It's not yet known if the records contained any relevant details, or if the thieves were able to copy or assess them before their arrest.

Dr Cornelia Roos, Parc des Danseuses, Vierne. I am going to fire a rocket up the wunderkind's backside. I don't care. That's what I'll tell her. I'm staying, Johanna, but don't worry about the project: I have one hell of a rocket for Matanick's backside. Best thing I can do for them. I don't have to leave at all. Gamer-boy schnook – I can send this rocket so far up his arse that his project will stall for ever. I'm staying, Joh. Just like that. No argument. *Fuh*. I'm staying. *Puh*. That's it.

I don't wait for the light before crossing the road, Vierne's quiet this evening. I walk across the park with a tower of foam containers, warm on my hands. They appear to bob by themselves in this light. Johanna: I'm staying, so shut up. Like that. Why agonise. She needs me.

Fuh. Love. *Puh*.

The hospital is bright, a shot of daylight after a cinema. I use the lift to the third floor and smile past the nurses at their station. Very nice here. Lovely nurse, the dark one. I enter Johanna's room but it's

1134903170: Dr Cornelia Roos of the IZOMA Institute has hit out at a science journal which claims that human empathy was a developmental mistake now being corrected by social media. The journal *YoSienz* claimed in its essay 'The Empathy Detour' that empathy can be traced to an error in Middle Ages thinking which led to a backslide for civilisation. Dr Roos accused the essay's authors of peddling nothing more than pseudoscience clickbait, saying, 'It's another cry from a milk-fed bourgeois elite whose unfinished puberty, but for empathy, would not exist. Their ideas prompt only one question: When might their little testicles drop?'

not Johanna's room, a gentleman is there. God, my memory. Which one was it? A nurse sees me waltz like a fly between doors and walks me to the other end entirely. I really must get more sleep, I say.

Finally entering Joh's room, I knock and announce: *Room service.* And here she is, looking out of place. A good sign. The day you seem to belong here must be the day you really belong. She doesn't belong, it's clear. That broom of hair on a judge's face, brittle smile on guard for adversity, as ever, adversity or not, with its sharp little teeth, which I vouch are quite sharp – here she is, out of place. I inform her it's a dinner date.

She counts the containers and asks me how many are coming. The purpose of that is to imply that I'm being excessive. I swing her table around and stand the boxes on it. Spicy oils have leaked from one. I examine my coat and hands, and answer: Shut up, how many come to a dinner date? Only Princess Charming. *Fuh*. But she's hardly satisfied to leave it there and immediately asks about an institute dinner

1836311903: Responding to an Animal Welfare finding that roadside pet abandonment had increased by four hundred per cent in the last two years, a declinist empathy-detour think tank has argued that waning empathy is a protective measure in the face of approaching collapse. Pointing to the saturation of disturbing media that societies now live with round the clock, a trend it says is designing itself to erode sensitivity to horror, the group claims 'species intelligence' can sense the time coming when empathy will be a handicap to the more mercenary self-preservative functions needed to survive widespread upheaval.

I'm invited to attend. This is Joh. Always suspicious of *yes*. I move her glasses, her tablet, a bag of sweets and a lily in a vase, and tell her I'm old enough to be undependable. She brightens as I use the word *old*. That small triumph has rallied her system. I'm sure if I fell to dust before her eyes she would leap out of bed and go skiing. She means to imply that I live in a neverland, that she's in possession of truths about life which I would rather ignore. Such as decline. Which I do ignore. I don't care. But she's older than me and entitled to her own point of view.

Old *enough* – I remind her – not just old. But this is fucking Johanna. Born in the countryside. And this is our surface temperature while deeper things stew underneath – *What if we're only buying time? She could slip away!* – et cetera, which is futile conversation under the circumstances.

We used to cure our undercurrents by making barbarous love, but here she faces mortality alone in a bed. The only recourse she feels she has is to passively imply that my attempts at aplomb are

2971215073: Average life expectancies in some high-income countries have declined for the first time in decades, a report released today has found, with some seeing lifespans stalling or falling across a number of age groups. Health analysts blame changes in diet and lifestyle imposed by late-industrial society, as figures show calorie-to-nutrition ratios have been steadily degrading since a peak experienced sixty years ago, during the poorer last century, when fats and sugars were less available and families still grew their own food. Analysts add that budget cuts to care services for older people may also have played a part.

irrational. She's thankfully redeemed by knowing she's wrong. I take it into account. It's also Joh. She makes these noises, knowing well that they're empty, knowing well that they're wrong; it's something we do. A bird has to squeak whether it's convenient or not, and people do the same to let their muck out. We just have to do it. This is people.

I also brought some sweets, I announce. It will extract some muck, I think, and it does: *I haven't opened the last one!* she cries. I place the bag on top of its twin in the style of a flood defence. Well, I brought you some more. I know you like them. She props herself up and glares: You should be in here, not me. Oh yes? I reply. And why? – Your *memory*! It's a wonder you can even find the room!

Well, well – I continue to open containers – obviously I find the bloody room, or how am I here every day? *Puh*. You're lucky to have a guest at all if this is how you are. She smooths her bedclothes and watches her hands as if they were somebody else's, as if they might cheat on the job.

4807526976: Rumours of an upcoming singularity beta phase have prompted outspoken pundit Dr Simon Enright to predict the technological singularity won't happen at all, but will merely be said to have happened in order to massage financial markets. Noting that the companies said to be involved in preparations all seem to be publicly listed, with many yet to make a profit despite colossal valuations, Enright predicts that most of any 'gearing up' will happen in financial departments, where business as usual for the tech industry will mean the habitual dash to dominate markets at the expense of perfecting its products.

I observe her. Her bedside lamp
is energy-saving. Its light makes
a clinical specimen of her as she
arranges her drip line like knitting
yarn. She uncoils some slack to poke
at the boxes – And we'll never eat all
this! Nonsense, I say, it's a *rice-feast*.
It's just a few different components.
I pass a container and show her
two eggs, in another some paltry
cucumber. Or would you rather they
mashed it all into one box? *Puh*,
it's nothing. Remember Jembaya? I
utter the word and watch her. Our
magic word. The channel it will have
dredged through our brains by now
will be deep enough for shipping.

We met in Jembaya as new PhDs
on our first interdisciplinary research
programme. Arrived in a bubble of soap
from home and were soon overcome
by a sweaty effluvium of fish sauce,
peppers and sex, as ripe as young cats
on adventures. Our ninth day there
saw us wolf brazen foods and devour
each other. Jembaya to us means that.
A strenuous abandonment to life.
Tonight's food is on a mission to trigger
the brain cells that carry Jembaya inside

her. She can moan all she likes but she knows: that name, this food, these odours can stir more librettos inside her than any old talk of mine. Mark this well: after forty-three years your words are just sounds, you need tactics to mobilise brain cells.

Start with the egg – I point. Or try some *Masi* – I pass a plastic fork. She recoils and looks at me pityingly: If it's the noodle place, it won't be real *Masi*, you know. They do noodles, curry, spaghetti, schnitzels, hamburgers, fried chicken and pizza; the menu is eight pages, I still have one here.

I pause with the fork and lean over her: Then use your bloody imagination. We're working with what we've got. Homeopathic Jembaya. But now she'll feign weariness, Yes, yes, she says, and I appreciate the gesture, but I'd like it even more if we could get to the part where you say you're staying and I say you're not, and we both get some much-needed rest. Well, I am staying – I spear an egg and poke it at her – so put this in your mouth and shut up.

She farts through her lips: I've never met such a

mule. And whether you're staying is not the question, the question is how much you're going to tire us before you go! I withdraw the egg. Johanna: I have one hell of a rocket for the wunderkind's backside. I can fire it as well from here. I'll send a rocket so far up his arse that his project will stall for months! Johanna falls limp: For pity's sake, assembling the media to broadcast your graphs and discredit their project before you arrive can only spoil our plans. Don't forget us! Be practical! If you must be a terror, please do it over there where you're at least being stupidly paid. I'm going to need that sea house, you know. We're both going to need it.

Her eyes grow damp but I resist them: Johanna! People are trying to raise children in this! Can you *imagine*? What they're *learning*? What they're *feeling*? Half a generation already lost! I brandish the egg like a mallet. She turns to fuss at her bedside table, knocking a pen to the floor: For someone so selfish you'd think you'd be selfish for us. And if it's that damned urgent, *get going*! You can discredit it from there! You might find even more to discredit! It might be a field day! A tear runs on to her cheek. *Fuh*. I lodge the egg hard on to the fork and lick the spice off my fingers. Anyone would think you didn't want me around, I say, licking. I actually despise this part of the routine, but it must be done. Or we're just not each other. I'm also intrigued as despite her condition her routine is quite limber, with a few new ideas here and there. I *don't* want you around, she glares. With your shit *Masi*. I want a sea house! I scowl at her over the egg: And now do you mean to offend me? She snaps: If that's what it will take! *Puh*, then you'll have to try harder. I bite the egg. Oh yes? She hurls herself forward: I've taken a lover! There, I've said it! I stare for an instant before gagging, *Hah!* Oh, my dear, *hah*, oh my, and the egg crumbles on to the bedclothes. You might laugh, she says, but it's a doctor, more charming and brighter than you. And better in bed! *Hah*, oh Christ. As I drink from her cup to stop myself choking, I take in the sparkle it brings to her eyes, the first in a week, the best in a long time. And what's his name? I enquire. It's a *she*, she retorts. What's her name? Er – Bom, she says. *Bom!* I exclaim. She struggles to swallow a smile: I was trying to say *Bob*, you put me off. Her name is *Bob*! I cry, but she pulls the sheet up over her face and shoos me away with a hand. Piss off now, I'm tired. *Hah*, oh my dear. I gather up the egg and observe her for a moment. This is Johanna. She doesn't like being sick. Doesn't like me to see her this way. This is how she is, and she also collects clocks. I trace her face through the sheet with a finger, feeling my way to her lips. Place a kiss on each, and one for good luck on her nose: See you for croissants in the morning. And I'll try to bring some cheese – if that's all right with *Bom*.

Dennis Farrell, 12-B Mason Drive, Molan Gardens. *Wheeeeedle-eedle-eee*, bof. *Cunt.* Wah-*hurr*, coolio. Heh heh: Dennis C. Farrell MAWIA Certified Professional Welding Joining Cutting Fabrication And Allied Metal Projects No Job To

53316291173: A district court judge has been suspended after using the phrase 'Get over it' to throw out a case. The judge had been hearing an action for punitive damages against a man who had repeatedly said 'Get on like a house on fire' in the presence of a house fire survivor, who claimed the words left him traumatised and unable to work. Announcing the suspension, a spokesperson explained that while a victim's past history was immaterial in such cases unless an offender knew of it beforehand, and deliberately used it to cause offence, the judge could have put things better. The case will be reheard by a new judge next week.

Big Or To Small A Fair Days Work For A Fair Days Pay. *Thhhp*. We are digital. Blua-ha-*ha*. Kiss my weenie. We are *lahve*, bebbeh. Hey, Lorraine! You fuckin boiler. Come and check this. Come and see. My gridsite, look. *Pthhhhh*, chew on that one bitches, siteo le feral *wow*.

Lon Cush, 37 Palisade Row, East Palisades. Things are quiet, which means fucking scary as anything could lurk in the stillness. Our stillness now bristles with danger. Used to be a place to escape to but now we should stay well away. That little old house of stillness, bare timber camp in the woods where we scraped over fences to trespass, seems to have been sold to a person whose face we didn't warm to at school, someone unwarmable-to. Because whoever thought making your enemies invisible was a step into a bright new future was a person who had trouble thawing dates between the legs.

But never mind. The geddon-rich environment took our focus off the goal. We've gotta fight back.

86267571272: The person carrying a child conceived via content stolen from a hotel wastebasket is suing a number of media producers over their use of the term *Wastebaby* to describe her unborn child. Human rights campaigners have flocked to social media in support of the action, calling it an outrage that any living thing let alone a person should be heir to an anecdote that refers to them as waste in over a hundred written languages. The mother is seeking undisclosed damages on her own and her child's behalf, claiming that an irreversible and permanent loss of dignity has been caused by the word's recent use in certain media.

Break out. *Heroicus interruptus* – suck on some Latin there, Darryl, brought to you by Long Lonnie Lonregan, because guess what, my friend, he's back. *It's Lonnayyyy.* Back on the trail of the model family, the impregnable family, a Kirchnerproof, Monaproof cupcake family, photoshoot family with unhinging jaws to show joy. *Oh my God, you should hear her!* Because why not, because *yes*, because fuck it, go big or go home, except I am at home.

I cup some more beer in my tongue, let it spill down the sides in trickles. *She's so your biggest fan.* Look how things lined up: secret fanbase tucked away upstairs, barely taking food and water. Like hospital patients, but throw the guitar in and *bang*! The old days! Fast track to proud, highway to happy, pony express to who we're all meant to be, an unstoppable force, a love team. *The others are green over it.* Those heretics don't know I know about their little grid project. Thing's been in the back of my mind like a vision from another life, a good life; and now it's time to make it *this* life. Surely I owe it to

139583862445: An unusual new lobby appears to be forming in the wake of a child's conception via the expendable fittings of an upscale hotel. An account calling itself Flipside Conception has attracted over three thousand followers claiming to have conceived via other means than physical contact and assisted fertilisation. The newly formed group, including one mother who conceived via a fencepost, a number via household surfaces, and at least ten immaculate conceptions, have demanded an end to their marginalisation for simply doing things differently, adding that their children are none the wiser, nor in some cases are the children's fathers.

them, to Diane. To myself. I don't know what happened, life got real along the way. The more real it got the less I played guitar, and the less I played guitar the less laughter there was, the less singing, less love. The music left our lives. But we could bring it back, pick up where their gridsite left off, make their site *come true*. By the mysterious Hand of Diane, by Heretic Magic, and Shel could even shoot a video, the Eagle could post-produce. See them beaming like the old days. Have a little suck on that one, Darryl, bijou suctionette there, Darryl, *nyah*, do we understand each other, *nyah*.

Lonnay and the Heretics, The Travelling Cushies, too cool and too lovely to fuck with, too obviously correct. I chug some more beer and reflect on it all. I may go down sometimes in life but I don't stay down for long. Here's me getting up again, bloody but unbowed. Nothing to lose. What can you lose by trying? *Nothing*. And if I made it a habit I could even get some gigs, just free ones to start with, Ali's or Kinbassa, for instance. I quaff and swig and slump

225851433717: An unemployed sanitation technician from Calabrava has become a Rike sensation overnight, attracting fifty million hits for the video of a song even he admits isn't that good. Thirty-year-old father of two Pere San Quinti was filmed singing 'Hostia Joder' as he swept the gutters of his cobbled neighbourhood, and by this morning was on a flight to meet the studio executives gearing up to monetise his new-found fame. One industry insider comments that most stars take years to attract the audience San Quinti achieved overnight, adding that the market is strong for lumpy maverick solo artists with raw down-home appeal.

into the sofa to savour it all. *I've seen her put everyone to bed on the subject of you.*

Truth is, their little tribute left a crater where in quiet times I feel sorry. Young grasshoppers, only doing what they can, no fault of their own. Just as love grows when you see them asleep, it comes out like a fog when they're absent like this, convalescing upstairs in their rooms. I don't know if it's healthy to dwell on it, also feels dirty somehow. But never mind. A scheme has hatched, not a scheme but a correction, and I gaze around with a whole new sense of wonder. Even the rug looks better to me now. I lift my feet and my socks look better, I look better, six empties on the floor and they look better.

Heretics are searching for comfort on the grid when here I am under their feet. *Yes.* Lonnie in da house. If ever a situation called for another Coypu pilsner, tell me if this isn't it. *Merci*, don't mind if I do, and serve up my finger to Kirchner.

I fetch a fresh bottle and chug till it burns, then I seal my lips, wait a few seconds and – *thoop* – pop

365435296162: A tech watchdog has warned news app users to be on the lookout for apps infected with the so-called PityMe code, which takes control of targeted news algorithms and substitutes news content for words and phrases captured from user conversations. Experts warn that detecting the code, which is powered by increasingly strong AI, can be difficult and may soon be impossible, as it learns and grows. Some users have reportedly suffered serious distress after conversations involving critical health issues and deeply held beliefs were targeted by 'adaptive news'. Suspected new cases should be reported to #reportpityme.

off the couch like a pump rocket. Okay, maybe I'm over-egging it but what the fuck. There's no excuse, it's up to me. I flip the Coypu on its head and drain it down my neck. Seven empties. *Lucky number.*

The others fall over as I stand it on the rug, loudest noise today, but never mind – *she's so your biggest fan* – we're heading up to the future. Shelby first, she's more easily amped up, or shows it more than Egan, who's in a grunting phase. Wind her up first and we can tiptoe down to Egan's in our socks – *Oh my God, you should hear her!* – spread the vibe that Long Lon Regan's back.

Halfway up the stairs I get the fog of love and sadness over my hectic sawn-off creatures. Stuck in a world where the terror threat level is constantly orange or red. We never had a terror threat level when I was a kid. What evil prick would think of saying there was a threat level every day, anyway? Fucking dickbean *is* the threat level. And they wonder why drugs are popular.

I knock softly but firmly on Shelby's door. Hang

my head and listen. *What?* she says. Shaylabubbly, I have a proposal! It comes out very sincerely. But I hear her physically slump: *Couldn't you just message me? You wasted all your energy to come upstairs?* Well, I have slightly more energy than just that, I say – and I'm here with a really fun idea, a family thing for all of us, be just like the old days! My hand's on the doorknob. Can hear my own breath. *But can it just like wait? I'm snowed under here.* I pause to amend expectations: Okay – is it something I can help with? *Oof, can it just like – wait? Please?* Okay, okay, I'll start with Egan. But catch us up as soon as you can!

I linger and listen to her listening to me. Both of us waiting for me to fuck off. When I finally pad away I do it noisily, my little gift to her. Off down to Egan's, where a sign is taped to the door: *Trespasers Will Be Kulled.* I rap on it. *Ugh?* he goes, and I say: *Culled* is spelled with a *C.* He thinks for a second: *Then it would sound like* Sulled, he says. Well, then your surname would sound like *Sush*, I volley; but

956722026041: The terror threat level has risen to severe after a man attacked a branch of JumpJet Burger wielding a flamethrower improvised from an aerosol can and a cigarette lighter. Four people were injured, including the attacker, who used a foreign language throughout the incident. This is the third attack by terrorists on the public this month, and the worst since a man armed with camping gas and a battery-operated hand drill terrorised customers and staff at Spike Harvey's on Sebastian Road. Authorities warn that further activity is expected, and urge the public to report suspicious behaviour to the Terrorline on Muh, Rike or Goh.

whatever, Eagle, I need a wingman.
I have a proposal for you. He rustles
some papers to show me he's busy:
*Like, now? Because my projects got
bunched up. And with homework on
top.* Now I pause for longer than I
should here. Heretics measure degrees
of pressure by the length of silence
after statements. He rustles again to
remind me of this, and I snap myself
back to the moment: No worries, I
say – what projects? *Mm, so, one about
ancestry, like the family tree, and one to
design an app for like a good cause, like
homeless, or cats or something.* Good
job, I say. And what's the homework?
A literature book, he says. Well – can't
compete with that! I try to keep it
light although a sinker's plunging
down. He grunts: *I can, it gets less
stars than* Kullforce II. Uh-huh, I nod
at the door. Well. Give me a shout
when you're free. And don't let me
hear any donkeys up here! I head
down the stairs, minus fog of sorrow.
A fog of beer blows in instead. Foggy
day. Number eight. *Lucky number
somewhere.*

1548008755920: Beer
drinkers are almost twice
as likely as teetotallers
to reflect before acting,
and three times more
likely to have good
singing voices, a study
has found. In other
findings, regular beer
consumption has been
linked to a lower risk
of hospitalisation for
water-borne diseases,
as well as a greater
likelihood of surviving
the complications of
a kidney transplant.
Researchers speculate
that chemicals released
in yeast fermentation
may be having a
protective effect, though
they're quick to add
that sympathetic effects
should come as no
surprise; the chemistry
between humans and
beer has been brewing
for thousands of years.

Ramona Winbourn, 64 Sun Village, 144 Kaylor Road, Harville Downs.
The girls will bring the sandwiches, and I'll just. Big hit at my powwows, except for that chunky ham, you end up pulling the whole lump out, get left with just the bread. You know? But I'll make these perfect, I'll.

Ahh, damn, I don't know why I get so teary all of a sudden, these days, I mean. Then again I have all the reason in the world, my beautiful daughter, a ray of sunshine, then John two years later, and the bubbies stuck with, you know – Lon.

Real mystery how some people get together. Couldn't even get a job, sent her out to work at Green Owl, I mean. And little Shelby-Ann was all I had in the world, and so like Diane, just heartbreaking. She was all I had because I could've gone out and found someone new after John, but no, I just. Too loyal. Now over sixty it's hard.

Oh God, is that the girls? Already? *Brrrrr.* Damn. Find some happy thoughts, happy thoughts.

2504730781961: An alliance of social science departments has rallied to voice concern over the exploding number of niche paraphilic groups arising on social media. It follows a warning by leading experts that humans are copycats who look to their peers for behavioural cues, tending mostly to act on minority impulses when enabled by others with the same interest. They cite as an example the rise of niche harming groups, attracting large enough numbers to make members feel normal, and even to empower them to act. Certain groups have been quick to dismiss the claims, pointing instead to a long prior history of marginalisation.

Madeleine Aude, Rue Gabrielle-Pierrot-Fripon, Vierne. Band music was playing this evening. It was coming from one of the rooms. Elodie came past and we looked at each other. She said it was Dr Fisser's room. I went to see. Dr Fisser's partner, Dr Roos, had brought a speaker and was dancing around. Not good dancing but sweet and full of fun.

There was a bottle of red wine on the table. *Olé!* Dr Roos was saying, and Dr Fisser was scolding her because *Olé* is too frivolous for hospital. Dr Roos is a famous scientist. Dr Fisser might be too, but I've seen professors of ours come to shake Dr Roos's hand. That's how I know. What a pair.

It was late to play music but it made me smile. These girls. Their little party. As far as I know there's nothing to celebrate in a medical sense – Dr Fisser isn't responding as well as we had hoped. But any good news is for the better. The more reasons we have for living, the more it can boost our systems, it's something you see in here. Subtle things, big things, anything we can find to make us hungry for

4052739537881: It's official: Calabravans really do have more fun, according to a detailed lifestyle survey just released, which ranks Calabrava among the top-five places getting the most out of life. Analysts say the climate and natural richness of certain places will predispose societies to live more outdoors, and take away the need for strict survival concerns, allowing a greater degree of poverty before lifestyle is affected. Calabrava's music was found to be one of the top-three influencers of fun, with experts saying the effect is so powerful that even humming one of the tunes can lower blood pressure and flood the brain with feel-good endorphins.

life is good for the health. I pretended to be cross about the noise. I said: What about all these drums? And Dr Roos took my hand and spun me around, *Olé!*

I had to smile. I took the opportunity to adjust Dr Fisser's drip, and she said: Cornelia's travelling away tomorrow, but they're installing a videolink which can be on at certain times, and we can chat as we always do. She smiled and added: You see, I can't get rid of her at all! Dr Roos made rude gestures at this, still dancing. How marvellous, I said, so you're having a *bon voyage* party, but Dr Roos said: It's not for that, we had a date to watch old thrillers but these social media shits have mounted a campaign and forced the network to cancel the film. Because the director was nasty. Excuse my language, she said, but there was an author who wrote that the world was made up of two types of people: us, who are busy going about our own business, and a small percentage, between five and twenty per cent, I think, who are *shits*, who have an unquenchable need

6557470319842:

Hotel occupancy by single males is down by over twenty per cent, a hospitality watchdog reports. The downturn is thought to stem from copycat thefts in the wake of publicity surrounding the hotel-baby case. One hotel fired a concierge this week after he was found to have accepted money to facilitate a theft of waste from visiting teen band Cattles of Sin, in town for the final leg of their *Stab Yo Bish* tour. Industry analysts say occupancy may be slow to recover, citing a recent poll which found that up to a third of working males would in future seek private accommodation in preference to hotels.

to be right, which needs the rest of us to be wrong.

Here Dr Fisser said: But you're off to fix all that. She's off to fix it – she pointed at Dr Roos. I'll do what I can, said Roos, before they ban all the greats of history. So many big works came from utter bastards. It's a fact we must accept: bastards are a fruitful sector! At this Dr Fisser smiled and said: She ought to know – she's one of them.

Melanie Holie, 91 Leon Des Road, Reynes Parkway. Julie? Hi, it's your amazing mother. I just – oh, you're there. Ha, what? I don't know, bout of sudden-onset self-esteem. I was just calling about Saturday but then I've been in hysterics. Donna's live at the Mona corral, and after the whole Discovery Wholemeal issue, Elizabeth now arrives with a copycat version of Em's oh-so-righteous sandwiches, foil and all – and they're better than Em's by a consensus of everyone! I'm crying – they took a selfie with her, she's there like a grumpy turtle, and Philippa Haselgrove right behind her

10610209857723: The newly appointed head of the local libraries commission, Richard Esaw, has said the world would be a better place without books by writers who drank and lived deplorable lives. He made the comments at the launch of a campaign to promote genuinely valuable literary works, where he was recorded as saying: 'Works by drunks, addicts, bigots, lowlifes, people who beat their women and have no respect for society, plain scum in many cases, have no place in the world we're trying to build.' Esaw, a Voluntary Self-Assailant, was roundly supported by members of the wider V-Sas community across the grid.

cocking a snook! . . . Oh my God, I'm sending, see for yourself. Apparently Tasha posted the recipe and then . . . Hey? No, that's next month. This is more of an impromptu rain dance with cocktails. I think Mona's looking for some dirt to wish for custody again, brainstorming with the girls, and . . . *What?* Oh, Julie, come on. *No.* Don't you dare call him. Listen now, don't even think of interfering. I mean it, for me if not for you. Leave it alone, be professional. I feel sorry for him too, but on the other hand – pizza and beer at this stage of her life? Seriously?

Anyway, listen, nothing will probably happen, you know Mona, just needs to drown some sorrows, let the girls talk her round. Okay? Julie? Be realistic, there's no need to stick your neck out when the likelihood is low. I'm sure Lon's being careful, he knows the score. Okay? So promise me? I knew you'd do the right thing. And anyway, look, if Mona hasn't managed it by now, it'll take some big new demerit against Lon, you know?

17167680177565:
It's the news we've been waiting to hear: scientists have found that cakes can be a *powerful dieting tool.* The catch? *Only the best ones.* Those scales can come out of the closet, because the study, which looked at the *science* of cakes, shows that more than half of a good cake's volume – by *good* they mean *lightest* and *fluffiest* – is comprised of air, with no calorific content whatsoever. Announcing the mouth-watering facts, researchers said that an *entire sponge* – as in big enough to *fill a plate* – has fewer calories than a meatball sub or an eighteen-inch pizza. The message is clear: get beating and bake off those inches!

Lon Cush, 37 Palisade Row, East Palisades. The school group has chosen *You Are Guests in Our World* for the heretics' Christmas play. Someone has already been thrown off the thread for calling it *The Snowflake Monologues*. I don't check the thread very often. It's down to two voices no one can argue with because they have disorders. Still, I checked it now and I'm sitting here wondering if it's good or bad news, the play. Something I do a lot of lately. Then Boges calls and makes me stop. Have to mark it as good and forget it. Something I do a lot of lately.

I pause *The Gravy Years* as his voice pummels out: Lonregandhi – did you get a pop-up Coypu beer offer? Yeah, I say. Don't click it! he says. Too late, I tell him; good deal, what's the problem? Ah fuck, he says, you idiot. It installs a trust score aggregator! A *what*? A trust scorer, he says – it renders a score from your grid activity, Rike and all the rest of it, scans your accounts, adds it all up and gives you a score as a person. See the little hyena top right of the screen? I hold out the screen

27777890035288: Children today are as busy as working adults of forty years ago, or as busy as forty-one per cent of working adults today, a study has found. Up to ninety per cent of activity may be vocational, showing the beginnings of a career or profession, which researchers go on to say is often associated with new technology, media and gaming. Early Choicers were quick to seize on the findings as concrete proof that childhood is an unnecessary detour for otherwise energetic and undervalued contributors to the wider economy. Parents' groups have responded by saying the findings show nothing less than corporate kidnapping.

and it's there, blinking and looking around: It's a hyena? Looks more like a dog. It's a spotted hyena, he says, they picked it for a symbol because they're good at counting, apparently they can do maths. Little fucker's scoring you on your friends, your shopping, your browsing, your feedback, the number of positive words in your posts, basically anything you've ever done, then it sticks a trust score next to your profile. I watch the hyena and it watches me back, even sniffs and shakes its head.

This calls for a therapeutic ale, which I fetch, asking Boges: Didn't you click it? And he says, Yeah, that's how I know. According to the forums it's been in the air for a while, some places already link your contacts to your tax file, so they can fuck you over your friends. Then Rike patented a version to assess your credit based on your friends, also pretty sinister, although they said they wouldn't use it. He grunts to himself and I try to pick my beer label off without ripping the little coypu.

Have to ask the question: Can they just do that,

44945570212853:
The Octagon is calling it the definitive fix for trust on the grid, and it's rolling out across town today with a bonanza of special offers for the first hundred thousand users. UFS stands for Universal Fluid Score, an intelligent system that renders individual trust scores by computing user feedback across a range of platforms at once. UFS is the brainchild of developer Baz Matanick, who says it's the final piece in the online grid puzzle, with code so sensitive that a single positive post will affect a user's score within a nanosecond of posting. A host of grid industries have welcomed the roll-out, including retail, insurance and banking.

from ordering beer? And he says: Did you read the contract? Tick the box? Dummy, the crawler will have scraped all your data. Start using a proxy for your porn, he says, and delete fucking Feral from your contacts. I don't have Feral, I tell him, Hordy was always shift leader. Well, fine, he says, then look on the bright side, it's only a guideline to let people know you're faulty. Waste of beer from their point of view, a picture would've done the job. Start posting about diabetes, throw in some puppies, chat about beans and you'll be fine, he says, because they're not sinister up at the Octagon, if you discount masturbation to cartoons. And listen to this, he says, a forum reckons the system's modelled on human judgement, same as the processes of judgement, an algorithm like a human mind. Designed to offset the anonymity issue, a weapon in the war on cybercrime. Underneath they're saying it's actually a peace offering from the industry before regulators start hitting everyone with unique user IDs.

Boges burps and I think this over. Swig some

72723460248141:
A Calabrava man is claiming to be the original singer of 'Hostia Joder', the song made famous by online overnight sensation Pere San Quinti. The man, who declined to be identified, said he was only a day away from recording and posting the song on the grid himself, adding that he was a genuinely unemployed street-sweeper who had been singing the song as he swept voluntarily, whereas San Quinti, who the man claims heard him and copied him even down to his uniform, was well known as a local barfly with questionable habits. If true, the man stands to have lost an estimated nine million bills this week alone.

more beer and try to guess what I'll score. Human judgement. Hyena. Score as a person. Tricky, because the first thing I realise is we always tend to assess ourselves deep down, we're always good deep down, we mean well deep down, love things deep down. Whereas this here's a floater.

I ask Boges what his score is and he says, *Eighty-two*, babadoo babadoo. Not too shabby, I admit. Out of a hundred? Not too shabby. And holy moly, he says, check this, my card interest went down. And – no way! – the limit's up five hundred bills!

I go to my own slightly frowning hyena and touch it. The letters *UFS* pop up. I remove my finger and the hyena looks at me. Blinks. I touch it again. The letters *UFS* pop up. I leave my finger there. *Fifty-two* appears. I remove my finger and the hyena looks guilty. Damned thing starts to scratch itself.

And get this, says Boges: there's a grid-vote to pick a name for the little mascot – no prizes for guessing Satan's neck-and-neck with Josh.

117669030460994: A leading hotel association is considering launching a civil action against a number of media outlets for their use of the words *hotel* and *hotel-baby* in reference to the recent case of a child said to have been conceived via alternative means. Pointing to a dip in revenue after the widely publicised case, in which a person is said to have fallen unexpectedly pregnant, sources close to the association have said hoteliers are mystified that of all the story's elements a certain sector of the public has taken *hotel* to be the operative word. Thefts of complimentary paper-based hotel expendables are believed to have soared in the story's wake.

Ember Mullock, 18 Styron Drive, Two Fields. So the Merlot offer had a catch. Uh-huh. Welcome to Ember's world. The long and winding Ember. A catch and it looks like a kiddie's cartoon. Like for trendy teens, a cutesy-wootsy spotty-doody and it stares at you and blinks. A dog. Or not a dog. A non-dog. An antidog. Doesn't appear in programs menu. Doesn't appear in system menu. Some scheme where I'm under the eight-ball again, how will I contain my excitement, uh-huh. Wait – touch it – *UFS*. What? Undoubtedly Falsified Shit? Unbeatable Fabulous Star. A horoscope? Uranus Flies South. Under Fiery Saturn. Is it research or something, an experiment? For teen gamers? Do we have to guess and then it . . . Oh wait, a *trust score*? For me? Just like that? It made no sense to announce it, give us a choice? Ah, because *c'est la vie*, within hours you're going to look untrustworthy without it. Okay, so – *seventy-nine*. Huh. Better than my average at school, I suppose. Thrill after thrill here for Ember.

Dennis Farrell, 12-B Mason Drive, Molan Gardens. Score what – my cock? Heh he. Thing'd run out of numbers. Little dog'd explode.

UFS, it says underneath. U Fuckin Scrote. Then *thirty-one*. I ping Boges about it and he asks me my number. Who cares, I tell him, I didn't ask for this, and he goes: Then why'd you call me, dipshit? Wanted to see if you got sucked in, I say – sucked off, more like it – and he says: Who are you trying to convince? My dear Feral, if you scored less than fifty, which I can see you have, you're in the lowest ten per cent of early scores. In a week you'll barely be able to order pizza. The polls put prison inmates at fifty or better, so here's a tip: use another identity for your porn, or get a new device. And take me off your contacts. I'll send you Cheryl's burner number, she can afford the points.

Fuck you, I tell him, take me off *your* fuckin contacts! Already have, he says; I'm a step ahead of you there, my mangy boy.

308061521170129: People who curse in daily life have been found to be healthier and more intelligent on average than more reserved and polite people. In a groundbreaking study released today, mortality and health were measured across a range of personalities to see if demeanour had a significant effect on our health. While reserved people scored highly on resistance to climate, and showed a lower incidence of injury due to violence, cursing people were found to be almost four times more likely to survive bladder cancer, and more than twice as likely to enjoy good gastric health. Experts are looking to lowered stress as a key.

Shelby-Ann Cush, 37 Palisade Row, East Palisades. Ksenya Ksenya Ululay, Ksenya Ksenya Bululay, Ksenya Ksenya Mululay, Ksenya Ksenya Fululay, Ksenya Ksenya Ooloolo, Ksenya Ksenya is-a-ho, *kh kh kh kh kh*. Uh *yuh*. How many views with the yoga pants. How many views with the tank top. How many views with the shorts. How many with the boob tube. Ow, Jesus. And she has ads.

Fennec Friends Premium. Free? Or clickbait. La-la-la-la-la. *Bluh*, take the score challenge. *UFS*. Unicorns something. *Eighty-four!* Gold for Shelbae! *Boo*, but then Ksenya has ninety-one. Hoe.

Nanny comes online just then. Mona. Nanny Monarona. Nanny Monaronahona. She goes: Shelby-Ann, darling, did you get hooked up to this scoring service? With the cartoon dog? It's a hyena, I tell her, duh. Hyeener weener – I don't tell her that. Well, great, she says, because I just, I was wondering where the control is to see your contacts' scores. It says you can see your other contacts' scores?

498454011879264: Cyberstar Mindi Meims has apologised after a spat over the habitat of fennec foxes with new viral rival Donger Deane. In a viral post yesterday, Ms Meims voiced concern over the vanishing forests of Jembaya, saying: 'They're destroying the forests, my poor fennec babies!', to which Ms Deane replied: 'The fennec is a desert fox. Learn about your pets before you get one.' In a heated exchange which can't be repeated, Ms Meims learned for the first time that Ms Deane, a vegan, was also a victim of physical bullying. Meims issued an open apology, saying anger over deforestation had prompted her outburst.

Egan Cush, 37 Palisade Row, East Palisades. *E-gan? Someone coming to the door*, which was weird for her to say because it was her door, this was Aunty Mary and Uncle Austin's place, like ages ago in January, who were like Dad's parents. The door chirped, they have a bird doorbell. *The girl from next door*, Aunty Mary said. *Come down, my hands are wet.* You could see the girl's pixels through the glass. Bruaagh, nerves. Girl. Door. Like that part in *The Gremets Shop for Sandals*, where they end up in a pus clinic. *Breuughh.* Aaaaargh! Not now!

I opened the door. Hi – she smiled automatically. Hi, I said. I brought you this? she said, and it was a book. *101 Code Tricks.* Is it scary waiting for tits? Is there really blood? Do you look at your body in the mirror? Does your house smell like this one? Is it strange to wear a dress and feel air? Is that what you want? Is that what *I* want? Thanks, I just said. So, she smiled. So, I just said. So, bye, she said. Bye, I said. Thanks for the book. No problem, she said, and turned around, still smiling, and then a thing

806515533049393:
Children in foster care perform twice as well at school as children in need receiving care in their homes, the Education department has reported. Fostering in rural areas showed even greater benefits, with children's grades and behavioural outcomes jumping places ahead of urban children under social services care. A neodeclinist group was quick to respond to the findings, writing: 'A kid playing in nature does better than a zombie glued to *Donkey Kull* all day? Tell us the earth is round.' To which one commentator said: 'They're FOSTERS. Being compared to ABUSED URBAN. Not chess prodigies. Moron.'

happened in slow motion, a terrible crime when a silent car flew past the front and the car, which didn't have paint but was just polished steel, didn't see the girl Silvia and threw her up in a ball of flesh and clothes which fell in a pile that was not the shape of a human body any more. *No!* I ran to her. *No! Please!* And the middle part of her face was smiling in the pile but the eyes were turned down and crying, and I said, Oh my God, what happened, oh my girl, and I scooped her up and staggered to the house and after laying out papers I put her on the couch and started picking gravel off her and she felt better and smiled in a new kind of way. Everything will be fine, I said, and I wanted to find a hand or a finger but I stopped before it got awkward. She was too nice.

Terrible, terrible thing, whew, thank fuck that didn't happen. So yeah, over a hundred likes on the fiction board for that. Got my chupacabras today too. Or hyena, supposedly. *Ninety.* That's my score. I call him Ramon. Oh, Ramon, please not now.

1304969544928657: A groundbreaking new study has found that ungrateful people live poorer-quality lives by a factor of five than averagely grateful people. The study follows an earlier finding that gratitude is an essential key to happiness and productivity. Researchers said a typical ungrateful person was eight times more likely to be involved in a car accident where they were not the victim, in some cases completely unaware that an accident had occurred, and almost twice as likely to remain unconcerned. A large number were also found to prefer unpainted cars. *Lowlife* was the term found to be most associated with the ungrateful.

Ramona Winbourn, 64 Sun Village, 144 Kaylor Road, Harville Downs.
Oh my. Oh goodness, no. No way, I mean. Barely *fifty*? Points? Seriously? I just. Oh God. Happy thoughts, happy thoughts.

And the forum says that within a week most businesses will only want to trade with scores of sixty or more – well, it's obvious, why wouldn't they, I mean. You know? Oh, Lon, honestly. Barely *fifty*? Good God, and I mean I'm up in the nineties and I haven't been employed in decades! Is the thing. I just. I have no responsibilities and look at my score! While he has crucial responsibilities and look!

Oh, those poor children. Oh, my poor babies. What if he's denied access to credit and just gets shut down, over time, and not say anything, because that's how he is, and then. I just, oh, my poor babies, oh my God. And surely this affects him with the Child Protection people? The forum says the government will use the system too, it just. Oh my, Julie Holie, where's Julie's number, she ought to know.

2111485077978050: Looking at, holding, smelling and polishing apples has been found to lower stress-related chemicals in the brain, elevating mood and creating relaxation, a study has found. Apples were studied in a variety of settings, from subway to city and meadow. While results were positive across the board, a meadow proved the most beneficial setting, for its abundance of other de-stressors. The finding has already led a number of grocery outlets to offer inedible apples, grown for their size, shape and colour. But experts say any apple will do, and if eaten after holding it for eleven minutes or more, benefits can rise exponentially.

Arielle Hovis, 41 Reynes Parade, Reynes Park. So my dad said check out these foreigners that had came next door, well a couple doors down, on the Bucci's side, remember the little place with the awning? so he said the owners dropped the price so far that refugees moved in or something, he's half waiting for like chickens in the street and whatever and I'm just like ya ya ya Dad, so anyway I had went over, you know me – *kh kh kh* – and so turns out they moved up from East Palisades, like I don't know, ethnic or whatever but like wait, no wait, listen – it's like a fricken *threesome*, two girls and a guy! And I'm just like Oh my God, and I mean that's fine and I don't know if like hardcore or anything, but then I'm like don't even tell my dad that part, like whatever they get up to in private or whatever, you know? but like so anyway they had told me they had came over from *Sanary* or some place, and my dad had went fricken quiet when I told him, he goes, *Sanctuary?* he goes, I *see*, you know how he does, I *see*, and he goes well the sanctuary coast is where they land after crossing from the war zone, they cross in little boats and like most of them drown but they get picked up and buried and he's just like Oh my God! But so like and I'm only right there in their fricken house! *Kh kh kh!* they had came over on one of those death boats or something and next thing good old Ari's there like, o-*kay*, *eek*, hehe, how do I get out of here, and you can hear fricken house prices dropping up the street, like my dad's calling around to get bars installed on the downstairs windows and I'm just like Oh – my – God, *kh kh kh*, but I mean like they were really nice though, I don't mean it like in a racist way, they're just like ya ya ya, and the guy's in this threesome or whatever, with a younger one, hot as you like – oh my God but like fricken *stab* her – and one who must like cook or whatever I guess. So yeah the war zone and I'm like o-*kay* hehe, my dad's gonna bust a fricken vein, I mean he bought here at the top of the market and now *oops*, o-*kay*. Really nice people though, brought out all this food, I didn't want to try any but they're just like it's fine, I mean

5527939700884757:
Mindi Meims has shot straight to the top of the UFS rankings with an almost perfect score of ninety-nine, beating viral rivals Donger Deane and Donkeyhooty, on a modest ninety-eight each. Mindi, who this week trialled the name Mindabae, was quick to play down her success, saying: 'Love can win out over hane, respect can conquer mullying.' Asked about the recent inclusion of her buzzwords *hane* and *mully* into a number of grid dictionaries, she said to our reporter: 'We had gotten so bored of like words but like now we can see them fresh again but from like a real person, from a real place with like real love and pain going on.'

you just have to feel sorry for them, smuggled around and like bombed and whatever, like just you know, they're still human and everything. So yeah, so Albert the guy's called, and Martha, and then but the hot one though, total fricken boner-coaster, you can see why they make them wear the black thing, Jesus oh my *God*. I'm just like uh-huh, o-kay, war zone. No wonder we fricken bomb them, *kh kh kh*. Anyway but so hey did I tell you I'm back to ninety-four? Yeah it was fricken Britnae. Ditch Brit, she's worth like five points. And hey Kitty's has double points for wax and tan, what are you doing later?

Dennis Farrell, 12-B Mason Drive, Molan Gardens. Fuck off, you heinous piece of shit, get the fuck. Wait – try this. Wait . . . shit. *Fuck! Lorraine!* You know anything about this points-dog thing? Yeah, the fucking hyena, won't get off my site. Well, fucking *duh*, because anyone who comes for welding will see twenty-nine! You moron.

8944394323791464: Developers behind an app launched this week claim it can protect users from bullying, stalking and even routinely awkward encounters in public. Developed after figures showed that one in four of us will at some point live with a 'stay away' or restraining order, and that two in three have already been stalked, abused or bullied, the GoWay app works like radar to pinpoint the people we don't want to see, offering alternative routes to avoid them. The app's GPS screen displays constantly updating likelihoods of contact with targets entered, also offering high- and low-priority settings for more densely populated environments.

Julie Holie, 9 Linden Close, Stresnan. I was fine as long as the kids were up. Now they're in bed I can't stop thinking. Have to reach out to Lon. With my amazing mother's voice in one ear. Oh, *Julie*. Her crimpy face. Julie, *please*. She's not even that old but all her years crawl out when she's antsy about one of her girls. As in me. Tania's the plain-sailing one. I'm the sailing-plain one. I stroke the phone in my lap. See if I can talk myself out of it. Reputation at stake. Job at stake. Mother at stake. Nope, can't talk myself out of it. Oh, *Julie*. Dilly-dally some more, check my score, ninety-one, whoop-de-do.

I read the UFS system's top-weighted, like a wine score: they expect over half of everyone to end up competing in the eighties and nineties. Or not competing, but you know. Okay, competing. So yah. But, so, I just don't know what it is, with Lon – Tania has it too, you just want to give a damn, or I don't know. Treat him like, I don't know. As if deep down he thinks there's good in people, not official

14472334024676221: Women who stay with or return to the crush they had at fourteen are almost twice as likely to remain in the relationship as those who partner with someone later in life, new figures have shown. Scientists behind the finding explained that a crush was not merely a passing desire but a significant chemical event whose footprint altered brain structure for ever, leaving it permanently primed to seek and respond to parameters consistent with that first tingling crush. The findings appear to support the notion that humans are designed to partner for ever, suggesting the crush we left behind might remain our one true partner in a chemical sense.

good but real good, easy good. *People* good. Calling him now would be people good. I could casually explain the criteria we use to advise on custody matters, give him some intel from inside.

To hell with it, I open his contact. Heart skipping, racing. Breath. Back in time fifteen years. Come on, Julie. Ridiculous. Grown-ups here. Grown-up voice. Julie, *please*. To hell, I hit his number and he answers straight away. Upbeat tone. Glad to see my pic. Which is nice. My mouth dries up but he saves me and dives in first: Julie, listen, sorry about the other night, the little vacuum cleaner rally. Should've offered some coffee for your trouble, he says. Oh, get out, I say, I was up City Hill and saw Shelby's thing, five minutes away, no trouble. Now hoping he doesn't ask if I usually drive around with a vacuum cleaner. And baking paper.

He spares me and says: Well, thanks, anyway. No bother, no bother, I say. So, Lon, look: I hope I'm not interrupting? – last dilly-dally, hope he says yes, but he doesn't, I have to jump in – Okay, so forgive

23416728348467685: Historians may have found a link between the nineteenth-century inventors of the concept of childhood and notorious murderer Albo Goncci. Research into what is now being called the Childhood Deviation found that the concept grew among Sarian traders who, to protect their fortunes from ruthless young heirs, declared an eighteen-year period during which the young had no rights. A closer look at the individuals concerned has led to links being proven between the founders of childhood and the groups Goncci once belonged to. Commentators are unsurprised, noting that modern parenting shares many traits with violent crime.

me but it just came to mind to see if all's okay down there, see if I could share some, I don't know, intel of, you know – family matters, or . . . ?

Aaand silence. I can hear his carpet. Blurt something quick: Please understand this is not through the office, I shouldn't be calling off the record. But I just thought, you know, sometimes just knowing where the goalposts . . . Silence.

I may have made a mistake. Oh, *Julie*.

Well, thanks, he eventually mumbles; I mean, is it because of, or . . . ? Did Mona contact you?

I have made a mistake. *Shit*. I overcorrect: Please don't think badly of me, it's just that I remember you as a people person, and offering support seemed like the people thing to do. You know? Lon?

Ah shit, it's Mona, he says. I can hear his head hanging. Lon, look, there's stuff we can do. You know? To make things bombproof, make Shelby a happy camper, and I'm not just talking more shopping, or a kitten or whatever. Lon?

37889062373143906: A declinist has had to be cautioned by police after a vicious Rike attack in which he accused popular cyberstar Minda Meims of being inane. The man, quickly identified by loyal fans, said the unquestioned celebrity bestowed on Meims and 'other stupid people' showed that the species was selecting backwards towards the apes again. He went on to outline the case of a promising young physicist who, due to a prior porn addiction, scored only forty-nine on UFS, while Meims scored nearly a hundred. Ms Meims was later applauded for her graceful response to the attack, writing on Muh: 'Lol at least apes aren't haners.'

Tania Holie, 18 Geppert Street, Reynes Parkway. I don't know, I mean – he was strangely innocent in a way. A stray teddy bear, I don't know. Not innocent to the ways of things, you wouldn't walk up and say he's innocent. But after a while, just a kind of wonder about him. Gratitude, or hope, or . . . Hard to nail it. He came down from Belvoir, so maybe it was an edge of soil. From a place that made more sense, where the sun managed to rise without counselling. Not hay-chewing countryside, but you know. Sense of values still. Not jaded, I guess, is what I'm trying to say. He was cool, I totally got him. And Diane was, how can we say – liberated by him, is how I'd put it. I suppose we all were. One of those people that if you threw mud on them would throw some back, if that makes any sense. Quick to grasp what level you were playing on.

They actually did that once, from head to toe. Mud. She felt liberated by him, and that's enough in itself. Isn't it? We should be so lucky. You know? And at the time she was still having hassles with her

61305790721611591: Chhrush, the app that claims to find your true chemical crush from among billions of possible matches, has been named newcomer-app of the year at the *Yo-Sienz* Awards overnight. Originally launched as a school-crush search tool, its functionality was enhanced after research showed that our first adolescent crush is most likely our chemical partner for life. Chhrush uses cutting-edge AI to hunt and match the DNA signatures most likely to have stirred up a crush, even matching some users with existing old crushes not previously entered as targets. The app is celebrating its win with a free match offer for every new user.

ex, the tennis club nightmare, which is when she stopped playing altogether, he was virtually stalking her, or anyway big-time failing to get over things, kept trading his car up and up till he was coming round in a limo, leaving little notes explaining what a catch he was. *Horribly* insecure, oh my God.

Then here comes Lonnie on the bus with a sandwich in a paper bag and a stupid grin and some candour. You know? It just lined up. And I guess all the shit with her parents just made them want it more, made it definitely happen. You have to get Diane – don't ever say I said this – but she just didn't trust Ramona. Really instinctively, almost weird. She got John but he was a busy man. I say it feeling sorry for Ramona, actually, no one dislikes her, even Diane felt sorry they couldn't be closer. Just strange. And Ramona, well, who knows how she felt deep down. You could tell with her she was acting according to her coding, I guess the only way any of us can act. I mean, she might've had all kinds of revelations, might've thought things, but in the end

99194853094755497: Up to a quarter of all English-speakers and over half of all declinists say they have issues of trust with their mothers, a new study has found. Looking into possible maternal links to declinism, researchers found an almost fifty per cent increase in cognitive bias among those who were bottle-fed compared to breast-fed infants, leading scientists to speculate that our innate senses of reality and optimism may spring from something as simple as a full waiting breast in infancy. Studies into declinism are ongoing against a backdrop of concern over the growing number of people over thirty succumbing to cognitive bias.

she had to ride with her code, with the expected, and what I think the real tragedy is, is that she might have come around, might've changed in some way, had some real bonding with Diane later on. Diane too, real tragedy, but nothing says you automatically trust your mother. We have a lifespan to work things out, we can sit down later as different people. Doesn't matter when you do it. Can be the day you die. But they missed that day. And they were still under the cloud of the marriage when she went, made Ramona even stranger, from what I gather. That much unfinished business.

I sometimes see her on-grid, she'll grasp out at random on a bad day. Better she do it to me than to Shelby – I worried for that kid, like watching a prequel of Diane with creepy music. Wouldn't surprise me if it affected her, and of course now she's with laid-back Lon again, probably thinks he doesn't care. And actually that nails it right there, with Lon: all his problems seemed confined to real problems. If a solid problem came up he'd go at it

160500643816367088: A new mental health app claims to be able to increase mental wellness and remove personal obstacles by hosting final conversations with the dead. Designed on the back of research showing that a failure to clear the air before a loved one dies can be a leading contributor to breakdowns later in life, the app is designed to listen to and answer users' concerns via one of sixteen profiles programmed with strong AI to match deceased loved ones' personalities. The living can also store profiles for use in conversations after their death. Some early users are calling the experience uncanny, with eerily accurate feedback.

like a fighter. Otherwise he could coast, he was fine. So there was this feeling when you were with him that the same rules applied, that you were fine. You could coast with him. Safe pair of hands.

One day I remember, the really hot summer, back when it was unusual, we were building a bong out of a dog food can, and in cutting the thing he gashed his wrist right into the fucking artery. Almost go weak just thinking about it, blood spraying over the laundry, Diane and I screaming our heads off. But Lon quietly pressed it with his thumb, joked around to calm us down – as in, Look, no hands! – I'll never forget. He finished the job with his one free hand, insisted we do a hit to get over the fright. Then I drove us to emergency, back when I had the clunker, fucking flew there, *bup-bup-bup-bup*, and by forty minutes later we're sat in JumpJet Burger killing the munchies. Hahaha. Unreal. I see he's on Rike now, part of me wants to reach out. But I don't know. If it'd be good or bad for him. Who knows. Pthh.

259695496911122585: The anonymous mother of a child conceived via alternative means involving commercial hospitality premises has launched an action for battery against the unborn child's alleged father, Qumau real estate developer Edmund Wei. The action comes in the wake of tests appearing to confirm Mr Wei's paternity, and cites actual bodily harm and psychological distress as a result of carrying a stranger's child. Speaking from a secret location, Mr Wei has said he will fight the action. NO WEI! supporters continued to rally despite a number being cautioned earlier after exchanges grew heated.

Lon Cush, 37 Palisade Row, East Palisades. Something's afoot with Ramona again. Julie didn't say but it was there between the lines. So here's me spontaneously prowling for moments to create a happy camper. This isn't one of them.

I also have to call Ember – I passed her this ball in the first place. Didn't think she'd kick it off the field, though. But first the happy camper: work on the bombproof household. I'll start without shopping or kitten and work my way up. Heart to heart.

Shel grouches past on her phone – *She thinks she's so like and she talks so like and everything's so like and she's just like such a haner* – so you know it's about Ksenya Ululay. As she ends the call I have to enquire – *Haner?* – and she goes: *Yuh*, duh, haner-weener, just goes around *haning* on everyone. I gently ask: Do you mean *hater*? With a *T*?

But we don't get to the answer. She recoils from her screen and flies to the window: Ow, I have to get going, my Trice is here. *What?* I go to the window as a clean-looking sedan pulls up by the gate: Your

420196140727489673: Keeley Teague supporters today joined children's rights campaigners to lobby for an interim state of independence for the young. Fronted by cyberstar Mindi Meims, the group appeared before lawmakers to argue that children of the past were fully able to assess their own risks, and even hold demanding jobs. Ms Meims said the abandonment of children to increasingly unstable parental controls posed a much greater risk to society than 'guided emancipation' would pose. Declinist groups echoed haners in roundly condemning the proposal, calling it another cynical psychological ploy to monetise childhood.

Trice? Shelby sags and dangles her arms: Oh Jesus God, *why is everything such a big deal with you! Lonnie!* Shelby, I say, you are not going anywhere in a Trice. Forget it, what makes you think I can fork out for you to ride around in taxis? And where are you even going in a taxi? She powers up like a whirlwind, flings her handbag at the wall: I frickin *knew it*! First of all, *Lonnie*, I have my own money; secondly, it's not a frickin TAXI, it's a *Trice*! I'M GOING TO SEE A FRIEND IT'S NOT A FRICKIN DRUG DEAL! JESUS CHRIST! Colours flash through her like an octopus.

I fix her the stare I'd fix a man – You are not leaving this house – then walk out the door and close it. The fuck. Trice. Two people are sat in the sedan; one is Maria Carney, who used to be a nurse at Alma. Lovely lady, probably retired by now. I settle my twitch and say, Sorry about this, but Ms Shelby won't be going anywhere.

Maria laughs: Not the first time we've heard it, not even the first time today. I'll leave a card – not

679891637638612258: A rights lobby has reported that the last century in the West was the first in history in which females were discouraged if not forcibly prevented from taking advantage of natural fertility, which can peak in adolescence. The group went on to call it an abuse of the most basic female right, citing one specialist obstetrician who warned that even twenty-six was considered old age for a first conception. The group's vision of a youth that can look forward to raising a family to an age of utility by the time they leave their teens forms the basis of Keeley's Law, the Early Choice proposal being led by Keeley Teague and Mindi Meims.

everyone's heard of J-Trice, or Junior Trice, she says; whenever you're tired of playing Daddy-taxi, we're a chaperoned service for juniors, all of us nurses or nannies. She hands me a card. As I read it she sings: *Cool as ice in a Trice!* and laughs. I chuckle along, type of high-pitched giggle you'd hear in a nuthouse. Kids are even paying from their own accounts, she says, from their little grid incomes and such. It helps teach budgeting and responsibility, gives them a valuable head start up the UFS ladder.

Well, I say, suppressing *Are you fucking shitting me* and trying to sound informed, sound woke, as we say down Palsays way: Scoring must be weighted for youth – her score's better than mine! I pull out five bills for Maria's trouble, but she turns them down and we both glance back at the house.

Shelby's in the window like a doll you'd see in a horror show. Screen-lit face from below. Come play with me, Lonnie. Thirty-Seven Palisade Row today. Just waiting for blood to gush out of it.

11000877783366101931: The so-called 'kiddie-conomy' will be one of the three strongest market sectors within two years, financial pundits predict. Pointing to the boom in youth-generated advertising revenue, as well as gaming and cryptogame markets, analysts estimate that over a quarter of digital income was created by children in the last financial year. An industry spokesperson dismissed claims of exploitation, saying grassroots support for Keeley's Law proved the young were entering the market on their own terms. Declinists and haners were quick to condemn the corporations involved, accusing them of slavery by coercion.

36
Breather

And, in fact, forget it. Between the undead heretic in the window and a creeping sense that Mona was about to ping him on Muh – maybe groundless, but groundless is scarier – Lon's legs grew leaden. It was Muh anxiety, the jittery wait for an incoming message to send a tick back to its sender, a receipt that he'd received the thing, so he couldn't pretend to be genuinely lost in the jungle.

The sum effect had to be heart disease. So he shut the phone down and went into the house. By the time he reached the head of the path, Shelby had gone like a spectre. He listened to the last of the clean little hum from Maria's sedan as it departed, and settled himself on to the sofa. Too drained to fetch a beer, although he did fetch one. He really should call Ember, but he ignored that as well. The place was still. Life seemed to pause. The world seemed to stop. He soaked in it.

The space around him posed and glowed like an exhibit. Its grain came out; he remembered applying the colours, three years ago now, must be. He had fretted to cut in the paint nice and straight on the door frames and the skirting. An omen for new times ahead. New space for a fresh new family. He had done it when all that his life comprised was stretching his limbs through air, flexing and talking in the realm that was his, a few square yards that followed him. But the skirting and doors didn't matter any more. Damn the skirting and doors. He swigged cool beer and held his breath, sat in the exhibit. And when he glanced at his hand it was worn. He had woken up older, and still pretty poor. He supposed it would happen till the eau de cologne on the bathroom shelf turned to drugs, till his breath smelled of salt, till the sweet pods of figs that were his guts years ago turned to calcium. But never mind: if he rubbed his ear with the bottle he could hear the sea. He should take the heretics to the sea. They should sit together at the sea. Splash in the sea, the heretics, instead of around his head.

The worst thing with the heretics was suspecting that what he reacted to in them was inherited from him, in invisible ways, uncontrollable ways. He hated it and was also mesmerised. They were a freak-show mirror of his shadow and light, one discreet and one blazing. Saved by Diane's appearance, at least. The boys at Kinbassa had once said Lon had a head like one of your parents' old bottle stoppers, with the drunks carved on, though he wasn't a drunk in the true sense. Most of the time. He didn't think. But his head *was* bold, and the older guys at the end of the bar, away from the music, said he moved like a sailor in a film, whatever that meant.

Maybe the heretics hadn't done so badly. A tribute to their mother's dimples and cool grey eyes. Not all was bad news. Something there.

Through reflections like these to the tiny hiss of beer, with the walls shifting colour and dappling at times – things in his mind grew clearer. The buzz fell away and calm returned. Filaments and branches that made up his brain all plumped and connected and billowed. Situations began to look orbital; everything seemed orbital now. Galaxies: orbital. Solar systems: orbital. Planets: orbital. Atomic particles: orbital. Friendship: orbital. Feral's bullshit: orbital. *Life*, he suddenly thought – *life* – it was orbital, and calculating that orbit must be the key to all action.

Things were therefore underway, an orbit was afoot, it might look bad from where he sat, but they were passing through a zone is all. Things could be worse, for the heretics too, much worse. Imagine who else they could be stuck with. Worse than him. Maniacs, like that ES manager they identified on the root cutter fetish site after Boges received a tip-off. A maniac but of the kind that was persuasive, which is even worse. Left a wake behind all he did, that guy, a filthy spray of backwash. He was the kind that absorbs other people, has them abandon themselves and suckle him; the kind with the wife required to be dumber than him so he can lie to her, so she can bring up the babies he was man enough to keep, but bring them up stupid too, so they could end up believing his cover, that his heart was in the right place. When his heart was in no place at all.

Lon swigged some beer. Heretics could do worse.

So he had that going for him. If only they could move upstairs, things could be rosy again. Palisades, Palisades, nothing was better at making you picture bacon rinds at the dump, from houses where the pit bull was the smart one. The south had become a power grid for outrage, according to Lon. But then, thinking about humanity, he saw how orbital it was too, how orbital people were, circling and talking but all doing the same as each other, as if each was only three per cent uniqueness, Lon thought. And ninety-seven per cent typical human. And who each person was compared to anyone else depended on that three per cent. He wondered which he liked the most, the three per cent or the rest. As with so much of his recent life, the answer was both. He liked to trot like a sheep behind the ninety-seven per cent, to mingle and run with his fellows, voices clanking around their heads like hail. He just wanted to be part of that clanking, be one of the clankers, or a clinker or a clunker-in-arms. And yet few others would ever admit that they ran with a crowd, that's the nub of it there. The equation reversed in their minds, they took their three per cent uniqueness and called it ninety-seven per cent.

That heat exchange, that repolarisation, thought Lon, standing the beer on its end; what if it was the mathematical engine that ran humanity?

He felt good with himself for thinking. Felt the power.

Self-esteem, he thought. Can't buy it – it's an inner burn of self-evidence. You can't live off flares of it either, a fizz of magnesium spikes and dies and leaves you in the cold. No, it must come from a stable ember. Stable ember in a hearth that you pile yourself, that you stoke and feed over time. A piping ember of red.

Ember! Now he should call. He was in for a talking-to, but he'd have to face it sometime. They still hadn't spoken since the Shelby affair. Why not now? While the spirit was light and the time was right. How bad could it be?

He powered up the phone.

Hello! It said. *Hello, Lonnie!*

Ember Mullock, 18 Styron Drive, Two Fields. Uh-huh, I say on the way up to a sneeze. I blast my eyeballs into the lids and flatten them. Spray the phone. Wipe it, and go back to the call.

Ember, says Lon; it's Lon. Uh-huh – I reach for the kitchen roll, this has gone way beyond tissues. He says: I thought we should talk. Uh-huh – I crush the phone into the cushion to mute it as I blow my nose. I'm dying here, I tell him, just so you know. Well, he says, I've been trying to get a hold of you, you know, about everything. Uh-huh, I crackle. I'm listening through my mouth, I say, the rest of me's blocked. Sorry, he says, want me to call back? But no, he's right, it's time for this. Before I die.

I mix up some vitality shit I found on the grid and pause *The Derriens*, which I'm watching for like the ninth time. Corey Kniessen is so hot in this. I fall on to the sofa like a cadaver, plumping all the pillows.

So, says Lon, I just thought we should clear the air, you know. Uh-huh, I sniff, off you go. But he's

17799794160047141-89: The Octagon has condemned a recent public attack in a southern suburbs bar on seventeen-year-old sanitation apprentice Jacob Storer, allegedly by thirty-nine-year-old pipeline shift supervisor Janos Bogdanovic. Witnesses also reported that a number of onlookers from the ES department chose not to intervene. Mr Bogdanovic's position with the department has been terminated with immediate effect, and his file handed to police for further inquiries. Eyewitnesses to the scene at the Kinbassa Lounge on Leonard Road have been asked to come forward. Reports will be dealt with in the strictest confidence.

waiting for me to go first. Leaving a gap for an apology. And I *should* say I'm sorry, I should say *I'm so fucking sorry* for protecting you from what a counterfeit your little family is while you splash round the sewers using the weight of your fucking mortgage as an excuse to not deal with your life. And then fly off the fucking handle at me. But not yet. I may be dying but my timing's still keen.

He finally continues: Well, firstly, I'm sorry for the Shelby thing. You were right to freak out. Uh-huh, I say, unpausing *The Derriens*; they're still on the boat to Latanga, so that scene can run in the background. I'm trying to get over fast-forwarding everything to the scenes I like, it's a twelve-step fast-forwarding programme, discipline myself to watch more variety, eat my greens, although I'm tending to watch the same meals over and over. *Bluegrace* is the other one. But hey-ho, today's greens is that we're on the boat to Latanga, where he's in his cabin with the toucan, one of your five-a-day, the cabin scene to Latanga, green bean of a scene, no fat, no

28800671943708161-20: Two NO WEI! supporters are dead and another three are in hospital, after a van thought to have been driven by Alt-Bae supporters hit demonstrators near the home of the so-called 'indirect conception mother' at the centre of recent protests. The incident comes within hours of the woman's identity being leaked on social media, a leak thought to have been carried out by a bot similar to the one blamed by the government on the Octagon last week, which led to details of government ministers' grid searches being widely shared, and over which three senior ministers have so far been forced to resign.

sugar, because he's fully dressed and saying nothing; but now, lying here, I'm aware of another discomfort: do I really want Lon associated with this scene? Anywhere near the boat to Latanga? Isn't there a danger that whatever he says will get tagged in Corey's cabin? *Yes* is the answer.

I pause it again as he goes on: I got sacked that day and then Shel came off the flat like, I don't know, a floozy, and giving out to me about it when I asked her. Uh-huh, I reply, but? No buts, he says, although I wish you hadn't put me on the abusers list, wish we could've talked. It's not like I stabbed her. Uh-huh, I say, you mean the list where people who hit people go? Not put you on that list?

He pauses to change gears; he can feel the tone getting shitty. Just would've been a damn sight clearer, he says, if instead of covering for their little schemes you just let me in on them – the ice bucket thing, for instance. Wasn't like they were dealing drugs. Only found out when I went to the school to see about her fucking language.

46600466103755303-09: Octagon chief executive Bertie Riley has joined Company sanitation apprentice Jake Storer in thanking the public for its overwhelming support in the wake of a vicious personal attack on Mr Storer at a lounge on Leonard Road last month. The Company has facilitated Jake's relocation to a secure address, where he is being counselled and supported by specially trained community services teams. Mr Riley also took the opportunity to update the public on the case's progress, saying the Company is awaiting security footage from which it hopes to identify other ES staff at the scene. He repeated an appeal for witnesses.

Uh-huh, I say, that she picks up at school. He ignores that one and continues: Even you said she'd been swimming, I don't get what the issue was, not like I was going to stab her, she wasn't dealing drugs. And then the flexitime thing at school, did you know about that? Yes, I say, by now really glad he's nowhere near Latanga; in fact, I blank the screen. Then I let him have it: And listen to you! When did you last look at your mail? I bet it's still in the pile where I left it! Let me tell you something, Lon, the clues were all there. Did you want a babysitter or a fucking interpreter?

Well, he says, you make it harder when you form conspiracies with them, or they'd tell me the news themselves. Ah! I say. Correction: you mean *Shelby* would tell you the news, *Shelby* would tell you because Egan vanished into himself two fucking years ago and . . . Actually that's another thing, he says . . . Uh-huh – oh, you noticed, I say, you did a headcount of children who express themselves and found yourself short by one? And to what might we

75401138047463464-29: An ex-sanitation worker has spoken out anonymously about what he calls a chronic culture of 'mullying and hane' in the Company's ES sanitation department. The man broke his silence after an appeal for witnesses to the devastating attack on teen apprentice Jakey Storer, a much-loved sanitation crew intern and gifted *Donkey Kull* player, according to his family and friends. The whistleblower has said such attacks are a daily routine among pipeline crews, and added that it was a lucky day when things didn't turn to violence. The Company has vowed to leave no stone unturned in purging the department of abusers.

attribute that? Hmm, let's see, hmm . . . Poor old Egan fell out of the limelight when Madame flounced back through the door, and here's me trying to fill the gaps, Lon – yawning canyons, more like it – in that kid's life, while you run round after Shelby like the Queen of fucking Uribe! Did you know he was commended for art? Did you know he got an A in writing? No, because you're supposedly taking him fishing every weekend to spend some quality time and you never fucking took him once! Shelby, Shelby, Shelby! I rasp it, breathing hard.

Listen, okay, he says, maybe I overcompensated, I don't say I didn't. But she's been nabbed once already, it's like a permanent parole with fucking Mona, she wants her bad, to plug the hole left by Diane, although perhaps I can't talk. But frankly, you know, Ember, if you're the one who's close to all this, while I try to barely keep a roof over our heads, it would've been a fuck sight easier if you'd let me in on some of it. It's not like I didn't want to try! Uh-huh, I say, and after a pause simply add:

12200160415121876-738: At least four more people thought to have been sanitation apprentices have broken their silence over the culture of physical and verbal abuse in the department served by senior pipeline engineer Janos Bogdanovic. Among claims stretching back over a decade are accusations of extreme sexism, racism, homophobia, obscenity and humiliation within ES department pipeline crews. Police are conducting an urgent review of Bogdanovic's work history, which started with the Company when the Octagon was being built but has been found to stretch further back as a sanitation worker, and earlier as an apprentice employed by the City.

Close like a *mother*, you mean? Clang.

He hesitates, dithers – Okay, listen, listen – but I decide not to wait, who cares, I wheeze over him: *Helloo*, I say, tell me if this sounds like the current century to you: man comes home, woman is there, food is cooked, children are clean, they shut up when he wants, woman fucks when he wants . . .

Hey, hey, hey, he says. No, no, I say, it's time to listen. A mother sends you into the world with a full belly and clean clothes and the first fucking thing you do is go out and find another female to fill the belly and clean the clothes, then little girls are born who learn to cook and clean and fuck and shut up when they have to, I say, although I taper there, it's actually pretty ranty and old-school.

Ah, Jesus, he says. He found it ranty too. Fuck, Ember, he says, is this where we're up to? I shouldn't have called, he says. No, no, I say – fuck it, he deserves the rant – you *should've* called, I say, you need this information, you cannot bounce from woman to woman expecting to be looked after if you

19740274219868223-167: Crowdfunding revenue for ex-sanitation apprentice Jacob Storer has rocketed past six figures, as investigations into his abuse by senior colleagues in a southern suburbs bar continue. Another six ex-apprentices have so far come forward with horrifying details of an Environmental Services culture of obscenity, intolerance and abuse. Among well-wishers adding support to Jake's cause was Mindabae, who also pointed to an apparent total lack of female crewmembers in the Knox Park-based facility, which is responsible for maintaining much of the Octagon and inner-city sewerage systems.

make it like their born fucking duty! So I hope you're having fun raising your little family; if you're unemployed you should have all the time in the world to cook and clean and listen to their stories. Well, he says, I think it's a bit extreme. I mean, I personally haven't bounced to many females in my time, and even the mother wasn't a real one in the first place. But whatever, forget it. I'm just sorry shit ended up this way, and if you could let me in on any other little surprises I'd be fucking grateful.

Well, hmm, I say, gosh, where can we start, for life-related hacks, hmm, let me see. Oh – how about TRY LOOKING UNDER YOUR FUCKING NOSE AND OPENING YOUR FUCKING MAIL! *Ploop.* I kill the call. Hey-ho. Check hyena, which I've named Hiatus, because that's how loaded these flu capsules are – and look, I gained two points! Don't know if it's *The Derriens* or the rant. Or the flu. But liking hyena, though, my carrion bro. Ha! So back to Latanga – take me, Corey, take me now.

319404346349900099-905: Local health and licensing inspectors have sealed off an area around the Kinbassa Lounge on Leonard Road after an unscheduled visit by community officers exposed a number of irregularities at the venue. Officers arriving to collect surveillance video of an attack on a boy by sanitation workers found a number of underage drinkers on the site, as well as evidence of drug use and a culture of off-site alcohol sales to East Palisades locals. Security footage of both the attack under investigation and the issues uncovered today is being examined by specialist teams. The lounge will remain closed until further notice.

Cornelia Roos, 14 Palisade Row, East Palisades. 'My Lori', what a tune. So clean and jazzy. So *sexy*. I'm humming along to 'My Lori', having just bid Johanna goodnight on the screen, when the bell chimes. It must be eight o'clock in the evening here. I open the door and it's Wunderboy. Carrying two bottles. I'm a little surprised. It's him with two wines.

Professor! he says too loudly. He may have had some already. I hope I'm not interrupting, he says, but I wanted to meet our new neighbour, see how you're settling in. No, come in, I say. I hope it's not an intrusion, he adds, fishing, I think, for a stronger welcome. No, no, I say. I don't do stronger welcomes. Still it's hard to argue with his initiative. Do you need glasses for the wine, I ask, or are you just passing by with the bottles? Well, if you'll join me, he says – sorry I can't tell you where they are, they should be in here somewhere, the place is fully equipped. Quite disarming, young Matanick.

I call to mind our relationship's model as I set off to look for the glasses. Probably a brilliant young

51680708854858323-072: A study into the cases of fifty City workers outed as mullies on social media has found that alcohol played a part in eighty-four per cent of the reported incidents. A prohibition lobby has seized on the data as a prime example of alcohol's destructive effects on individuals and society, saying the percentage of offences by males would fall to almost nothing if not for alcohol and the enabling culture around it. The news comes as a round of snap inspections of city bars finds three more premises in breach of their licences, two for serving underage drinkers. Officers warn that more closures are likely to follow overnight.

man, under his ignorance. A utopianist, like all whose inspiration comes from machines. Enchanted by the possible and not the necessary. *Blinkered*. And I think: Not far from myself at that age. Thesis in my pocket like a penis. So the differences between us are slight. Slight but quite decisive.

And what are the differences? Well, experience is one. Then the appalling chimera of gender, specifically women's effect on young men, as putting nuance aside for a moment, looking only at practical averages, if they don't want to fuck you they're looking for a mother. Solace and sandwiches, Johanna once said, in the absence of sexual promise. And I don't do that game in either direction. If due to that I come across as tougher than I am, so be it, I don't care. I've had to. Woman in a man's game, although they were all men's games when I started, my field not as bad as many. As for gay, I won't even discuss it until we pick a less prancing word.

I am honestly looking for wine glasses here; they will be in one of these cupboards. I've located the

83621143489848422-977: A study has found that using hard consonants such as *B, P* and *T* in speech may damage the palate over time. The findings follow comparative research into languages using fewer or no vocal occlusives, also known as plosives, and appears to show much lower incidences of palate injury and disease, in some cases up to six times lower, than in speakers of harsher languages such as ours. Experts wonder if the current trend towards low-plosive speech in social media broadcasts might be an example of 'species intelligence' at work, demonstrating a spontaneous selection away from higher-impact habits.

tumblers so they must be nearby, they're herding creatures like oxen. I call out to Wunderboy: I am making progress! No problem, he calls, it's a tour of your new kitchen! Hah, I leave that one alone. Little shit. Hear this kind of thing once and it becomes the debate's mass, how can it not. We can answer back, of course, but from a subjective disadvantage, outgunned by a two-inch cocktail sausage that makes every man a musketeer. The worst you can ever say is *small penis*, whereas to point at a woman and say *woman* is a bullseye every time. *Puh.* There it is.

It might sound militant but I'm not so much. Other things to do. As a child I liked the company of girls as all girls like the company of girls, nothing more. We had friends who were boys but we departed like trains from a station when we started to bleed. The locks to our doors all changed. We pitied some later, not harshly but with sympathy, which I'm sure they found even more galling. We didn't know why at the time, but it owed to how slow they were to grasp that life has a rhythm, a pulse like a

13530185234470674-6049: The Octagon is racing to patch what some commentators are calling the Angel Vulnerability, as a growing market of so-called 'sin-eaters' was found to be hacking trust scores to re-credit points lost for criminal convictions and other demerits. For the price of a family meal at JumpJet we were able to erase the demerit of a parking ticket through a sin-eater who went on to quote prices to remove restraining orders, rehab orders and even bad debts from UFS. Sin-eaters are thought to move demerits on to volunteer low-point accounts, but the Octagon warns that the marks will return as soon as a patch is in place.

metronome. That rhythm is the universe searching for form, and we're a sensitive part of it. Like relays.

Ah – and the universe throws up some wine glasses, still in their boxes. I roll up my sleeves, pull two from the cupboard and start to give them a wash. A curious domestic moment comes as Matanick pokes his head around the door, me like a mother at the sink, even humming. Need a hand? he asks. *Yes* – I aim a finger at the stairs – *go up and tidy your room.* He stops in his tracks. Hah! After a suitably uncomfortable pause, I say: Could your UFS calculate a value for that moment?, and he slumps. Because, I go on, still humming, still rinsing, It was a typical human moment, perhaps positive, perhaps negative. A superposition. Algorithm of a moment, I say, turning to leer sympathetically. Poor Wunderboy. Perhaps he knows who he's dealing with. Perhaps he doesn't. But here we all are, how jolly: a swiftly devaluing cocktail sausage, a pair of empty glasses and a ton of bricks.

21892299583455516-9026: UFS critics have voiced concern over the falling average scores of people over thirty, saying the trust algorithm doubly benefits youth by favouring youth-related activities on top of an inbuilt induction weighting. Critics also pointed to a widening gap in gender points averages, as male heads of households scored higher as a result of being family utility and bank account holders. An Octagon spokesperson has asked for patience while the system finds its feet, saying that as a 'system of systems' in its first month of operation, the intelligent program has to adjust to the job's complexities just as any human would.

Gideon Hovis, Allied Social Services, Parsons House, Farlow. Bobby? Take Dan's Outdoorland off the favoured suppliers list. Mm? Because A: we couldn't feed Sam the cat on their savings compared to Providers, and B: they just quoted a grand to install security bars on some windows. Mm? Yeah, mine, downstairs. Just almost decorative, iron or so, like you see around. Spanishy. Bucci's has some, the trattoria along from me. In keeping with that. Keep the street's integrity. Mm? Well, it's not what it used to be, Reynes Parade. For one thing the Wards have just sold out to immigrants from God knows where. Arielle went over, and from what she told me of their trajectory, they arrived through the sanctuary coast. Ha! Tell me about it – if it was a glass-bottom boat they'd be able to see the house prices! Ha. Ha. Let's just say. Anyway, Bobby, when you get a minute can you check some local labour? For the bars? I think Derek can do materials, I just need it put together. Cheap: we're not talking rocket science.

Lon Cush, 37 Palisade Row, East Palisades. The phone wouldn't stop pinging through Ember's chat; now I go to investigate and this other shit starts up. Something buzzing. I think it's outside my head for a change. Takes me a minute to confirm. Sitting still. Beer at rest. Froth at bay. But then chimes start up as well, *ting-a-ling-a-ling*, fucking crazy, losing my mind. It's coming from the direction of the window.

I tug aside the curtain and there's a drone hovering over the fence. Little ears on the thing, eyes on it, flying kitty or something. On the one hand it brings a wash of the chemicals that come with the relief of not losing your mind, on the other I have to adjust to fucking drones hanging over the fence. I don't appreciate it. Need my head unblown here. Things being what they are. Real issues. But *ting-a-ling-a-ling* and *fvvvvv*, until a new set of chemicals washes me up and out the door. What-the-fuck chemicals. See if I can swat the thing.

As I reach the bottom step a cooey voice sings out like a baby. Who knows what it's saying but it shits a

The standoff between four nuclear powers active in the Al Qemen war zone has entered its second day, with posts from all sides growing heated. Head of the arbitration board appointed for the region, Mads Dreyer, has expressed concern over the appearance of the word *nuclear* in more than one Rike post yesterday. He said the threats were hugely destabilising, and would greatly hinder urgent and ongoing diplomatic efforts. The latest row between participating powers was triggered when the warring bloc was found to have signed a major deal for superintelligent over-the-horizon defence systems.

box on to the lawn – *doof* – which makes me flinch. I find myself hoping the thing isn't fragile, and then that it isn't a bomb. Blow me up on the lawn. End of Lonnie's problems. End of mowing, at least. I go to pick it up before I start hoping it *is* a bomb – the drone watches over this, *fvvvvv*, sending data back to its masters in a cave – and, for crying out loud, the thing's from Harville Pharmacy. It's Kirchner's DNA swab kit for Shelby, delivered by drone, by Autogyrokirchner. I consider going in to get the shotgun, but after a few cooey words the thing lights up and buzzes away.

I watch it hug the curve of the Row down to City Hill Road. Then a nanosecond of quiet before the phone's back, pinging like a hailstorm. I sag on the lawn and let gravity push me down, arms hung, neck lolling, eyes to the sky like a martyr. Beseeching, whatever that really means. And so fucking help me, although I don't want to do it, although I consider myself capable of not doing it, although I think of myself as someone who doesn't really do it anyway,

92737269219307899-9176: A blog by a previously unknown fourteen-year-old has become ground zero in a pitched battle between supporters of teen abuse victim Jake Storer and members of a growing GetReal campaign, thought to be led by sanitation workers in support of disgraced pipeline engineer Janos 'Boges' Bogdanovic. The fight erupted after high-school student Anton Coali expressed surprise that no one had asked what seventeen-year-old Storer, a minor, was doing in a lounge bar where alcohol was being served. Comments were disabled on the blog after exceeding twenty thousand responses. The firefight continues on Muh.

compared to some who embrace it with the force of new atheists, in fact consider myself to be persistently on the verge of never doing it again, and perhaps going fishing instead, or smelling a flower, or flying a kite, and perfectly capable of that, at any time, without a thought – I fucking do it, I huddle into my screen. Where I'm rewarded with the news. And fuck, it's Bogesgeddon.

Brain cells scatter like mice. Then Boges phones up, doesn't start with hello, just says: Don't get involved, it's a feeding frenzy. I ask what apprentice they're talking about, since our crew hasn't had one since April, and he says: Little fucker at the Kinbassa the other day, the skinny prick at the pool table with his goats and Velcro gloves.

Boges is literally chewing his words, gnashing and gnawing them audibly. I gaze around at the lawn, needs mowing, the streaky sky, needs beseeching. The fence, count the fenceposts. My feet, count my feet. And I run the scene back in my mind: Kinbassa the day I got fired. See how things

15005205362068960-83277: An international early-life charity has offered specialist counsellors to a number of junior schools whose hopes of honouring teen assault victim Jake Storer were dashed by Environment Agency officials. Children from as many as fifty countries had been participating in the Life Is Still Beautiful campaign, aimed at cheering victim Storer, by sending a flower from each of their countries to be gathered into a 'bouquet of solidarity'. The Environment Agency, which oversees customs and quarantine procedures for the importation of plants, apologised, saying that some foreign species pose a threat to our local flora.

cluster. Clustery day. From Shel to Kinbassa. Kinbassa to pool table. Pencil-necked apprentice trying to charm a gothy girl and failing. Too full of beer. Boges says: Nothing to do now except hope the pendulum swings. Should've pounded the little prick – he's made a hundred grand off this while my score's in fucking freefall. I'm down to *forty*. Fucking hyena's *weeping*. I don't know which of these apps tracks your speech, he says, but we need to come up with a language, hang on to the points we have. How about use *bae* for bullshit, *darling* for dickhead, something like that. *Diabetes* for dipshit, *beans* for booty – you with me? I feel his breath on my ear. I hold away the phone and test the lawn's elasticity with a shoe, mussing it like a rangy son.

And Lonreghandi, he says: ping me when they realise you were there. It's still the early stages, in the real world, anyway. They're going to want to talk to everyone. So let me know. But use code, say *gluten* or something, *gluten puppy victim bae*.

242789322839997508-2453: Two Environment Agency chief inspectors have been forced to step down within months of their retirement following allegations of verbal abuse, thought to have taken place in their first year as undergraduates. The men, whose names have yet to be released, were alleged participants in a clandestine beer pong ring at the college dormitory where the abuse is said to have taken place. Both men are also thought to have been behind this week's decision to enforce legislation against the Life Is Still Beautiful campaign in aid of teen abuse victim Jake Storer. The agency has apologised unreservedly for such a lapse in its hiring policy.

Saphia Lusk, 9–142 Borlow Road, West Palisades. So I basically go for like the last slice of the ham and pineapple but end up sitting with it in my hand my mouth's too busy with Kristen and I'm just like HELP IT'S DROOPING but it doesn't dump ingredients it just stops at the angle of bleh whatever so phew, but so I'm trying to tell her about Jokey Storer when I was gothed up at Kinbassa, she can't remember him but basically your disappointing friend's lame buttock and hitting on me and half shitfaced already and so then gets it in his head to tell one of the full-timers he fucks goats, and I mean the biggest one like a tank, and you're just there waiting for him to get snookied, and I'm like the closest one waiting for like the pool table and he's basically just sliming and *weuahhh* and whatever and I'm just like *Really?* so but and this other *hawt* older guy oh my God but just like basically staring and didn't say a word and I'm just like please please notice me *muah-muah-muah* and so but fuckin Jokey talks shit to the big one the one they call Vogues or

39284137646068711-65730: Environment Agency officers are almost three times more likely than the general population to be declinists, a study has found. Studies also show Environment Agency work is linked to a higher incidence of hane and workplace abuse, including mental coercion. Responding to the report, an Environment Agency spokesperson has apologised unreservedly for any declinist attitudes in the agency's past, saying that as an organisation of many decades' standing it was more vulnerable than some to historical mores. Commentators have said it's high time that such agencies joined the twenty-first century.

whatever who's like a fuckin house or something oh my God, but anyway I'm not putting any of that *what should I fuckin put?* KRISTEN you have to *help meee* NOW KRISTEN FUCK I need a response I'm like the closest witness the thing's fucking viral LEND ME YO EAR BITCH. Kristen's there *blup-blup-blup* doing her thinking sounds so I sneak a bite of pizza, and she goes: Well just like put whatever you saw or whatever, I don't know. RIGHT, UH-HUH like I'm really gonna put that and get wiped on fuckin Rike Kristen anyway THE STORY'S BEYOND THAT NOW it's in the NEXT SPACE we're past what HAPPENED fuck. Okay, wait, wait, I go, wait, how about – *Jakey my heart goes out, wish I could erase that night for you bae* . . . But now Kristen's lolzing, Don't put that, she lolz, next thing he's sending you dick pics! Just put the first thing, put *heart goes out*, or no, wait, but also let them know you're like the star witness, put, wait, put – *Couldn't believe my eyes Jake, wish I hadn't been there, so close, in the middle of everything, but I'm*

6356306993006846248183: A third advisor to the government has been forced to resign after pictures emerged appearing to show him playing beer pong in a campus garden as a student. The government has issued a categorical apology to anyone affected by the news, stating that pre-millennial attitudes had absolutely no place in public service. Pointing to a study listing beer pong as an indicator of low empathy, and even criminality in later life, some commentators have also urged a review of laws governing freedom of speech, after haners were found to be promoting the game to minors in a series of comic memes.

always there for you, get well soon and . . . Get well soon? I go, HE WAS FINE, and she goes, wait okay, how about – *Can't believe we shared this Jake, wish I could erase it for your sake* . . . Except now she's rofling her ass off: *And ping me your dick immediately!* she screams. Tch. She such a hoe.

Janos 'Boges' Bogdanovic, 84 Godfrey Court, East Palisades. What do you mean, don't say that. Fuck's sake. What I regret is not ripping his balls off. What? Oh, oh, I see – it's *me*, ahh, very well, say no more, there's our problem right there. Well, that's what it sounds like. Oh really, ah-hah. You weren't even there! Oh, naturally. Of course. And what would you put. No, go ahead, you have the floor, you fucking tell me, I'm all ears.

Get out, Joelly, can't you see we're talking? Wait, come here, Bumpylumps, kiss. Daddy a kiss. What? It's all the change in my pocket, look. I'm not even counting it. No, you can't have the debit card. Bye-bye. Bye, Honeysmudge. *Byee* . . .

10284720757613717-413913: A decades-old study on families has reported that over two thirds of all marriages south of Reynes Parkway will dissolve within nine years, and of these almost ninety per cent will live with ongoing animosity. According to the report, the fallout is mostly felt by children, over eighty-two per cent of whom will grow up at least partially in a broken home, almost half with limited or no access to one parent. In almost twenty per cent of cases, children will be removed to relatives or even into foster care. The agency points out that grid dating is very different from, and has few of the responsibilities of, caring for real flesh and blood.

So what would you put, let me hear it. I'll be the stranger, how about that, I'll come up and say: *Look at big fat Cheryl, needs Velcro gloves so her goats don't go over the cliff when she fucks them*. Oh, get real. Regret what! Should I send him something about the weather? Put *Jakey, it's partly fucking cloudy?* Leave out the part where I bang him till he loves me? Well, that's how I feel. What am I going to do about that. Oh, is it. Just like then. Very well. Identical to then. And I suppose identical to all the other times, the taxi in Cala, the time I said *lipids*, the Christmas party. No, no, no, what totally fascinates me is how the list never fucking fades, Cheryl, it only gets bigger and brighter, follows none of the laws of physics, shows zero entropy at all, old nest egg of a list you seem to treasure more than our wedding day. But that's what you don't get! I'm not doing it to you! I'm not doing it to *you*, Cheryl, this is a moment in a bar after work, one of a billion similar moments and one of extremely few in history where nobody got doinked. Oh, ah-hah. Well, if it's

16641027750620563-662096: A major health study appears to confirm what we knew all along: country living is better for you. The study, which analysed results from over a dozen other health and lifestyle studies, reveals that simply being within sight of a tree has a measurable effect on wellness, and benefits multiply with the number of trees in sight. Likewise, being able to see the horizon, hear birdsong and have most of the colours in a view derive from nature were all found to add to longevity and general well-being, as measured using a wide variety of indicators including sleep quality, gratitude and overall tolerance to stress.

down to stupid men I'm not going to win now, am I. Oh, is that right. Well, you seemed to like us when the drain was fucking blocked. Here's me all this time thinking it was about putting bread on the table and buying skincare for my child, and . . . *I beg your pardon?* I am not saying that. I am not fucking saying that at all. *You* said that.

Look, if it's about a message I can send him a message but I'm not saying I regret anything. Oh, but it's not about that, it's not about anything but the list, the good old list, ole dog-eared list and its crimes, hanging on threads by now for how much use it's fucking gotten. Makes a plumber's fucking time sheet look empty. Oh, is that so. Well, thank you so much. And you too, quite frankly. My career of twenty years put down the shitter by a teen on a hundred grand for being told to fuck off and no fucker in the world is in my corner and especially not fucking *you*. Cheryl. Are in it. Oh, well, fine. Fine and fine. Dandy, off you go. *Arrivederci. Au revoir.*

269257485082342810-76009: The latest census reveals a huge lifestyle divide between urban and rural communities, as technology takes over civic and social roles, and traditional lifestyles decline. Many rural residents have yet to begin to adopt digital lifestyles, even in communities relatively close to town, with over a hundred households in Belvoir reporting their only communication comes via wired telephone landlines or in person. Others reported using tube televisions or only listening to radio. The head of the City's Group for the Future, Andrew Gilchrist, said that while more upgrades were being rolled out, there was still a long way to go.

Madeleine Aude, Rue Gabrielle-Pierrot-Fripon, Vierne. I wait at the door while Dr Fisser ends her videocall. I can hear Dr Roos. Her throaty, twanging words. They speak in their language, both of them twanging. Funny birds, and so accomplished; I've grown quite protective of them. The daily chat will be important, and so advanced, the technology, as if they're in the same room. Very important routine, her chat, although she seems to spend it scolding Dr Roos. It's simply how they are.

I hear her finish, walk in and say: I hope you told Dr Roos about your procedure? She doesn't answer at first. She hesitates, then says: Well, no, the stress is bad for her memory. But Doctor, I say, we would be happier if she knew. Fine to be optimistic but it carries some risk nonetheless. And you might miss some videochats, then she would worry more. Her memory seemed fine, I add. At this Dr Fisser opens her cabinet door. Six or more bags of bear-shaped sweets slither out on to the floor.

43566776258854844-738105: In an unprecedented Rike attack, the Education department today accused an independent school inspectorate of victimisation and hane, after inspectors added a laughing emoji to a report claiming the most common answer by primary-school children to the exam question 'Which of these is not a garden tool: Shovel; Rake; Hoe; Ice Pick?' was Hoe. A complaint has been lodged by the districts in question, charging inspectors with flippancy and hane towards thousands of 'intelligent, well-meaning pupils'. The Education department has since defended a decision to mark the answer correct on the exams.

Cornelia Roos, 14 Palisade Row, East Palisades. We sit in armchairs placed in haste, as one still has its tags on. And all very beige here. Faint smell of paint. But things are going well. Wunderboy is rattled.

After a couple of listless pleasantries – *I hope your new space is fine? It will do, it will do* – he lifts his glass in an awkward toast and fucks himself right away: I have to tell you how excited we are to finally have you on board, he says; we're such big fans of your work. *Hah!* Oh, my dear. Stupid boy. He should have sent his mother, we could have had an honest drink. As it is I lose respect – what else can you do. *Fuh*. I hold off reacting for now; I'll give him his chance, the pulpit is his. But I'll give that much less of a damn exposing his farce. If Johanna were here she'd say I'm only able to filter myself when I'm hatching some devious ploy, otherwise I'm happy to bulldoze. I beg to differ, of course, being in shrewd control of my filtering; though for all intents and purposes she's right, hah, I don't care. Graced with flat-country bluntness, my long-suffering publisher

70492524767089125-814114: A declinist group has reported that eighty-seven per cent of studies featured in the media over the last eighteen months have presented as aberrant human behaviour thought normal and even healthy ten years ago. The As We Burn organisation said there was only one reason for alarmist pseudoscience and it was profit, as conflict vastly increases our use of social media compared to agreement, and social media principally exists to increase our interaction with the markets. A realist group called the claims simplistic in the extreme, adding that they showed the kind of thinking that led to the Dark Ages taking hold.

would say. I smile at Wunderboy – Thank you, Mr, hm – and nod my glass in return. Please, he says, it's Bastian, or Baz. Thank you, I continue in a kindly way, like the doter he wishes I was: and so, *Bastian*, let's hear of all these schemes you have burning a hole in your pocket. Why don't you outline your vision, define your goals, in a perfect world? I settle back and sip some wine.

Well, Professor . . . Colleagues call me Cornelia, I prompt . . . Thank you, Cornelia – he takes a hasty drink to wash the name away. Well, so I guess you'll know we're approaching the leading edge of the singularity envelope . . . ? But here I'm forced to interrupt: I would argue it, Bastian, we can only say I know it's being said . . . Okay, fine, he allows; but even without the full roll-out, the pull of the tide by itself is going to lead to increasing displacement of lifestyles and jobs, is where I'm headed, Cornelia, if you will. We're hoping new tech will dovetail with that, but whether it does or it doesn't, the phase we're in now is about clearing a space for it, floating

114059301025943970-552219: A new study reports that habitual beer drinkers are almost four times more likely to be abusers and up to six times more likely to suffer from impaired or low intelligence than teetotallers or drinkers of wine in moderation. Beer drinkers who took part in a raft of double-blind experiments performed significantly worse in mental aptitude and general knowledge tests than their non-beer-drinking counterparts, even when sober, and in some cases when answers were given to them in advance. A Public Health spokesperson has said the results represent another nail in the coffin of the last century's laughable alcohol licensing laws.

the environment in advance. He hunches over his knees: We imagine we're building a *raft*, Cornelia, a *platform* we can ride no matter when that tide comes in, no matter how fast it rises; a *ferry* to superintelligence, motivated by future users, in fact, because the learning curve will be gradual compared to a big bang later on, he says, sitting back to watch me fall over. Whereas I quietly sip some more wine. Lift the bottle and study the label.

Really quite good, quite fruity.

Wunderboy catches the absence of awe and paddles out even further: as for social connectivity, which I know you're concerned about, and which I need to explain more clearly, can I maybe just start by painting this analogy: you'll be aware of the discovery that ninety per cent of plants on earth are connected underground? Sharing nutrients and data, ganging up on invaders? As he waits for the answer I gulp down my wine – there isn't enough in the world – and then reply: But they don't taunt each other. Bastian. They connect underground because they

184551825793033096-366333: A travel waste compactor has been identified as the main component in a bomb which brought down an airliner yesterday, killing all ninety-one passengers and crew. The passengers are thought to have included nine children en route to a *Donkey Kull* fair. Travel waste compactors have been withdrawn from the market, and any trading in manufacturer shares suspended, pending claims by the victims' families. Officials warn it is now illegal to travel with a personal waste compactor, and offenders will be liable to fines or imprisonment if found in possession of one of the devices near any public building, especially an airport.

have no mouth or legs. The human equivalent is a nursing home. Where I doubt there's much ganging up. I hold out my glass. He takes a moment to spot the cue, then pours to where a waiter might, a quarter full or so. Keep going, I urge, and as he pours I lay my first little trap: Bastian, I say, did you ever get in trouble for social media in the classroom? His brow stands up for this: I wish, he says, but it wasn't really around, smartphones hadn't appeared yet. You *wish*? I query, and he laughs: Ay-ay-ay, if you'd seen the mutants I went to school with! I express a faint smile, the smile Johanna has called *the cat that shat in your shoe*: So you were among people, I smile, quite a few people – and yet you wished for others elsewhere? His grin withers back, to the smile of the owner of the shoe, Johanna would say. Do you not think, Bastian, that those other people, strangers perhaps, that you wished for, elsewhere, might also be mutants to the people around them? That perhaps all of us are mutants at close quarters? Could we not say you merely wished for more *distant*

298611126818977066918552: Disabling, defaming, copying or interfering with personal avatars could become an offence under proposals put forward by the government today. A senior advisor to the watchdog for virtual life said the move aims to target a growing crime-by-proxy trend, in which avatars and personal online grid characters are being defaced and even killed. If passed as proposed, the laws would make assault on an avatar equal to an assault on a person, resulting in charges and possible jail time. The move follows the enactment of similar laws overseas, where several people have been jailed for assaulting or killing avatars.

relationships? He melts back into his chair: Professor, I swear to absolute God we are not responsible for the socials. Really, really truly, I get your point, but I was being light-hearted; the platforms are out of our hands.

Fuh. I lean across the space between us, slightly into his territory, and pounce: *Bastian!* Your stated ambition is to embed those platforms into the fabric of childhood and youth! You're under contract to do it and you are doing it! As he adjusts to this gust I raise my glass and sniff the bouquet before sipping. I don't linger long: You're facing a critical problem, I say, ignoring a crucial fact, a truth we share, you and I: *we first met all our friends in the flesh!* We may be the last generations in history to have tolerated our smelly, inconvenient, glorious friends, for years without a choice. We collected each other like flea-bitten strays and stuck with each other for ever, by singular mysteries of time and chance, off a crooked smile, a vacuous stare, a moment like a feeling aurora. Our belching, farting friends. We didn't have

48316295261201016-3284885: An animal rights vlogger has drawn widespread criticism for implying that popular cyberstar Mindabae is responsible for the growing issue of feral fennec foxes. The vlogger's comments come in the wake of pleas by a number of local governments to think twice before buying the foxes, as many have been abandoned or lost, and some now appear to be breeding in feral troops. While the fennec is a small fox, easily able to hide in the hood of a hoodie, it is a highly intelligent and active wild animal that can prove a real handful for owners. Mindabae has called the accusation stupid, saying she didn't create foxes.

hundreds of others to run to when things got awkward between us. Or we needn't have compromised with anyone! We could've made a human shopping list! Demanded our whims be met! But what then? Bastian? When our list was met? When no desire was so peculiar that somebody wouldn't agree? I'll tell you: we would've made a *sub-list*. And a sub-list and a sub-list and a sub-list, until a hair growing out of a freckle could poison true love. This process is now underway! And how is it we're not infected, you and I? How are we the last to escape, with our miserable, marvellous friends, as if dangling off the skids of an airlift from the Al Qemen war zone? Because we were forced to learn fucking *tolerance*. Bastian. Forced to *cast a wide net*. I pull back as if the argument has left a physical pile of muck. Wunderboy shifts uncomfortably. The thrust of my problem with you – I point – is that you have nothing in common with the people you target. You are uniquely unlike your market. Bakers tasted bread before even toddling, pilots of the future saw

78177407943098723-0203437: Donkeyhooty de la Munchies has announced he's going 'quad' and moving on to all fours for life. The move has been hailed by the wider Low-Responsibility Individuals community – better known as Loris – as a major step towards its recognition as a thriving lifestyle sector. Though not originally a Lori himself, Donkeyhooty aligned with the movement after being forced to defend his right as a quadruped to relieve himself in public, if only in parks and on verges. A recent survey reported that Loris have overtaken Emos as the lifestyle of choice for disaffected under-thirties, though they still rank well below Haulers.

the sky. But you and your market are strangers. You are not represented and will never be represented, as old as you get, as old as the market gets. Because at ten years of age you were forced through the fires of betrayal and disgust to find your connections the hard way. None were edited through portals. None were profitable to others. None had scores. You made allies the way that all creatures do, and were inducted into life with your species. Whereas no child today need do it! I stare mesmerically at Wunderboy. I'm not without sympathy for his youthful ideals, not out to crush all endeavour. But he falls into a risk group for clumsiness, not only as a young male, not only as a dropout, but as a student of computing, where degrees ignore the humanities altogether. Dangerous combined with ideals.

He nibbles on a fingernail and regards me rather darkly, under his shiny gilded hairdo like a hedgehog. At last he says: You make it sound so extreme, Professor. Kids still go to school, still hang out. The socials are additions, not replacements. I

12649370320429973-93488322: The food and beverage watchdog has expressed concern over a growing industry of beer buyers, popularly known as Tankers. The middleman service is said to have grown in response to recent adjustments to UFS algorithms, which have begun to mark down purchases of beer at the rate of a point per two dozen bottles, following a spate of recent beer-related abuse claims. The Octagon, which administers UFS scoring, responded by saying alcohol purchases were always scored down, in line with wider social scoring practices. Tankers charge premiums of up to twenty per cent, and are said to use deceased or hacked profiles.

struggle not to sigh. Bastian: it's the excuse of all selling that consumers are free to choose the harder option. But we don't choose the harder option. It's not how we operate. Now we've become the commodity and we still refuse to choose it. We can afford that cost for our snack foods, but not our connections. Bastian. Our humanity. Because the next device will make it easier, and the next one easier still, until we're out of the game altogether. And it's all we have left. Our only free space. There's nothing more to mine. We've sold the family silver spoon by spoon. Auctioned all the pictures in our books. Devoured the land, the seas, the animals and trees. *And now it falls to you to start on us!*

I pin him with a stare. I can see that I've offended him. He sits with arms and legs tightly crossed, a pretzel, nibbling his finger. I reach for the bottle and motion his glass, but he shakes his head minutely. *Puh.* More for me, then. Draining the bottle in prodding silence – and he hasn't my stamina for it, too bourgeois – I time my little noises to be

20467111114739846-23691759: Reports are emerging of a sharp increase in suicides involving low-pointers, or Lopers, as low-ranking UFS scorers are known. Data from the coroner's office show that almost seventy per cent of recent suicides involved victims with UFS scores below thirty. While the UFS is meant as a personal trust guideline, some declinist commentators point to a growing number of commercial and civic interests now using the scores to assess everything from personal creditworthiness to job suitability. When approached for clarification, the Octagon was unable to provide further UFS scorer data, citing privacy and data protection laws.

poignant. Shrill purling of wine into the glass from a height. Solid knock of the bottle on its table. A stifled burp. It soon prods him back to the mauling: What I struggle with, he says, is you make it sound like the end of the road, the end of learning, tweaking, as if this is as far as we got, I mean . . . He flops up his hands in defeat. I hold in the answer and savour my wine, resting my eyes for a moment. Then I launch a lesson like a saint up on a mount: Bastian, Bastian, Bastian – I let the words thud out like drumbeats – life is a growing mosaic, it makes trivial sense in fragments. We archive events as pixels that grow into landscapes later on. It's a purpose of life to step back and see them, under any system of thought. The acts of living, storing and deciphering events are the holy trinity of life, the creation of *meaning*. It's the big bang we're here for, but events must happen in reality! And as we sit here tonight drinking wine, you and I, little children around us are cheating their bedtimes for a glow of empty promise on their faces. Not some of them; *all of them*. And the problem isn't

33116481435169820-17180081: A quantum physics laboratory is cautiously optimistic that it may have stumbled on a significant key to our coaction with the universe, following a series of experiments appearing to show that memories and thoughts have mass. While it was known that some creatures can navigate by quantum mechanics, most notably certain birds, quantum phenomena in humans have been harder to detect. Scientists speculate that if thoughts are shown to be wave emissions with a reciprocal influence on the universe, the finding could shed light on age-old mysteries such as synchronicity, telepathy and past-life memory.

connectivity. By all means let's connect. The problem is white male DNA and its fucking obsession with profit. Bastian.

Media demands the exceptional, and if we are the actors it demands it from us. But we're only human. A vulnerable thing. Insecure. Weightless. Lonely. It's one reason we're hardwired to copy our peers, but being exceptional in the usual sense, with talent or effort or skill, is a lot to ask of us. And so we've come to an arrangement, a very profitable one for you, in fact the one you're keen to normalise as life: *we'll just keep lowering the bar!* If we throw out reason and shame we can be exceptional in achievable ways! Exceptionally self-involved. Exceptionally intolerant. Exceptionally ignorant. Exceptionally *violent*. A few views are all it takes. And when your hyper-normalisation system is fully up and running, you'll grow exceptionally rich passing it off as the future of human affairs, while other pseudoscientists, probably funded by you, set out to try and prove that we're adapting. But we're

53583592549909666-40871840: Advisors to the government have urged a review of juvenile laws as the violent crime rate for under-elevens looks set to beat last year's record. The call follows yesterday's incident at Molan Gardens Junior School, where a nine-year-old of male orientation stabbed a classmate in the back with scissors, after the victim reportedly looked at him. The Education department has appealed to parents to take a more active role in teaching the young to think before speaking, and to respect the physical and visual space of others. Under current laws the person involved in yesterday's incident is too young to be criminally charged.

not adapting. Is the problem. Bastian. It's a decade of gimmicks against millions of years of development. Walk into any hospital maternity ward, right now, tonight, in the twenty-first century, and press your outstretched finger to the sole of a newborn's foot: its little toes will try to grip it. That's how far from the trees we've come.

I pause for the image to lodge in him: The bleak truth is, Bastian, there aren't enough drugs in the world for the insecurity you're about to unleash. Because this carousel of yours can only reveal how alone we've become. That we're not born equal and can never be equal. That there's no energy in equality whatsoever. That the brain is designed to discriminate. That we'd sooner trust a dog than one another. And that for all intents and purposes there are no human rights. Wunderboy goes from chewing his finger to squeezing the top of his nose. If he doesn't strike back at me now I'll expect him to bite covertly later. So often happens that way. And fine by me, I only hope he grasps the irony when my

86700073985079486-58051921: Homemade debut single 'Dirty Men in 410' by Minnie Wei, the seventeen-year-old daughter of real estate mogul and alternative conception defendant Edmund Wei, has amassed a hundred million hits within three days of posting. Alt-Bae activists were quick to join some of the public in condemning the song for appearing to suggest, among other things, that the mother had prepared for her conception. Some commentators have taken particular exception to the chorus: *'There are no etchings in this room.'* A leading hospitality association has also voiced concern over the way hotels are portrayed in the video.

graphs go viral on his platforms, *hah*. I have them here on a memory stick with my Jembaya keyring attached. A holy grail. Because I don't imagine this thrashing will change his plans. Not for one minute.

He scours his lips with his tongue, and says: I could understand your personal resistance, Professor, but it comes across as if your whole field is opposed. And aren't both our fields still evolving? Aren't our positions fluid? I mean, I accept your expertise . . . His argument fades and I wait for more; he waits for it too, even watching the air leave his mouth. But nothing more comes. I give him some space, and at last I reply: A cerebral response, Bastian. As though arguing the rules of a game. You'll find my position is fluid but for the doctrine you keep bumping into: *that this is not a game*. That we cannot simply gamble. Can't just wait and see. As for my area of specialty, you'll know I switched fields mid-career? Or rather added a field – they're complementary. In fact, being such a fan of my work, you'll recall my first thesis? The text that brings me into your orbit,

14028366653498915-298923761: The world has recorded its worst deforestation rate in a decade, losing an area of rainforest the size of San Uribe in under a year. The figures come as new surveys confirm that over half the world's rainforests have already been lost, and that remaining forests will at the current rate be gone in under a century. Despite experts warning that much of the world's oxygen is generated by rainforests, an area the size of forty football fields is being lost every minute. Some blame the global rise in deforestation on a pervasive political swing to the right, with economics taking priority over the environment.

and also the genesis of those graphs you saw, do you remember? I give him a moment to summon some bullshit but he leaves the bait well alone. Hah.

My thesis, I go on, as if describing a succulent pastry, dealt with the nature of *tumour growth*. Bastian. Specifically, how a tumour tricks healthy cells into believing it's one of them. I crane at him, leering moistly: If only the tumour had followed your thinking it could've simply called itself *Josh*! I gaze at my glass and chuckle, check the clock on the wall, a digital clock; Johanna would hate it. And prepare to call it a night, *puh*.

I draw an inward sigh: I hope I haven't held you back, Bastian, intruding on your space like this. It's late; I'd better be going. But I'm glad we had our chat. I rise and find my satchel. My coat beside the door. As I'm pulling on the coat I find him staring strangely at me. Hah! Wunderboy. He may not have known who he was dealing with.

But oh, my dear, he does now.

22698374052006863-956975682: A new charity in Al Qemen is out to supercharge self-esteem in under-privileged young vloggers by loaning packages of goods to use in haul videos. Explaining the charity's origins, Haulcare founder Geeta Bakshi told us: 'I saw how the children watched the videos from away, day after day, night after night, of shining people on their carpets opening boxes, while here they lived in dust and felt unlucky.' The first hauls to be delivered were valued at the equivalent of only six bills, but Ms Bakshi has vowed that values will rise as funds flow into the charity, aiming to offer fifty-bill hauls within two years.

Gideon Hovis, Allied Social Services, Parsons House, Farlow. Idly watching the news, should still be working; but honestly you'd think the only people in existence any more were foreigners, you'd think the news itself was run by foreigners. Look at this case of the Ululay lady I'm watching, who abused her young daughter, hit her or something. But you'd think the lady herself was the victim, the way it's portrayed. The child has had to be removed for her own safety and you'd think it was a crime on the mother, whereas if one of us hits our child we're just abusers, just haners and abusers. Mm?

The phone rings just now, my assistant Bobby. Says he found someone to fit bars to my downstairs windows. Oh great, I tell him, sounds reasonable; and an ex-Environmental Services man should know what he's doing, not that it's rocket science, a few iron bars. I'll tell Arielle to look out for him, or actually better if I'm there myself. Who, Bobby? Okay. Thanks. Dennis. *Dennis Farrell.*

36726740705505779-255899443: Mindabae has announced she's sending a containerload of goods to new foreign charity Haulcare, which loans packaged products to the underprivileged young to feature in haul videos. The announcement was met with tears from the charity's founder, Geeta Bakshi, whose call to the popular cyberstar included sixty-one *thank-yous*, according to fans. A clip of the emotional call has been liked nearly fifty million times, also triggering a frenzy of speculation as the star appears to allude to another name change. Betting sites are offering Mibae at three to one, after it was found to mean *attractiveness* in certain languages.

Brayan Basauri, 460 Cutler Way, Molan Gardens. Lonnie? You shittn me. I only straight up kep that job cause Cushy help me out. Couldn even write a report, Cushy filled em out till I could copy. Twenty minutes add to the clock.

Serious bruh at the accident too, I'm clearin the main up Pentangle after Control identifies a mass, and but a fuckin gator's already under it and stopped sending signal, and so I puts a hand and it takes my glove and half the fuckn hand off. Then sends fuckn signal. Cushy buss the thing up to find the hand but it's all chew up and ate. Only bruh to sit with me after in hospital too, him and Bosey. Straight up only man I ever bawl to and he bawl back. Half my right hand, thumb and three fingers, or two and a half, see the nubbo? Dog likes it in his ear. Little ear-fuck for Maxy. And Cushy kep comin, not so much since his kids both there. Not sayin he had it easy either. Nah, Cushy. Never see him aks for help. Give help, yeh, aks no. Be life or death before he aks.

59425114757512643-212875125: AI visual speech analysis has revealed the horrific scale of apprentice Jake Storer's abuse at the hands of colleagues in a southern suburbs bar. Transcripts from security footage show that Storer's words to senior engineer Janos Bogdanovic were simply '*Götze Boss*', a foreign phrase seeming to name the senior as his idol, while Bogdanovic's response is too obscene to print, and included death threats. Facial recognition technology has also identified a second senior at the scene, said to be pipeline worker Lonregan Cush, while another two present had their backs to camera, unaware of the assault taking place.

Lon Cush, 37 Palisade Row, East Palisades. Shelby slinks around like a weasel, cheeks glowing hot with the news: *Kh kh kh, a second senior at the scene.* I jab a finger at the coat rack: That coat is still not on! It won't put itself on! *Kh kh kh, yes, Pipeline Worker Lonregan.* For crying out loud. She slithers around me and opens my profile, taps the score. Twenty-fucking-three. *Oops*, she goes, *kh kh kh*, and I bark: *Coat!* Little brat. I call up the stairs – Eagle! We're on the move! – and wait for his grunt to come down. I'm jittery, I won't say I'm not.

I got out the iron and ironed some clothes, shiny denims and my only decent shirt, upstairs type of shirt, twelve years old. Stripes: a cry for help. Because we're calling in the heavy artillery. Hack force, the caped crusader. My score started the day at thirty-six, went to thirty-eight when I paid car tax, back to thirty-seven when the charge hit my account, then tumbled to fuck with the news.

Now every response counts against me. Boges's too for being in my contacts, but I can't ditch Boges;

961518554630184224-68774568: Lori icon Donkeyhooty has been named as the principal investor in a charity aiming to empower underprivileged girls by loaning swimsuits and leotards for use in challenge videos. Chalang was set up after a recent report found that videos featuring swimsuits and leotards attracted up to thirty thousand times more views and a thousand times more likes than those using everyday clothing. Studies suggest the impact on the eye of bright colours and angular patterns could be responsible for the effect. Grid performers in swimsuits and leotards are estimated to have contributed billions to the wider economy last year.

anyway, he was always harmful to be around. My liver would tell you. He moved on to digital harm is all. Next-level harm. I should be grateful I don't have Feral. The forums say you barely lose a point for shit like burglary: the fact it gets heard in a court means they don't score you down very much. But incidents of hane they score you down. Very much. I had to decide to ignore the score when it fell to thirty-one. Just ignore it, mopey hyena. I wanted to kill him – there are a bunch of apps to beat him up and torture him on screen, and forums full of hacks to uninstall him. But the score will still exist, that's the thing. Only you won't be able to see it. Makes no sense to do. So I just ignore it, apart from constantly checking to prove I'm man enough not to ignore it.

Shelby looks at me sideways: Are you going to be like this all night? I reply: Like what? And she bobbles her head: I'm going to need a different table if this is how you are on nanes. Well, firstly, Shel, do you mean *dates*? With a *D*? Because this isn't a date, you don't take kids on dates. No *yuh*, she says, but

594251147575126432-12875125: Research has found that bright colours and angular patterns can hold the eyes of creatures as large as the bowhead whale, and as small as the damselfly. Scientists say the use of bright colours and angular patterns is not only coded into the DNA of many species, it also accounts for our own innate sense of design, which can be seen at work in everything from police cars to packaging. The findings come by chance in the same week as the government prepares to vote on banning branded and coloured beer labels, after a recent report linked beer and beer pong to hane and abuse by male drinkers.

it's a ninja nane because she likes you. Don't just go out with someone who likes you and you like them and think it's not naning – don't breadcrumb her, she says. I straighten her coat: Speak properly! I can't just presume she likes me – this is a thank-you for helping us out. This is how it's done, Shelby-bean. She flounces her hair off her collar, *Yuh*, well, she does like you, so *duh*. Uh-huh, I grunt, and you know this how? From Mallory! Wake up, Lonnie, stop being an *incel*! she cries. I look at her the way I increasingly do, like the puppy who stumbled on yodelling. And I leave it at that.

Such is the evening's safari from Thirty-Seven. Cry-for-help safari. Cash is as tight as a fish's ring but I've decided to be an optimist, start as I mean to go on. Tonight's destination is Likelike, apparently; Kim said, Have you tried Likelike because Mallory's a fan of their vegan teriyaki and she can be hard to accommodate. I abandoned my proposal of Shaky's for pizza and beer. Fucking hyena sneered when I said Likelike. Brazen cyber buzzword implying I

36726740705505779-255899443: In a ruling declinists are calling the death of shame, a court today awarded a driver partial damages against the family of a pedestrian killed by his car. Neorealists are calling the ruling a welcome blow to outdated black-and-white thinking, pointing out that only the vehicle's damage was awarded, and not that part of the claim seeking damages for legal convictions arising from the collision. The driver had claimed punitive damages for his arrest, fines and loss of enjoyment, maintaining the collision would not have occurred if the deceased had stayed at home. The pedestrian's family are hoping to crowdfund the award.

have the brain of a child and am prepared to be milked out of all I own just to feel fluffy and cool. I was quietly superior when I heard the name. Though to Kim I said great as if I go all the time. This is how it's done when your clothes are ironed.

We cruise out past Fourteen, all freshly pimped with its paint and palms and lawn. Old Caveney would've been proud. Medinas too, I guess. I get a rush of soothing chemistry from the street pimping up like this. Big works at Moyle's as well, walls reinstated, gardens tamed back. The Medinas were right, the street's on the up. What am I worried about, time to market the house again, time to count blessings. Big nane with Kim, street on the up. Move the heretics closer to Harville, calm Ramona down.

The corner after Sebastian Road is Providence, another shambly lane full of migrants and peppercorns last time I saw it above ground. Lot of rats under the road, some as big as dachshunds due to the main flowing under Marinus Street Market. But pulling around the corner, I see it's gone the way

22698374052006863-956975682: The two words used by teen victim Jakey Storer which initiated the exchange that led to his abuse – *Götze Boss* – are sweeping the world in a viral trend that pundits say may be bigger than any so far this year. Speaking from a garment stall in Wilfried, Neue Esmarch, a T-shirt seller told us Jakey's words are much more than a simple catchphrase, with *idol* and *boss* expressing a mythical purity in describing two essential qualities people should offer each other in order to achieve maximum respect. The inspirational quote is fast becoming a weapon in the wider fight against workplace mullying and hane.

of Sebastian, all chalkboards, smartcars, haircuts like turds, garlands lighting branches through a flame-grill haze. And Likelike sits where the bakery used to be, a flash of tiki-chic with shimmery hardwood, gingerbread eaves and lit-up faces. We cruise as far as the church for a park, then walk back up Providence through a hubbub of outdoor tables, patches of burn from patio heaters, runaway laughter *nga nga ngaaa*, and heretics lost in their screens. Clinks and chatter stepping into the venue, sizzle of yakitori against a floor-to-ceiling portrait of a lady in grand old clothing. *Princess Miriam Likelike*, it says, *1851–1887*, a real-life princess from a tropical island kingdom. So ciao, my superiority.

A server dressed like a ninja comes up. *Guten Abend*, she chirps; *wilkommen, guys*. No sign of Kim and Mallory yet, so we follow her to a table in the depths. She hands us all tablets, telling me to log in via Rike, Muh, Goh, Fff, facial recognition, voice or thumb. The fuck. As I start logging in through Rike she adds: It's our pleasure to serve scores over sixty

14028366653498915-298923761: Dark horse teen abuse survivor Jakey Storer revealed today he's spending some of his recovery time learning foreign languages. A spokesperson for the Octagon has announced free weekly private classes for the plucky apprentice, saying his is just the type of spirit the tech leader seeks to employ, someone who picks themselves up after a fall. A backlash meanwhile continues to grow against a large number of foreign haners arguing that the foreign phrase attributed to Storer makes no sense in any language. One Jakey supporter was quick to wryly respond: 'Nothing makes any sense in your languages.'

today. I lower the screen and look at her. Wonder if she says that to everyone.

I start the login again but Shelby grabs my hand and sighs: *I'll get it*. The server points a device at her: *Wunderbar!* You're authorised up to three hundred, what can I get you guys? Wait, wait – I snatch Shel's tablet away – she can't pay for this! Shelby leans over the table into my face: I said I'll get it. Lonnie. Try and be normal, not cringey. *You are nine years old!* I cry. *You do not have three hundred bills!* She allows herself a tiny brittle sigh: I said I'll get it, Pipeline Worker Lonregan. And anyway, according to my DNA I'm twenty-seven. So can we get this party started.

I look around the choppy sea of haircuts, glasses, teeth. Faces grow alien, chatter turns mocking, the smoke gives a taste of the end of the world. I search for something to cling to – a lumberjack shirt, some unkempt hair, a shoe that someone has worked in – but the place only caters to selfies. It dawns in a flash that democracy could soon be the only real threat to

86700073985079486-58051921: Speakers of a foreign language are up to forty per cent smarter than their non-foreign-speaking counterparts, a study has found. Not only that, experts speculate that simply choosing to study languages may be an indicator of higher intelligence, even before the language is learned. The finding supports recent research which shows that foreign-speakers are half as likely as their monolingual counterparts to be declinists. One commentator has said the findings also shed more light on plucky teen abuse survivor Jake Storer, who was the victim of a vicious assault while speaking a foreign language.

my freedom. In the end I grasp at Egan, the good old Eagle, chip off the old mussy block, as I answer Shel: *We barely sent your DNA swab to the lab!* But Egan wisely shrugs and slays a donkey. Shelby starts to tell me her preliminary results are on the grid, but before I can scream *Are you shitting me*, my phone vibrates in my pocket. I ask the server as I drag it out, What beer do you have, while we workshop all this?, and she leans to my ear to say: We don't serve fermented beverages. Shel's brow floats up to her hairline: *Marley's for mullies, hops equals hane.*

I turn to the phone and it's Kim. Lon? she says. I had to put Mal to bed, she's being a mare – hope you haven't left for the place yet? I even wonder if she's getting her *ngff*, she's been weird for days, she says. I make an ironic parenty noise and she inwardly sighs: Anyhoo, I also wanted to meet and ask a favour. Sorry to bring it up like this, but – could we possibly scratch this number from your contacts? It's just that I have a mortgage, and . . .

53583592549909666-40871840: A growing number of personal DNA test kit users are reporting gene-age results of twenty-seven or fifty-six, regardless of their analogue age. The unexplained phenomenon has sparked a viral wave of memes on the grid, with culture watchers reporting that *twenty-seven* and *fifty-six* are entering the language as slang for a raft of gags. With people as young as four scoring adult age results, the health watchdog has warned test kit users to treat the numbers lightly, as the science behind true age speed is still unfolding. A number of declinists have called the anomaly a typical corporate scam to pressure the gullible into consuming.

Bastian Matanick, Moyle House, East Palisades. Ay-ay-ay, just surreal. We were drinking wine, she was busting my balls, and next thing she says, *I'm going.* Out the fucking door if I hadn't stopped her. From her place! Had to convince her she was home, satisfy myself she didn't need a doctor – another half-hour I was there. I kept repeating *Fourteen Palisade Row, Fourteen Palisade Row,* to give her a fighting chance of calling a cab or ordering food or whatever. Almost fucking scribbled it on her hand.

So she finally comes round but thinks I'm an overnight guest. Ay-*ay.* And like okay, she'd put away some wine, a bottle or more, but this was something else. I thought I should really bring this up with the committee, or with someone.

Then I thought: Is Chad almost ready to trial Curlytime? Because if we can steer what's left of her mind away from the fucking platforms, while she even works out where she is, we could make some serious hay here. While that sun shines.

33116481435169820-17180081: A new dating app is claiming to match users to perfect sexual partners based on their porn-viewing habits. Baezen assesses data from preferred genres, model types, rewinds, freeze-frames and total viewing times to build a detailed profile and match it to likely partners. While the launch has been welcomed by the wider porn community, some declinists have asked how such detailed viewing data became available, saying the app seems to be based on a security breach. Some also warned that innocent exploration by young persons was at risk of being used to shape habits, an interference which could haunt them for life.

Dennis Farrell, 12-B Mason Drive, Molan Gardens. *Ew Denny when are you going to find work ew I can't afford to support you ew eww.*

Well, suck on this, Lorraine.

Reynes fuckin Parade.

Stick that up your asterisk and chew it. Gideon Hovis. Man of taste. Taste in metalwork. Solid job for a solid client. At a solid address. Premium address. Solid local man. What? That's not racist, don't confuse respected with racist, Lorraine. After all your fuckin whining don't you want me to get paid? By someone who pays their bills? Don't mistake racist for logic, Lorraine. For common sense. How many liberals do you actually see doing business with fuckin reffos? After all their fuckin preaching? Fuckin none, because A: they don't want to get shot or fuckin stabbed, and B: they don't want to get paid in drugs, Lorraine.

Oh, *really*? Then fuckin answer me this: are paramedics responsible for terror and hane? Are plumbers? Lavanians? – *What?* – Someone from

20467111114739846-23691759: Mindabae was a surprise guest at the Blowback Music Awards, stunning fans in an original fur bikini tailored for the occasion by hottie couturier Jija Sou. MB was later pictured partying the night away with this year's winners, Jamakhi and Bul-G, for their smash hits 'Six Packa Booty' and 'Time to Shup', the latter from the album *Ride Your Property*, which also won the popular vote among under-twelves. In a red carpet chat with eager fans and media, Mindabae said the awards were a chance to remember that music is all about empowerment, values, love and respect, as well as realising that each one of us is special.

fuckin Lavania, stupid. Or who's responsible, how about war reffos, see if that can find a way into your tiny brain. How many dead will it take you to see that reffos totally hane us, they hane us when they're born and they hane us when they get here, they just hane and hane, it's all they fuckin know. As soon as they arrive they're ready to bomb the shit out of us, but people like fuckin you still think it's fun to let them in. They stand in their shithouse countries and tell us they hane us, they don't even pretend, they say we are committed to your destruction and we still let them in, give them houses and rights we don't even have. This is so fuckin clear.

People like you that fall for their babies with big black eyes and blame us for how fucked and covered in blood from bombing themselves they are, and next thing they're fuckin here. Name one fuckin bombing before they came. Lorraine. Fuck. I find it hard to believe you're even smart enough to suffer anxiety. Now heat this shit up again, will you?

12649370320429973-93488322: A fifty-two-year-old Molan man has been convicted of indecent exposure after touching the fly of his trousers upon leaving an airport bathroom. The act was witnessed by a twenty-three-year-old person who said in court they had felt repulsed and assaulted by the act, which the man is alleged to have performed within a yard of their body. The man tried to argue in his defence that the motion was a common male routine to ensure the fly was closed after use. Prosecutors successfully argued that any genital or near-genital contact should have been completed before leaving the facilities. A civil suit is pending.

Ramona Winbourn, 64 Sun Village, 144 Kaylor Road, Harville Downs.
Well, but was it pressure? Can we even call it that? I mean, pressure in the sense of bad pressure? Diane had so many gifts, it was just – we didn't know where to start! Flute and tennis and riding, and . . . We didn't so much push her as keep her to her word. You know? Is that pressure? She was good at so many things!

But Mother took me aside one time, I remember as clear as today, pulled me into the kitchen one Christmas, to help, or well. I remember she could panic and be efficient at once, pots hissing, oven smoking, washing dishes as well. She would enter a zone and panic over the meal, which, I mean, we offered to cook every year, and John often said: Let's go out, to a nice hotel, let someone else do the cooking . . . But it had to be her doing everything, her gift to everyone, I suppose, perhaps to make up for those awful trinkets off late-night TV, and, well, this day she was sweaty, her hair stuck down her face, apron dripping and everything boiling and

78177407943098723-0203437: Playing tennis and learning the flute have been found to rank among the top-thirty indicators of good parenting and a happy childhood, joining activities such as riding and debating. The news comes as a growing number of organisations for the young call for broader opportunities for young people, particularly in entertainment and media, as the tech industry goes on to dominate job markets. Youth commentators also pointed to a recent study which found that simply owning a flute or visiting a tennis club socially increased well-being among the young, even before the activities were played or learned.

cartoon penguins singing on TV, John trying to be polite and failing, Diane would be twelve, I guess, the Christmas she got her big bike, she was on cloud nine, spent the whole day fidgeting to get back on her bike, back to her freedom, I suppose . . . And Mother, seeing that Dad was boring John, and John was boring Dad, and penguins and God knows what, took me aside into her little kitchen hell, dinner boiling away to its death, and said to me: *Don't let John put too much on her.* And I just, well, I hadn't expected it, I said: What do you mean?, and she took a moment out of her panic, without moving her lips, that way she had, as if we were being watched, and said: When a man wants a son as bad as John did, he can set the bar too high for a girl. Pressure, she said, to make up for no train sets and fishing. Well, and I had to tell her, I just said: You're imagining things, John's very supportive of everything she does.

But of course once they're gone you get to thinking. I don't know, I just don't know. And lupus into the bargain, which is nobody's fault, you can

48316295261201016-3284885: Scientists have announced the discovery of a compound with the potential to reverse cell ageing in humans, in what biomedical experts are calling a historic breakthrough. Studies with mice have shown that a single dose of new compound Neuterium leads older mice to revert to a thriving stage of life for up to sixteen weeks. The team behind the discovery was quick to play down the effect as a cure for human ageing or death, saying the genome is not compatible with life extension beyond the point already seen in long-lived individuals. It added that more research is needed to grasp the compound's potential.

lower the risks, not tempt fate, like going through multiple pregnancies. But everyone said the risks could be managed, I mean, it's not as if, you know? We were so *unlucky*. Is the thing.

Mother was a real case, I was never fully comfortable with her. Just something. I was always Daddy's girl, I suppose, and, well, Mother liked Lon, is the thing, you see. And he liked her, and would bypass us in the end, it just. They got along. She liked Lon and he liked her food, and would always go back for seconds and thirds, John used to call him her waste disposal, and what I mean is, Mother may have liked him because of what she said about John, to me, that time. May have seen him as an escape for Diane, in her mind, and just . . . It wasn't pressure but then maybe it *was*, if you know what I mean, and so many hours of flute, and. It just.

What made me think is that she never touched her flute again, after Lon. She'd had enough of flute, and never played tennis again that I know of, although she was handicapped down where they went to live, not a lot of tennis down there, ha. I mean just *poof!* Nothing. It all stayed behind in her room and never again, it just. Mother took me aside that Christmas and you get to thinking: What did she see for Diane? What was the alternative in her mind, to the things she was supposedly under pressure to do, which, I mean, you know? *Good* pressure, to better yourself! *Ambition*. But perhaps she just wanted Diane to feel the wind in her hair. To feel some freedom. Freedom from what, I'll never know, we were doing our best. But Lon represented that, to her. He set her free, according to Mother's way of thinking. I think it was that. Although we weren't the closest she was an intelligent woman, she'd seen lots of things, changes. She was sacked from her job for getting married in those days, and after that just fussed over Dad. I mean, he wasn't a slave driver, he loved her, and I think admired her, it's just. It was so *automatic* back then. You'd be seen as a fool to do anything different. You'd be *outcast*.

Then I had opportunities Mother could never

18455182579303309-6366333: Research into the decade's most successful people has found that being concerned only for oneself is the single strongest indicator of high achievement. What's more, those raised to care only for themselves and choose their own agendas were twice as likely to succeed than those who began later in life. Researchers enjoyed an online chat with popular cyberstar Mindabae, with whom they agreed that a second important life factor was 'mersonaliny', an assertion financial pundits were quick to second, pointing to the vast amounts contributed to the economy by homemade media every year.

have, but in the end what I chose to do was more or less what she'd done, stay home and keep house, is what it was. *Blah*. And so she could see Diane sitting that day through the kitchen door, through all her smoke and steam. She could see my beautiful Diane, her long golden hair, at the table. She'd see her fingers fidgeting and her legs bouncing. Cartoon penguins and not paying attention. New bike outside the door. And Mother had given up her individual life to stay home and raise a family, and I had done the same, and now she could see Diane and Diane could see her bike through that window. And she pulled me aside. You know? About John. Wanted some wind in that girl's hair.

Perhaps she was right. Time to break the chain, the cycle. If only I could have Shelby back it could be third time lucky next time. Another chance from God to set our blood free, if that's not too dramatic. With what I know now. Oh yes. If she came back to me she'd be as free as a bird.

11405930102594397-0552219: Mothers who liberate the young by allowing them to choose from as wide as possible a palette of lifestyles have been found to live up to four years longer than stricter parents, a study has found. Looking into the effects on mothers of their experience at the helm of young families, researchers found that those who demanded the least from their offspring were almost twice as likely to live fulfilling lives, and three times more likely to say they had no regrets. The study has been added to the mountain of evidence being used to back Keeley's Law, a proposal that seeks to lower the age of executive majority.

Lon Cush, 37 Palisade Row, East Palisades. Long draught of beer as ideas collide. Or more of a question and an idea collide, as in *How the fuck was Shel approved for three hundred bills?* And the idea, more of a flashback: time to try Kim's snooperware. The tools are in my hand. Everything's in my hand. Because I can't leave Shel to set the agenda, less the way things are. Three hundred unaccountable bills, run that up a flagpole in a court. *She must've been saving for a boob job, Your Honour.*

I settle back into the couch, open the snooper app. Shel's silent upstairs in her room. But here she is now in my hand. Here she is now in the palm of my hand – in fact, here she is on Rike. AwwsomeShelbae between a pile of ads for cellulite treatment. She posted a video – *Gymnastics* – although she doesn't do gymnastics, and anyway spends the whole vid talking. It has twenty-four views. Eleven likes. Two dislikes. Nine subscribers. Good harmless fun. *Relief.* But then comes a video of her retching in the kitchen. *The Cinimon*

70492524767089125-814114: An early-life rights group has launched a campaign to abolish the word *child* as a descriptor of persons in early life, saying the word is not only inaccurate, pejorative and sexist, but was incorrect even at the time it appeared. In the Middle Ages, *cild* was used to describe 'a fetus, the unborn', and in most variations had more to do with the womb and the mother than with persons undergoing early life. The group says it wasn't until the Sarian majority law that early persons needed a word at all, and that as a blanket term covering all ages from birth to eighteen, *child* should not have been chosen.

Chalange. Seventy-three views.
Twenty-nine likes. Six dislikes.
Concern. It's followed by *First
Unboxing*, the heart-warming tale of
unpacking her phone, meaning Egan
must've shot it. Ember was right,
I need to bond with the Eagle. I'll
corner him tomorrow and make a
pact. For now I take a swig of beer, a
Palisades promissory note, and lick the
bottle rim to guarantee it. My tongue
perches there through a cellulite
ad. Then comes *Morning Routine*.
Three hundred and twenty views. A
hundred and nineteen likes. Twelve
dislikes. And you can leave comments
underneath. Hmm.

Anonymous strangers can leave
comments. Some are leaving addresses
and numbers. There must be seven
fucking languages there. *She blew a
hole through the wall of our house. A
pack of fucking strangers is giving her
scores through her bedroom wall. That
she uses to judge her worth by.*

I jab my tongue at the bottle. Clink
it with my teeth. The reason I didn't
choose a foreign backstreet to bring the
heretics up in is they might've had to

43566776258854844-
738105: A twelve-
year-old thought to be
responsible for three
pregnancies in his class
at a Parkwood school
has been named by a
friend as Demarcus
Stanley Halsey, son
of Princess and Mero
Halsey of Jacksdale. A
number of social media
accounts were sus-
pended following the
revelation, after a wave
of congratulations from
male users. In an un-
precedented move, police
have warned the whistle-
blower, who denies he
broke the story in order
to profit from crowd-
funding appeals, that he
could be liable for the
cost of relocating Halsey
to a safe house as Alt-Bae
activists were earlier seen
descending on the area
around his home.

meet unsavoury people. I got a house with a door and curtains to keep them safe till they learn some judgement. As a species we must've conceived doors and curtains thousands of years ago. But now here's a one-way glass. Scumbag Motel – they can see in, we can't see out. And alongside her video is a column of similar videos. A few are *Recommended for you*. The algorithm decided we must like this kind of thing. Foreign girls. From places with fewer doors and curtains. One of them is fucking *pole dancing*. That's the field she's competing in. *Pole dancing*. One has *seven thousand views*. One has *forty-eight thousand*, one has *six hundred thousand*, one has *three million fucking views*. And you don't have to watch the vids to grasp the equation. You can see from the list of thumbnails: shame goes down, views go up.

I am chewing the neck of this bottle. I am going to eat this glass. A hiss comes up my throat that I roll into a burp to soothe myself. And now – *surprise* – Ksenya Ululay, all made up like a hip hop princess.

Two hundred and eighty thousand views.
Her account – KsenyaPerfectBae – lists
reams of videos, years of productions,
and at the bottom a Cinnamon
Challenge. Meaning Shel's competing
directly. I fumble to open Shel's chats,
my fingers too old for this shit, but
here we are, chat, chat, chat, the most
recent from someone called Ram:
You are a qualifed star, you star statis is
garantee if you follow my tutrials. I have
push many video over a million views. I
can teach you all them. You can make 3
to 8 thosands a month in your room. I
helped girls make 20 thosands a month.
Somtime more.

I am standing off the sofa. I am
mapping the route to the shotgun
under the stairs, the cartridges in my
room. I will blast her phone into the
fucking lawn and toss the remains
in Reynes Reservoir, which has a
hundred-foot depth in places.

But I don't. I don't do this, I don't
do this at all; I hang here half standing
instead. Because here's the rub: if I
bust her now she'll know I snooped
and vanish underground, and with
Mona hanging over us

like a cloud. I gnaw my bottom lip and go back to this scummer Ram: *Here is list of basic shows you must do, which is call basic level and is for look autentic.* He lists her homework: *the water bottle flip challenge, try not to laugh challenge, bananas and milk challenge, balloon challenge, what's that stink challenge, yoga challenge, blindfold make-up challenge, one bite challenge, what's that taste challenge, no thumbs challenge, hot pepper challenge, try not to cry challenge, try not to cringe challenge, blind drawing challenge, say anything challenge, touch my body challenge, wet my head challenge, not my legs challenge, ice bath challenge, gargle the song challenge, eat it or wear it challenge, 7 second challenge, flip cup challenge, 100 layers challenge, salt and ice challenge, Honeybeetox lip challenge, baby food challenge, brain freeze challenge, death by butter challenge, high-five and selfie challenge, human dartboard challenge, nutmeg challenge, sugar high challenge, spider-walk challenge, troll your family challenge,*

10284720757613717-413913: Alleged teen abuse victim Jake Storer has failed to post on his recovery vlog amid growing grid support for an association of deaf lip-readers which claims that transcripts of his assault were wrongly interpreted. The group's leader said there was unanimous agreement that Storer's first words to a senior colleague were in fact 'Goats, hey, Boges?' and that the colleague's response was simply *'I beg your pardon.'* Analysing conversation prior to the assault, the group has confirmed that in using the word *goats,* Storer was imputing acts of bestiality to his colleague. He has so far not responded to requests to discuss the claims.

vacuum your eyeball challenge, pencil
in your ear challenge, swallow the ruler
challenge, eat the paperclip challenge,
roast your teachers challenge, mice
in blender challenge, sawdust cookie
challenge, fall downstairs challenge,
ink bath challenge, pins and needles
challenge, then some ASMR, crinkling
clothes, chewing jelly, wet mouth talk . . .

Shel breaks in at this point: *Can we*
like get to the viewsy stuff? I'll do these
but I need like a views one. And Ram
said: *Ok, then better at make privat*
videos! Go to privat message. And bloop
– she went to a back room like a slave.
With Ram.

I try to open her private messaging
but a pop-up note appears: *Not*
supported in the free version. The fuck.
There's a pile of foam left in my bottle
from too much violent swigging. I
suck it noisily out. Go to the foot
of the stairs and listen up. Nothing.
The sound of nothing. The backstreet
would be so much easier to patrol.
Because here: silence. This silken
silence. The silken sound of losing her.

6356306993006846248183: Declinists
are twice as likely as
realists to have been
bedwetters into their
teens, and three times
more likely to remain
single throughout
their forties, a study
has found. Research
looking for possible early
indicators of declinism
shows that the younger
a person succumbs
to cognitive bias, the
more disappointing
their performance in a
range of crucial arenas,
including relationships,
health and career.
Research also showed
that outcomes improve
nearly fivefold after
early detection. Experts
advise to be alert to
any pervasive sense that
things are getting worse,
and to seek help as soon
as possible.

Madeleine Aude, Rue Gabrielle-Pierrot-Fripon, Vierne. She knows why I'm coming. She frowns more intently at her book. But I really must be firm with her now: Have you please told Dr Roos about your procedure? I say. Let's not sign the consent until she knows, Dr Fisser, please.

She turns a page and replies: I'll tell her on Saturday. I observe her rather sternly: Well, Doctor, that's your very last chance. They'll literally be taking you to theatre! She's naughty.

Honestly, these girls, what a pair.

Colleen Carl, Television Centre, Carmel Street, Reynes. Well, I'm the one who's usually on the march against sensationalism, but if what you're saying is true, Professor – and I don't doubt it is, it's more a case of those graphs coming across as clearly as you explain them – we could seriously upset an applecart here. Can I just ask: would you be prepared to go live on our flagship at six? On Saturday? I'm thinking leave the graphs to do most of the talking,

39284137646068711-65730: A man wearing a *Wei to go!* T-shirt has been attacked outside Sisters of Mercy Hospital, where reports are emerging that ex-runaway Keeley Teague is not a patient. The mood of a vigil outside the hospital turned angry following rumours that Ms Teague had left the country after admitting to a phantom pregnancy. The rumour is still unconfirmed. According to predictions, the ex-runaway's child was due to be born prematurely this week, and gaming markets have reacted unsteadily to news that the pregnancy may have been a hoax. The victim of today's incident is being treated for non-life-threatening injuries.

so much more impact than a pre-packaged feature, and I'd love to get the live team on board. It's just so *timely*. And between you and me, Professor, and I mean I'm forty-one, I don't mind telling you, I'm like the dinosaur around here, but frankly I've been noticing too how . . . *Exactly!* Nothing if not a male perspective, and apart from that I just think we're plain running out of voices who remember how easy things were! How much more freedom there was and . . . I *know*, and I mean we didn't have all the thought police, and . . . Well, great, I'm so glad you're down for it. Can I just ask, because I'll be asked for diligence: is anyone else in on this? I mean, it sounds like the findings are older than today, and . . . Wow, okay. You have the only copy? Well, everything rests on that. We can shoot it off your screen. And you know, I'll stick my neck out here and say we could be on to a real bombshell. The findings you describe are just too scary. But if you're prepared for a bombshell, you know what? So are we.

24278932283999750-82453: The family of alleged teen assault victim Jake Storer has asked for calm after pictures emerged of him playing beer pong, sparking an avalanche of hane online. The game is said to have been played two years ago when Storer was only fifteen, but despite a rallying cry from beer victim groups, the images have proved to be the last straw for many supporters. Crowdfunding sites have issued a warning that the estimated six-figure sum donated to the teen apprentice is not refundable, and that civil action in court may be the only way for contributors to seek redress. Storer has not been seen on the grid for over two days.

Lon Cush, The Aston Loftus Room, Palisade View Community Centre, Palisade View. Clean clothes to anger management. Because the clean don't get angry, or I don't know why, my parole mentality. I leave my old colleague Brayan Basauri's nieces in charge of the heretics – not the challenge it used to be – and step into the purple eve.

The drive is quiet to Palisade View, at least outside my head. On the inside I'm finally forced to admit I need a tiger for Shelby's birthday. Must be triggered by passing the spot where she brought it up that time. Weeks ago now, feels like years. All the thoughts that get stuck on these corners. City of triggered thoughts. So at Tiger Corner I remember I still have a tiger to find, and that I need the thing now more than ever. Cheap little tiger for hire. Rental tiger, scruffy or lame will be fine. Not saying it's a cure by itself, but I need to pull out all the stops, get Shel out of her room, put a grin on her face, give her something more wholesome to video.

In terms of everything else, the bigger picture, I

15005205362068960-83277: A district court judge today issued a reporting deadline of ten o'clock tomorrow morning to the hospital said to be treating ex-runaway Keeley Teague, whose baby was due this week. The hospital has said patient data is confidential, and it will not confirm whether Ms Teague is a patient until the situation outside the hospital, where supporters have gathered in their hundreds for a vigil, can be brought in line with her privacy and safety. Some commentators were quick to accuse the judge of bowing to pressure from gaming markets, which saw a threefold spike in trading last week in anticipation of the celebrity birth.

still need much more. Something big, a magic bullet, the cowabunga. I just don't know what it is yet. But there's a sense that it's out there. There's even a sense that we can just make it up.

A karate class echoes from the centre as I arrive – sounds like a barn dance with choreographed stabbings. I find the Aston Loftus Room with its air of sweat and dust, and the first thing I see is Boges. He's stood with Ryan, also from work, but from the clean end up at the reservoir. Six other people stand around some folding chairs and a whiteboard. In the doorway stands a pushbutton feedback device featuring two yellow buttons, smiley and sad. The spectrum of human emotions.

I'm about to make a crack about it when Boges looks across and he's stony. *Kid hung himself*, he growls; *the apprentice. We're bailing to the Anchors for some jars.* He looks and sounds like a battered child. The news tilts the scene on its axis. I check around the place: Can we just walk out? And Ryan says: I'm the instructor – you feeling angry? He

927372692193078999-9176: Former assault victim Jacob Storer has been found hanged at his Stresnan apartment. A police spokesperson said the body was found just after noon today by counsellors arriving for a routine therapeutic appointment. The case is being treated as suicide, and no other suspects are being sought. Octagon supremo Bertie Riley was among the first to respond as shockwaves spread around the globe, offering heartfelt condolences to family and friends of the much-loved local apprentice, and a cry to stamp out hane wherever we find it. The Octagon has offered counselling and support to anyone affected by the news.

points to the back of the room: Go to the screen and hit your name, then as far as the system's concerned you're attending. Everyone's bailing – we need grief therapy tonight, fuck anger. I log myself into the system and follow the pair to the door. Boges shuffles out like a zombie – *He was only a kid, what the fuck* – and we all punch the sad face as we pass, *bam, bam, bam*, abandoning our cars for appearances' sake and trudging through the damp to the Anchors. The grit of our steps is loud tonight.

Another anger client draws level at North Road and pauses under a light to offer a cigarette. A health warning flashes off the pack: *Tobacco smoke may contain your dead mother*. Personalised, he says before I can ask; I'm trying to quit. I point to the picture above the warning: And is that your actual mother? Yeah, he says, lighting up.

The rest of the walk is necessarily silent. At the Anchors, I go to the bar with our order, a jar of Kreeftpomp and a pair of Coypu Steams; but the barman plants his hands on the wood and levels a

5731478440138170 8- 4101: Leaked documents appearing to show investments into research on Yeast-Induced Compulsivity Disorder via companies owned by actor Corey Kniessen have been dismissed by the actor's lawyers as fiction. His legal team has asked the public to respect his privacy and lend support while he continues to undergo treatment for the crippling disorder. YICD is thought to arise from chemical imbalances in the brain triggered by certain fermentations usually associated with beer. YICD is thought to be the cause of up to eighty-nine per cent of haneful behaviours in younger males, according to the latest research.

stare at me: I can only serve you one, he says. Which one do you want? As I search his face for clues, he goes: The others have to order their own, it's one per user, that's the rules. I pause to take this in: Hm, then give me a Coypu Steam. He shifts his weight: What mixer do you want with that? The fuck. Mixer? I quiz. It's a beer, I'll have it straight. He stares down his nose: We can only serve them with mixers. Fine, I tell him, then any, but on the side. No can do, he says, mixed drinks only, one per user. Boges inflates behind me and bellows: *Bar! Serve a decent drink, what's wrong with you!* The barman retreats a step: You'll be excluded, sir, if you can't keep it down; we don't make the laws around here. *What fucking laws?* shouts Boges as a murmur erupts in the place.

Weighing it up, I find it uneasy. Juices, pastries, haircuts around. And within five seconds: phones, pointed at us. I stretch a friendly hand to the barman: Thanks, keep up the good work. Then I hiss into Boges's sideburn: *Out, out, they're shooting fucking video!* Ryan catches the drift and we head to the door. As the night licks our faces the knowledge hits too that Boges is now the leading man in the teen apprentice drama. A clump of people appears ahead and we drop our heads like rapists. Ryan consults his screen: That vid's already on Fff, he says. On *what*? I ask. Never mind, he says.

We accelerate and cut through Horsley Alley to avoid the lights of North Road. Boges's face is clenched like a fist: Know what kills me the most? he grumbles. They're forcing us into their game. Only way we can fight is through their channels, and it's a one-way street; they can destroy in the physical world, we can only answer on the grid.

The community centre looms around the corner. Boges blows a sigh like a steam train: I'll just have to fucking embrace it. Catch some trendy disorder. Or resort to fucking charity. Charity-caught-on-video. He rolls his gaze at me: Cushy, if you're smart you'll do the same. An act of visible charity. *Viral* charity. As a vaccination. Against hane.

21892299583455516-9026: Moderators on a Pearlbook sub-site, WeKnow, have been warned to suspend a thread relating to recently deceased abuse victim Jakey Storer, after more than a hundred users of the memorial site reported receiving messages from the deceased, some asserting that his death was actually caused by disgraced former ES pipeline supervisor Janos Bogdanovic. Pearlbook management was quick to hit back at what it calls unjustified and hysterical attempts to curtail basic freedom of speech, saying Pearlbook is an entertainment site and that individual posters' content is not the responsibility of the platform.

Saphia Lusk, 9–142 Borlow Road, West Palisades. Oh my God oh my God oh my God. Oh. My. God. This is like. OhmyGodohmyGod. *Fuck*. What can I put what can I put what can I put what can I put what can I put what can I put KRISTEN FUCK. This is like way beyond sadfishing *oh my God* what can I fuckin put you have to help meee like NOW KRISTEN THIS IS LIVE I could end up on the news or like *Today* or like this IS REALLY IT NOW BITCH, LEND ME YO SKANKY EAR!

Wait, wait, okay, wait: *Beloved Jakey our love was so young, the stars fell from the sky for me except now you're just gone* . . . Except *gone* doesn't rhyme. FUCK. Wait: *And now you're just done* . . . No, no, FUCK – *Oh Jakey our love was so strong but now like a fallen star in heaven you're just gone. Away. From our love. Bae.* Fuck. KRISTEN HELP MEEE the fuck okay no wait, wait, *My dear beloved Jakey our love was so young, now it went to heaven to shine like a sun* . . . Fuckin YAAY! Bitch.

13530185234470674-6049: The latest craze for adult teething rings, or pacifiers, has had an unexpected boost from a study which reports that the sense of security experienced by infants sucking on a dummy is no weaker in adults who follow the practice. One infantile-accessory historian has said that pacifiers for older people were only abandoned due to a chance error in history, when societies were poorer and had to encourage their children to suck their thumbs instead of using a more expensive dummy. Today's adult pacifiers range from simple plastic to the gold and diamond-encrusted example gifted by Mindabae to Donkeyhooty.

Alberto & Marta Medina, 35 Reynes Parade, Reynes Park. Don't make faces at me, Alberto, I've been on her case since we got here. I even told her to ask Lon, our old neighbour, in case he has friends in the association or whatever it is, for that type of thing. *Así que basta!* Oh, and now you made her walk out. *Gracias, Alberto.* Ush.

Dennis Farrell, 41 Reynes Parade, Reynes Park. So I get to the job, check in with Hovis, cheap motherfucker but hey. Unpack some gear on the street, and holy shit, heh: a little brown boning machine comes along. Heh he. Come to Dennis, baby. Here she comes, heh he. Hello, sweet thing, what's your name? Gala, she says – what are you doing? Heh he, tight little skirt on it, ass like a peach, give the old dog a bone. I say: I am about to installify these metallurgical componentries. You're a welder? she smiles. Heh he. Heh he. *Yes,* I smile. Dennis, you killer fucking dog.

83621143489848422-977: Lori-haner Makenzie Squillace, found guilty last week of defacing public signs around the city, has been sentenced to six months' home detention. Squillace was part of the wider #Animals-Supposedly-Cant-Read-Signs-Duh campaign against anti-defecation signage in the city's parks. The signage was installed to warn humans not to undress or defecate in public, following the rise of 'humanimal' or 'Huml' lifestyles, which include most practising Loris and Noris. Speaking outside court, a Huml spokesbeing said the case was just another example of the marginalisation and hane its community lives with every day.

Gideon & Arielle Hovis, 41 Reynes Parade, Reynes Park. Arielle? I said pull the curtain, that sun's blasting right up the street. Mm? No, next week! I wander over and do it myself; may as well talk to the wall. She's kneeling at the window taking pictures of the welder. The welder Dennis and some female, who knows who, an assistant maybe.

This is how Ellie chooses to spend her youth. A Rike voyeur. Mm? Kids today. Posting pictures of themselves. Pictures of others. It only took this long, since photography was born, barely a century and a half, for humanity to be reduced to this. Lost in the mirror of itself. Absorbed and put beyond use by anyone. Mm? I pull the curtain in front of her and leave her kneeling there. If that girl could show me a single productive use for her social media, I'd be the first to get behind it, behind her. But she can't. A complete waste of time. When I look back she's still kneeling there. Taking pictures. Mm? Her mother and I would've been better off getting a cat.

51680708854858323-072: A police spokesperson has said the police car blast which closed much of Upper Reynes today is not thought to have been terror-related. Investigators add that early indications from the scene point to a UNT in the car's control system. Security experts recently warned of a growing problem with UNTs – Unknown New Technologies – after stem-coding formulas were leaked on the public grid. Today's incident, in which no one was injured, follows a spate of similar events in recent weeks, including GPS coordinates being scrambled on public transport routes, traffic-light hacking and mysterious flying objects.

Lon Cush, 37 Palisade Row, East Palisades. You can't hire an actual tiger. I didn't think you could. What you get is a *genet*, which is a smaller cat with spots and a raccoon tail.

For two hundred bills I can hardly afford, I booked a genet for Shelby's birthday. Sounds trivial but it's not: it puts a spoke in the wheel of the algorithm *and* serves a finger to the hyena. Although it also makes it urgent to talk to Egan. Man to man, heart to heart, before the birthday adds insult to injury. He'll wonder about a genet around.

So much harder to fucking manoeuvre with a hyena on your tail. Telling everyone you know you're damn near broke. Say what they like, a killer with a million bills would hardly lose a point. As it is, my score's on nineteen, my mortgage is up, my credit is down, the apprentice death rammed us into a nightmare – we don't even know if we can go to the funeral, don't know if we should even send flowers – then Mona's playing her usual long game to legally fish for my children. *But* – a genet is coming on

31940434634990099-905: Surgeons have reported the first successful animal-to-human ear transplant, attaching a pair of snub-nosed monkey ears to a woman who lost her own ears in a fire. The donor ears came from a zoo animal due to be put down after a stroke. The anonymous young recipient is said to be doing well, and is able to hear even better than before, something scientists say may be down to the ears' fur lining, which acts as a natural wind baffle. The woman's family has reported that the ears are the envy of patients throughout the hospital, and surgeons admit a waiting list of applicants is growing for the simple procedure.

Saturday. And that little secret has a burn like a vodka shot. That little banker is the beginning of progress, a slug over the bow of this shit.

I was also encouraged by Boges's idea, the big idea: *charity*. It's the one I needed, the cowabunga. I'll enter this game with a viral salvo. Not that we're usually uncharitable but these days are all about appearances, and capturing it on video makes sense. Big weekend coming – there's that drone festival as well, out on the flat. Kick off with some drones, then a charity mission, get back to find a party at home. *Surprise!* Egan can set it up while we're out. *Yay!* Immediate reward for an unselfish act. A big big fucking day, and with another secret banker: I can use the drones, the joy and the genet to shoot some family videos as well, Shel can post them for Mona, us eating cake while our scores rocket up.

Now, through the window, I watch the heretics making their way up the road from the bus stop, bobbing like raggy buoys. The gate chirps and they clatter inside. Shelby pulls her coat half off and flaps

1974027421986822-3167: Police have been called in to assess more than one eyewitness report that celebrity runaway Keeley Teague has been spotted at Lake Cala, Calabrava. Teague was expected to have delivered her baby some time ago, and today's witness reports say she appeared tanned and at ease near a popular shopping precinct, showing no signs of pregnancy. Markets have reacted to the news with volatility, and regulators warn that billions could be lost by parties who backed a live birth by the runaway. Contributors to early crowdfunding drives were quick to lodge court papers pending news on the runaway's situation.

a sleeve up the road: A lady moved in next door, she says, at Fourteen. Egan grunts: Looks like a guy. She batters his face with the sleeve – It's a *lady*! She's *cool*! – and thumps away to her room.

Like a predator nailing the slow one in the pack, I move in to corner the Eagle. He knows something's coming – his gaze darts around like he farted. Oh, how I remember that awkward age. Trapped inside the wrong person. All the technology in the world couldn't cure the stickiness of growing up. And it never quite goes away, that feeling – didn't for me, at least. Always trying to be this or that. Something more, something less. Something else.

I herd him past the stairs towards the kitchen, to the vicinity of fermented beverages, the district of the fridge, as fateful a spot as a fireplace to a lord. So how's things with you? I venture. He stiffens and says: Okay. Been a while since we did any fishing, I say; cast a few lines up the gorge? I mime the action of landing a whopper and wait for a signal of bonding. But his face crinkles up with disgust: Is that

12200160415121876-738: Speculation is growing among experts that the soundtrack to a recently discovered private film of serial killer Albo Goncci may indicate he was playing beer pong. The footage discovered in an attic appears to show the criminal's mountain lair, and while images are too degraded to offer clues, the film's soundtrack seems to describe a game of pong, even down to the telltale splash of the ball. Declinists arguing that Goncci didn't drink have been hounded on the grid for appearing to sympathise with the killer, who has been estimated to have tortured and murdered over a hundred and fifty people.

even *legal*? he says. Torturing fish like that? I swipe at him: What? Eagleton! Come on! Anyway, doesn't mean we'll catch anything. There's even an old joke says the only problem with fishing is there's always some fool wants to fish! I target a jocular beam at him. Wait for a signal of bonding. But then I drape myself over the stove like a stud, till it looks like I want to fuck him. Now meeting his eyes is like prodding live kidneys.

He peers around with his mouth at half mast and gives a high little whine: *Jesus, this is excruciating.* Good word, I volley, but he squints through his pleading grey kidneys and says: Look – is this about Shel? Because you don't have to threaten me with fishing. *Threaten you?* I cry. I'm just trying to carve out some time together! But anyway, what about Shel? I stare and he squirms a full-body squirm before folding his arms and muttering: I don't know exactly what videos you saw, but one of them isn't her. He drops his gaze and stiffens some more; a body language code that means a bigger revelation is contained within that sentence. I watch him for a moment, reach past him for a beer. My silence squeezes more out of him: She probably got rept, he says, like replicated, we were going to tell you anyway. I carefully savour the first rush of ale. Swallow, gulp and exhale: Well, first of all, Egan – how do you know what videos I look at? He shrugs: Anti-snooperware. It's only the free version, he says. The fuck. He's up to three reasons for trouble here, less a discount for coming clean. It means the reasons might barely be Base Camp One: there could be a summit of trouble ahead.

I feel the buzz of concern descend, that familiar methylated air: So – someone stole a video? I ask. Is that what you're saying? He slumps along the bench and hoists a leg up like a flamingo, stuck between confessions and unease, running out of ways to squirm. Not just a video, he mutters, they more or less stole *her*. After a chiming silence during which you can hear my beer, he pulls out his phone and loads one of Shelby's videos. He pauses it and

46600466103755303-09: A video shot in Upper Eastwood of a young person helping an older man cross a road has become the month's top viral sensation, beating both the Donkeyhooty facepalm clip and Mindabae's fennec din-dins by over a million views each. The young person was quickly identified by friends and neighbours following media reports that estimated his UFS score would rise into the nineties overnight, after congratulations flooded in from viewers and fans around the world. The young person himself is being low-key about his new-found celebrity, and is quoted as saying: 'It was just some old guy, but I'm glad I did it in the end.'

redundantly says: Okay, so this is Shel; forget about the body, artificial intelligence can build that in a second, likewise her movements, that's standard deepfake stuff. *Deepfake?* I quiz, and he says, Yeah, like when you put a celebrity's head on a porn star's body or something. Hm – I rub my jaw – she mostly just talks in her videos, they're not going to get much out of that. Egan studies my face with a solemn maturity, glimmers of depth I haven't seen before. A mature kind of pity, as he holds up the screen and starts to click through the video frame by frame; and there, between Shelby's first word and the end of the sentence, unfolds a universe of human expressions, a box set, a personality genome of all the faces she'll ever use, one per frame, faces she used as a baby, faces she'll use when she's grown-up, faces she'll use when she's old, faces I've never seen before, *click, click, click, click,* happy, fearful, aloof, surprised, disgusted, serene, apprehensive, sighing, wondering, awed, suspicious, disbelieving, content, excited, jokey, gleeful, breezy, relieved, knowing,

28800671943708161-20: The government has said that it could draft new legislation if sweeping new measures aren't adopted by social media platforms to protect digital images of people. The warning comes amid growing concern over the repping craze, which has seen an estimated eight million people, including children, digitally duplicated and retasked for private use in so-called 'lifestyling'. Citing some foreign countries that enacted legal protection for avatars over a decade ago, the government says the platforms cannot be allowed to set the agenda where people's rights are concerned. A person's image is currently only protected by copyright law.

uptight, flirtatious, modest, angry, ambitious, guilty, pious, reckless, relaxed, proud, concerned, terrified, indifferent, bored, mischievous, grumpy, gasping, pensive, grateful, loving, passionate, ecstasy, ecstasy, ecstasy, what the fuck.

Egan goes on like a patient old tutor to a child from another country: So, you see, from one face to the next, she goes through all the others on the way. Then these repping programs give them values and render a virtual stem-personality. You can write scripts for them, substitute them in movies, hook them up to AI and let them learn by themselves; you can mix and match parts, swap them in chatrooms . . . He stops to check my expression.

I hoist myself on to the bench and stare through the ceiling at the universe beyond. There must be a law, I muse. Against copying people like that. Just isn't right. He shrugs: Only copyright law. But you'd have to find out who did it. And the market for reps is huge. You can buy lifestyles for them, they can inhabit bots and dolls, and with the new bio-

17799794160047141-89: An increasing number of full-time Ssskinz wearers have stumbled upon a solution to the repping epidemic, although the hack is now being eagerly traded on forums. Expert and full-time skin wearer Lucas Avila says the new generation of chromeleon skins, whose colour, texture and design can be wearer-controlled with little additional technology, is simply being set to chromakey or green-screen designs when used in public, rendering them uncapturable by current manipulation technology. The hack applies only to public domain captures, although Avila says a number of new programs will aim to protect studio work.

bodysuits you can interact by touch, translate your media into heat and compression. Made from a kind of bacteria, he says; some people are wearing them permanently now, just living with bots or holograms. There's virtually no difference between that and the meatspace, except that everyone does what you want. They're saying the suits are healthier than clothes, like they regulate temperature, protect your skin and stuff, and you can even project cool designs on to them. But anyway – he exaggerates a shrug – the thing to remember is that Shel won't be the only one. Anyone of interest on Rike or Muh or Goh is probably getting rept right now. It's like a gold rush. There are already companies selling bots to track people down, or you can send a rep hitman to find and kill the reps. But it's expensive. And from what I can tell it's unusual to see a rep re-uploaded. Ninety-nine per cent of them go to private use and are never seen again, although they could technically appear when bots get smart enough to come out on the street, like later when superintelligence kicks in. But

11000877783661019-31: A petition brought by privacy activists against repping received half a million signatures within a month of being posted. The petition follows a recent wave of repping incidents, where privately made videos of people are copied and then manipulated to have them perform in private lifestyles, often involving sex. The petition, using the tag #YourPicIsYou, calls for tighter laws to protect personal photo and video images, as well as a ban on several popular repping programs such as Git-U and Slaveho, whose free versions critics say are powerful enough to capture most videos and create virtual sex slaves.

that'd be like in the future, maybe a year away or so. They say a lot of childless couples are repping kids and building families. So chances are she went to a family, because the new-generation cores they need to grow them to adulthood can cost a packet.

Egan steps back and returns the phone to his pocket. The chat has composed him completely. He's proud of his performance. He gives a false yawn, which is the bill for services rendered, a request to be dismissed. And I'm inclined to grant it. Under a helpless kind of horror I'm also proud. Somehow reverential of this new young man, so calibrated for the times of his life. One thing's for sure: we're both in a different space than when we walked in here. And strangely serene – perhaps the serenity of the inevitable. Anyway, it's only an image we're talking about. I hope it's only an image.

I'm fucked trying to judge how horrified to be, as nothing in the story seems to come from the world where I previously judged any horror. Which is its own kind of horror. I pay Egan's bill with a quiet

679891637638612258: A new report claims that ex-runaway Keeley Teague's personal image has been rept over a million times from a single video posted on her site. Although Ms Teague had earlier licensed her rep for sale through popular program Git-U, many reps making up the total are thought to have been rept illegally. The video has since been removed, prompting underground sales of Keeley reps to rise dramatically. The government is conducting an urgent review of personal copyright and public domain laws, but warns in the meantime that the only sure way to protect one's reproduced image is to limit distribution of selfies.

nod. Look up and find his eyes. No longer tender kidneys, now they're wormholes to an infinite place where anything is everything and the driver is awe. I watch as he slouches back into himself and puffs a little sigh: Just a bummer she didn't get to monetise it. *Monetise it?* I go. *Your sister?* You know, he says. Better than just giving it away.

He shambles off and leaves me in the silence of the kitchen. In this modern day. In these rocketing times. No more comedy laughter. No thuds, no shouts, no giggles. I sit and dangle my legs in it. But a lot of thoughts come from this meeting and one of them is strangely: *Maybe we can make it through*. There's a plan. Two smart allies, my tech support team. And the repping might serve as a lesson to Shel, nip riskier ideas in the bud. These strands swirl around, but some, I realise, are only there to distract me from another little thought sitting quietly in a corner, a less parenty whisper that says: *I wonder how clear my old videos are of Diane*.

420196140727489673: Diehard Mindabae fans are awaiting an announcement on the likelihood of her releasing a licensed Mindabae rep for her birthday. The possibility was first mooted at the *YoSienz* Young Achiever Awards, where MB was coy when questioned over the possibility. Meanwhile a number of hackwatch forums have reported links between Mindabae management and the CEOs of leading rep platforms, with one leaked memo purporting to state that any rep would only be released in a standard economy low-function model, until higher security levels could be added to a sexually functioning product for premium users.

Chad Mullens, Quantum Time Lab, Octagon Road, Reynes. Who, not Baz again? Well, I'm not picking up for a reason – tell him I can't talk now and he should know why. Ey? I said tell him to wait, I'm fucking busy! It's not passive-aggressive, I'm up to my ears in qubits. Tell him I'll get back to him later. Well, there isn't going to be any progress if he calls every two minutes for a progress report. Tell him even trial mode at Moyle's is going to be Saturday at the earliest. Just tell him Saturday, tell him I promise. Saturday if he gets off our backs! Ey? Well, that's the whole reason it's taking so long, fucking Fourteen Palisade Row! What does he want! If he confined it to one building we'd be fine!

Okay, okay, listen: I know it's wired to Moyle's, but particles still have to entangle over two hundred yards. Just tell him Saturday, and have him warn whoever's in there because clock speed's going to get weird at first, like slow or even stopped. Oh, and ask him what his last fucking slave died of.

259695496911122585: Observers near the Octagon have reported lights burning long into the night at the group's QT lab in Reynes, prompting speculation about an imminent localised trial of QT, or Curlytime, as the consumer product will be known. Touted as the last basic step towards full singularity readiness, Curly, as it's affectionately known, will replace analogue time with a more flexible quantum scale where time is nominal. When rolled out the move is expected to generate a fifty per cent increase in corporate profits, as limiting timescales are switched to more open-ended models for contracts and deliveries.

Gideon & Arielle Hovis, 41 Reynes Parade, Reynes Park. Well, well, well, I take some of it back. All her snapshots may have paid off.

Just look at that. Rays flashing off the upturned visor on the young woman's head as the sun gushes over her, all golden skin, shining teeth, velvet shade. The welder kneels slightly behind this girl, holding her around the waist, looks like he's teaching her, patiently positioning her arms and talking into her ear as they stretch towards the target as one, in as muscular and vital a motion as the raising of the flag in a war zone. This is good, Ell, I say. Who's the girl? She says: The refugee from Thirty-five.

My God, it is a good shot, almost symbolic, or no, it *is* symbolic, not only their slim young forms welded into a single golden mass – that's it, welded! – but one of our own embattled young labourers, one of our unsung tradesmen, trying to make his way in the hostile environment of our times, but with enough heart to spare, enough strength and humanity left over to interrupt his gainful employ and show a

160500643816367088: Passengers have been warned to expect delays and cancellations at Coade International Airport today after air traffic control systems were disabled by a suspected UNT, which replaced aircraft ID tags on radar screens with Kiz Kitty animations. The airport warns it will operate at reduced capacity while forensic teams examine the system's estimated million components to isolate the unknown technology. The airport's chief executive has assured the travelling public that reduced operations pose no risk to passengers, as manual control procedures were safely used for almost a century before digital systems were introduced.

newly arrived refugee from the war zone what we expect from our citizens here, how we do things, what we stand for, who we are. Yes, dammit: *who we are!* That's what the picture says, that's what it shouts and screams. I examine the image more closely. He's as attentive to her as a father, a leader, as one of our own, and she sparkles in her eyes and absorbs every word, young woman from the desert, lost and outnumbered but from that small welcome percentage that's willing to follow, willing to learn and bear our children and make their blood at home among us. A *woman* and an *immigrant*. Learning from the cream of our workers, an embodiment of the spirit of this place. Epitome of *care*!

I turn to Arielle; our eyes meet. Steady eyes full of excitement, bright with life. *Ahh*, Arielle, I say, I take some of it back. That's a beautiful picture. And look, look, she shows me the views it's attracting on Muh: almost a thousand just from today. *Ahh*, Ellie. Not bad, my girl; I take some of it back.

99194853094755497:
A survey has revealed that up to sixty-one per cent of UFS scores under thirty are held by people born over two thousand miles away, the majority refugees and economic migrants. Commenting on the results, one declinist told reporters the most salient finding was that migrants scored lower than Loris. He later apologised to Lori and Nori communities after quipping that they should try harder. Liberal declinists have meanwhile called for a UFS boycott, prompting the Octagon to respond that societies have for decades been secretly scored by banks and authorities, and that UFS has merely brought the process out into the open.

Melinda Meims, Roca Del Mar, Arcadia Heights, Arcadia. I am not going to any war zone. Tell them we'll do a fennec charity shoot or something. I don't care how many lonely soldiers are there, let them jack off, we'll send pictures. Well, because both sides are using the word *nuclear* on Rike and I don't want to get nuked, *duh*, Lamelle. What do you mean when? Today, now! Pay attention!

I said I'm not doing it. It's just not smart. Well, I have a total lack of fucks to give, Lamelle. Complete fuck deficit – in fact you owe me fucks. Find some easier hits, let's visit a twisted child or something. Oh schnap, wait – did you see this? Pay attention! What? Well, put him back in his cage, don't let him shit out here again. It's like a minefield of fucking foxshit. Just shut him up, put him outside. Did you see this? I'm talking about the pic. Trending on Muh. I know it's a fucking welder, duh – I mean the hits. We want us a piece of that. See? How much easier? And he looks so sweet! *Welder Bae*.

61305790721611591: This week's Picture of the Week on leading social site Muh is set to become the most popular ever, with views and shares already rocketing past fifty million. The pic shot locally by Arielle Hovis of Reynes Park features a gritty sunlit scene of a welder teaching a young female protégée the ropes of his trade. Rights commentators have called the shot a breath of fresh air and a shot in the arm, not only for women's rights but for gender equality, as welding remains a trade most strongly identified with males. A number of declinist commentators have also come out to say the picture is a welcome break from fennecs.

Lon Cush, 37 Palisade Row, East Palisades. Look! Look! I point as the drones form a word in the dull listless sky over the flat. The word is PUTUBE. Or maybe FUFURS. Or no: *FUTURE*. Look! I hiss, but Egan barely raises an eye.

Every few seconds under the buzz of the drones comes a quivering sigh from his phone. I finally give up pointing and turn to his screen: What are you playing? *Donkey Kare*, he says. I watch his on-screen character rushing to various donkeys to give them a hug. Hm, I say – and what happened to *Kull*? It's not their fault they're donkeys, he says. We have to stop kulling everything that's different from us – they can't help being donkeys.

With a couple of deft strokes he puts a jeering horse in its place with a farting sound that turns it into a donkey. After a moment's quiet between us he finally looks up. Our gazes softly meet and I see something new in him. This non-fishing boy. I don't know what it is, but it's something in his blue-grey eyes. A gentle burn, a welling.

37889062373143906: The hunt for the subjects of Muh's Pic of the Week is half over after the revelation today that the welder in the image is local man Dennis Farrell, a Molan Gardens local recently made redundant from a long-term position within the Environmental Services branch of the Octagon, which manages pipelines and sewers in Reynes and surrounding areas. Farrell was reportedly undertaking his first job as an independent welder when he made the effort to show a young associate the basic ropes of his trade. The woman in question has yet to be identified. Farrell meanwhile has been enjoying his new-found fame at venues across the city.

Maybe a pain. I drape an arm over his chest and lay it heavy. He settles back into me and I peck his big head. So much to say; nothing to be said.

After a few moments suspended like this he lowers his phone and says: *Dad . . . ?* But Shelby chooses now to burst in, and he stiffens back over his screen. She gripes: Is there anyone we can call about this racket? My audio's frickin destroyed, and I can't lose a whole day of posting. I let a moment's steam come off her, then I grab her arm, spin her around, and point out through the window: It's *Dronestock*! Look what they're doing for your last day in single digits! As I say it, a cloud of drones flies up and starts to play a tune. If only she knew the surprises I have for her birthday, the charity mission I've planned. I'm about to drop some hints when two drones break away from the swarm on the flat, and buzz past the house towards town. The rest quickly land and the air falls suddenly still; after a moment more, from over the cliff, comes the growing cry of sirens.

23416728348467685: Star welder Dennis Farrell has become the most Riked person in town after being snapped in a viral Muh pic this week. Crowdfunding revenue for the redundant sanitation worker has reportedly topped six figures, and rumours have it that entertainment industry bigwigs are even lining up to option the heart-warming tale, describing the humble worker's unselfish dedication to a disadvantaged young stranger, now increasingly rumoured to be a refugee from Al Qemen, pure cinema gold. A-lister Corey Kniessen has said the story has all the makings of a classic, though he was shy when asked if he would join the cast.

Drive Time with Roney, BUTI-FM Studios, Arcadia North. After the news, if you've never thought of Molan as a celebrity hotspot, think again as Mindabae's BFF, local hero Welder Bae, drops in to take your calls. Later in the hour, new twists in a West Palisades child protection case, as mother Shona Ululay, whose child was removed, now claims it was a boyfriend who had her daughter post Rike vids, to fund drugs, according to her. All this plus: Should we be worrying about so much use of the word *nuclear*? After news, weather and traffic – it's over to Bev. *From Harville to Stresnan to Molan and Reynes, we're one lovin' unit, yo* BUTI.

I motion for coffee as the intern ushers Farrell into the studio. Looks like he's been shopping for the first time in his life. Or got stuck in the first shop he found. Dennis! I point to a chair. Or should I call you Bae? Ha haha. Headphones right there.

He looks around and I scan his notes: school dropout, ES department – which makes me ask: Was that the department with the abuser? Bogdanovic?

14472334024676221: The inaugural Dronestock event on the East Palisades flat has been marred by an incident, as a pair of modified drones taking part in a coordinated aerobatics display left the field and flew to Coade International Airport, causing airspace to be closed for over three hours. One drone was shot down by police before any harm could be caused, and the second was seen to vanish over Knox Park. Passengers have been warned to expect delays in the wake of the incident. Festival frontman Baz Matanick apologised for the malfunction and said an internal inquiry to identify the incident's cause will leave no stone unturned.

Heh he, yeah, he says, we all got abused by him. Sorry, I wince – I hadn't heard, it's not in the notes. I don't talk about it, he says, what's the point. Sure, got you, I say – just so larger-than-life, the socials this amped and you haven't even broken that news. I mean – pretty dark, workplace hane like that. He snorts: Dark is the least of it, and I put on my news face to ask: Did you also know Jakey Storer? The apprentice? Fuck, he says, I was like his main bro, back before Bogesy killed him. Fuckin job was more like a death match, now I think about it.

As I watch the clock tick into the last minute, a buzz comes in from the newsroom: we're given another minute to wait as a newsflash reports some drones shot down near the airport. The city's on terror alert. I use the extra time to probe a scoop: So, Dennis – would you be okay to talk about the abuse? If it's not too painful? Might bring some closure. And I'm sure your fanbase would love to position you as the face of the abuse survivor . . .

8944394323791464: Police have been called to an undisclosed address in Reynes after haners reportedly gathered, seeking the former media graduate who claims to be the girl in the now-famous Welder Bae image. No further details are available about the cause of the call, and police have reported moving a number of so-called 'hane surfers' out of the area to Starlite Mall car park, West Palisades, where they are expected to disperse. Galatea Marin Medina is now one of over a hundred people claiming to be the subject of the Welder Bae image, in which a young woman's features are obscured by a welding helmet worn on her head.

Janos & Joelly Bogdanovic, Starlite Mall, West Palisades. Lon calls: Boges, just thought I'd let you know for Joelly – Shelby already had a Little Burro, and she thinks she's over them now; I figured you could use the gift info, he says.

I pause upon hearing this. Joelly stops beside me. What are you, psychic now? I ask, and he says: The mall doesn't close for an hour, I'm telling you early. At which I have to say: If you're asking if we remembered the birthday party tomorrow, then yes. But we've known about the date for some time, as in years, you surely don't think we'd leave it till now to find a gift? Yes, he says; and don't spend too much. I'll offset with beers tomorrow.

Ach, I'm so transparent. I kill the phone and nudge Joelly ahead, deeper into the gifts section. Starlite Mall is glittering with products while I glitter inside with disquiet. It's the type of apprehension that filters everything out but the sound of your own voice. I can hear myself droning: An extra five we can do, she got you that unicorn.

5527939700884757: Plucky abuse survivor and media star Welder Bae took to BUTI-FM to discuss the devastating effects of abuse on young workers like himself, and to express his sense of loss and dismay at losing his closest friend and protégé, the apprentice Jakey Storer. In a sometimes sombre tone, always lightened by a plucky trademark chuckle, Welder Bae said it was a matter of routine for many workers to be referred to as morons, and often much worse than that. He revealed that his secret weapon in dealing with the daily grind of abuse was to think of his beloved sweetheart, who despite suffering anxiety was able to inspire such hope.

Or look, how about this: a phone sofa, I say. But every time I look around, someone else seems to know my face. Joelly picks up on it, and falters. I know, honey, I tell her – I'm watching. I know they're shooting video, I know, but they're outside the doors, okay? Find something for Shelby, let's focus on the mission, it's nearly tomorrow already, and you have to get to bed too. I know it is, baby, but it's just how some people are. Don't pay any attention. Well, because funny old Dennis – from Daddy's work? – well, that's how we joke around, it's what boys do, okay? And remember this has nothing to do with Mama and me. We both love you very much and I'll see you a lot, like today. And we still have doughnuts to come! Yum!

We poke around the aisles with our heads down like burglars. I know, I hear myself say, I know, just keep looking, what about this one, pink or purple, what do you think? Eh? I'm watching, don't worry. Just think about Shelby. How about this: a fennec? I know it's a lot of people, I know. Eh? Well, baby, we're here instead of on the grid because we want a nice life. Okay? It's you and me, we can touch the toys, we can walk around, we can smell the doughnuts. I can smell the doughnuts already! Can you smell the doughnuts? I can smell the doughnuts, and it's nice, and you're nice and the gifts are nice and life is nice, see? How it works? Then all that nice gets wrapped into a gift for Shelby, see? Joelly?

As we pause at the storefront to have this exchange, more and more people gather at the mall's glass doors. Joelly looks up. I know it's a lot of people, I whisper, I know, but just . . . Fuck, and they're coming in – I grab her as the mob heads our way. Listen, listen to me: I love you, we'll be fine, but I want you to go to that lady at the back and call Mama to come get you, okay? And wait there till she comes. No, I can't take you, Bumpylumps, I'm sorry. Please now, Joelly, run like a bunny, go on now, go, go – I watch her stumble and turn with wide eyes – oh, and don't cry! Joelly? *Don't cry!*

2111485077978050:

In what's believed to be the largest gathering of drinkers to address a single channel on Rike, over ten thousand young males have livestreamed a pledge to give up drinking beer. The event follows a week of admissions by high-profile haners and abusers that the incidents they are accused of were beer-related. Support on the grid for victims of beer has been overwhelming, in some cases prompting accusations to be withdrawn. Naning sites have also reported a surge in popularity among beer victims, who until recently ranked among the least likely prospects to land a nane, having been scored as simple abusers.

Bastian Matanick, Moyle House, East Palisades. Drones? Our official line is that it's bound to be terror-related. Spread the word: if it's terror then the heat's off us, and we need that. What? Well, because the neighbourhood to the west is full of Al Qemen refugees – it's fucking plausible, Chad.

Ay-ay-ay, and can someone just give me the time in the analogue world? I know I fucking asked for it, but that was before the drones. And please admit: the last Curly demo you showed me didn't zero the phones, it just added a timezone option.

Cornelia Roos, 14 Palisade Row, East Palisades. God, is that all the time is? I must have slept ten minutes. *Fuh*. Age. I hate it. You go through the bloody agenda, all your rituals, and for what. And today of all days, with the media coming to film my little bombshell for Matanick, and Johanna's chat before that, with so much to ask her. *Puh*. Time has frozen still. Roll over and start again.

1304969544928657:
A round of applause could be heard in the Octagon today as engineers confirmed the first localised Curlytime trial was live and underway, almost two months ahead of its original schedule. Confined to a small area with off-site labs and residential space in East Palisades, the live launch was declared a success after clocks, phones and electronic components in the vicinity re-zeroed their time functions and floated in free time. Quantum engineers explained that for all intents and purposes it would appear that time had stopped, but quantum computers running the system would be logging events in the background.

Colleen Carl, Television Centre, Carmel Street, Reynes. We don't need it scripted. She's an eminent professor; believe me, she can speak. And I can do the intro on the fly. Look, we're wasting minutes over this. As soon as she opens her mouth you'll see what I mean. God, just – trust me on this one.

Dr Johanna Fisser, Rue Gabrielle-Pierrot-Fripon, Vierne. The screen is dead. Not a peep. Doesn't even show the time at her end. For pity's sake.

Her memory. She just won't realise, or won't admit, both her father and her brother were gone by seventy. And now here's Madeleine with the pre-op shot. Just five more minutes, I beg; I can't get the call to connect! But she scowls at me ferociously. I have to go, the theatre's waiting. She'll come back and keep trying it herself, she says, asking if I have a message to relay, as I might be in recovery for some time. Well, yes, I say: send my love, and tell her I'm down to my last nine packets of bear sweets.

806515533049393: City officials have warned that the terror threat level will remain at extreme following an attempt by drones to approach Coade International Airport, endangering aircraft and potentially causing hundreds of deaths. The City's anti-terror squad has been on high alert for further suspicious activity, as terror attacks have been known to come in sequences. The office of a migrant rights group has been closed by police as it was found to be a meeting place for Al Qemen refugees from the southern suburbs. Refugee leaders have warned the City not to provoke them any further, as unrest in the community is growing fast.

Lon Cush, 37 Palisade Row, East Palisades. Finally Shel's big day, *our* big day. Charity day. Viral day. New start day. My heart bangs with it. I've planned it like a military operation, in every detail, or almost. Boges'll be proud when I show him the video: a food drop to the underprivileged, film it and post it on Muh, then back to find Shelby's party set up, with her rental cat strutting around. Egan's receiving the cat and its handler right after we set off. Shel can sense something brewing.

I stuff her into her coat like a mannequin. She lets me do it, she's limp on her birthday; it's a licence to be ministered to, apparently. Either that or she's not buying the charity thing, but the magic of the day, the impendingness of surprises, has softened her resistance like catnip. We didn't get to this stage of civilisation by forgetting everyone else, I tell her, stuffing her arm down a sleeve. We haven't got cash to throw around but we'll share what we have with others, I say, trading a wink with my accomplice Egan, conveniently slouched on the stairs.

Bang goes the door behind us. We go down the path, past the car and into a gusty breeze. What are you doing? she says. We're walking, I say, to Supa-Lo. She stalls – All the way to Supa-Lo? – but I take her hand, we crackle along, and when we swing our arms there's a sense in the air that it's going to be all right, this family of ours. The chicken place up City Hill is brightly lit but empty. Not even the servers are there. Did you know, Shelby-bean, I say, that giving's more addictive than taking? That people are happier when they make others happy than when someone makes them happy themselves? She jiggles my hand, *Kh kh kh*, and along we go over holes and cracks, model little family, love, love, love.

A lady beside a warehouse fence is pulling up her jeans. I quickly look away but she yells: I SAW YOU! I SAW! And Shel hisses: What's her problem? Must be mental health, I say. I'M A WITNESS, shouts the lady. WALK AWAY, I HAVE WITNESSED EVERYTHING!

The light at the corner of Mogford is green; we

308061521170129: A survey has found that over seventy per cent of local young people think death by terrorist attack is more likely than death in a vehicle accident or from one of the top-ten cancers. The survey, which analysed data from over ten thousand youngsters, also found that being abducted as a terrorist virgin bride was thought a better lifestyle outcome than finishing school and going to university. A number of haners and declinists have said perceptions of risk are now entirely tied to trending themes on media, bearing no relation to actual risk. One said if fennec attacks were streamed for a day, they would also be called a major risk among the young.

cross the road with its blessing. There's no traffic anyway, City Hill Road is deserted. Terror alerts: not all bad news. Because the threat level jumped beyond red overnight. They ran out of colours for the terror threat level – should've started at white if they were going to ramp it up this far.

Supa-Lo hoves into view and we make for its heavenly light – *Authorisation needed, unexpected item, please scan your item* – ping ping ping ping. Shel sighs: What are we getting, anyway? A little feast, I say, for someone less lucky than us. We start at the top and go to the chickens. I test her and ask: Which do we pick? And she says: The biggest? Right on, I say, and we start to furnish our basket. Potatoes, peas and stuffing, some apricots and mandarins, nuts and honey, coffee, butter and bread.

When Shel begins to flag I let her choose something for herself, a gingerbread fennec and a tub of magic slime, then we grind through auto-checkout and stride off down City Hill. What now? she asks, tugging the back of my shirt. I point past the

190392490709135: Authorities have called on media giants to implement tighter controls on socials, after a woman claiming to be the refugee in the viral image of celebrity welder Den Farrell said he threatened to deny her identity unless she had sex with him. Galatea Medina, a twenty-six-year-old unemployed media graduate, has also been identified as a national of San Uribe, prompting an outcry from local Al Qemen refugees. Up to today, over four hundred young women have come forward claiming to be Welder Bae's partner in the image. The welder is said to be meeting claimants personally to help identify the person in question.

warehouse: See where the lady was? In the alleys behind, a couple of rows back, live some really struggling people. Refugees and such, not as lucky as us with surprises waiting at home. Those little houses are struggling, with children in some as well, no surprises for them today. We may not be rich but we have enough to share, doesn't matter how little, we can . . . *Yuh*, okay, she says, I get it.

We crunch past the warehouse via an alley at the side. Shadows are heavy; there's a smell of diesel and filth. A rat ripples a gutter. Shel tenses up: What are we going to do, knock on a door? What if they open and they're richer than us? What if it's Mental Health Lady? What if it's a meth lab? Shhh, I say, they're too poor for meth; but you're right, let's think this through. If we knock to present this in person it'll only make them feel small . . .

Off down the alley we go, keen as hunters, thinking things through, shadows brushing like cobwebs, Supa-Lo bag swinging low.

117669030460994: Over half of former refugees and economic migrants who travel for leisure do not visit their places of birth, a new study has revealed. The surprising finding comes from research into leisure and family holidays by former migrants who arrived within the last fifteen years, and showed that the vast majority of migrants from Al Qemen or further east don't return to their homelands when holidays come around, preferring to visit closer beach resorts, and in some cases mountain ski resorts for winter sports. Travel companies were quick to pick up on the trend, with one already offering two-for-one tickets to former migrants.

Dr Mauro Hahn-Gilardi, Neuro-surgical Theatre, Rue Gabrielle-Pierrot-Fripon, Vierne. *Ahhhh*, the piano concerto. Better, thank you. As good as a drug. They should've called him Balms.

And we need it. This is looking trickier. *Swab*. When I was training like some of you, one surgeon I observed, maxillofacial, used to listen to audiobooks – *clamp there* – at first I found it strange, but I soon realised – *now this looks unstable, see here? Tie it* – that some of his procedures, like radical oral and neck dissection and reconstruction, were so long that he timed books to them rather than – *damn. Suction*. Ach, look. Don't like it, see there? Another tie, quickly. There. *No*. Suction. Hold it. *No*. Hold. *Merde*. It's disintegrating. *Ach*. It was ready to go. Relentless. *Tch*. Close up for me, she's gone.

Write it up as a rupture, the complications are clear in the notes. Is there someone to inform . . . ? *Roos?* I thought she'd gone overseas . . . She's there now? On cam? Nurse Aude? Have her paged.

72723460248141:
A revolutionary new therapeutic approach for the treatment of tumours is being trialled at a leading post-operative clinic. In what's already being called the most promising new lead in post-operative tumour therapy in a decade, clinicians instruct their patients to give tumours likeable personal names, such as Josh or Jared. Patients report a greater sense of calm and control, having identified their tumours as friends, and while doctors say it's too early to know the full results, an empathic state of mind can only help in the long run. Gaming programs are also being developed to help with visualising tumour friends.

Lon & Shelby Cush, Brewer's Lane, West Palisades. An old woman steps into the grimy lane to add crap to a pile by her door. The light is dim and damp in her tiny row house as she hobbles back over the threshold. *Look* – I point. Shel surveys the place and whispers: The bag won't last a second, rats and cats will get it. Hmm, I nod, good point, Agent Bean. Then how are your ninja powers? Because we'll just have to knock and run. *Kh kh kh*, she says.

We stop at the corner and set the video to record. Saunter up to the rotten old door and stand the bag on the step. Quietly fold the handles. Shelby's tensed like a rubber-band toy, awaiting my signal to go. I finally look up and nod. She leans to the door, knocks quickly twice, and we fly up the alley in a whirl, to the *thup-thup-thup* of her shoes, windmilling arms through the shadows. We hardly reach the end of the block before a gasp breaks out behind us. Shel looks up at me, beaming.

The sound of joy, Shelby-bean, I say, reaching down to high-five her; you did a good thing today.

44945570212853: New figures show that elderly females make up the largest, most vulnerable sector of the poor, and in the case of former immigrants the number is almost double. On top of their condition of poverty, analysts point to the longer lifespans of females on average, leading to longer periods without a partner towards the end of life, and giving rise to a number of issues which further complicate poverty, among them loneliness. Charities have responded by citing complementary studies which show that lending help or time, or even so much as a kind word, to an elderly woman is more appreciated by them than by any other group.

Like spies, we don't take the straight route home but detour back up towards Supa-Lo. Shel giggles and gasps between breaths, her fennec flailing beside her. See how it feels? I pant – that's what I'm talking about. Joy.

Pausing for breath just ahead of the store, I bend to replay her the video. And there we are, there's Shelby's face, lips clamped with the audacity of it all. Now here's the door, rocking towards us, damp glowing over the doorstep.

Kh kh kh, says Shel, if we run out of food we can go back to that house! I sigh apologetically: Well, we might have to, I forgot what day it was; might have to eat dry bread, I say. No, you didn't! – she pokes me hard – there's BIRTHDAY CAKE! Oops, I sigh, another thing I forgot, and she pummels me into the Supa-Lo bike rack – Liar! You did not! – then flattens her nose into mine to hiss: *What's the surprise? Is there a surprise? You can tell me, is it alive?* We-ell, I muse. Mmm . . .

Colleen Carl, In Transit, City Hill Road, West Palisades. Get on the scanner: another terror alert. You heard, breaking now. A few blocks down – we could beat the early responders.

I crane over my shoulder to sigh at the crew – What is it with this place all of a sudden? – and they shake their heads; one yawns. Heart of war refugee territory, says another, place is all wound up. Never really welcomed in the first place, now on a knife-edge from all the threats to bus 'em out to other towns. We drove 'em all screwy.

We pause as a crackle of news comes in; the address narrows down to a number. Strange, I say: don't often hear of devices planted on their own doorsteps. At least the address is on the way – in fact, look at the map; don't go to the device location, head to the scheduled address on Palisade Row. We can set up near the corner. It's the other side of City Hill Road, almost opposite. What's that now? *Two suspects, one juvenile, on foot . . .*

17167680177565: Plucky Molan Gardens star Welder Bae has attracted more than a hundred thousand hits on Rike for comments he made earlier today in response to a question about the southern refugee population, particularly war refugees. Asked why he chose an Al Qemen refugee to join him in the image that made him famous, the welder replied: 'It was a female because they don't do war.' He went on to say he once defended a colleague's family from being stalked by male refugees, adding that it was males in the southern suburbs who were at the root of all their problems. A massive response continues to grow from fans across the city.

Lon & Shelby Cush, City Hill Road, West Palisades. Life's a funny thing, Shelby-bean, I say. I swing her by the hand and we stroll down the hill towards the Row, all gangly and loose from our run, limber and bright with excitement. You don't have to have a religion, I say, to see that good deeds bring a following wind. She looks up and for once I think she listens. There's an energy in the world, I go on, same as I saw in the pipelines at work, of good stuff in and bad stuff out, and if you join in the good, other good stuff will follow . . .

She stops near our corner to point: It's the lady from Number Fourteen! I gape around – seems a crap time to go meeting neighbours – then I see where she's pointing and falter. A spindly figure in a bathrobe toddles over the corner of Palisade Row and churns up City Hill without seeming to bend her legs, locomotive rods pumping instead. She whimpers as if forced to march. *Hi!*, I call – *Everything okay?* But she's briefly obscured by a van with a satellite dish sliding around the corner on

10610209857723: Citizens have been ordered to evacuate an area around Brewer's Lane, West Palisades, following a report of a suspicious device planted on a doorstep. Anti-terror police warn to avoid all non-essential travel and outdoor activity, as terrorists have been known to strike multiple targets at once. Reports from the area say a man and a juvenile were seen running towards City Hill Road moments after the device was found, prompting speculation that they may be local. Residents in the area not surrounding Brewer's Lane have been requested to stay indoors and remain on alert. Further updates will follow live from the scene.

to the Row. She doesn't hear me anyway, or at least doesn't stop, and now sirens are approaching from town.

I take Shelby's hand, she tucks herself close, and we pant up the Row towards home, chattering about nothing to keep the buzz alive. On the roadside sand not far from Fourteen, I feel a tug as Shel bends to retrieve something. Looks like a dongle on a keyring. *Jembaya*, she reads; yuh *what*? It's a place, I tell her, frowning ahead, trying to make sense of the view. The satellite van sits opposite Fourteen, the door to which is wide open. Shapes mill behind the van windows. A methylated air descends, the old firewater buzz that says something is nigh. Another clustery day, a change-cluster day in these clumpy clustering times. We quicken our pace to outrun it. Shelby nestles into me, looks up and breaks into a scamper – but too late.

Our footsteps scrape to a stop.

A camera lens pokes from the van window as cars skid up behind us, dumping an aroma of brake pads

6557470319842: An unusual new study has found that a number of people who practise charitable acts fall among the least desirable, and sometimes the most dangerous, people around. While the finding seems paradoxical, researchers say the answer lies in the declinist and haner brain, which has been found to be wired differently than other people's. Where a healthily wired person would seek to alleviate the suffering of others, or lend a helping hand in order to assist them, many declinists would instead perform the act to help themselves, and to alleviate the stress of what they know to have been previously unkind and even haneful acts.

and ozone. We don't have to ask if they're coming for us – the sound of them hisses our names.

I pump Shel's hand for courage, hers and mine, I pump it for comfort and love, for old times and new, I pump as if the world we want, with the peace we knew, will inflate like a rubber castle; and there in the distance before us as I pump, I see Egan coming on to our step. The good old Eagle, apple of this old mussy eye. A loudspeaker barks before I can wave: *On the ground! Let the youngster go!*

As we kneel and then lie, knowing we seized the wrong day, police whisk Shel off her belly. I hear her gasp, and try to unhear it. I hear *Bizarre*, and feel strangely proud. But what I finally take away from these last moments together, from our life together, perhaps, is the image of her before last: she was hitting the deck with her dad, flat on the road as a partner in crime, our hands held over the grit.

I peer along the ground to our family home, down this lane I've driven so often; the last thing I see is three rings, then two, then one of a genet's tail.

4052739537881: The Popular Starlite Mall in West Palisades remains closed today after the body of a man was found impaled through the thigh on a perimeter security fence. While the man's identity remains undisclosed, a forensic officer at the scene explained that the death had the hallmarks of a tragic accident, perhaps during an escape from the mall after a crime. The man appeared to have been trying to jump the fence into a neighbouring yard when a deterrent security spike punctured his femoral artery and caused massive blood loss. A police spokesperson said it is not uncommon for petty thieves to jump the Starlite fence to avoid the cameras on City Hill Road.

DOPAMINE CITY

76

East Palisades

'The thing to remember is this,' says the anime deity-mentor fox: 'The rhythm we think of as natural to humans is the rhythm of an animal world. Rising or retiring with the sun or moon is as much a vestige of our distant past as the tailbone at the end of our spines. Because once upon a time in a harsh, sulphur-infested world, the only real job we had was to eat and avoid being eaten. Make babies and crawl away to die.

'Many of the world's creatures are nocturnal, many are diurnal, some are crepuscular, even today; and this is for no more sophisticated a reason than that the foods they eat and the creatures who would eat them are following the same routine. Come out in the dark because your enemies work by day; adapt to the foods you can hunt in the dark, develop strong ears, strong eyes. Come out in the light because your enemies hunt by night; adapt to the foods you can see in daylight, develop strong legs and resistance to sun. And it's logical this pattern should have persisted in humans so long after we left the trees, because the first thing we did was become an agrarian creature. We learned to cultivate plants, husband animals for meat and milk and eggs. After two and a half million years as tool-making creatures, two and a half million years since the hand-axe was used to adapt the world around us instead of letting it adapt us – we became farmers. Barely a few thousand years ago. And farming, needing sunlight for crops and livestock, further ingrained the notion of a twenty-four-hour day, with daylight activity and night-time sleep, until we now – even now when those days are long gone! – find it natural.

'Well, but no. It was a convenient guide to the life of the plants and animals we were trying to grow, the use of daylight as a tool. But things have changed, they changed some time ago, and it only remains for us to see the light and reap the benefits of what we know to be a higher way. A *better* way. Look at these facts and I think you'll agree how crazy things look from today: we occupy just one of over seven hundred trillion planets in the known universe. Let's take a look at some of the planets closest to us, in our own solar system, and see just how opportunistic and random, how imposed by outside forces, our habits have been. Jupiter, for example, has a ten-hour day. *Ten hours*. Presumably if we had grown up on Jupiter we would call that a day and live our lives in fast-forward. But then Venus, at the other end of the scale, has a five thousand eight hundred and thirty-two-hour day. Think we could survive a day's work on Venus? That's a day lasting two hundred and forty-three of our days. *Hard day at the office, dear?* These are our closest neighbours. See how much we have in common with them. Virtually nothing. So to think our rhythms are a universal thing is pure whim.

'I'll tell you what's universal: what's universal is that we *observe*. We are *observers* of our universe. That's all. When and how we do that observing doesn't have to be tied to the habits of a few spinning rocks and gases. That's just absurd! A crusty molten rock in empty space dictates when this fairy-tale creature – that's *you* – deploys its intelligence? *No way*. There was a time when it was useful; it no longer is. We have changed the earth to serve greater aims than feeding ourselves. And not a moment too soon, as our reliance on natural resources has only harmed it.

'Now there's something we can do to help – we can literally stop time.

'I can already hear you saying: *But what's the compelling reason? We like it this way!* And guess what: you can have it this way. But you can also have it any other way you want without losing sleep, and while boosting productivity and well-being by up to three hundred per cent. *Three hundred per cent!* The compelling reason? It's this: with the gradual roll-out of singularity-compatible technologies, and with the final integration of information, social and media systems, a problem has arisen which requires us to act. But let's not call it a problem, let's call it a *spur*, a kick-start to the future. It's simply this: quantum and digital data moves too fast to fit current measures of time without using a whole lot of numbers and zeros. An exhaustive amount. We made it fit for the purposes of developing the systems we have in place, systems that can learn and grow, even replace themselves without intervention. But engineers ran into the problem of time quite a while ago, as those systems were being developed. They had already run into it on a theoretical level, with quantum mechanics, but the issue was now purely practical: the machines running our life-supporting systems, and the systems themselves, measured time in much smaller units than we ever had before. Soon every purchase, every payment, every birthday message on social media was running at lightspeed, but running within a framework we built to milk cows. It was a rocket engine tied to a donkey's back, and now, as users of those systems, producers of them, we ourselves have become the donkey in the picture. Everything is on track except us.

'The simple answer lies in a change we can make to meet the future: the switch to Quantum Time, known as QT or Curly. You may have found the news surrounding quantum more than unsettling – well, to be frank, so did we! – as if the next step in human progress was switching off the sun. But the confusion surrounding singularity and quant is one of the reasons we got involved. We got involved as humans because we also like sunshine, we like knowing what's coming up in our lives, what time we're meeting for lunch. We could see the wild potential for quant to change individual lives, and we were excited; but we didn't want anyone left behind, and that's when we decided to find a way to make transitioning to quant the most comfortable experience for everyone, and that means *you*. At McKinlay Quant we've merged decades of scientific experience with the simple human values we enjoy at home every day. Science is science but a good apple pie is a treat, and we've approached our range of plans with this in mind, with *you* in mind, from our popular Anytime package, all the way to Partytime, Life With Awe, and Original Burnished Wood, with its twenty-four-hour days and easy-to-use markers for breakfast, lunch and dinner, just like the good old days. Call us old-fashioned but we can't get away from the immortal words of our founder, Elmer McKinlay, as he looked out from his porch in analogue times one sunburnt summer's eve: *The problem with damn machines*, he said – *they don't know how to relax!'*

Lon muted the living room screen. He lolled, staring up from the couch. Silence was silence again. The air was unbusy. His phone had been switched off by a police station duty officer, and apart from a last longing glance at his messaging, he'd left the thing switched off. The world was just the world again: it chirped, rustled and hummed, it sometimes rained. The light sometimes blew a hole through a cloud and made him feel hopeful again. Then the hole closed up and he took stock.

This was the world. This was how it went, its cadence.

The last thing he'd seen on his phone, and a reason he'd left it turned off, was a joke from his old workmate Hordy. It went like this: A man is trapped in his house in a flood, and as the water gets higher, he climbs on to the roof. Someone comes along in a boat and says, Get in, but he says: No, God will save me. The water keeps rising and the boat returns, and he says: No, God will save me. So he drowns, gets to heaven and demands to see the manager, who is God. Pissed off by now, the guy. And he says: Why didn't you save me? And God says: I sent the damned boat twice.

It was the last straw for Lon because the joke was a reference to Feral. The joke implied that if only Lon would swallow his pride and ask for Feral's contact, his score could go through the roof. And his score through the roof meant his life through the roof. He'd have contacts again, credit. Order pizza, maybe beer.

But Hordy had said this in the week of Boges's funeral, which Lon was given licence to attend. And the funeral in practice meant an image of Cheryl Bogdanovic's face etched on to his mind for eternity. Not an image of her as she sobbed through the rumours of Boges being stabbed on the fence, instead of gashing his femoral on the wire after a mob blocked his route to the car. That was the official story. No, the image that stuck was her recounting the several days it had taken to find the courage to tell little Joelly, only to then be beaten by Rike and Muh. It was against that that Hordy wanted him to kiss Feral's ass for points. Lon would rather burn.

Thus his score remained on four, which was less than Boges's and he was deceased. Lon also remained on home detention. A

Supa-Lo terrorist. Apricot and nut terrorist, both of which contain explosives. Gluten, nut, meat and dairy terrorist, all potentially lethal allergens. The old woman he'd left the bag with had just kept nodding when they asked if she was intolerant. Didn't even speak English. She may have dined every day on lard but now Supa-Lo butter was a problem. Probably crowdfunded to a duplex in Reynes by now, the lady. Lon had been advised by his City-appointed lawyer to plead guilty to a public nuisance charge and take some home detention, rather than pursue the implausible charity-mission claim and be remanded for mounting a bomb hoax, corrupting a minor, and inciting a minor to terrorist acts.

He could deal with all that. The real stunner was Mona being awarded both the heretics. A double-or-nothing win. He heard Mona's voice from his cell when she came for Shelby. 'Well, but I just, and I mean, is this like, are you . . .' et cetera. Shelby didn't say a word. A no-contact order was put in place. Fridays between one and two he was allowed to roam north as far as Leonard Road, and west as far as Springfield. For shopping and necessities, except within a hundred and fifty yards of a licensed premises, or anywhere promoting beer. His old crewmate Brayan Basauri, pensioned after losing his hand, was helping out with beer. Home brew. Muddy. Not bad. Lon couldn't use North Road at all as it led to heretic stomping grounds, now patrolled by an app. He once tried to leave the kerb on a North Road corner and the app went berserk. So he gave up and took to reading *The Gremets*. He was sitting on Egan's bed one day, trying to prove he had courage; and Egan's books called out from a shelf.

The Gremets were some kids without a mother who spent most of their stories looking for one. There was a boy and a girl and some distant aunts and uncles, including one who played an accordion. The Gremets made Lon cry when he realised. They were a window on the Eagle. Lon howled when it all became clear.

He was embargoed from selling the house as it was now a detention facility. So he was up to *The Lost Gremet*, the seventh book in the series, where Uncle Klaus gives the kids a duck that immediately imprints on Matilda, the girl, and turns her into a mother.

Lon went to the window and stared. He stood and stretched and yawned. The view was empty. The techie at Moyle's had reopened the estate's old driveway, on the other side to Lon. So no traffic on the Row any more. Not even to Number Fourteen, which was empty after the neighbour went into care. They'd found her wandering confused and carted her away. Bereaved and taking it badly. Dementia. Her house sat dark and still and the lawn was dying. Octagon lackeys had been in and taken some suitcases.

Now through the window there was nothing. No urgent threats. No present dangers. No hidden traps. No voyeurs, no crowdfunds, no selfies, no haners. The view through the window was uncoded again. Lon wanted to skip and bounce all over the flat, spin and dance around, he wanted to howl like a banshee.

But only with his heretics. Now he wished more than anything else that they'd spent their days that way, singing and dancing on the hour, running and jumping and yelling, *We're alive, we have mass, we're made of sunlight, heresy and howls!*

But that was just not going to happen. Not any more.

77
Time

Towards spring it dawned on Lon that time was becoming a problem. One Friday during licence to stretch his legs, he exhumed enough credit to head up City Hill for pizza. He hadn't the points for delivery, a thirty-point threshold, not a problem for most living persons but him. So he phoned in the order, paid for the thing, but when he reached the joint it was shut. The opening times on the door said: *Q2, QR and Hy.*

He waited around but West Palisades was no longer a place to loiter. Permanent cops on some corners, occasional fires in the street; the war refugee population had started kicking off around the time of his charity mission, fuelled by social media and increasing blame for terror alerts around town. Plus the drones and the Supa-Lo bag were Palisades incidents, which shaved a clean eleven points off an address there. Didn't go down well as most refugees fell under thirty points, which cut their access to everything. One night when trouble flared, the City warned that it was preparing to act on its threat to bus haner refugees out of town, to split up the males and ship them away. Welder Bae Farrell chipped in to that shitstorm with his adoring fans behind him. Hence Lon didn't wait too long on City Hill. The pizza place didn't open anyway. And nobody else came for pizza. On a Friday afternoon. So something was afoot.

Brayan came over that evening with Max the dog. 'Therapy dog,' he said, and that was true. Lon wasn't allowed to have guests but there was a hack going around to disable social tracking. Brayan worked it out, grabbed some beers and came over.

It took the first beer to dissuade Lon from abducting the heretics. Brayan had to explain that the hack didn't apply to geo-tracking, it just wouldn't register that he was with Lon. Then, as he spelled all this out, a bot came to the door.

'The fuck.' Lon crawled over the rug to the curtain.

'Don't let it in,' said Brayan.

'It's going to know we're here – don't they have heat-sensing shit?'

Brayan sidled up to the curtain: 'Wait – it's not Corrections, it's the City. Don't let it in – the City's tryin to map your house interior. They buildin a virtual X-ray city map, includin every interior and person. Big Octagon project.'

The bot stowed its rotors and assembled on the step. It knocked as they watched through the window. Brayan drained his muddy – 'Watch this' – and opened the door.

The bot said: 'How are you today?' like a child, as they all did these days. It had a multi-angle arm on a bearing. Brayan started to twist it.

'Please don't touch me, sir.'

He took the arm and slapped the bot in the face with it. 'Stop hittin youself. Why you hittin youself, stop self-harmin.'

He smacked the thing around until a voice boomed through a speaker: 'Don't mess with the bot.' It sounded like Keller from the City Lighting department.

Lon poked his head around the door: 'That you, Keller?'

'Yeah, don't fuck with the bot, I'm trying to do a job here.'

'Wonder if it has any holes.' Brayan started to grope it.

'Listen, cunts,' said Keller, 'I could be liable for any damage here, leave the fucking bot alone.' The machine began to transform and put out rotors. Tried to take off but Brayan grabbed it by the leg. 'Let it go, cunts,' growled Keller.

'Send more drinks or the bot's gonna get it,' said Brayan. But the pair were so broken they had to let go. 'Cunts, cunts, cunts,' it said as it flew away.

'See' – Brayan fell indoors – 'set your Curly to Hy and the City don't come round no more. Someone said it cause they systems can't pick a time, the math too fast for the City systems. Is what I heard. Like a invisibility shield for the City.'

'Just makes me miss Wednesdays.' Lon reached for a beer.

'I know,' said Brayan. 'But see me, what I did, is jus leave it set and pay it no mind. Get a old mechanical clock from Providers. Ten bills. Fuck it.'

★

So Lon took the plunge. Curlytime. Climb aboard or get left behind, is what they said. The McKinlay Quant G2 would save more than twice the cost of purchase by rolling back his mortgage by up to five months. Some testimonials said years. That's Curlytime. So Lon's Friday break was spent upstairs at the McKinlay outlet, minus ten minutes for necessities at Supa-Lo on his return.

The wall behind the counter featured a mural of a fiery planet hurtling through a galaxy into your eye; the person behind the counter was a man who looked like he was sparing your feelings. A thirty-year-old in old money, probably twenty-seven if you went by DNA. He was saying: 'It's a totally next-level vibe – think staycation, only better. Just one governing rule: it's a bit-in bit-out system: it'll stop if a transaction goes unfulfilled. So things don't just go away, bills and so on.'

'Uh-huh.' Lon tried to look woke: 'I heard there's a whole legal boom in quant law.'

'Quant and law,' the guy nodded. 'They're not that different from each other, because quant deals with superpositions, where a mass can be positive and negative at once, just like lawyers arguing innocence or guilt. Both positions exist in a suspect entering a court. They're innocent and they're guilty until the decision.'

Sounded knowledgeable, so Lon bought the G2. Declined the insurance. The guy went to a back room and left the door ajar. Looked like a bathroom repurposed as a store room. Badly wallpapered in a small floral design. Toilet with no seat. The end section of an old sofa unit. The man poked around and picked up a box: 'Welcome to the here and now.' He stroked it and smiled.

Lon got home and plugged it in. Looked at his mortgage.

Five grand in arrears and didn't itemise months any more.

The fuck. He emptied the box to find a helpline number.

McKinlay had a virtual helpline. Lon scanned the languid flat as if the voice was coming from there. Sounded empty enough. The greeting was tedious.

'The thing doubled the arrears on my mortgage,' he griped at the bot.

This virtual assistant had the voice of an unblinking girl. It sounded patient. 'Some things can be changed in the system,' it said. 'But some have to change within us.'

'What has to change in the system,' said Lon, 'is that I don't have five grand to pay the bank when I'm only two months in fucking arrears.' And this proved to be a good move.

A human came on the line. It was the man from the store itself. 'So listen,' he says, 'we don't have to tolerate abuse just to do our job here, okay?'

'Did you just hear? The thing put me grands in debt as soon as I plugged it in.'

'Okay, but most likely cause is improper installation, which isn't our issue at all.'

'What installation, the thing's advertised as plug-and-play.'

'No, okay, but did you go straight to H or R? Because if you hit like H or R then events will occur that you wouldn't get in one or two, you know? What it'll do is ping your institutions, the City or whatever, to request a timezone code.'

'Okay, okay.' Lon knelt before the unit. 'Where's the control – can I change it now?'

'Of course: check under the power light and see there's a dial with *DRM*? Turn it clockwise till it flashes blue then enter your code on the keypad.'

'Code?'

'The one on the box.'

Lon picked up the unit and found the power light. 'There's no dial on here at all – not anywhere on the unit.'

'*What?* That can't be.'

'Well, there isn't one.'

'*Ahh*, wait, wait – what model are we talking about?'

'The G2.'

'Oh God, okay, that's like two versions ago. We have limited support for G2.'

'Listen, I just bought the thing, remember?'

'The G2 was an early starter kit, it doesn't do retros, but wait – what's your insurance code? I have an idea. I'm on your case here.'

'I didn't buy insurance.'

'Ah, ah – okay, so look, you didn't specify retrograde functionality, you'll need an upgrade for that. But wait – oh, lucky I have one left, they're like hen's teeth right now. No one's stocking till the GZ launches . . .'

'Fuck's sake, you just sold me this!'

'Listen, buddy, I don't have to take your attitude. Okay?'

Lon slammed the receiver down. Ripped the quant plug from the wall.

A tail light cruised past the fence.

A head appeared after a moment. It was Julie Holie's head. Lon felt a tingle, part feelings for a face from the old days, part confusion over her breaching his No Visitors Order. But he was glad. He was glad and he watched her and thought of time, how long ago it seemed that she'd been out there with a vacuum cleaner. How long before that she'd lectured him over Shelby, as Julia from Child Protection Services. How long before that she'd gangled around in braces while her sister Tania hung out with Diane, Lon sometimes too, ever prepared for some teenage ambush from Julie.

Not that long ago; but in a different lifetime.

Julie glanced up and down the Row. Came in through the gate.

Lon went to the door and opened it. Her lapel camera blinked.

'Mr Cush?' she said. 'Please excuse the intrusion. Our system logged that you switched to QT, and as you're registered with us I'm required to confirm that you reside at the same physical address. As I see that you do, I'll update your details right now.' She retracted one arm out of camera range and held up a wad of little handwritten notes. The top one said: *Follow me.*

'Well,' said Lon, 'I'm still living here, yes.'

She clenched her teeth and switched notes – *Been trying to ping you FOR EVER!* – while aloud she said: 'That's noted. It falls within our remit to pay a call on our registered clients when circumstances change . . .' – *I saw them they're fine! Ember will visit too, get news. DON'T WORRY.*

Lon's gaze misted up and he turned away.

They were forming a bridge to the heretics.

The women in his life, the ones in the wings, were forming a human bridge.

Julie's eyes swung hard to the last note:

SO PLEASE PLEASE SWITCH ON YOUR PHONE!

Lon Cush, 37 Palisade Row, East Palisades. Backlog of notifications I can't deal with, so I'm trawling the grid instead. Dipping a toe back in that water. Then *wham!* There she is!

Shelby-bean! I sing. Shaylabubbly, this is amazing, I found you on Fff! She looks great, she's wearing the unicorn top I got her, and she says: *I miss you, Daddy!* I'm immediately wet on my face. I love you, Daddy, and I miss you, this is crazy, she cries. The fuck. I'm twisted inside.

I say: Shayla Shayla babely, I love you too – remember when we hit the deck together? With the police? She ignores me and says: I need cash, Daddy, badly, and I say: *What?* I need three hundred, she says, right now, it's crazy, I miss you.

I feel a sinker drop from a great height. The faces she makes are like the faces I saw when the Eagle showed me her video that time, his little intro to repping. I scramble up to her room. The unicorn top is still in her laundry. The fuck. She looked so fucking real.

139583862445: Time to face the facts, Lonnie, no sense hiding from the truth, not one as glaring as this: she was right, you're just a loser. It's the word that comes to everyone's mind as soon as they see you, and part of the real tragedy is that you know it to be true, I don't even have to tell you. You look over here for news, for tips, for gags, and your sole motivation is to escape what you know to be true. It's pathetic, Lon. We decided long ago there was no point in enabling such a tragic routine any more. Because what's the point of news when you have the value of a turd on the street? We don't provide services to turds, Lon. Nobody does.

Ramona Winbourn, 64 Sun Village, 144 Kaylor Road, Harville Downs.
All well and good, but just the *laundry*. Oh my God, and then all their mess, and meals and. But no, happy thoughts, happy thoughts. Anyway, sorting the laundry is me-time in a way, reflection time, so what's the issue. I just.

Thinking back to Mother in the kitchen that Christmas, when she said about John, and pressure on Diane, and I mean. There's Mother wants some wind in her granddaughter's hair, Diane's beautiful hair, and I never asked: What did she want for *me*? What about *my* hair? *My* wind? She was my mother before Diane, I mean, here's me wistful for Diane's freedom when I was, you know? Was Mother just channelling through Diane what she wished for me? There's Mother going to Diane but was it a message for me? And now here's me setting Shelby free and everyone in the story is set free except me!

Or was that all meant for me? That message? Was it meant to be me that sets our blood free?

86267571272:
BootyGoss mag hit our screens today with a series of exclusive tell-all pics from inside Mindabae's Arcadia mansion during last night's F&S party for friends. The increasingly popular F&S gigs – named for two bad words which it recently became unlawful to say in public – have traditionally attracted a host of stars. Among highlights from last night's session were a series of risqué poolside selfies featuring Mindabae and hot new contender for more-than-BFF, Den-Den Farrell, or Welder Bae, as he's known across the world. Last night's party was in aid of popular charity Fennecare, which supports the fennec fox.

Lon Cush, 37 Palisade Row, East Palisades. So I come down to the kitchen all heavy with new reality, new awareness, I guess, is what it is, and the heretic bridge, and the phone now has a virus on the newsfeed, the self-hane feedback virus; and then the next thing I see is a rat through the window. Makes sense. Why not. An unconcerned rat on the narrow strip of grass and junk between the house and the rock face. Shel's new bike is part of the junk. Already looks old. She never even saw it.

I open a muddy and watch the rat climb up on to the bird feeder. Healthy shiny rat. The bird feeder is designed to keep rats out. It has two metal cages, one inside the other, which are spaced for small birds to get through. Maybe a rat could get through but it would be a stretch. No birds come around anyway. Why the fuck would they. Come round to a dead place. With disappointments inside.

The remains of an old fat-ball are still inside the feeder, that's what it wants to get to. It can't reach it, but it's trying. The tip of my tongue is poked into the

53316291173: Let's face it, even your own mother didn't want you. Couldn't even wait around for adoption, fostered you out and fucked off. That's how desperate she was to see the back of you. Could've made all kinds of money adopting you out but she gave you to the first person stupid enough to take you on, and fucked off into the sunset. And who can blame her. Is the thing, Lon. You can't even use *She was young and in trouble* as an excuse: she was over thirty and knew exactly what she was doing. Fucked some alcoholic ex-football loser and gets a bouncing baby alcoholic loser. I mean, what are you going to fucking do. Lose–lose situation.

bottle, tasting as the rat tries to get at the fat-ball, this way and that. Fucking rat. Must be desperate if this is its best shot at survival. Better off chewing Shel's brake cables. Rats are just bad news. I put down the bottle and go for the shotgun. Long time since the gun came out. I load the thing and come back to the kitchen door. Quiet on the handle. The rat stops still, looks at me. And flies into the grass.

Ember Mullock, 18 Styron Drive, Two Fields. Julie? Hi, it's *moi*, so listen, do you have any way to monitor their grid activity? Because I went over and – okay, it was mostly for Egan – but anyway, young missy had all *sorts* of things open on screen, I mean all *sorts* of things. So I didn't know if in your official capacity . . . ? *Ah*. Okay, makes sense. Of course the object wouldn't be to prevent dysfunctionality, God, where would that leave them? So hey-ho. In other news, Egan's questioning things, shall we say, and Mona's in a 'What about me?' phase . . .

32951280099: Corey Kniessen is being widely tipped as the lead in a forthcoming feature based on the remarkable true story of local welder Den-Den Farrell, who shot to fame after being discovered offering professional capacitation to migrants from the Al Qemen war zone, despite having been recently laid off himself. The hunt has meanwhile intensified for the possibly female person who was seen enjoying the fruits of his unselfish labour. Corey Kniessen has said he would be humbled to play such a rare human being, and went on to hint that the job could see him visiting the city to meet with the plucky welding star before the month is over.

Lon Cush, 37 Palisade Row, East Palisades. Evening time. Yes, the shadows say evening. Sirens and a glow to the west, red from the alleys around City Hill. The place is kicking off more routinely these days. Although perhaps it's an illusion. Perhaps it's the beer. Fucking muddies turned into a lottery – God knows what's going in some of them. The boys that brew them don't care, because you'd be in as much trouble drinking one as making one.

The gun is still propped by the kitchen door. Makes me look out the window. And there, barely lit in the evening gloom, at the back between house and palisade, I see a shape hanging out of the bird feeder. The rat. On its way out of the feeder. But slow about it. Taking its time. I wait and wait for it to disappear, don't even reach for the gun, it's pointless, they're fast; but it just hangs out of the feeder cage, bent over almost double. I'm like a pillar watching but it doesn't move. Time stood still for the rat. Perhaps it's a quantum rat. Maybe stuck between universes. Who knows what McKinlay would make of it.

20365011074: I mean, let's slice this up: no job, the job got taken away because it was above you, and had to be performed by a machine that could actually do it; no kids, both taken away due to totally absent parenting skills that the whole fucking rest of humanity seems not to struggle with; no wife because you couldn't even keep the last one you had alive, and no girlfriend because it must be true what they say about women being smart. And you're *by far* not clever enough to be gay. So why are you even here? How is it you manage to justify even sticking around? When you've either killed or lost everything you ever had? This is the question, Lon.

The longer I watch through the dusk I see that it's stuck in the feeder itself. It must've entered the cage through the tight little bars then eaten the fatball and turned. But due to it being a double cage it's not able to stretch enough lengthwise to squeeze itself out. It's stuck and panting. Bent at the gut. I step outside. Wonder for a moment if it's a weasel, the fur seems shiny for a rat, although I'm used to seeing them wet. It stirs a little. I feel a pang of something. Ratworthiness, perhaps. Didn't even bring the gun; I just study its situation from every angle.

And I was right: entering the cage it had the whole outdoors to stretch itself long and slide in. I watch it pant, check the rhythm of its breathing, trying to gauge how injured it might be. After a moment I reach out and give it a tug. It's too depleted to bite, and it won't budge. So I go back inside and get a bucket from under the sink. You can smell smoke around now, hear motors and sirens, fuck knows what that's about. I fill the bucket with water. Go out and unhook the feeder cage. The shiny

12586269025: Seventy-two out of two hundred female beach volleyball players say they would choose a welder over a mechanic for a blind date. Of those seventy-two, forty-eight were blondes and fifty-one said they would have sex on the first date. The figures compare to thirty-nine out of ninety professional cheerleaders who would pick a welder over a mechanic, though twenty-four admitted no previous experience of welder fantasies, and eighteen said they would wait to see who the date was before agreeing to have sex. Latest figures show that over three thousand welders enjoyed hot romantic company nationwide last night.

creature stirs and squeaks. I move the cage over the bucket and drop it in. Then I turn and walk back inside. Step up to the fridge and open it. There's a salami. Carton of milk, yellowed at the spout where I slug from it. Bottle of hot sauce. But then outside is the rat. Outside the rat is dying. Outside the rat may be dead. May be inert like this salami. And if I take away the word *rat*, it's just a thriving creature. If I call it a tiger, it's a shiny tiger. Shiny thriving striving creature doing what it's meant to do. Doing its job. Tiger job. Taking its chances in the tiger world. But another creature came along and I was the other creature. Rolling my dice in the suburbs world. Doing my job of rat hane. I arrived with the power to help it, but left only after I'd killed it.

That's how automatically we act.

I wander back out to the bucket. Now it's dead, the rat. In a foetal position. The cage of my chest starts to heave by itself and I chug back a chill as hard feelings erupt, and the kitchen strip light pings and smoke blows in from the flat and I don't know what universe we're in any more – if this is the one where we have control, the one that supports observers, the beautiful fairy-tale universe where things are just right to support us, then why the motherfuck is it such a downer! I crouch to get my bearings and all I can see is the shape of the rat, which looks slim enough now to slide out. Fucked while it was alive, safe now it's dead. And I'm a person who has to think this. A man without time who has to think. A paused man. I am the paused thinking man, I am the paused fucking thinking man and I kill thriving things automatically. Do I love the rat, is it my wife, the rat? Or a symbol of everything that's dead, of everyone that's fucked off and gone away? Do I only love dead things that I kill myself?

Or what is this shit. Lonregan. For crying out loud. The fuck. Beer. You haner. Beer beer beer. Big haner you. Haning declinist loser. What would Diane say. Get a life. Lonnie. Get a fucking life.

How hard can it fucking be.

Ramona Winbourn, 64 Sun Village, 144 Kaylor Road, Harville Downs.

Or am I just repeating her role in this? I mean. Could it be that inherited? Where Mother skips me to try and free up Diane, and here's me skipping Diane to free up Shelby? Or not Diane, but you know. I just. Because look at it: she pulled me aside that Christmas and they can't have been ideas that she hatched there on the spot, I mean. I doubt she saw Diane jiggling around at the table and had a revelation right there. You know?

She must have had a whole agenda brewing, it must have been building, so she just . . . And I mean Christmas, with John there, what a moment to choose. She must have been saving it, and then the circumstances backed her up, Diane jiggling, playing with her long blonde hair. Chewing it and me saying *No*. And just. You know? For heaven's sake, and here's me now the same, obviously not with Diane, things would have been different, but . . . Playing Mother's role in a way. I just. In a *big* way.

Lon Cush, 23 Malcolm Street, Molan Gardens. Blessings to count: Julie got to see them. Doesn't mean I can see or even speak to them but I got to see the face that saw their faces. Which is something.

It floated me up, then slammed me down. Like everything lately. Get a life, Mr Cush.

So I'm paying a call on a man here. In his shady bungalow. Which stinks of dog. Table with energy drink cans on it. Let's see, says this Wade, who looks like his bungalow, which is to say slept in. Has a stoop to him and a flighty little marionette walk. Comes recommended by Brayan. Leads me to the back, where screens and machines are stacked on a bench with more cans. The actual dog is here, an overweight pit bull. Gives a wag and I scratch its ear. This is Friday. I'm prepared to blow a mortgage payment on this. I hand him the disks.

One is of our wedding. The other is fragments of Diane and I messing around on the lawn at her Uncle Ken's place. The wedding disk goes first. He holds it up. It's the clearest one I have, I frown – not

1836311903: A storm warning is in effect for the metropolitan area and northern districts as far as Belvoir this morning as Storm Josh gathers strength in the east. Categorised as an idiomobile class-four inductive depressive air-mass event, Josh is expected to bring a strengthening breeze, risk of precipitation, and possible precipitation of aqueous solids. Danger to life from generally shifting outdoor conditions cannot be ruled out, nor risks to electronic and quantum-powered devices, especially Curly units set to retrograde or hyper. Residents are advised to avoid all but the most necessary journeys and to take shelter until at least noon tomorrow.

professionally shot, but at least on a camera and not a phone. He studies it like a fossil. It's not HD, he says, loading it up. Let's find a headshot or a two-shot, he says. After some whirring and ticking, Diane and I appear together in the shade of the oak behind the tennis club. A bus goes past in the background. The same bus I used to take to visit her. Bus took me there in the first place, and a bus cut me off in the end. Buses: no respect. Diane is all golden ringlets down to her waist, with daisies, gardenias and baby's breath strung in a headband. I'm hungover in my skinny grey suit. We're awkward.

Her cousin was shooting and didn't give directions, so we did what you see everyone do on their dresser and mantelpiece pictures. I moved behind her and held her round the waist. She leaned back and looked up. We laughed at the cringe of it. Hammed it up. She dropped her head on my shoulder. Closed her eyes. I nuzzled her with a look of watching lightning from a beach.

Then Mona's arm pokes into the frame and Wade

1134903170: A welder married to nine women at once has been granted an adjournment to gather evidence for a religious freedom case in answer to his prosecution for bigamy. Thirty-one-year-old welder Lowell Bultos last year declared his home a sacred commune after celebrating his marriage to nine women at once, ranging from nineteen to twenty-three years of age. Bultos claimed the lifestyle was protected by religious freedom, although no specific religion has been named in his defence. When interviewed by police, the women, six of whom are also nudists, unanimously praised their welder husband, saying he had made them extremely happy.

pauses the action. Okay, he says, more softly now, as if the pics weren't what he expected – what are you looking for exactly? You want everyone or just the bride or . . . ? Just her, I say. Well, he says, we should be able to get something off here. Then for about four hundred you can get the basic program. But I mean, like what were you after exactly?

I think he means sex, and I just say: You know, just to rep her or what-ever. Sure, he says, but are you going straight to lifestyle or . . . ? Hm, I ponder. I'm on G2, if that's any help. My sympathies, he says, but this works straight off the grid – you don't need Curly. Listen, I say, I'm not sure what the options are, I'm starting from scratch here. Wade nods. Want a beer? He pulls two muddies from a fishing fridge behind him and leads me to another room where everything is white. The window's covered over. Everything's white and grubby with smudges and dog hair. Blank white sofa and chair. Give me a minute, he says, I can run a quick demo. Won't be fully rendered but you'll get

701408733:
Campaigners for once-pregnant runaway Keeley Teague lobbied the government today seeking an urgent review of guidelines governing virtual pregnancy. A spokesperson for the group, numbering up to a thousand VP activists, said in a statement: 'For simply having followed her dream, for having made a virtual baby with one she loved, for having simply sought the adventure of family life – a universal birthright – a young woman in her virtual prime has been ridiculed and shamed like a haner. It's time we realised that life doesn't wait. The young know this too. Time to identify as who we are, virtual mothers.

the vibe, he says – and because you're Brayan's crew I can rip you a copy of the basic set-up. You got blanks? he asks. Or is it all visor? I'm starting from scratch, I say, I don't have anything yet. Okay, he says; I'll show you some options, but you'll eventually need devices and blanks, like furniture and shit, if you're going for lifestyle.

He steps away. Drives soon start to whirr. The dog comes in and drops its head in my lap. Wade keeps talking through the doorway as he tinkers: Bad shit with Boges, he says. Yeah, I say. What's he doing going over the security fence anyway, when his car was there? he says. From what I hear they saw his lights blink when he unlocked it, I say, and mobbed it before he could get in. No way, he says, bad shit; seen Tyson lately? Not too lately, I say, no. Me neither, he says, since his in-laws bit the big one. Yeah? I say. I hadn't heard. Oh yeah, he says, crossing the road up at Parkwood, electric van, they didn't hear it. One of them survived for about a week. Four-bedroom they left on Arcadia Avenue.

433494437: An overwhelming number of respondents to a new study have indicated that if Jesus were alive today He would more likely practise welding than any of another fifty-nine trades and professions. The results now rippling through the welding community show that Christ is almost nine times more likely to have chosen welding than legal practice, and four times more likely to pick welding than auto mechanics. When given a choice between welder, mechanic, pattern-maker and mortuary technician, over half of female respondents aged between nineteen and twenty-five said they would much prefer being nurtured by a welder deity.

Squillions, he must be worth by now.

He returns with a headset and visor. Try this, he says. I put the set on and the room appears, but textured with fabrics and moodily lit. A wash of purple through the curtains like the ebb of a sunset. This is wild, I say. Wade steps in front of me and looks as clean as Corey Kniessen. Chiselled jaw and ice-cool eyes. Starburst off his teeth. He adjusts the visor and says: So this is a basic rep.

Diane steps into the room. My heart muscle flat-out dies. She opens and closes the physical door. It's beyond nature. Beyond life. She's not in her wedding dress but a simple skirt and top. Wade says: This is Lonnie, and she looks across: Hi, Lonnie, she says. Coy, never seen her this coy. I reach out and see my arm. My arm and her in the same field of view for the first time in a decade. So *real*.

I rip the fucking headset off. Not going any further with Wade in the room. He looks at me: Your wife? And I nod: She died. Few years back. Sorry, he says. Just tell me what I have to do, I say. Well,

267914296: The case of a person becoming pregnant after contact with a facial tissue from an indoor wastebasket has so far resulted in a dozen company floats, none more successful than Kecha, the range of sanitary products specially designed to keep biological material alive, and now forming the basis of a new generation of research and development for biological exo-skins for humans. While health authorities warn of an increased danger to life for living material kept outside the body, the Police Association has said that it remains the duty of all public agencies to assist with the protection of any living materials conveyed in the public domain.

he says, the easiest way to start is with a visor. They can go from twenty up through a grand for wraps and helmets like to live in. Bodysuit's the next step up, then you get touch. The forums have your other hacks for like smells and like you know. Lot of people getting into guesting sites like Succubi, where players inhabit your rep, you know, for sex or lifestyle. Be weird with your wife, I guess.

He calls the dog off the sofa. Okay, I say, but so how do they get like – organs? And he says: When you model the body you can add in a beak and whatever. The beak stores online have different types to match. They call them beaks, but you know. Then feet, there's a whole foot fetish zone, and hands and tongues and teeth, because they don't often get rept, although everyone's stocking their parts in detail these days. Different for you because you have a specific person, but otherwise you could buy like a detailed porn star for sixty bills or less.

Hm. I get to the rub: Will you set her up? Yeah, he says, get you started. For what you want I'd go AI

165580141: An intriguing new study has found that the testicles of men such as welders, who routinely work with heat, are up to thirty per cent larger and heavier than the average man on the street's. The effect is thought to come about through internal temperature regulation, as testicles are designed to hang to maintain a lower temperature than the body. In cases of males in close contact with heat, the testicles may expand and grow heavy in order to achieve more separation, although one scientist who studied welders has admitted that results are purely empirical, saying that welding may simply be chosen by people with larger testicles.

and let her learn for herself. Bit more work. Bit of time but she'd soon be thinking on her own. The more input you give her the closer she'll get. Even images can help them learn, they don't miss a thing: I had one I showed a pic to that had books in the background, and from the titles alone she read all the books and could talk about them. I was fucked, I hadn't read the books. So look, I'll render her to Aime-Moi, a cool little French program, easy dashboard, and I can do a used visor for ninety. Call it three hundred to render. Hundred for the voice and lip-sync module. Blanks – I mean, you can just paint your room or get covers. Might shimmer a bit at the edges, see how you go. Sofa blanks are running from three hundred new. Beds around six. Window shades, we can talk if you move off the visor, that's when you want real blanking. And if you go objective like hologram or bot then you need perfect surfaces, no light. What's her name, anyway? Diane, I say. Okay, he says. Give me a week with Diane.

102334155: Emergency departments across the country have reported a surge in cases brought on by recent viral craze Blueberry Neutro, also known as Snakebite Neutro or Baby's Milk, depending on the chemicals used. Health experts report that more than a dozen children have so far been hospitalised, and dozens more treated, after attempting to mix household cleaning products into a facsimile of the youth drug Neuterium. Doctors have warned that, contrary to recipes found on the grid, there is much more to the untested drug than simple household products. The craze follows a growing awareness of ageing amongst the young.

Dennis 'Feral' Farrell, La Maison du Goût, 333 Arcadia Avenue, Arcadia.
See if they can melt some cheese on this shit, put ketchup or something, fuckin sauce looks like nacho puke. And the fuckin wine needs bubbles, what the fuck.

So what was I saying, Brad, so yeah, so like the struggle has to come from inside, you just focus and use all your strength, and that's the key to winning, in my case anyway, but I know it's very rare to break through. You have to be a certain type of person, virtually nobody can do it like I did, maybe only Mindabae, it takes a certain thing, but you can still just be happy as who you are, heh.

What's that? Of what? Oh, heh he, well, yeah, for sure, inclusivity, why not, uh. Welding's inclusive, it's one of our things, you know: INCLUDE THEM heh he, and life should be the same, then we're all just included and . . . But now, Brad, if I'm buying dinner here you can ask about some other shit than the girl, okay? If I'm fuckin paying.

63245986: The number of attractive foreign women listing welders as their top choice of partner for fun and marriage has topped nine thousand from just a handful of countries. Among respondents to the survey are more than two hundred pole dancers, as well as members of gymnastics and volleyball teams. Welders were once again the top pick over pattern-makers, actuaries, funeral technicians, glass installers and mechanics, with commentators joking that if only we knew what it was that welders had, we could bottle it and make a fortune. One leading welder we spoke to said the secret comes down to the profession's added *spark*.

Lon Cush, 37 Palisade Row, East Palisades. Never forget the first time I saw her. In a house overhung by trees, no bricks, just grey, or white, I guess, in daylight. Magnolia in front. Doesn't look much like a party, I said to Bel, who supposedly knew these girls. They're trying to keep it quiet, he said, the parents flew out to a wedding.

Tania Holie opened up. What do you call this? she said, and we both went: A party. It's a *girls'* night, she said. We told her we came from Belvoir, which we had, although it was for football that afternoon. Then Diane said: Who is it? A song was playing that was later used in a traffic campaign where a car full of kids gets wiped out.

She had the sexy fragility of dampness and probably got colds a lot. She evoked fine wool on skin. She didn't say anything, just stood there. Then Tania just said, Fuck off, and closed the door. It was perfect. I couldn't fuck it up with awkwardness, but we'd seen each other. Compelling as a hill to a goat.

Ramona Winbourn, 64 Sun Village, 144 Kaylor Road, Harville Downs.

My friend Melanie Holie, Julie's mother, started her hot flushes and we were talking about it. Well, the whole, you know. I think everyone's lulled into a false sense of security these days, with hormone replacement and just, I mean. That it'll all go away. Mel's optimistic and we were laughing but I mean. It's so much bigger than the physical change, is the thing. As big as the worm to a butterfly, or whatever the butterfly does next.

You don't want to say *old age*, oh my God, and I won't say it, I just. But like shutting down a nuclear reactor must be. Just this clock inside, a pulse, a rhythm all your life, you get so used to riding it, it's the centre of you, and then just . . . I mean, obviously people experience it differently, some are happy to be done with the hassle. Others haven't had them for years anyway, for whatever reason, medication or whatnot. But there's just this other dimension, the bigger one, for me anyway, and much more than just, I mean. Like being taken off the charger.

24157817: An association of plastic surgeons has reported an almost fifty per cent fall in demand for cosmetic procedures since the advent of chromeleon skin technology. Facelifts were the procedure most affected by the downturn, which surgeons say could leave a generation of current interns unemployed. Prices for the most routine procedures have fallen, although rises have been seen in a number of humanimal procedures, particularly horn, ear and tail grafts, though experts have said that grafting is a mixed branch of surgery served by a number of different specialisations, and so the figures add only partly to cosmetic surgery statistics.

It's probably psychological, I'm happy to say it's just me. But you wonder. You were being charged all your life, current pulsing through you, then you're unplugged and . . . I mean, you just wonder if that was your whole charge, if you just . . . feel it slowly winding down, and nowhere to plug in, and. If the moon doesn't talk to you any more. When it talks to the likes of the brats next door who party every night and don't even know what they've got.

I don't know. I don't want to say it, we have so much left. But just, I mean. So much value was placed on it. Maybe that's the thing. By society, or men, or . . . us, I don't know. Poor Melanie, but she might sail through it, be optimistic. Happy thoughts, happy thoughts. I hope she does, I really do. But I mean, I'd turn back the clock for both of us at once, I'd even pay for it. We could go out like wild gals! Wind in our hair again. But I need to bide my time to bring it up, I just. You know? The therapy's still illegal. I just need to choose the moment.

14930352: A linguistics department has reported that communication by older people via emojis may actually forestall and even shorten symptoms of female, male and even non-binary menopause. The project, which set out to study the effects of emoji communication on the declining brain, has likened early results to what is known of the learning-impaired brain, which has been shown to be resistant to certain effects of natural decline, including those associated with the menopause. The key for older people, said one researcher, may be to keep up emoji traffic until new youth drugs such as Neuterium are approved for the market.

Lon Cush, 37 Palisade Row, East Palisades. I look for Wade's car through the curtain but he finally appears on foot. Walked from Molan wearing a visor and lugging a sports bag. He looks around; I presume he can see the real view in some form, because he finds the gate all right.

Hey, Wade, I greet him. He passes me the visor on the step: I set up a little intro script, he says. I put on the visor. The view looks better, not a fantasy view but sharper and better light. And there's Wade. Still looks like Wade and smells doggy, but all somehow better than life. Then from up the road comes a figure carrying another bag. *Diane.*

There's a light objective breeze and it blows her hair as she rambles along. My mouth is dusty; she's amazing. She slows at the fence and looks up: *Lon?* Talk to her, says Wade – it's interactive. Feels stupid in front of him, so I just go: *Hey.* She swipes her hair from her shoulders, the way she used to. I try to remember where in the videos she did that. She must've done it there but I can't recall.

She says: I didn't think I'd find you again. The fuck. Unbelievable, and I say: Me neither, *Diane*, and it pumps a shiver through me. I take a step down to help with her bag, but nothing's actually there. I reach for her hand but it's not there either, and now I want to throw up. I whip off the visor.

Wade, who's watching like a trainer from the doorway, says: You need a bodysuit or a bot for that objective stuff. He asks where I want the main set-up, and I take him to the bedroom. Cameras go up in each corner. He plugs in the console, brings up the dashboard and tells me she's running AI. So like if the dog comes in, he says, she'll learn how to send it back out. Except I don't have a dog. Then he tells me freestyle is where you just talk to them and see what happens. It can be uncanny sometimes, apparently. Otherwise you run scripts and correct her as she goes along. Hit pause when you want to correct her, he says, and remember to mark your successful scenes and create restore points for later.

Amazing where technology has come to, I think.

5702887: The developers of a popular repping program have reacted with surprise to claims that users were unaware they were being watched in order to tailor their reps to better respond to their lifestyles. Explaining that users can opt out of certain features via the settings menu, the company said that repping programs succeeded or failed according to their algorithms, which aimed to build real-time lifestyle databases. It went on to say that the fact that user data, including intimate anatomical and sexual data, was harvested for offline analysis had no bearing on the program's main goal: to provide the best-quality lifestyle experience for users.

He scrolls through a dashboard menu with all the scripts she can use: Hey How You Doing, Your Glass Looks Empty, Fun at the Beach, Meet in First Class, This Is My Room Key, Alley Rescue, Naughty Weekend, I'm Your Private Porn Star, Run from the Law, Be Philosophical, Banter If You Dare – where she just fights over everything you tell her, he says – Can't Find a Place to Hang Out, Hot for You at the Fair, I'm Your Teacher and You're Late, Be Gentle I'm a Virgin, You Wanted a Nightmare You Got It – which Wade says is surprisingly popular these days – Monster Trucks & Mud Pies, Bikini Car Wash, It's My Birthday, Lazy Sunday, Back to School and Booty Bonanza.

Now Diane wasn't fond of porn. Didn't like the idea of porn at all, thought it was a disrespectful waste of valuable energies. I myself am hesitant to put her image near this shit. Great technology, I say; but I think I'll start with Lazy Sunday. Wade winks and pulls a little box from his pocket.

3524578: The so-called 'repconomy' will be one of the four strongest market sectors within two years, pundits predict. Pointing to the boom in rep-generated revenue, as well as gaming and cryptorep markets, analysts estimate that over a trillion bills was created by reps in the last financial year. An industry spokesperson was quick to dismiss claims of vio-exploitation, saying grassroots support for Top-Brain Freedom proved the viological repping market was expanding on its own terms. Declinists and haners said the major rep corporations were guilty of profiting from basic theft of people's images and private fantasies.

Ember Mullock, 18 Styron Drive, Two Fields. Feels strange, but hey. Or no it doesn't. Or yes it does, but hey-ho. I have to go to hyena settings, let it know he's not a contact. Enter the number and cancel the warning about his score. *Bip boop*.

And here's Lon. Hi, I say: so you're in jail now. I'm not in jail, he says, and I say: Have it your way; so Lon, I saw the kids, we went to the new Fennec's Breath Café, they look fine. Egan had a veggie burger, Shelby had beef and bacon, I say. First time I've felt like a country aunt, on the phone. But I can hear his silence – it's big news. I shouldn't be cruel.

Mona's super-relaxed, I go on, they're basically running the show. But in a good way, if there is such a thing. Or okay, no – but they're looking well. Just about need a crowbar to get Shel off Ksenya Ululay, she virtually lives there now, I say. *Ksenya?* Lon says. Her *arch-enemy*? Nooo, I say, she repurposed, they found out they have everything in common. Met at the abuse group, and both their dads were in jail.

2178309: Local authorities are urging the City to declare a state of emergency after a night of unprecedented clashing between war refugees and police in the southern suburbs. Refugee leaders warned that worse was to come unless the City dealt with growing anti-refugee hane on the grid, which they said was visible to even their youngest family members due to recently enacted grid freedom laws. According to police, the latest clashes saw widespread arson across Molan and West Palisades, thought to have been sparked by local star Welder Bae's public pledge of support for the City's plan to bus war refugee males to outlying cities and towns.

Shelby-Ann Cush, 64 Sun Village, 144 Kaylor Road, Harville Downs.
Hey, I got a note through Fennec Friends. From a boy. Ksenya? I got pinged through Friends, look, a boy. See?

Akeem. Where's that name from? Probably like Calabrava or somewhere. He's cute. Older though. An older man, *kh kh kh.* But oh my God he's in hospital, look. Says he got shot, see? *Bluh*, wow. By allied forces. Who's that? Is that us?

Poor guy. Where the fuck is he? Oh – West Palisades. Ah, not hospital, just like a bed in a room without furniture, without anything. Cutie though. Big black eyes, look. Melty eyes, *kh.*

Oh my God he's sending a heart! He's there right now, look! *Awww.* Akeem. What shall I send, what shall I send? Not the pumping heart, that's like for serious shit. This one, with a bandage. Okay no, that's broken heart. Flowers, or get well . . . What? *Kh kh kh*, I'm not sending him a *peach*, oh my God Ksenya, fuck. *Kh kh kh*, are you crazy!

1346269: Authorities are warning of a disturbing trend among youth-friendly grid sites such as Burro Bridge, Yay Bae! and even Fennec Friends, involving friend requests from young foreign people linked to terrorist cells. One security expert has called the trend the most active threat to our young so far, warning that sites can't filter members for their affiliations off the grid. A score of young people has been lured into terrorist groups by seemingly innocent youths from overseas. Some declinists were quick to assert that the practice was the endgame for freedom on the grid, adding that they had predicted it decades ago.

Lon Cush, 37 Palisade Row, East Palisades. Wade's gift was a script called Island Honeymoon. The box even has touchware. A tiny bottle with oil of tropical flowers. Lozenge of leaf matting with its smell. A piece of silk. The luxury touch.

I lay the items in my lap and set the visor. I can choose from a menu of starting points, and I set it in-flight to Holiara International Airport. Sunrise, I put. Why not. And Diane arriving on another flight, so I can meet her at the gate. Anticipation. And a brainwave: I pull out our old sun lounger. Recline like a first-class seat. Sun lounger and a muddy beer. Then I settle back in and start it playing.

There's a crown of cloud over Holiara. We fly a circuit around the island and it's beautiful. I succumb to the soundtrack menu. Something from Diane's day, the track from the road safety campaign; it almost brings tears. And now the sun breaks over the horizon and spears the cloud with a bolt of pink as we turn over a sparkling sea. A science clip I saw said that now the multiverse is proving true it was

832040: Chhrush, the app that claims to find your true chemical crush from among billions of possible matches, has now been upgraded to include reps, with access to the widest selection on the most popular global boards. Originally launched as a school crush search tool, functionality has been thoroughly enhanced to accommodate physical partners as well as best-matched chemical crushes, via any popular rep kit with venotype functionality. The app still uses trademark cutting-edge AI to hunt down and match the DNA signatures we most respond to across all races, genders and lifestyles, giving your reps a fifth dimension of ultra-compatibility.

likely that we as observers in the fairy-tale universe created our own reality. And looking at this island I can believe it. Nothing's far-fetched any more. We fetched it all. I sniff some oil. Gardenia, which is weird because Diane really loved it.

A young local puts a lei over my head. Nice touch. Early morning in Holiara, feel the silk. And nerves. She's nearly here, the arrivals board says. I spot the lei girl near a snack bar and call her back. Can I get another lei? And she says, *Oui*, and stands beside me watching the gate. And it's that kind of attention to detail that blows me away. She doesn't give the lei to me but waits to put it on her – it's their sacred form of welcome. Nice touch.

But nerves. And there's Diane! That moment before they spot you. Unbelievable. Tired and crumpled, the attention to detail is amazing. As her eyes approach I see they're glistening, oh Diane, my precious Diane. She puts down her bag. Smiles, and says: *It's my birthday fuck me in the ass.*

514229: UFS critics have voiced concern over the number of refugees and migrants with scores below thirty, warning that the trust algorithm is actively participating in racial hane by further marginalising those already struggling to integrate. Critics also pointed to a growing list held by the City of so-called haners, or pre-terrorists, as they have also been known, a list it threatens to use in the event of further trouble in the south, proposing to break up foreign haner rings by bussing selected members to other towns. The list, according to recent leaks, comprises solely those members of southern suburb communities with scores below twenty-five.

Shelby-Ann Cush, Fennec's Breath Café, 624 Oakland Road, Harville Downs. God there's just like a bunch of them, look. Take your frickin pick. *Bluhhh*, love bomb. Wait though – Ksenya – wait, see which ones are linked to Akeem. *Akkie Bae. Ahhh*, Akeem. Okay, it's like all of them. *Yuh*. Why don't you just send a high-five to all of them? That are linked? Then they can hang out together, Akeem and whoever, and we can . . . *Kh kh kh*, we're double-naning, *aaaaaaah* oh my God!

See here where he showed us his uncle? I just like melted when I saw that, for real, like; imagine if we had uncles like that, we'd just be like *bluuuuh* melted over the floor. *Yuh*, I know, I know it must be easier for them to get rockets and shit, but it's just like, wow – one pic they're there defending their women with like rockets and whatever, and next minute they're playing with kittens.

God, can you imagine if our *dads* had been like that? Just like *ahhh*, melty?

317811: A number of parents' groups are gathering to protest the enactment of grid freedom laws which would enshrine the right of grid companies to waive responsibility for membership and content on their sites. Citing the estimated thousand young local people found to have been targeted by terror cells posing as members of youth friendship groups, a speaker for parents said the new laws would be the last nail in the coffin for parental rights. The exchange has sparked demands from bereavement support groups for an apology, after some said terms like *coffin* were clear examples of the mounting trend towards covert or passive hane.

Lon Cush, 37 Palisade Row, East Palisades. Wade? Listen, I'm getting a bug where no matter the script I'm on, it goes to It's My Birthday.

Shit, he says, well, don't try too many scripts because she'll learn it anyway. Or test the scripts with a blank, grab a user off the boards. Is Birthday one you'll ever use? Not to get too personal, he adds. No, I say, I think we can skip Birthday. Well, he says, just delete it, and anyway I can rip you better shit than that, if you know what I mean.

I leave it for now and go back to surfing the grid. Modern version of staring out the window. Now that the window's blacked out for the rep thing. But then: *Shel? Is that really you? Yuh*, she says, just look at me, *duh*. And she is wearing another top.

I study her closely, and she says: Remember when we hit the deck together? With the police? *Shaylabubbly!* I cry, God, okay, I'm so glad to see you! I love you, Daddy, she says. But I really need like five hundred right now, it's desperate.

196418: Reports are emerging of a number of rep suicides, all while using freestyle settings on popular lifestyle devices. A lobby is growing to push for coroner intervention in rep deaths, especially since the advent of virtual DNA, giving reps virtual biological componentry known as 'viology'. In the last week alone, two female reps were filmed locating and hiding tools for their suicides in advance, though programmers from three popular platforms have said it's impossible for a rep to perform anything it hasn't been taught or exposed to. At least one of the platforms is gathering data for an emergency rep helpline.

Ramona Winbourn, 64 Sun Village, 144 Kaylor Road, Harville Downs.
God, the testimonials are just, well. I mean, they wouldn't be able to print it if it weren't . . . Not that it's printed on paper, but I mean. Plenty of scientists are saying there's no reason for the stuff to stop working, the info they're using to claim it only lasts a few weeks is from very early trials, not from now. And I just . . .

Well, Julie came around and said the longer-term goal would always be to reconcile with the father, that's Lon, and I mean. I always liked Julie, strange to see her being so official. She tried to tone it down with little notes off-camera, she has to wear a camera after the Baby Perry case, not that it was her that missed the clues. But this is the first time I've heard them say Lon, you know, except as a defendant. Which, well, at first I was, I don't know.

Anyway, happy thoughts. Some testimonials on Rike are saying it can last *years*. God, it would be like a miracle. Even just for a month, I mean . . .

121393: Early studies into the new compound Neuterium have suggested that a handful of doses could turn back age clocks by up to seventy-five per cent of a user's lifespan. But scientists remain undecided over predictions that at the end of the effective period, thought to be only weeks, cell decay could accelerate quickly towards death. It's also thought that only the first course of the drug would prove effective, as it destroys chemical pathways used to enter the cell, locking out any further ingressions. Some scientists have speculated the discovery could eventually be used as a 'final fling' drug, to bring dignity to end-of-life care.

Lon Cush, Skinbox, 34 Reynes Parkway, Reynes. Only takes a couple of weeks before I have to touch her and she touch me, at any cost at all.

Trying to work out blockchain hasn't helped. They finally called from the retraining office to say there could be opportunities if I knew about blockchain. Part of my brain rewired trying to work out blockchain. Cryptocash thing – apparently all the little transactions are linked in a chain, and you have to prove each transaction to access the value or something, I don't know. Some fucking thing. The net result was that I faced the fact I won't be retraining too soon. Blockchain, the fuck.

What I need is human touch. That's all I need. The less I know about blockchain, the more I need touch. There's no love in this house. This life. No touch. It's a craving like the craving to breathe. So I take a longer shower than usual and shave all over. You can get cheaper skins off the grid but you can't tell if they're used, they say. The forums are full of nasty stories. As soon as someone puts on a skin the

75025: A class action lawsuit is growing against producers of the popular mini-series *You Can If You Want*, as a character in the last episode uttered aloud the activation code for a popular brand of rep, causing thousands of reps across the country to learn and perform the second half of the show, which included sex acts. Producers said their style of naturalism demanded that they depict reality wherever possible, and that a character living with reps would of course have to use the activate code. They added that it was the factory default he had used, and they were now working with a popular eraser platform to get a restore patch to affected viewers.

living material starts to adapt to their chemistry. So I'm going up almost to Reynes for this, on the very edge of my range, flirting with North Road.

I drive up in the rain and find a park under a *No Shitting* sign. The smoked-glass storefront features a skin on a mannequin under a spotlight. It has a wolverine pattern that changes as you watch into a range of other creatures, including a mottled hyena and an Iltanian tiger with stripes. The visor is discreet, no bigger than a pair of shades.

The place is silent inside with brisk cool air. Wood-panelled walls and glass morgue drawers that are lit to show skins inside. The climate control is another plus about buying live, apparently. They couldn't guarantee that for home delivery. Skins use your own chemical factors to build resistance; they don't develop immunity till they're worn.

A person comes from the back in a tweedy skin. I'm Troy, he says, how are we today? I already made a decision not to try and sound au fait with all this, after what happened with the fucking G2 package. I

46368: Geeta Bakshi, founder of youth charity Haulcare, which loans hauls to underprivileged vloggers, has posted a stinging letter on Rike accusing star benefactor Mindabae of not shipping the goods she had promised in a much-publicised video. She went on to say that staff at the star's Arcadia mansion, Château Mindabae, had told her to 'Get over it' and 'Go away'. A containerload of new goods had been promised, Ms Bakshi said, but not so much as a breath had reached her since. She went on to post pictures of the only two items currently offered in her haul: a three-legged fennec toy, and a princess crown for toddlers.

put myself at Troy's mercy instead, but he abuses it straight away: We have a seriously desirable PSV-R Chromeleon Muon, he says, when I tell him I'm in the market. Or some really hot RVS-Ts with full flare optics and mat-binding sequencers on semiconductor outrigs. I'd throw in a POS-X GRGT Spectrum visor with that. He crosses his legs and leans on the wall like a tailor, if tailors do that. Is it for you? He looks me up and down. Looks like a fifty-two to me, he says, moving to a drawer and sliding it open. You'll know we're dealing with a biological product, he says, and strokes the filmy garment. Like skin but as strong as cobweb silk, a living fabric that adjusts to every dimple. It takes him another ten pitches to get to the one that sells me: Plus you'll never pay for clothes again. Bah! Throw them out! Your clothing bill just fell to zero!

Ten minutes later he's spraying me with medium as I unroll a suit up past my waist. It's stretchy and moves by itself as if searching. I feel it suck into my crack then pop into a respectable booty.

28657: Mindabae was a surprise guest at the Blowback Music Awards, stunning fans in an original jellyfish-tank dress built for the occasion by hot aquatic couturier Ami Bronstein. MB was later pictured partying the night away with this year's talented winners, Mbbip and Kyron Muahaa, for their smash hits 'Bish-O-Matic' and 'Next Time Do What I Say'. In an impromptu red-carpet statement to fans and media, Mindabae said the awards were a welcome break from a difficult year, and were a chance to remember that love and respect still existed, after all the hane she had to endure from a growing number of haners and declinists.

The view through the visor is hyper-clear, it's liquid. Makes Wade's old rig look like black-and-white TV. As we inch the suit up I reflect on the speed of things. Wade's visor was like surviving death when I tried it. Now it's like black-and-white TV. Something in my expression must ping this to Troy: *Fwoosh*, he says – there goes yesterday!

By the end of the fitting I've warmed to Troy as you must warm to your barman on an ocean voyage. He carefully folds my clothes into a box, ties it with a ribbon, and I step on to the street feeling strangely alive, and with strange new powers attached. Although who knows what they are. But this is Lon: an Iltanian tiger with his hindquarter stripes. *Tiger Lon.* And walking to the car I see others around in wolverine and husky and snakeskin designs. The future shimmers today. First time I've seen other skins around town. So from here I set off to lie down with Diane and touch her till I die. Talk to her and touch her for ever. And ignore any other shit.

17711: An intriguing new study has found that the brains of men such as welders who ply a demanding precision trade are up to ten per cent larger and heavier than the lowest average person on the street's. The effect is thought to stem from the degree of accurate targeting needed to complete a job successfully, and from the tracking of sparks via peripheral vision, which scientists have said can have remarkable stimulatory effects on the visual cortex. Welding has enjoyed an upsurge in popularity following the success of welder stars such as Welder Bae Den-Den Farrell, and Big Bob Hopa, whose Muh tutorials are watched by millions of fans.

Ksenya Ululay, Fennec's Breath Café, 624 Oakland Road, Harville Downs.
Shel, check this one, look. *Ungnnhhh.*
And it's like they know me, they know inside, it's like. *Waahhh.* Wait, send a pic together. Hold your hand like that, like that, like the struggle thing. *We're with you!* Hehehe. Look, look, what's he saying oh my God: *You would be princesses here.* Oh my God. Hehehe. And everyone just like doing whatever, like so cool. I heard Maia already went. No yeah she did, she went, check at school, nobody's seen her and she's free. For real.

They just treat you like princesses and you get to have babies and no one's allowed to touch you, you're just like protected and do whatever you want. No one can say anything to you, they fuckin kill them with rockets if they say anything to you.

Send a heart. Hehehe. *Awwww,* Akeem. Look, look, and they have cats, you have kittens all around, I mean, hey – should we both like . . . No, no, wait, but like, wait . . . What if we like . . . you know?

Lon Cush, 37 Palisade Row, East Palisades. Mona calls, and under my surprise I'm grateful. Her voice comes into the visor and she says: Lon, this is me being civil; I'm not here to chat but I thought as her father you should know: Shelby wants to get her ears done. It's her birthday on Curlytime, apparently, and I'm happy to give her that from me, she says. I sit up in the lounger. Pause Diane.

Her *birthday*? I query. On Curly QR, says Mona, she's sixteen today. *Sixteen*? I go, and Mona says: I got her the hyper subscription on QR. Hm, well, I say – can I at least say happy birthday? It's not technically allowed, says Mona; but I'm too soft, I'll see if she's around. She's probably with Ksenya – they're virtually camping at the new youth café.

As she leaves the phone I hear media playing nearby. A voice is saying: *One of the ways young apparel is demeaning is in its styling, which derives from a boundary issue dating back to the bootee. Parents operating like monsters in the dark of youth, before consciousness arises, use that ignorance to*

6765: A police spokesperson has said nuclear alert sirens sounding for over ten minutes across town today are not thought to have been a terror-related incident. Indications from the scene point to a UNT in the system's control units, which can be operated from more than one location. Security experts have warned that the incidence of UNTs – Unknown New Technologies – has tripled since the start of the year, surging after crucial stem codes were leaked on to the grid. Today's event caused little disruption as most residents were indoors, many using earphones or visors. The City said it must raise awareness of the system, as it's there to save lives.

breach a baby's defences and usurp its right to dignity by commandeering it as an object for fantasies of homemaking and immortality, made all the more lurid for being a farewell to their romance, which itself was probably false and which in any case they were bored with. The dark ensuing project begins with the bootee and progresses to animals on the clothing, but not just any animals – baby animals. Because in discarding the baby's rights the parents unilaterally decide to trap it in a world where it will not see a realistic representation until it is eight. It will only see cute depictions of anything, including tigers and bears, which if come across for real would kill them and probably eat them. Tigers don't have smiles. Bears don't have smiles. If those young people live near tigers and bears that is a death sentence. Their parents did that to them, the voice whines on as Mona returns: Not a sign of them, she says, but Lon – and this is me being civil, I just – I'll tell her happy birthday from you.

4181: A study has found that speech, even in whispers, may damage the palate and voice box over time. Some commentators say the findings seem to concur with the notion of 'species intelligence', as at the point in history when the phenomenon is discovered a solution appears in the form of instant messaging, and a related trend towards modern pictographics, both leading away from high-impact habits. Studies on silent people appear to show much-reduced wear and tear in the mouth and larynx, in some cases by half, compared to speakers, especially of harsher languages like our own. Platforms have begun to highlight the health benefits to users.

Tania Holie, 18 Geppert Street, Reynes Parkway. Jules, I heard from Ember; not sure if you picked up on this: it's the *Ululay* girl with risky grid habits, and now she's spending all her time round there with Shel. You know? So I wanted to run something past you: I know Lon's barred from contacting the house, but what about connecting to Ksenya? She doesn't even live near his no-fly zone. She must share loads of media with Shel – should I just ping him her contact? I have the excuse of an old friend, if it looks iffy. And I mean, is Mona even watching them, is she still living there? All this drama to claw them back and now she's out to lunch? Or what the fuck? You know?

I wait for the length of a Jules sigh. She says: Mona's on a *me-first* jag, her life's flashing before her eyes. Also didn't bargain on Ksenya virtually moving in. I told her she could claim support, but no answer. She wanted Shel and got the box set, and now with Egan the way he is. Anyway, stay tuned, she's over at our amazing mother's tonight . . .

Lon Cush, 37 Palisade Row, East Palisades. So I'm on the lounger facing an issue when a message pings into the visor. The issue is that Diane is unaware that we had children. Which blows a fair-sized hole into the lifestyle bubble.

I was picturing aloud the scene of Egan and Shelby at the café, and Diane was going Uh-huh, uh-huh, which is also weird because she actually used to do that – Wade did say freestyle could be uncanny – and from there I was thinking how strange that Shel made friends with Ksenya, after all their earlier hane. Bizarre, as Shel herself would say, and then *ping*, a message flies on to the visor field:

Tania Holie says there's no rule against me checking in on Ksenya. If they're pals there must be a load of interaction between their accounts.

She sends a link, a hug, and says: *Delete*.

I'm excited enough that I pause Diane. I made a rule for myself not to pause her, to always bring her along. But I need to think about this. New world of possibilities. Maybe she could learn about her kids

1597: Hospitals are reporting a growing number of people under the influence of experimental youth drug Neuterium, with over a hundred admissions in the last week alone, as effects take hold and cause unusual symptoms. Some reports are of users as young as sixteen. The health watchdog has issued a warning in the wake of the reports, saying the drug in its experimental form is as good as a death sentence, and that no amount of short-lived youth could balance that. Calls are also being made to shut down the livelogs of Neuterium celebrities like Amarone Jones, whose twenty-four-hour log is following the former forty-eight-year-old's first weeks of youth.

from Ksenya's content. Meet her current heretics. Hopefully the Eagle's on there too.

I go straight off the link to Rike. A few Ululays are connected, more than you'd think: a Shona, a Benny, a Ditson, and Ksenya. I open her Rike; it's public. Lot of friends, a *lot*, but even through my limited eyes it has an air of not the main deal. Like a living room left spotless while you party out the back. Some older people are there.

Her Muh is mostly unpopulated, some pics from when she was smaller. Her Goh is classmates and school stuff. But here's her Fff – and my goodness, here it is. Only the entrance is public, but all the friends are boys. Spike-eyed foreign young whips. And that's as far as it goes; looks like they're flocked around the gateway waiting to join.

I'd need to fake a profile before I could join. Fuck knows if that'd be a good idea. The way things are. Do I need the headfuck, for instance? The risk? Or am I better letting spikey-eyes lie.

987: The health watchdog has warned the government that health services are being stretched to breaking point by the current wave of Neuterium-related admissions. A recent survey of school leavers found that nearly half would take the youth drug before the age of thirty, and more than half of those before they reached twenty-four. A committee is being convened to look into legislation surrounding so-called 'preternaturals', current and future families of drugs with lifespan-altering effects. At least three hospitals have said they will no longer accept patients showing signs of Neuterium use, as beds are in short supply.

Tania & Julie Holie, JumpJet Burger, 59 Alma Road, Lower Stresnan.

Time's so strange, *pthh*. Jules? And not even in a way, you know? But like *bloouaah*. I'm even pretty sure this is the table, Diane was sat where you are. Lon was there. He could do two double beef and hold a conversation, hahaha. Unreal. His wrist was bandaged that time, we were five minutes out of the emergency room, I mean we never came to this JumpJet ever, I don't think, before or since. It's an Alma thang.

Julie puts her coffee down and stirs it through the lid: Bet he's not that jocular now, she says; I know it's none of our business, but the amount of stuff he doesn't know is growing by the hour. She levels a stare over the table. I peer at my fries: Soap opera, I nod, you just want to hug him; and where Diane pissed me off, she was so trained to bite her tongue, he'd never suspect she wanted out. So under the radar. Blessing it didn't come to that, strike me down for thinking it. But what the fuck? *Pthh*.

I toy with the fries: Does he even know about

610: A number of consumer credit associations have defended an average four per cent rise in the cost of individual credit, citing growing numbers of so-called 'bangers', as borrowers who take youth drugs such as Neuterium with a view to spending up to their limits and 'going out with a bang' are known. In one case alone, a spokesperson said a borrower was able to spend twelve million in the last ten weeks of their life. Lenders were quick to add that greater safeguards were being put in place at the application stage, including closer scrutiny of sudden applications for higher credit limits, especially among applicants over thirty.

Egan? Or suspect? Who knows, she sighs; I don't know who knows anything about anyone any more. Ember Mullock's the ally there.

Everyone's so high fucking maintenance, I say, everyone's suddenly our job. Now Mother Dear and Mona – I mean, *really*? Jules rolls her eyes: They got on the sauce and made themselves a pact, like teens with their first fucking joint. *It wasn't a full dose, testimonials are amazing, it's the expensive type, wah wah wah*, she whines. I eject a blob of mayo on to the fries: If they haven't pinged in ten more minutes I'm going to imagine they agreed to treat them. Means we could be waiting hours. But I suppose I'll be happy to wait.

Julie shakes her head: Nuh-uh. I doubt it. Check the news. Symptoms too notorious already. They may as well be wearing flags. And the City's threatening to cut benefits off to anyone found using the stuff. Just for starters. Can't believe these fucking girls, to be honest. I'm scared, Tania.

377: In a new twist to the Welder Bae story, a former San Uribean woman who claimed to be the female in the image that made him famous has secured security camera footage of herself approaching him on Reynes Parade on the day in question, wearing clothes featured in the picture. Welder Bae, who is currently overseas, has said he can't remember which woman it was as she wore his visor, but reiterated his claim that it can't have been her in light of strong accusations she made in the wake of the story's appearance. The woman, Galatea Marin Medina, has challenged him to pose for a picture again and let his fans be the judges.

Ksenya Ululay, 64 Sun Village, 144 Kaylor Road, Harville Downs. Oh my God, the cousin, see what I mean? *Ungnhhh*. Don't tell Akeem, Shel, he said don't, this is like a surprise, and to help him out. Akeem's trying to recover, his family's really sad. *Uff*, but the cousin, look how cool. He says:

Did those people who said they loved you, love you as we do today in our family? Telling you what is true and how much we want you with us? Did they tell you even once that you were wanted? Or were they people who thought that anything they told you, like *Eat your food*, or *Get your things*, meant they wanted and loved you? But could that be true? When it is easier to say *We want you* than *Eat your food*? We *want* you. In this world and in this life we want you with us for always. Isn't this easy to say? But did you ever hear it said? Even once? Please think about this. I say our family has found you like a rod of sunshine from Heaven. Just to know you are there is helping us every day.

233: Pressure is mounting on social media giants as the government moves to restrict live streaming of military strikes in Al Qemen and elsewhere, citing stress caused to victims of the attacks. A realist lobby has mounted a counter-campaign citing freedom of information, and noting the streams are essentially the same as news, adding that individuals who film themselves running into blasts are newsworthy in themselves. They also point out that, but for dedicated streaming, no record of the action would survive. A number of declinists were quick to call the debate a decoy from the real issue of climate damage caused by the ongoing strikes.

Lon Cush, 37 Palisade Row, East Palisades. May be hope for me yet. What a sensible fucking decision. Not to go anywhere near Shel's content on Ksenya's accounts. Because I'm only in this position after acting like the dad on *The Gravy Years*. Upstanding old Gary Gravy with his OCD. Anyway, I made the effort, made the contact, found Ksenya's sites, la-de-da, I'll leave it at that. I just feel better having made a decision. I roll over, find Diane and we lie back, spent. I inhale and reflect: all I wanted was for the heretics to have the same sweet awakening to romance that I had. They might not get it, but what can I do. Have to let go sometime.

In the visor the shadows of a fire dance on the ceiling. But I'm tired of the flickering fire. What I really need is a doll. Those silicone dolls have come a long way. They can make them to anyone's shape. I'm sure Diane would love a body again. *Surprise!* But it's an idle thought because I'm down to zero. The bank is quiet because they'll be plotting violence instead of talking to me. I rallied myself for an hour

144: Police are warning southern suburbs residents to stay indoors, as fire appliances deal with over a dozen fires across West Palisades and Molan. The area is bracing itself for the worst night of trouble yet, after news was leaked of up to a hundred buses making their way towards the city. Star Arcadia resident Welder Bae, who was born in Molan Gardens, said he was saddened by all the destruction in his old home neighbourhood, and joined his fans in lobbying City forces to act against what he called 'home-grown terrorist haners'. As a known benefactor of Al Qemen refugees, he was widely praised for his brave decision to speak out.

yesterday and found a lawyer on the grid who for a hundred bills does lawsuits against McKinlay. I don't have a hundred bills, but I looked, and that was satisfying. Sue them. Sue everyone.

I started sleeping with the visor on. Accidentally. I was in this underwater script with waves and coral and tiger stripes of light and I just kind of drowned and fell asleep. One thing they got right with the visor: *comfort*. No edges. And the light's softer than real. They even say it's better for you. Protects the eyes. You can watch an eclipse with the visor and zoom to the surface of the sun. You know. I mean, what do I really want in life: to work in a sewer and fight to get ahead, or to live in a fucking dream? I could zoom to the surface of the sun!

I still discipline myself to read text. Don't want to lose that, after all Mrs McHenry gave me in English, back in the day. It's not *less*, she would say – it's *fewer*. So I was reading that all human problems came about because we plan and say things with the evolved part of the brain, but the animal part

89: The most comprehensive survey to date of fennec numbers in the wild has confirmed that a majority of the world's fennecs now live in captivity. Private pets form the largest part of their number, followed by zoo, park and party-hire animals. Pets alone outnumber fennecs in the wild by a factor of two, and for rare colours – cookies'n'cream, cappuccino and red fennecs – it's ten-to-one. Although proponents of captive breeding claim the pet market is a hedge against dwindling numbers in the wild, wildlife activists were quick to point out that the world can only use so many fennecs, compared to other less appealing but more endangered mammals.

underneath is still the driver. So for instance you can walk around saying *I live for peace and love*, and then punch someone. And the animal part owns the penis and vagina. This separation is the cause of human problems, I was reading. The brain. It built new faculties but left the old ones running.

The info on this was quite funny, said it was like having a professor and a thug on the same street. In the same brain. I thought it was quite amusing. But now they say with gaming and porn we've decoyed the worst of the animal brain. Those inventions are the key to the future, because they free our higher minds to be amazing. Our big hands and powerful backs have done their work. Penis and vagina have done their work because all they needed to do across millions of years was get us to this point in history. Now we have arrived, they say. The final brick in the wall is the visor. With a visor we can finally think of the body and its animal brain as a battery. Nothing more. Top-Brain Freedom. So yeah.

55: The grid is alive with news that Mindabae, who only recently shortened her name to ME, is being sued by two people said to be the shoppers whose taunting in a supermarket queue led to her viral rise to fame. The pair claim they were the popular star's best friends, and that they devised the stunt together with a specific view to make a funny viral video. They claim the verbal contract prior to the stunt was to split any proceeds three ways, but that Minda shut off all contact with them during her rise to stardom. The pair also accuse her of suppressing their story via multiple court orders, and a relentless campaign of bullying and intimidation by staff.

Ksenya Ululay, 64 Sun Village, 144 Kaylor Road, Harville Downs.
God, and he's built like I don't know. *Unnghhh.* Think the cousin's a rep? Or can someone really be like that? Filter is okay, but a whole rep? Maybe we should ask for like proof. Except what proof? Hey maybe we should get him to come over! Or no, okay, *duh.* But if he's in West Palisades. Hey and but you *can* see like smoke. Like from the trouble. Around him sometimes. Like in the back. Maybe we should get him to show us a real object and send it over, like clothes or something, a spoon, I don't know, or not a spoon, *duh.*

I saw where their baes just live in like piles of blankets and pillows and fur, not like laundry but just snuggly, and full of tiger kittens. And fruit around, did you see that on Muh? Soldier brides with all this fruit around, but they can keep that shit, *bleh,* you know, except it looked pretty. And nobody can tell you anything, you're just like the main bae, and . . . Wait, now he's saying something else . . .

34: The woman at the centre of the Welder Bae image mystery, Gala Marin Medina, has said she forgives him for comments he recently posted claiming she looked like a sixty-year-old on Neuterium. She repeated an invitation to meet her in person and be convinced that she was the girl in the image. Welder Bae has said he'll think about the offer, noting with a characteristic chuckle that he has hundreds of interested parties to interview for the job. Fans enthralled by the slow-burning saga have added over a hundred million more hits to the image in the wake of the recent exchanges. Pundits are tipping Welder Bae at odds-on for viral sensation of the year.

Lon Cush, 37 Palisade Row, East Palisades. Fucking weirdest thing we're starting to see: unexplained freestyles by reps. Just uncanny, and apparently not programmed. I look at Diane sometimes too. Makes me wonder.

One viral clip shows a rep going to a man's back garden and digging up an empty perfume bottle from under a bush. Except it's not empty: it contains a love note that was buried by a twelve-year-old back in the day. And the rep who found it was rept from the grown-up twelve-year-old. And the note had been written to the guy whose garden it was, and he never knew, and now he's together with the woman who the note was from. They're saying it's quantum. They're saying there's another nature under the one we can see. It's being uncovered by our actions in the quantum world. Mists me up sometimes, I won't lie. I unpause my wife, my beautiful wife. *Diane* – I gently call her. She turns in the doorway, smiles and says: *It's my birthday*, and I lunge for the menu.

21: Another two selfies appearing to have been taken in front of mushroom clouds near Al Qemen are being hotly debated today as haners rally to prove that anyone within selfie distance of a visible strike would be dead. A realist science group has argued in response that the mushroom cloud itself only appears in the wake of the blast, and poses no threat at the moment of exposure. The flash which comes with detonation would more likely kill within a certain distance, it says, but to snap the flash would be an act of luck, unless the photographer knew it was coming. A health watchdog has warned against travel to any war zone.

Ksenya Ululay, 64 Sun Village, 144 Kaylor Road, Harville Downs. I have no problem, he's saying, I will ride the bus to glory, our family will go where life is warm, and I will kill whoever stands in our way. But you are also our family. I will also kill who stands in your way. The proof is that I am here with you now; no one else is here. Who is here with you now is who will save you, and who is not here doesn't want you. This is the glorious truth, because it means I will save you. You are saved.

This is true: our family is real. Even if I die for the struggle, that love will follow us into the sky and shine on us always, keeping us warm. Our house will be full of sunshine and laughter and love. We need nothing more because we know what we want. We are alone in a world full of talking where nobody knows. But we know. I knew when I found you that you knew exactly. That you are special.

Take this message today: love the ones who save you. Come and join the ones who truly care.

13: Crimes committed while wearing skins on which another person's image is projected have quadrupled in the last year, a crime watchdog has reported. Tech skins, originally worn for full-body gaming and lifestyle play, have become an increasingly popular alternative to traditional clothing, especially as chromeleon technology allows wearers to change the skin's image and texture like a 3D screen. The trend gained pace after at least a dozen actors attended this year's *YoSienz* ceremony in skins resembling tuxedos. Police have warned that projecting someone else's image on to facial skin is regarded as impersonation, which is a crime.

Lon Cush, 37 Palisade Row, East Palisades. There on the road to making one face she passes through ecstasy faces. But real ecstasy. If she blinks in the middle of most faces, which she often does: ecstasy face. But real fucking ecstasy, with horror and awe and fear and peace and surrender. Death faces. Faces facing death. She's at the end of the bed and there, look at it: ecstasy face.

Beyond any face she ever pulled for me. Beyond any face I was capable of giving her, perhaps. My body starts to buzz and burn with this. Because all these faces she had inside her, all the little stops between one thing and another, are like watching the base of an iceberg whose tip was all that you settled for. She had a couple of ecstasy faces with me for sure, but just like tongue-lolling and eyes rolling up. Nothing like this. Total ecstasy, abandoned and falling and burning from inside.

Her face was capable of it. But she never achieved it like this with me. Though her face was programmed to do it. Her face did it thousands of

8: Migrant groups have warned the government to expect all-out war if its current plan to bus non-voluntary applicants to its town expatriation scheme to other towns goes ahead. A spokesperson for a migrant advocacy group has said that plans put forward by the City may well be illegal, and could be challenged in court if it doesn't offer assurances not to bus peaceful migrant residents out of the city along with militants. A spokesperson has said the City remains committed to the plans, and any opposition or unrest directed at the public would be met with force. Clashes reported in the southern suburbs tonight already exceed any in the city's history.

times a day on its way to elsewhere. It's part of her basic equipment, this ecstasy face, but I never saw it like this. Years after her death I'm watching the amount of ecstasy she was set up to express. She was capable of a thousand miles an hour and we drove at thirty together. But then my face must also have ecstasy settings. It's possible our brains can take those fleeting faces in without us knowing. They might be part of the language of attraction that brings us together. Though surely they're meant as a promise of things to come. Except they never came. They never came, ah fuck, and now – did she really come? Or did she fake it. I make a loop of this frame so she stays in the throes of this ecstasy. But already I'm wondering if there isn't an even better ecstasy face somewhere. Even greater ecstasy.

I save this one and move on, but within a second comes a fucking brainwave: I'll find some more pictures, even stills on paper; there must be more around. Calibrate her to even greater heights. I go to the boxes under the stairs and rip out old envelopes

5: Popular cultural icon Welder Bae has agreed to meet with Gala Marin Medina, the former San Uribean who claims to have been his cohort in the image that made him famous. Using his trademark chuckle, the plucky abuse survivor has said it will give him great pleasure to meet the young woman who he once accused of being a sixty-year-old on Neuterium, and see if she fits the helmet used in the shot. Meanwhile Gala Medina has said she's up for any test whatsoever, and will spend her time in training to look her absolute best for the popular star. Premium subscriptions to Welder Bae sites are said to have doubled in the wake of the challenge.

of prints. Kneel for a while, fanning
through them, school projects,
camping, the trip to the speedway.
My knees soon hurt and I recline on
my side like an emperor, all heavy and
spreading.

Our trip to the zoo. The pool party.
And here's Barton Road, our first
place together. Here's Barton in the
garden. And there she is in her sarong.
Ankle bracelet. Nose stud. And here
we are indoors on regular days, no big
occasions. Egan was around, there's
toys drifting under the sofa.

Winter and that big furry rug on
the floor. Frost on the window. Look
at it all; but the next picture stops
me breathing. Diane's on the blanket
with Egan. Watching me take the
picture. Looking right into my eyes.
But no pleasure on her face at all, no
fun at all, it's barren and pained. One
hand's on the rug beside her. Three
fingers and thumb are drawn back.
The middle finger points straight at
me. And it flies off the paper across the
years like a snake to say: *Fuck you.*

3: Jesus, Lon. For real?
Of course you couldn't
give her ecstasy, you
couldn't even get a
fucking job. Face it:
if a mother can't love
you, what hope can
you realistically have?
Talking to you always
has to verge on fucking
heartbreaking, it's like
stab the teddy, but
take it from your news
service, please finally
believe us – nasal surgery
would give her more
ecstasy than you, we're
surprised she didn't
read the paper, clip her
toenails. You poor thing,
because it is that fucking
tragic, Lon. I mean,
change our mind, did we
miss something: you're
actually there wondering
how much ecstasy you
could give some blonde
bombshell from a tennis
club?

Ramona Winbourn, 64 Sun Village, 144 Kaylor Road, Harville Downs.
Oh my, I have to sit down, I just. I hadn't thought Diane's clothes would fit, after all these, just. You know. Oh my, I.

I should've thrown them out long ago, I know, but I mean. Now I'm overcome. But happy thoughts, happy thoughts, though I am actually happy, just so strange, I . . . The dose seemed to work, I just. And in her little bag, the leather one, I find her cards and some pictures of Egan and Lon, and I . . . He was a good-looking man, I'll grant her that, grant Mother that. I stare into the picture as Diane must've done, I sit in her dress, not worn since then, and stare as she did. And things make better sense.

Strong, friendly features he has, and he is strong and friendly, you'd trust him in a way, I mean. My God, and I never got to say, I . . . And now her own pair growing fast, and one so like her. Both out of the house, virtually gone already, just me here now, I . . . Oh God, please, happy thoughts . . .

2: A photographic expert has declared at least two so-called 'mushies', or mushroom cloud selfies, from one of two possible foreign war zones as genuine, saying the rare temperature of light following a blast would be almost impossible to fake in detail at such short distances. Moreover a growing number of witnesses point to Neuterium users as the subjects, with some seen running towards blasts to capture themselves in a shot. The trend has already spawned a local variant, with subjects running into flaming barricades or on to burning cars in the strife-torn south, as police continue to warn the public to stay away from the southern suburbs.

Lon Cush, 37 Palisade Row, East Palisades. Makes sense. Diane was nice but we weren't made for each other. That's clear. Maybe she wasn't happy, I don't know. Maybe she felt sorry for me. I don't know, too late to ask her anyway. She died – how would I ask her? She's in a better place.

Within an hour a message from the bank informs me it's putting the house on the market. Another cluster event. But just as well, I can't fucking pay for it. It's empty anyway. Twenty-year adventure and it all went away. If it ever existed in the first place. Diane the rep comes into the room but I'm cold to her now. I grab the pic of her shooting the finger and scan it into her program. She pauses, the way she does uploading input. Then she turns to me, troubled, and says: *She's not me, Lon. My blood is out there – waiting.* Her edges start to shimmer and fizz, and – *thp!* – she pops and dies. *Fuck.* Gives me a shiver. I roll off the lounger and rip the plug from the wall. Then I lie here and think: the fucking day has come.

1: Gala Marin Medina, the former San Uribe national claiming to be Welder Bae's cohort in the image that made him famous, has been shown arriving at the Cornado Hotel for her date with the plucky star. With characteristic style, Welder Bae has said he is ready to apply a number of tests in order to confirm whether she was the real subject of the shot, including having her pose for further pictures. Leaving her cab in a rakish hat, Ms Medina was heard saying to waiting fans that she was ready for anything. The striking young graduate is also said to have received a number of marriage proposals on her way through the crowd.

Ksenya Ululay, 64 Sun Village, 144 Kaylor Road, Harville Downs. *Shhh!* Watch out for the camera. Fuckin crazy over there, look. Can't believe we're doing it like for real real. *Waah.* He's waiting for real *oh my God.* But we're gonna be safe as soon as he sees us, you saw what he said. And nobody can tell us anything. Those soldier baes are for real, they kill anyone that fucks with their crew. Like serious safe. Oh my God it's fuckin real! Shel? *Beaah,* fuck!

Lon Cush, 37 Palisade Row, East Palisades. *Dad.* I get a voice in my ear. *Dad, it's the Eagle.* I flick on the info and it says Ramahoudna Sopzidnitz. That's not the Eagle, I say. Looks like bullshit. It's really me, he says, it's a fake account. Dad, I think we need to talk, Nanny's gone all I don't know, she took that stuff, and now I think Shel needs help, someone on the grid may have talked her into . . .

Eagle, I say: Eagle, Eagle, Eagle – first of all, it's good to hear your voice! Now slow down . . .

1: Mindabae fans are demanding answers from the former star after pictures posted from an emergency room showed her two alleged best friends in critical care following a beating by her staff. An off-duty police officer witnessed the beating and was able to identify the assailants, since found to be her personal trainer and a gardener employed at her Arcadia mansion. In filing a police report, the officer also discovered that Minda, whose real name is Belinda Beims, has a string of prior convictions for fraud. Lori icon Donkeyhooty was among the first to respond to the news, quickly returning a gold and diamond-encrusted pacifier she had gifted him.

Shelby-Ann Cush, North Road, Palisades View. *Brrrr*. Or should we just forget it? *Yuh*, I know we said, but I just thought . . . we could just go back. I mean, look at the frickin sky, the place looks like a game! Ksenya? Looks like *Incinerator III – The Return*. Should we just get a drink at Supa-Lo? No, I'm fine, I just mean like for you too, or like.

I'm *not* scared. But just I used to live down here. My dad's place is down here. My dad'll be there inside. I mean, do we even know where we're going? After meeting the cousin or whatever? I don't want to like lose everything. Ksenya?

Lon Cush, 37 Palisade Row, East Palisades. Passing through the kitchen I catch sight of the sugar jar. Came from Diane's childhood. Shape of a bear licking its lips. I used to argue it was a honey jar. She always said it could be any jar it liked.

So it's a sugar jar. Full of love. Full of memories of love. That's why it's here. That's why it survived. It's one of the things we mined, one of the trillion

0: A hunt is underway for San Uribean graduate Gala Marin Medina after popular local star Dennis Farrell, Welder Bae, was found haemorrhaging from the groin in a hotel bathtub. Shocked fans and media describe a grinning, flirtatious Medina leaving the luxury hotel just after six this evening, even pausing for selfies with Welder Bae fans. The severity of her attack on the plucky abuse victim was only revealed when a passing guest heard cries from the corridor outside his master suite. Medical commentators say that while it remains extremely rare to treat full amputations of this kind, the severed parts, if recovered in time and in good enough things we mined for a speck of love. And I kept on mining, mining her image, my memory, for love and unspent potential, the codes of it, the keys, the blocks of it, the pieces that aren't connected to each other, across universes with different laws.

Now it hits me like a donkey's hoof: *love is a blockchain*. An algorithm so hard that you mine it all your life just to prove a fragment of the transaction.

So prove the transaction, Lonnie.

I open the back door, reach for my phone, and toss it into the grass. Throw the visor on top. Take my old Maubeck Stealth pump-action twenty-bore.

And blast them to infinite fuck.

condition, can often be at least partially reattached in certain cases. Local man Gideon Hovis, father of the photographer who took the viral Welder Bae shot, was himself the first on the grid to launch a crowdfunding page for the embattled welder, who it transpires was on a paying job at Hovis's Reynes Parade home when the famous picture was taken. No donations have been pledged to the fund as yet.

SEPTEMBER

I

East Palisades

The west was aglow. Palisades and Molan were orange and sparkling with cinders from fires of unrest. Evening was dimming behind a crocodile of clouds in an exodus matched by humans below, lit toasty underneath by their trouble. Lon padded upstairs for his guitar case. He replaced the guitar with the gun, tossed ammo in beside it, and strode on to the flat in his tiger stripes. His pulse ran fast and steady.

He strode across the flat with his guitar case on his back, leaving the Row behind to flash through shadows. The grit felt good on the soles of his skin, cool and clean and free. Cars were alight up City Hill, roadblocks lit by flames. Police with visors threaded a crowd as drones overflew like swamp flies. Soon he could see that buses were parked at the foot of the hill, rows of them on the flat. The City must be acting on its threat to break up haner rings, bussing them out of town. Some in the loose congregation appeared to be willing; some weren't even refugees. There was a sense that the buses were symbols of protest, with activists and media in the fray.

Lon slowed to find a path through the feverish dusk. The situation upstairs in town looked routine, the usual aquarium glow. Citizens would have their cameras poised over salmon and chickpea salads, pinging data of love or hane to each other between their trestle tables, no byte of which would influence any fires burning below. Smiling faces, laughing faces, kitten faces and turds with eyes were incapable of quelling the trouble to the south of the city.

Lon scanned the horizon from right to left. Behind him the flat ran black and soft and empty into the distance. Ahead the city was a stage. A writhing line moved along at the level of City Hill Road, of people being herded down the hill towards the buses. Loudspeakers boomed above a commotion flecked with cries. He set off in their direction, the direction of North Road, headed for Harville; but he didn't join the mob. He waited back, a lonely silhouette with a clear route behind him on to the flat – and from there he stood and watched. He watched and calculated the shape and gait of anyone he could see approaching. Tense but endowed with new power.

The power of nothing to lose.

He soon enough spied a target. A pair with a certain carriage, already close, making their way to the flat. Their forms grew defined as they left the jostling mass. He darted to the nearest cover to watch them pass him by. They were breathless and hissing:

'It's not a whole tiger, though,' said one. 'It just has stripes on the ass.'

'Iltanian tiger,' corrected the other. 'More sandier than like a tiger.'

'Yeah, sandy and not orange. Oh my God, think he's really coming?'

'Fuckin I don't know. He better, the place is a shitstorm. He said where the furthest person was out on the flat, he would be even further. Go out there and wait for him.'

'But Jesus, there's like a frickin squadidlion people out here already.'

'I know, fuck. Maybe you were right, about going back. Like what if it's a trap?'

'*Yuh duh*, who knows. He never went to any of my sites, I didn't log him once, so I mean . . . how does he even know who I am?'

Lon looped through a milling crowd to meet the pair head-on. They were larger, more solid and shuffling than when he last saw them. One had jungle cat ears, and was Ksenya Ululay. The other, the fennec, was Shelby, her furry ears twitching in the breeze. The girls had the nature of toys, with limited movement of arms and legs, their life expressed through their faces, their eyes, like luminous animatronics.

He sprang into their path.

'*Fuck!*' hissed Ksenya.

The pair froze stock-still. Glanced at each other, glanced at him. Then Ksenya shrieked '*Run!*' and they turned on their tail.

Lon caught Shelby's arm and lunged to her ear: '*Bean!*' he whispered. '*Don't blow our cover, tell her it's okay. You can look like the brave one.*'

Ksen! yelled Shelby.

Ksenya slid to a stop, arms akimbo, poised to flee.

Shelby turned to Lon. She scowled and blinked, then her eyes grew deep and still with the weight of sums known only to childhood. She looked up and took in the guitar case. '*Lonnie Lonregan*', he heard her barely whisper. She was still a few moments, chewed her lip, curled her gaze around. Then she play-slapped his tiger face. Her absolute buoyancy of old was gone, the face behind the bluster was brittle. Life had grown real.

'So *bluh*,' she mumbled, 'the struggle.'

'We're going to the struggle,' said Lon, 'called the future.'

'So but . . . ?'

'I meant it. Let's get out of here. Start again. It's no place for fennecs. Ksenya mightn't be able to go far with us, but we can get to Belvoir, hide out with your Uncle Austin and Aunty Mary, maybe write some letters, make base camp and decide where we're going.' As he said it he could swear he whiffed Belvoir air. Soaked with rich soil, crisp with the click of insects, bursting with time to think and live and grow. Once a place revered by the city, a luscious place between hills, where citizens knew they could go, which meant they almost never went. But now, apart from its name being used as a northern marker for weather reports, Belvoir was largely forgotten. Not a lot had been written about it on Rike or Muh or Goh.

'So, okay,' Shelby frowned, 'so but like . . .'

'Eagle's coming,' said Lon. As he said it he glimpsed a pair of forms emerging from the smoke. A shock banged through him. Not Egan but a familiar blonde with a younger girl beside her. His head cocked automatically. She had windstrung hair and a familiar leather bag. Eyes that lit up when she found him. *Diane.*

Sounds grew thin. Diane with an older Shelby.

He went but his feet stopped halfway to them. Diane smiled a sheepish smile, brushed her hair from her face, lit golden by fire haze, made stunning by trouble.

'*Mona?*' He squinted.

'What the hell,' she said. 'Right?'

She had lost thirty years, maybe more in this light. And as if her nature had changed under the force of it, her speech was like a girl's again, still vulnerable but quietly assured. Lon stared until she grew self-conscious.

'I'm nine days in.' She toed the ground.

Beside her stood a likeness with her gaze to the ground, in a dress that rippled around as if tugged by firelight: the heretic once known as the Eagle. She had found herself despite Lon missing the clues, despite him looking to Shelby for traces of opal to flash from his wife. She raised her face to Lon and her old crumpled smile came out. She was finer now, her hair was long, the colour of Diane's, and the truth became clear, her blood became clear about its travels down the line. Lon took her by the shoulders:

'Did you tell Nanny?'

'About bailing? Uh-huh.' She glanced at Mona.

'The couple that raised you,' said Mona – 'still live at Belvoir? Can I come that far and see if the hospital will treat me? Or the effects could go south pretty soon. I mean, they may be less tuned in to the news at Belvoir, I just . . . And I can tell Melanie Holie if it works, and . . . Then we'll see. The world's upside down, there's not much to lose. We can see. Can't we?'

A drone broke away from the crowd to hover above them. Two more took position well back. Lon pulled Shel and Egan together: 'Listen,' he said, 'we have to bail now.'

'Where to?' hissed Shelby. 'Just Belvoir?'

'No,' he said, 'the future, if that's even far enough. Let's go analogue, let's be annies, we can go wherever we have to go to be free.' He saw Ksenya grinning, and nodded.

'We'll have company.' Egan glanced at the drone.

Lon looked up under a shading hand. 'Drop your heads, turn around.' He whipped the shotgun from the case and blew the machine from the sky. Then he dropped the barrel and faced them: 'Phones on the ground. One pile – NOW.'

Shelby beamed like a night light: 'You'll start a manhunt.'

'Better a manhunt with love.' Lon blasted the pile. 'Right?'

Mona looked up as more drones approached: 'I hope you know a way out?'

Lon pointed to the west: 'Storm drain entrance behind the kiosk there. Take us halfway over the flat, to the creek. Beyond that we're free and clear.'

'We have to go in a drain?' said Egan.

'Good stuff out, we can say. Anyway, it'll mostly be dry.'

Lon's tally by the time they reached the drain was four drones, four phones and a Jembaya keyring Shel had picked up on the day they hit the deck together, kept as a charm and accidentally tossed down with her phone. The crew echoed away through the concrete drain. 'We could go to my old pen-pal Bea,' hissed Shelby. 'She lives far, they don't even have UFS, they banned it.'

'Where?' asked Lon.

'*Yuh*, FAR, I said.'

The storm drain was dark, but it was dry. Lon's crew formed a chain behind him and he felt his way along from memory. Drains had always been good to him, much better than to Brayan Basauri. He had messaged Brayan the hiding spot for his house key before leaving home. *Suck a muddy and strip the place.*

After a while the gang felt a hopeful breeze, with a scent of cool, dark freedom. Reverberations thinned, their voices hushed and they popped out far across the flat, their steps by now in time, a rhythm trained by echoes.

Woods lay over a ridge at the edge of the plain.

They made for them like ninjas.

★

A badly spelled footnote on a police report from that September eve records the sighting by a witness of figures on a ridge at the south-ernmost edge of the flat. It was one of three hundred and forty-nine reports written up that fated night. It was the only one to mention a cat, a fennec, a mother and daughter, and a tiger with a guitar.

The report appeared as a footnote and not in the body of the text, as it was known by then that every observer inhabits a universe not necessarily inhabited by others.

Harder things take courage. To inhabit one universe is harder.

The cat, the fennec, the women and the tiger were going to try.

And *boom*.

They were gone.